A Twisted Arrangement

Twisted Vows

J Wilder

Editing: One Love Editing

Editing: Steph Rawlins at RawlsReads

Cover: Y'all That Graphic

Join Group

Join J. Wilder's Readers' Group Join the Wild Ones readers' group if you love giveaways, polls, teasers, quotes, early access to covers, blurbs and all kinds of other things.

The Wild Ones - J Wilder Reader Group

Dedicated to the readers who would go with their kidnapper willingly if they said they had books.

Author's note

A Twisted Arrangement is book 2 in the Twisted Vows series.

It can be read on its own.

This series is on the darker side. One may say *Cozy Obsession* or *Cozy Dark*.

I wanted to create a book for readers to have a good time and have fun with it.

Trigger warnings:

- Manipulation
- Kidnapping
- Birth control tampering
- Knife play
- Childhood trauma
- Violence

Chapter 1

Matthias

You might say my obsession has become a compulsion in the way I need to know everything about Scarlet Laurent. That even though I've stepped into the background, I could never look away from my Little Sparrow. I watch as she maneuvers through the restaurant, her honey-brown hair catching the afternoon light streaming through the windows. She looks elegant in her ice-blue shift dress that highlights her eyes. It glides over her body, giving the barest hint of her curves. There's no doubt it's perfectly tailored just for her.

An older gentleman and his much younger wife approach her from the side, fake smiles plastered on their faces. A line forms between Scarlet's brows, and her fingers tighten around her champagne flute.

My teeth creak with the force as I clench them together. I want to go over there and squash whatever bullshit they're saying. Before my feet can move, Scarlet's demeanor goes cold, a warning and a threat.

She may have been away for the last seven years, but she's still from one of the ruling twenty-six families of the Order of Saints. For the first fifteen years of her life, she'd been raised to live up to the highest form of society etiquette. Which, for the Order, includes knowing how to put someone in their place without breaking her outwardly perfect demeanor.

I smirk when the man bows his head and pulls his wife with him as he practically flees. Scarlet doesn't need me to intervene, never has. That won't stop me from tracking him down and fucking with his business profits for upsetting her. As a Lord in the Order of Saints, I'm more than capable of ruining him.

"If you stare any harder, she's going to burst into flames," Damon says, keeping his voice low enough for only me to hear.

"You're one to talk." I follow his gaze to where it's trained on his own wife, Misty. Her pale lavender hair brushes back behind her shoulders as she laughs at something our younger brother says, causing Damon to stiffen.

I'm about to tell my older brother to fuck right off when Liam Dupont approaches Scarlet, wrapping his hand around her waist as if she belongs to him. The only thing stopping me from going over there and crushing his fingers is the way she pulls away, breaking contact. This asshole showed up while I was out of town on business and managed to fit in three dates before I could get to him.

Unlucky for him, I'm here now, and there won't be a fourth date. Not if he wants to live.

"What's wrong with you? You look like you're about to kill someone." Damon hands me a crystal tumbler filled with amber liquid, and I toss it back, savoring how the alcohol burns my throat as I finish it.

He's not far off from what I'd been thinking.

I don't reply, too occupied with tracking Liam's movements. There's something off about him today, like a poorly hidden excitement in his actions. During the week I was out of state, I used my experience as the Order's technology expert to pull up every spec of information I could find on him. He's an only son, from a family with ties to the Order of Saints, but they aren't members. Bottom grifters greedy for power who try to get close to anyone who can provide them influence.

On paper, he's smart. A Harvard alumnus, but he made a crucial mistake coming after what's mine.

Scarlet's the last remaining Laurent, leaving her seat open in the Order, and it's clear this asshole thinks he has a shot at it. He's sorely fucking mistaken.

"Are you going to tell me what's going on?" Damon asks, his eyes hot on my face as he examines me.

"No." I haven't told him any of it, and this isn't the place to explain now.

Ten years ago, when I was sixteen, Scarlet's family attempted a coup, killing my father and abducting me and my two younger brothers, Bash and Xander. They'd locked us up in their estate in an attempt to draw out Damon and finish off the Everette line entirely.

My family has maintained the position of Lords in the Order of Saints for over a century, and that was the first time anyone came close to taking it.

I'd never told Damon the way Scarlet took care of my wounds, kept me fed, or how she held me together, fierce arms wrapped around me when the sound of my brothers' screams pierced my ears. She repeated over and over again that they were fake, that her family was trying to get me to break. She checked on Bash and Xander, and they were safe. She's the only reason I didn't shatter that night.

Her father sold her off to the patriarch of the Vasiliev family, at least forty years her senior.

Scarlet's dad had no issue with the depraved marriage, knowing the combined power of the Laurent and the Vasiliev family would only come second to my own.

So when she tried to escape, they trapped her in that castle like us. A little sparrow caught in her cage.

Yet, she still took care of me. Made sure Bash and Xander were safe and risked her life to tell Damon where we were being held.

I could have loved her just for that, but it was those quiet moments when she snuck through a hidden door to visit me that had me falling for her. It was the way she'd give me shit for splitting open the cuts she'd glued

together and sit with me for hours, chatting awa,
a minute, keeping my mind from tumbling into my darkness, that was my undoing. She'd captured my heart, and
there's no getting it back.

At fifteen, she'd orchestrated our escape and aided
the downfall of her family. She'd done it knowing she'd
likely be executed along with them.

Damon protected her as the Lord of the Order of
Saints. Kept the Laurent seat in the Order for whoever
she marries. He'd thrown the Everette name behind her,
making it known anyone who dared to approach her
would have to go through us.

I'd have taken her away the second we'd escaped that
hellhole, hidden her like a fucking dragon in my cave, if
it wasn't for the wish she'd made. The one that's
governed every breath I've taken for the last ten years.

I'll never forgive myself for the things I said to her
to push her away. The way her blue eyes had shined
with unshed tears will torment me forever. I've asked
myself countless times if it was the right decision, each
time coming to the conclusion that I would give my
Scarlet anything she needed, even if that meant letting
her go.

"What the fuck is he doing?" The low warning in
Damon's tone pulls me back to the present. The muscle
in his cheeks ticks as he looks across the restaurant.

I follow his gaze to where Liam lowers himself to
kneel, holding out a ring. The color drains from Scarlet's
face when she looks from him to all the eyes on her.

She's trapped again, society trying to force her into its box.

What the hell is this asshole thinking? He must be desperate to propose after only three dates. I should have killed him the second I got back, then I wouldn't have to do it so publicly. Ringing fills my ears as my vision goes red around the sides. It's okay, Scarlet. I'll wreck him for you.

"Fuck that," I hiss, moving toward them, and Damon grabs my arm, holding me in place.

"I want to kill him too, but she's got this. Scarlet's able to take care of herself," he says, fingers tightening their grip.

"Don't you think I know that? That doesn't mean she should have to," I growl. I hate everything about leaving her to deal with this asshole alone.

Damon's right though. She can handle it. She's wearing her polite smile like a mask, but I can see the rage behind her eyes.

Damon claps me on the back. "Relax, brother. That was the biggest mistake that asshole ever made."

His wife, Misty, waves at us from across the room, and Damon immediately stands taller.

He gives me a quick glance. "You good?"

"I'm fine. Go see your wife."

He gestures from me to where Scarlet's standing alone, Liam nowhere in sight. "Don't think I'm letting you off on explaining what the hell was with you today. You've been acting weird ever since Scarlet came back

from college, and I'm done waiting for your explanation."

I raise one brow at the threat. Damon's the head of the Order of Saints, but he's never held it over my brothers and me. So I know this command is coming as my brother and not his position.

"Fine. Later."

"Later." He nods.

I know he'll hold me to it. I just need to make sure I'm ready when he does because he needs to understand.

I let her slip through my grasp once. This time, I'm never letting her go.

Liam doesn't notice me until I'm less than a foot behind him. He turns toward me, eyes going wide, and I close the distance even more, keeping my voice as low as possible as I warn. "You are fucked now, Liam."

"What?" He stumbles back, and I grip his arm, holding him in place.

"Take this as a warning. Never show your face again, or I'll make your life so miserable you'll regret each breath you take. After all, some things are worse than dying, and they happen to be my specialty. So run along before you learn exactly what I mean."

I let him break free of my hold, his mouth dropping open, then closed several times before he can speak. "You're insane."

A dangerous smirk curls the corner of my lips. "I'm glad you're finally catching on."

Chapter 2

Scarlet

My GAZE SKIMS over the crowd of impeccably dressed attendees. Unsurprisingly, the event is being held in one of the best restaurants in the city, privately booked, just for us. There can't be more than fifty people here, our community purposely kept small.

Today's luncheon kicks off the Order of Saints' summer social season. For the next several months, I'll be subjected to any number of galas, balls, or archaic rituals, each one hidden under the guise of charity, but in reality, it's just another game of influence and money for the Order members to flaunt their power over each other.

I managed to avoid attending the last seven seasons while I studied at Stanford Law. I chose the West Coast so I could get as far away from this world as possible. I couldn't avoid it forever. Even with Damon's protection, I had to come back. There are expectations for members,

15

and even though I technically don't have a position in the Order, my family still holds a seat.

The Saints stand tall with stunning women draped over their arms, their Unsainted offspring a step or two behind them.

I inwardly roll my eyes at their pretentious titles. Saints are full-fledged members of the Order, and the Unsainted are the initiates. The entire thing makes me nauseous. There was a time I looked forward to this, when excitement filled my veins at the idea of dressing up and spending the evening dancing, but all that changed when my family betrayed the Everettes and turned my world upside down.

I curl my fingers to stop myself from fidgeting. I don't belong here, and they all know it. The Laurent name has been tarnished so badly I could never be anything more than a pariah, and the worst thing is it's justified.

What my family did was unforgivable, and even though Damon appeared to have forgiven me, I can't help but think there's hidden resentment there.

I'm lost in my thoughts when an eerie hush falls over the room, making my hair stand up on end as the crowd gasps in unison, all eyes pointed behind me. I spin in place, hands fisted at my sides and my heart racing in my chest, ready for whatever I'll find.

At least, I thought I was.

Adrenaline shifts to annoyance at the sight of Liam kneeling in front of me, a giant diamond ring held out

between us. We'd barely gone out a handful of times, and his transparency of wanting my family's seat in the Order makes me sick. I should have known better after meeting him through an Order contact. All they ever wanted was to get my family's seat in the Order of Saints.

Which won't be this asshole.

Unfortunately, I can't just turn him down in front of all of these people. That's not how things are done in this world. No, it's whispers and secrets. Closed-door conversations.

No doubt why he chose this as the perfect opportunity to pop the question.

Too bad for him I have no problem turning him down the second we're in private.

"Of course." I put on my fakest bright smile and take the ring box from his hand, not letting him put it on me. I'm seriously starting to regret moving back here. Life was so much easier when I'd been three thousand miles away.

Liam pulls me into a one-armed hug while I comfort myself with all the countless ways I'm going to humiliate him in the future.

Not yet though. Not here.

This man has some audacity. We haven't even kissed yet! The only reason I'd dated him in the first place is he appeared to be an easy lay, and as a nearly twenty-five-year-old virgin, I've become desperate to get it over with.

Of course, every man that approaches me is looking for marriage, not a one-night stand. My life would be so much easier if they'd stripped the Laurent name of their spot. Instead, they're holding it for whoever I'm unfortunate enough to marry. Of course, that doesn't explain why I couldn't find anyone to date while I was at school. No one knew my ties to the Order of Saints, and I made sure to keep it that way.

I smile and accept congratulations from the people who hate me. I nod and laugh at their fakeness, just like they do for me.

No one wants me here. The feeling is entirely mutual.

This bullshit is all because the ruling families insisted if I'm going to live, they're going to keep a close eye on me. Of course, they hide it under the facade of kindness, letting me bounce between their homes until my family's money switched to me when I turned eighteen and I disappeared to college. My dead father's money felt dirty, but after everything they'd done to me, I figured it was my right to spend it.

I'd gotten out of here the second the money hit my account like I was being chased by the devil himself, holding the secret of which college I enrolled in under lock and key.

I've been told I should be grateful. That I'm lucky, but what is luck?

Was it lucky to have my entire family killed if it meant escaping them?

A sane person would say no. That nothing could justify the cruel bloodshed that happened all those years ago.

But I never claimed to be sane.

I helped free the Everette brothers, and in exchange, they freed me.

Just like I wanted.

Needed.

I'd spent my entire childhood with the invisible collar around my neck and bidding wars behind closed doors.

Everyone wanted their shot at marrying the little helpless Laurent daughter and to take advantage of my family's place in the Order of Saints. Although my older brother, Christopher, would have taken the head seat as the Saint representative for the Laurent family—that is, if Damon hadn't blown his face off—whoever I marry would still become a Saint.

The appeal to marry me is even higher since whoever does will control the seat. Which is no doubt why Liam took the risk to publicly propose.

I killed my father to escape, and Liam better watch out because I'm more than happy to do it again.

As if sensing my thoughts drifting, my fiancé turns to me. "Smile. You said *yes*, remember."

Oh, too bad for him that's not binding.

I slip my hand down my dress to where a knife is hidden in a custom pocket. A little poke in his side

should shut him up, right? No real harm, a little blood and a ruined shirt.

After what my family did to me, I swore to never be that helpless again. I enrolled in every self-defense lesson until I was more than capable of protecting myself.

"I'll go fetch us some drinks." Liam escapes just in the nick of time.

It's for the best. There's no way I could jab him without him screaming.

"I've been dying to meet you." A cheerful voice pulls my attention toward them, and for the first time today, my smile turns genuine.

Damon's standing in front of me, face stern as his wife, Misty, grins. She's stunning with her lavender hair bouncing around her shoulders, dressed in bright colors that both have no business here and completely belong.

Damon's watching me, cautious as to how I'll respond. Will I try to snub his beautiful wife, like no doubt countless idiots have done since she's been intro-duced to our fucked-up society?

I grab her hands and pull them into mine. "I can't believe you married this ogre."

"He's not that bad." She laughs.

"*Sure.* I'm excited to get to know you. Whoever tames this guy must be amazing."

A slight blush covers her cheeks. "I'm not sure I had a choice in the matter."

I freeze at the idea of another girl being stuck in a

forced marriage, but her tone is light and playful, earning a smirk from her standoffish husband.

"Well, I owe Damon a lot." No doubt the only reason I wasn't murdered along with my family. "So I'm happy to see him so content."

I point at him. "Don't mess it up."

He wraps both arms around Misty's shoulders in an affectionate display that stands out here. "Don't worry. I know exactly what I have. So, you're getting married? I didn't think that guy was really your type," Damon asks with one raised brow.

I shrug, not bothering to lie to him. No point anyway. All of the Everette brothers can spot them.

"He's not... Surprise proposal. I'll deal with it later," I grumble.

Misty snorts, and her smile takes up her whole face. "I hope to see more of you. You should come by sometime."

"Yes, that sounds great," Liam says, appearing out of nowhere. No way he'd miss his opportunity to speak directly to a Lord. Too bad for him Damon's looking at him like a bug to squish.

"You weren't invited," Damon says, voice flat.

"Of...of course not. Girls' date, right?" Liam tries to recover, poorly.

Damon talks circles around my soon-to-be ex-fiancé, who has no idea that he's being repeatedly insulted, as I let my gaze drift over the crowd.

Pretending I don't know who I'm looking for, I scan

the room. No matter how hard I try to forget Matthias Everette, I can't help but search him out. From the second he'd dismissed me all those years ago, he treated me like I had some kind of plague, and it pisses me off.

A hint of movement catches my eyes, and for just a second, I think I see the unmistakable curve of Matthias's jaw. I blink, and it's gone.

"Scarlet. Are you listening?" Liam cuts in, annoyance edging his tone at my inattention. "Mr. Everette asked you a question."

My head snaps back to a smirking Damon, who's looking over at my shoulder to where I'd been staring.

"What?" I huff out, tired of everything that's happened today.

"I said if you need anything for the wedding, let us know." Mischief is evident on his face. He's making fun of me.

I wouldn't call us close, but he's always taken an interest in watching over me from afar. As if he owes me for helping him find his brothers.

He's wrong. It's my family's fault they were taken to begin with.

"I'll make sure to take you up on that." My voice is soft and serene. Everything a society lady's should be. Which just makes Damon's grin grow wider.

"It was great meeting you," Misty says, glancing behind me, then back to me again. She can't hide her curiosity when she says, "Let's have lunch."

"I'd love that." She smiles wide, pouring a

welcoming warmth over me. Her good mood is addictive, and I can see exactly why Damon's drawn to her.

Once they're gone, Liam relaxes, letting his arm drop from my side.

"Congratulations!" A man with nearly white hair claps Liam on the back. His hair stands out in a way that doesn't match his young face. He shakes my soon-to-be ex-fiancé playfully, and his sleeve lifts momentarily, revealing what appears to be a family crest tattooed on his wrist. "You should have told me."

"I didn't want to waste time." Liam shrugs, then looks at me. "I've told you about Trip, haven't I? We went to Harvard together."

I internally roll my eyes. We've gone on three dates. When exactly would he have told me about his friends?

"I'm sorry, I must have forgotten." I reach out a hand to Trip. "I'm Scarlet Laur—"

"Laurent, I know. Liam's told me all about you. I'm hurt that he hasn't mentioned me."

"Knock it off. I'm sure she's just forgetting," Liam responds.

Now this asshole is really pissing me off.

"Do you mind if I steal your fiancé? We have some pressing work things to take care of." The look Trip gives Liam belies his lie.

"Yes, that's no problem." I leave out the fact that I don't want to be near him either.

"Perfect." Liam kisses my cheek, and I barely suppress my shudder. "I'll call you."

I'd really appreciate it if you didn't.

It's clear now that Damon's gone, there's no point in him sticking around. He's not even bothering to pretend he's here for me. Which is good because it would just piss me off even more.

I guess I won't be dumping him tonight. I down my champagne in two swallows before grabbing a replacement from one of the trays circling the room. I'm going to need to dull my senses if I'm going to be stuck here for any longer.

"Shouldn't you slow down?" Oliver, my burly security guard, says in an even tone. Like he's saying it out of obligation, knowing I won't listen to him anyway. He's been with me since I moved out on my own; pretty sure he's given up on trying to talk sense into me. Oliver is in his late forties, and there's been more than one occasion I caught him questioning why he took this job.

The Order stuck him with me without asking if having a guard is something that I want, but apparently, as someone who's "unprotected" by men in my family, it's not a choice.

"What? You don't think I should celebrate this happy occasion?" Sarcasm drips from my lips, and I take another sip to wash the taste out.

There's no teasing in Oliver's eyes like there was with Damon. He doesn't like what's happening here any more than I do.

"Relax." I grin at him. "It's either drink or commit murder. You decide."

Oliver hands me another glass, taking my empty one. "That's what I thought."

It's not long before a fuzzy contentment takes over me, and I begin to sway with the music. It's been a long time since I let my guard down like this in public, but there's only so much bullshit I can take, and Liam hit my limit.

Of course, the happy feeling doesn't last long as the crowd's whispers reach me. I'm not surprised they're talking about the proposal, but it's the way they point out he's only marrying me for my place in the Order that has me annoyed.

My stomach flips at the idea of marrying any of these men. I want to get away from these stuffy people as fast as possible. I take a step toward the hall, but Oliver's gentle grasp on my arm stills me.

"Where are you going?"

"The little girls' room." I huff out a breath, the alcohol making me sound more like a child than I care for. He's being a little too overprotective for where we are, but he's also my ride out of here. "Actually...grab the car, and I'll meet you around the front."

He examines me for several seconds. "Are you sure you don't want me to walk you?"

I raise one perfectly arched brow, and he just shakes his head, taking a step back. "I'll meet you out front."

I turn before he can say anything else and slip

through the groups of chatting people, trying my best to ignore the whispers as I go.

"They should've ripped the Laurent seat from her years ago."

"There are several families who are a better fit. Now we have to deal with Liam Dupont."

A lady meets my gaze, but that doesn't stop her from saying in a hushed tone, *"I can't believe he went as far as tricking that useless girl. She should know better than to think someone at this level would want to marry her for anything other than her name."*

With each word, my steps turn more frantic, needing to escape. I much prefer when they gossip behind my back.

I'm still looking back at her when my foot slips, tipping me forward. I brace for impact, knowing in this tight dress, there's nothing I can do about the fall, when I slam into a wall that wasn't there a second ago.

My hands go up to catch myself, and they're met with hard muscle under thin fabric. I follow the path of pearl buttons, a black tie and crisp collar, all the way up a thick, tanned neck and pouty, curved lips, a hint of a grin curling the corner.

The air whooshes out of me as I meet a pair of familiar brown eyes with gold-rimmed centers. He looms over me, several inches above six feet, his broad shoulders double my width.

Matthias.

I jolt back, but his arm bands around my back,

holding me in place. My heart ricochets against my ribs, fluttering in my stomach. How can being held by a man I haven't been close to in a decade feel so good?

For a brief moment, I allow myself to relax into him before reality comes crashing back.

"I'm so sorry," I rush out.

He's made it perfectly clear he's the last person who wants to see me, and embarrassment, mixed with something I refuse to examine, crawls up my neck into my cheeks.

He dips his head to my ear so only I can hear him, and I can't stop my shiver when he says, "I've caught you, Little Sparrow."

Chapter 3

Scarlet

"You know, you could be friendlier," I say as I sway against Oliver's side, desperately trying to distract myself from the mortification threatening to take over. I frantically search for something, anything, to take my mind off the overwhelming embarrassment that threatens to consume me. The moment Matthias spoke, I ran away from him like a frightened little bird.

He meant that he *caught me* as I fell, but it triggered memories of the brief period when I thought he wanted me. That I was somehow special to him. The last ten years did a great job of proving me wrong.

I stumble on the next step, and Oliver steadies me easily, putting several inches between us as we walk up the five steps to my front door.

"See. It's like you think I have the plague. You've been my security guard for a freaking—" *Hiccup.* "—decade."

Oliver grumbles something under his breath, and if I didn't know better, I'd swear it was about not losing his fingers.

"Silly. Why would you lose your fingers?"

He blanches but just shakes his head at me as he unlocks the entrance and heads inside before me while I wait patiently in the entry. This is the way it's been ever since that guy broke into my place and lay in wait for me. It had left me feeling vulnerable, unsafe in my own house.

Honestly, prior to that, I kinda thought having my own security was excessive, but he saved my ass that day. So here we are. Me against the exposed brick wall, trying to convince myself I'm not as tipsy as I am, while Oliver goes and searches my place for *bad guys*.

The attempts to trap me into a marriage to claim my family's spot have calmed down since then. I guess the sight of my potential kidnappers' mangled face put a dent in their plans.

Well, that is, until tonight's proposal. I guess he thought if he came at it sideways, that would somehow make his attempt more likely to succeed.

I huff out a breath. All it did was piss me off.

My cozy home is shaped like a long, narrow alley-way. I renovated it when I got back from college, doing my best to keep the charm intact. The original red brick wall runs along one side, serving as a focal point for the furnishings. The kitchen is in the middle of the layout. It's small, less than ten feet wide, but functional, leading

into a dining nook at the back. I embraced the vintage charm of the space and went with a Victorian girly theme, keeping the original crown molding and wainscoting intact. But to add some drama, I painted the walls a deep, rich green color that makes the space feel warm and inviting.

"All clear." Oliver says the same words he does every evening.

I make my way into my living room and try to escape the confines of my dress. It's pretty, I'll give it that, but I haven't been able to take a full breath in the last hour. My fingers fumble with the black clasp that needs to come undone before I can slide the zipper down, but the thing will not unlatch.

"I'm off." Oliver's already walking to the door.

"Wait! Help me get out of this first."

His feet pause midstride, and he turns to me with a look of horror. "You can't just...tear it?"

"Are you kidding me? This torture device costs a fortune." I reach back as if showing how impossible the task is. "Just undo the top clasp, and you can go."

He looks out the window before his shoulders hunch over as he walks to me. Jeez, you'd think we were strangers with how he's acting.

I turn to give him my back, trying to make this as easy as possible, and make a mental note to not wear this type of closure again.

His fingers don't so much as graze my skin as he makes quick work of it, sliding the zipper down a few

inches, finally giving me enough room to inhale properly.

Oliver's phone rings, the sound shrill in the quiet, and I turn to face him.

"Hello." His face drains of all color as he listens to whoever's on the other side. "Of course, sir."

He's already walking backward toward the exit by the time he hangs up. "I'll lock up."

"I know." We've done this countless times. I tilt my head to the side. "Are you okay? You look sick."

"I fucking hope so."

"What's that supposed to mean—"

The door slams behind him before I can finish.

Strange. Something's off with him. My skin starts to prickle with anxiety, but the champagne is dulling the sensation until I brush it away.

I tug at the back of my dress, letting it fall to the floor, leaving me in nothing but a navy blue bra and panty set.

Chapter 4

Matthias

I WATCH from my car as Oliver checks Scarlet's place exactly how I trained him while she waits patiently by the door. I'd hired him the day she decided to go to college. I despised the idea of her being out on her own where I couldn't be nearby, but as a Lord in the Order of Saints, I couldn't leave my responsibilities for more than the few days I went to watch her every other week.

Oliver works as my eyes and ears when I can't be there myself and was the only reason I didn't go insane the seven years she was gone.

Another light turns on in her place, illuminating it all the way to the back. It's impossible to see her from where I'm parked across her street, but after a year of this, I know her habits. Drunk Scarlet will be leaning against the wall, head tipped back, unwilling to admit to herself she's unbalanced, even in her ridiculously high shoes.

Tonight's pair are a navy satin that looked sharp enough to kill. I'd picked them out specifically because they reminded me of knives, and I have no doubt my Little Sparrow would happily use one to defend herself.

I've been sending her things under the guise of designer freebies over the years. The fashion houses are more than happy to play along with my little secret, so long as I make it worth their while. Over the years, I've sent dresses perfectly tailored to her dimensions, shoes the rich would be jealous of, and purses worth more than cars. Dressing her has been one of the small indulgences I've allowed myself. Spoiling my girl even before she's mine.

Seeing her wear something that I've picked out has become an addiction. I've spent hours meticulously choosing each item to perfectly suit her.

Each time, it makes me want to buy her more. To spend more time learning every little detail about Scarlet's likes and dislikes until I know her better than she knows herself.

After years of being starved of her touch, I nearly came undone when she fell into my arms tonight. I shouldn't have been there, but I can't bring myself to regret it. Everything I've done since she'd been the reason we'd survived her family has been for her. I will do whatever it takes to make her happy, even at the cost of my own sanity.

She'd looked up at me with wide doe eyes, bottom lip caught between her teeth, when I wrapped my arm

around her. If we'd been anywhere else, I wouldn't have been able to stop myself from taking her mouth. Resisting her has become excruciating, but she's not ready for me. Yet.

The way she reacted to my touch sent a thrill down my spine. She may not understand why I've stayed away, but her body wants me. I can work with that.

Seven more days until the agonizing ten years of waiting for her ends. I'm going to use every single one of them to warm her up to the idea.

Countless times over the years, I've wanted to say fuck it and break the distance between us, but I've always known once I get close to her, I won't be able to let her go. She'd told Damon if a guy really wanted her, they'd wait. So that's what I've been doing. That all ends the second the clock ticks twelve on her birthday. Then, she's all mine.

Scarlet steps into view of the picture window that takes up the majority of the front of her brownstone. She's struggling with the back of her dress, and my fingers itch to go in there and be the one to snap the clasps and slowly slide the zipper down, running my knuckles along her sensitive skin as they move along her spine.

I'm getting hard just thinking about it.

Oliver comes into view and blanches at something she says. He shakes his head *no* a few times, but she raises a brow, head tilted at him like he's being ridicu-

lous, and his shoulders visibly slump as he walks over to her.

He raises his hands to her upper back, and my entire body stiffens.

You've got to be kidding me.

I hit Dial on the console just as her top comes undone, the fabric opening several inches. Leather squeaks as my fingers grip the steering wheel to keep myself from crashing in there and ripping him away. I don't give a shit that he works for me. He knows better than to touch her.

"Hello?" Oliver answers unsteadily.

"Get out here, now." I can't keep the growl out of my voice, and he visibly flinches in response.

The way he scrambles out of there would almost be comical if I wasn't fighting back the urge to slowly cut off each of his fingers.

I've hunted down any men that are close to her. I was more than happy to fly across the country anytime Oliver informed me of her dates. I'd enjoyed pulling them into alleys and beating them within an inch of their life for daring to get too close, not letting them leave until they've sworn never to go near her again.

Is it fair to Scarlet? No. Do I care? Fuck no.

The passenger door clicks open, and a nervous-looking Oliver climbs inside. His face is turned toward the windshield, throat bobbing with his swallow. I don't miss when he curls his hands into fists and protectively pushes them deep into his jacket pockets.

"You touched my girl," I growl, low in my throat.

He flinches. "It's not like I wanted to. I'd look like an asshole for turning down her request. She probably thinks I'm some kind of perv that can't get close to women."

"Why would that matter?"

That startles him, his gaze snapping to mine. "What?"

"Don't worry about it. You've been working for me since she was eighteen. She'll understand soon enough why you can't get close to her."

A thrill rolls through me, knowing I'm so close to getting what I want. My eyes scan over Scarlet just as she lets the dress slip off her shoulders.

My cock hardens as I let my eyes skim down her supple body. Her long, lean muscles are defined from years of working out.

When Oliver told me she wanted to try kickboxing, I arranged for her to go to the best gym in town. They had additional lessons in self-defense, including how to use a knife. The trainer bitched about it being beneath him, but he shut up when I showed him what I'm willing to pay. Wasn't long before he was sending texts talking about how well she's doing. Of course she is. My girl's a fighter.

Oliver's eyes are trained on his lap, like he's aware he'll lose them if he so much as glances up. It's nice that he knows me so well.

Scarlet disappears upstairs, and her guard's already climbing out of my car. "She has an early appointment."

I pull up her schedule on my phone and see it's for waxing and lift one brow at him.

"Hey, now. I don't book them. I just bring her."

I don't bother replying, and after all this time, he knows not to expect one. He disappears into his car, leaving the responsibility of watching my girl to me.

I've lost countless hours of sleep sitting here in my blacked-out Range Rover, but it's been worth every second. I've learned she midnight bakes when something's bothering her. That she prefers oversized T-shirts to pajamas. Luckily for her, she receives some for Christmas every year. I make sure to wear each one so they smell like me, and I've caught her lifting them to her nose more than once.

It's been hours of me sitting here, long after her lights have gone dark, when my phone rings.

Answering, I say, "I expected you to be back in hiding with your wife."

Damon grunts. "You're so fucking jealous."

He's not wrong. I'd kill to hide away with Scarlet.

"What do you want?"

"Reminding you there's an order meeting tonight and to check up on you. You looked like you were going to kill Scarlet's fiancé earlier. I'm just checking if you need me to get a body bag." There's a teasing tone to my brother's voice, but I know he means it.

"He's still alive. For now."

"Fuck...you sound so ominous."

"Your wife looked happy tonight." I switch to his favorite subject. He's been head over heels for that girl since they met. He did some shady shit to get her, but I can relate. There's not much I wouldn't do to get to my Little Sparrow.

"Don't try to distract me." Damon's sigh comes out clear through the speakers.

"Why? It's working."

"Tell me what's up with you...I thought you wanted nothing to do with her, but you watch her like she's the fucking air you breathe." His voice turns low, edged with a deeper warning. "We don't keep secrets from each other."

I drop my head back to rest on the seat, knowing that explaining everything is long overdue. "I've always wanted her."

"You could've fooled me. Tell me. What's going on in that screwed-up head of yours so I can help you out."

I know he means it. If I asked for his help, he'd do whatever it takes, even if it meant breaking a few moral rules.

I flick my lighter—open. Closed. Open. Closed—until Damon's about to lose it, then ask, "Do you remember what she said to you the day she saved us from her family?"

"I remember you disappearing for a month and scaring the shit out of me." He sounds pissed but waits for my response.

"I didn't leave right away. I'd planned on cornering her when she was alone. I needed to own just how badly I'd messed up. I needed her to know that I'm so sorry."

It would take more than just an apology to get her back, but fuck, I was desperate for her. I still am.

I was willing to fall to my knees and beg. Everette family pride could fuck right off. Even at sixteen, I knew she was the one for me. I'd always hate that she had to go through all of it, but I'd be damned if I wasn't grateful that it bonded us together.

It was fate, and I wouldn't let go of that without a fight.

I roll my neck, the crack relieving some of the tension, and check her window again. Still black. "When I found her, she was with you. Smiling with her head tipped back, blue eyes shining."

I can still remember her words from back then, the joy in her voice.

"She asked you if you were going to marry her off, and you told her she saved our family. You'd give her whatever she wanted. Do you remember what she asked for?"

"No, but I'm guessing you do?" His voice sounds shocked, like he's learning a whole different side of me.

"She told you she didn't even want to think about settling down. That she wanted to go to college, get a job. To stand on her own."

I roll my tongue in my mouth, swiping it over the sharp edge of my teeth. "You asked her what she wanted

if someone approached you with interest." I pause, taking a breath, knowing the next thing held me back for the last ten years.

"She told you she didn't want to hear about it until she was at least twenty-five. That if someone was truly interested in her, they'd be willing to wait."

Her response echoed what she told me in that prison cell of a room. When I'd thought I was about to die and none of it mattered. She'd kissed me hard, saying she didn't want it to be anyone else. I wanted to believe I'd be the one to marry her anyway. Even if it was just a delusion.

"Fuck, Matthias." Damon whistles low.

I don't say the next part out loud, not needing Damon to know just how gone I am for her, that I keep these words tucked away in my chest, reminding me of what she wants.

I want to live in an eggshell-blue house with a wraparound porch and a tire swing hanging from a tree. I want to be chased around my backyard by jelly-covered faces. Is that too much to ask?

"She was so happy talking to you, dancing around like she might levitate off her feet." I rake my hand through my hair. "How could I take that from her? She needed that freedom, and I knew the second I got close to her, I wouldn't let her step away."

"So you ignored her for a decade?" It's easy to hear my brother thinks I'm an idiot.

"How long do you think you could've stayed away from Misty once she was within arm's reach?"

"So, what are you saying? You've been waiting for her?"

"Ten fucking years, Damon. Her time's almost up."

"What's that supposed to mean?"

"That my Little Sparrow is about to be mine."

Chapter 5

Matthias

BLACK HOODED ROBES pulled low over silver-masked men line both sides of the stone aisle. The swish of heavy fabric is the only sound filling the underground cavern as they bow in unison when Damon enters the path, leading the way for me and our two younger siblings.

Sweat builds at the back of my neck, my own black robe suffocating in the heat. The string tying my gold wolf mask snags in my hair at the back of my neck, and I grit my teeth against the urge to correct it.

For how much I hate all of this, I respect the fact that there is power in ceremony. The men bowing around my brothers and me are the Saints, each a member of one of the twenty-six ruling families in the Orders of Saints.

Centuries of tradition have led us to this day, where billionaires bow their heads willingly, knowing that their service to the Order will be repaid.

47

Behind the silver-masked Saints, the Unsainted kneel, heads bowed nearly to the ground. As merely initiates to the Order, they are allowed inside the Vaults but are to be invisible. They are observers, men here to serve quietly in hopes to one day be brought in by their family as a Saint.

My boots click against each stone step as I climb the dais to where four thrones stand tall, Bash, Xander's, and mine slightly behind Damon's.

It's only when we take our seats that the men around us take theirs.

The image laid out on the floor four feet below us perfectly represents the hierarchy of the Order of Saints.

One Saint from each family is seated while their remaining Saints stand behind them, and the Unsainted remain kneeling further back.

Damon leans forward, his gold wolf mask glinting where it catches light from the lanterns hung overhead, and lets all eyes settle on him before speaking. "Today, we have a treat. There's a change of power in the Montave family. You may approach."

There's a gentle hum of excitement charging the room as two men step up from the back. Until recently, the Montave family risked losing their representation in the Order of Saints. A seat is forever owned by the family so long as there are living members, but only a male can occupy it.

They risked it all in order to bait in a bigger family to

unite with theirs, and the plan worked. Earlier this week, Chloe Montave's family sold her into an arranged marriage to the Ledukes' eldest son. Unlike other marriages, the young Ledukes' son took on his wife's last name, following in the Order of Saints tradition.

The two men approach the foot of the dais, where there's a long, thin table. The low murmuring turns dark when the newly minted Montave son removes his hood, revealing a maskless face. There are very few opportunities for a man to skip the Unsainted and go directly to Saint and, in this case, take the family seat.

I can practically feel the jealousy from the Unsainted, who will likely wait years to move up. There'd been a rumor that Chloe was going to marry one of them, but I knew that wouldn't happen. There's no point in marrying into another Order family; the seat would remain open until a male descendant was born. No member of the Order would give up their last name.

"I formally abdicate my role as the Order of Saints representative for the Montave family. I present to you my succumbent member, Noah Montave." The elderly Saint lifts a knife from the ceremony table, slices through his palm, and lets the blood drip into a silver bowl before passing it to his heir.

Noah pauses for a moment, as if debating if he's insane, before slicing his own palm.

"Bow before me and take your rightful position in the Order of Saints." Damon's voice is a clear demand

that causes any lingering complaints to go silent. Once he's spoken, all descension is out of the question.

"Thank you," the older Montave replies and leans on the younger man's shoulder. It's as if he'd been holding himself together all of this time just for this.

Sick fuck, selling off his own daughter. It reminds me entirely too much of how Scarlet's father tried to use her similarly.

A smirk threatens the corner of my lips at the memory of the deviant girl dressed up like a princess. She never did marry the man her family set up for her since her betrothed died suddenly.

My eyes trail down the line to the one open seat. Laurent's.

We killed off every surviving member of her family after their attempted coup.

Every last one of them, except for my Little Sparrow.

Chapter 6

Scarlet

THE DOOR ATTACHED to the cafe rings as Liam steps into the small building. His features twist in distaste at the overcrowded decor. No society member would dare to be caught in a place like this, which is exactly why I picked it.

Plus, it's cute. It reminds me of a similar cafe I would study at for hours near my school.

Liam stands at my table, looking down at me like the ass he is. Of course he wouldn't act like a normal person and just take a seat right away.

"Sit down," I say, tone crisp.

"You're my fiancée now. There's no ordering me around."

I huff out a laugh. "Yeah, about that. I'm not marrying you."

He jerks back like it's somehow a surprise that I'd turn him down now. An idiot could've seen this coming.

53

"I thought you were smarter than this, Scarlet." He moves to sit across from me, keeping his voice low.

I glance to where Oliver stands far enough away he can't hear what's being said, but his entire body is tense, no doubt just waiting for the opportunity to take this guy out.

"You made a mistake cornering me. It's going to be all the more embarrassing when I dump you." A smirk curls my lips. "I can't wait to hear the rumors about why I'd leave."

A muscle ticks in his jaw, and he leans forward, elbows on the table and phone in his hand.

"I was really hoping it wouldn't come to this, but you *will* marry me, Scarlet. I've been waiting to join the Order for entirely too long."

"Well, you should've come up with a better plan because there's no world where I marry you—"

He slides his phone toward me, a video already playing. It's fuzzy, but the audio is crisp.

"Honey, you're hurt. Just put the gun down, Scarlet. We can sort everything out. You don't have to marry anyone you don't want to, I promise," my father says, *voice placating me, but even with death pointed at him, he still can't hide his condescension. Even then, I knew I'd never be anything more than a tool to grow the family's influence for him. I cock the gun.*

"Oh, this? Don't worry. The blood's not mine. Your son made quite the mess when he died."

The grainy image of my father's last steps has anger

searing in my gut as I watch past me fire off round after round. I remember feeling like he was some kind of monster, and I was worried a single bullet wouldn't kill him. In the end, he was just a man.

That night feels like it happened in another world. I'd grown up with that misogynistic bastard as my father, controlling everything I did, but I'm no longer that little girl. I've left her in the past, where she belongs.

Oliver moves toward us, but I hold my hand up in a symbol that I'm fine. The last thing I need is for him to make this more complicated than it needs to be.

I glare at Liam. "How did you get that?"

"You're not the only one with connections."

I rack through my head, but I can't think of a single person who would have access to the security cameras that night.

I huff out a breath, fingers drumming on the table. "What do you want?"

"It's simple. Marry me and this little video stays between us."

That's the type of power a man like this will hold over me for the rest of my life.

"Let it leak."

He jolts back in shock. "What?"

I take a slow slip of my coffee. "I said go ahead and share it."

"Do you think your lawyer buddies will let you work if you're a felon?"

A muscle twitches in my neck. It's not like I don't

know reputation is as important as education in this field, but I'll never let anyone control me like that again.

I lean back, resting my hands in my lap demurely. He doesn't realize he's playing a game he can't win. He picked a fight with me, but I'm the one who's going to choose when to strike.

"Of course. I'll start wedding planning right away," I placate, donning my softest smile. The one that says I'm the docile, submissive girl he thinks I should be.

Appeased, he smiles at me. "I thought you'd see it my way."

Little does he know, I'm planning his murder. After watching that video, he should've known better than to back me into a corner.

My biggest problem is getting all the copies erased. There's only one person who's capable of wiping all of the evidence from existence, and he's the last person I want to owe.

The last real conversation I had with Matthias ended badly. I'd been a foolish girl with a naive crush, and his words tore me apart.

His cold eyes locked with mine as he said, *"Let me make it easy for you. I don't want to see you, hear your voice. I don't want to be in the same room as you."*

The bond that felt tied between us, shaped by a world we barely survived, frayed with his words. His only response when I asked him why he was doing it was to say, *"You may have helped us, but you're still a Laurent."*

At the time, his words shredded through me, but I'm no longer a foolish girl anymore. Matthias Helios Everette isn't ready for the woman I've become.

"What's gotten into you?" Mark says as he ducks another one of my kicks. He's been on the defensive since I landed my first one.

I like sparring with him. In his midforties, he's more collected than some of the hotheads in here. Most men see me in the ring, and their first mistake is to underestimate me. It's no fun if I win too easily.

The gym's walls are made of concrete painted white, allowing each hit and grunt to echo around the room. The facility is pristine. Even the ring itself has new ropes that are changed at any sign of wear. Speed bags, weighted punching bags, pads, and weights are neatly arranged around the walls.

This place is designed to train the best in the city, which should make me feel out of place, but it's one of the only places I feel like I can be myself. I'd been shocked they accepted me so quickly when I returned to town, but they've shown me nothing but respect.

The scent of sweat weighs in the air as I jab forward and duck to miss his answering swing.

Irritation grates at my nerves at Liam's audacity to try to coerce me. I throw my fist forward, and he jumps back, dodging my blow.

"What can't you take a punch?" I say, doing my best to keep my breath under control.

His deep brown hair drips with sweat as it falls into his eyes. He does his best to brush it back without letting his guard down, knowing I'm fast enough to take advantage of any mistakes he makes.

Mark's not afraid to throw his weight around but also respects my ability, making him my perfect opponent. Unfortunately for him, I have a whole lot of frustration to work out today, and he's currently my outlet.

He dodges my punch, catching my arm in a move that has me flipping onto my stomach. Normally, this is when he'd pin me down and make me tap out, but he just stands above me. "Next time, warn a guy before you take out your anger. At least then I could've come in prepared."

I roll over onto my butt, and he reaches a hand down to me. "I'm sorry. I guess I got a little carried away."

He wipes blood from the corner of his mouth. "It's alright. I can take it. I'm just happy I'm not the person you're really pissed off at."

"Alright, you two, off the mat," Coach calls from the side. He's an older Black man who, even in his late fifties, still carries at least fifty pounds of muscle.

I'm grateful that he took me in; I needed a way to fix that helpless feeling that had been ingrained into me after years of living with my family. Even though I had the last laugh in the end, that kind of trauma sneaks up on me.

I've made it my mission to never be that helpless again. I'm not dependent on anyone anymore, more than capable of defending myself. I've learned to fight, to take advantage of my smaller body and speed. Hours at the shooting range honed my aim so I'll never miss.

I'm proud that I can take care of my own problems, which is why it pisses me off that I have to ask Matthias for help.

I'll never admit to keeping tabs on him, but it's impossible not to hear about the Everette brothers. Rumors have spread that Matthias is the head of their technical security, and he's been scouted by the CIA. Not that he'd ever choose to work with them.

Making him my best and likely only shot at neutralizing Liam's threat.

I hop down from the ring and grab a white towel to wipe off my face and go to follow Mark out when Coach stops me.

"You were sloppy out there by the end. Got something on your mind?"

"Nothing a little time on the mat can't fix."

He hands me a bottle, and the water's cool on my tongue.

"Want to talk about it?"

"Not particularly," I grumble. A part of me would love to lean on him. Over the past several months, he's become somewhat of a father figure—a slightly grumpy one that makes me run my ass off if I mess up but caring when I need him.

I can't though. He's not in the Order of Saints, and no matter how much it's tried to take away from me, I'm still at least somewhat loyal. Things have definitely improved since the Everette brothers took over.

Which is why I can't very well tell him I'm being blackmailed into marriage. My family had tried to force me into a loveless relationship with a pedophile pervert. That man was at least ten years older than my father. I'm never going to let anyone attempt to coerce me into marriage again.

I'm just not quite ready to speak to the person who can fix it, and that's assuming he'll even let me get that close.

Not that I'll give him a choice.

Chapter 7

Matthias

"WHAT'S GOTTEN INTO YOU?" Bash asks me, his voice bouncing off the polished black walls of our private room in the Elysium club. He's sprawled out on a leather lounge chair, a crystal glass filled with whiskey dangling precariously from his fingers.

His sandy-blond hair is disheveled, falling loosely over his eyes, covering the gleam in them. He's the youngest Everette brother and somehow the loudest. Xander sits beside him, his hair several shades darker, perfectly styled off of his face. At only eleven months apart, they're thick as thieves. Xander's the more sensible of the two, but Bash never fails to drag him into trouble.

The two of them are several inches below where I partially rest on the back of a chair. There's too much energy running through my veins to allow me to relax.

Tinted one-way windows line one wall, overlooking the dance floor below, the noise from the club muffled in

the soundproof room. We'd purchased the club several years ago, and Xander handled all the contracting to make it perfect, including this room designed specifically for my three brothers and me.

I glance up from my phone, where I've been looking at a picture of Scarlet leaving the gym Oliver sent yesterday. Her white shirt is see-through where her damp hair rests on her shoulders, and I can't decide if I'm turned on or pissed off about it.

Things have been slow ever since the Ricci family's failed attempt at a coup that nearly cost both Misty and Damon their lives.

We stripped the Ricci family of their seat in the Order of Saints, completely wiping them from existence, Sending a clear sign of what would happen if anyone else thought they could fuck with us.

My two youngest brothers are bored out of their minds and the bane of my existence. In the next few years, they'll have to step up and take an active role in our family, but for now, I want them to have the freedom that was denied to Damon and me.

"You've definitely been distracted lately," Xander adds, taking a sip from his amber-filled glass.

I've always been distracted by Scarlet. I've just been better at hiding it, but as the days tick down and I get closer to everything I've been waiting for, it's been harder to keep from them. At least Damon's still too preoccupied with his wife to give me a hard time.

"The both of you can fuck right off." I flip to the next

picture, done caring that I look obsessed. It's about to become insanely obvious anyway.

"Come on, big bro. You can't leave us hanging like this. The way you're staring at your phone has me dying with curiosity. Do I know her?"

"Who says it's about a girl?"

Bash snorts, and Xander smirks, giving me knowing looks.

I crack my neck. "Yeah...you know her."

"Hmmm, that's surprising...I haven't seen you interested in anyone...unless..." Bash's eyes go wide, mischief filling them. "It can't be?"

For a little brat, he's become more observant. I'm still debating how much I'm going to let them know when the door crashes open.

Scarlet's holding a purple key pass in her hand that only our security has.

"Sorry, boss." Our six-foot-four bouncer comes rushing in after her. His hand covers his nose, where it's leaking blood. He's looking down at Scarlet like she's a viper and not the elegantly dressed woman that she's projecting.

He looks almost as scared of her as he is of us.

I lean forward, captivated by her. She's wearing a red dress that perfectly contours her curves, showing off the dip in her waist and the roundness of her hips. Hell, I even love the little softness showing in her stomach.

I had full intentions of tracking her down, but I'm enjoying the fact that she came to me.

Bash smiles up at her. Those two have a special relationship. They aren't close, but he's made sure it's no secret that anyone who messes with her has to deal with him. Hell, all the Everette brothers have.

She marches right up to me, hands on her hips. To anyone watching, they'd see the adoration written across my face, but she's blind to it. She's sexy as fuck, standing inches away, chest heaving with her breaths. It's clear she came here for a reason, and I'm dying to find out what my Scarlet needs.

This is the first time she's actively sought me out since I was an asshole to her at sixteen, and I'm quickly realizing I would have caved to her immediately if she'd asked.

I lean back, opening my knees wide, enjoying how she steps between them without seeming to notice. There's a pull between us that I've been fighting for years, but I'm done with that, and I'm more than willing to succumb to it now.

Scarlet came back from the West Coast, fierce and determined to take the world on her own. The way her blue eyes narrow on me has blood rushing to my cock.

She has no idea how close she is to me losing control.

"How can I help you, Little Sparrow."

Her eyes widen briefly at the nickname before a wall closes, blocking out her thoughts. "I need you to do something for me."

I cock my head to the side, loving the sound of that,

but I also want to see how this plays out. There's a lot of power in a favor.

I stand, crowding her back until she's trapped in my stare. "What's that?"

Pure blue eyes meet mine, the shield she just put up instantly gone. Curiosity, heat, and hurt swirl around her pupils as she studies me, weighing whether it's worth the cost of asking. "The guy who proposed..."

A muscle ticks in my jaw. I definitely thought she'd have gotten rid of him by now. I'm fully aware that they'd only gone on a few dates. He just so happened to propose the day I planned to dispose of him.

I tilt my head to the side. "What about him?"

"He has a security camera video of me killing my father, and he's trying to blackmail me with it."

"Oh shit," Xander and Bash say in unison. There's a pang of jealousy, knowing they'd been there to witness my girl finally get her revenge.

The muscles in my neck strain, and my teeth grind together as I process what she said. A lot went down the night the Everette brothers eliminated the Laurents. None of which we want records of. Not that we couldn't bury them if they ever did surface. I don't tell her that. It's much more fun to see how this all plays out. I rock back on my heels and grin.

"Is that all the help you need, Scarlet?" I move closer until the scent of her perfume fills my lungs with every breath.

"Y...yes," she says barely over a whisper, her chest rising and falling rapidly.

She's temptation incarnate with red-painted lips that are begging me to take them. I got around in my youth, but I haven't touched anyone since her, and like hell I'm having my first kiss in ten years in front of my brothers.

I've saved it for her all this time. I can wait six more days.

"Consider it done."

"That's it? You'll just take care of it?"

"Of course not." I chuckle. "You'll owe me."

"What?" Her mouth curves in an adorable frown.

I run my thumb along my bottom lip, thinking of all the ways she can repay me. "I'm sure we can think of something in time."

She huffs. "I'm not agreeing to that."

I tilt my head to the side and raise one curious brow. "You don't have a choice."

She looks at my two brothers, who are luckily smart enough to stay out of this, and crosses her arms in front of her chest.

I wonder if she realizes that it's pushing her already full tits up for me.

"Fine, just make this go away. Try not to kill him."

I smirk, having no intention of fulfilling that request. "We'll take care of it."

Her shoulders sag with her sigh, all the spirit washing out of her.

I'll make sure she knows in the future, she never

needs to be tough with me. It's my fucking pleasure to take care of her. I'm happy to be the devil she can lean on.

As if she finally realizes exactly where she is, her body goes stiff. "I...I have to go. Let me know when it's done."

"Don't worry. You'll know."

She practically scurries out of the room when Bash whistles.

"So it *is* her."

My gaze cuts to him. "Fuck off."

Matching smiles form on my brothers' mouths, more cruel than happy.

Bash claps his hands together and gets up. "So let's go make this asshole pay."

"We're not really going to let him go with a warning, are we?" Xander asks as he follows after his brother.

"What do you think?"

"I think he's going to regret this for the short amount of time he has left."

Chapter 8

Matthias

"Is that him?" Xander slows down, pulling his Range Rover closer to the curb. Sure enough, that asshole Liam is striding down the street toward a bar. There's a girl hanging off him, and he lets his hand slip over her ass.

"The fuck?" Bash says from the seat behind me, his voice dipping dangerously. The air in the car is practically crackling with just how pissed we are.

"I'm getting out. Don't follow me," I say, eyes still trained on the dead man walking.

"Are you kidding me?"

I turn toward Xander, who leans away from me, hands up between us. "Fine. Happy hunting."

I chuckle as anticipation grows in my chest. *You can run, but you can't hide, Liam.*

Following close enough not to lose him in the crowd but far enough he won't notice, I have time to see just how slimy this asshole is. He's smiling down at this girl,

71

his mouth more leer than anything, and I start to debate the merits of beating his face in, right here on the street.

Sure, it would bring bad press, but nothing we couldn't handle. I move faster, the idea of grabbing him by the collar growing more appealing by the second. They aren't moving fast; the girl is unstable on her feet, and she's leaning more of her weight into him than should be necessary. This man better not be trying to get with a girl too drunk to consent.

I stop when a shoulder slams into mine. The guy's face is relaxed with alcohol, a too-wide smile across it. "Sorry, man—" His words cut off as he takes me in and swallows hard, backing away instinctively. "Shit...I mean, I'm really sorry. Um...yeah...please don't kill me."

All of my brothers have been told we're intimidating. It's something inherent to the Everette line. Born and raised to rule over the rich, we've defended our position as Lords of the Order of Saints with blood.

I raise one brow, and he shifts backward before practically fleeing. It would be comical if it hadn't distracted me from what I'm here for, and Liam's disappearing through the entrance.

The bouncer looks at me before bowing. "Mr. Everette, to what do we owe this honor?"

I don't recognize him, but if I had to guess by his attitude, he's an Unsainted, an unvouched member of the Order who hasn't gone through the initiation yet.

"I'm here to catch a rat. The man who just walked in. Don't let him in again."

"Of course, sir." He holds the door open, fingers trembling on the handle. "Have a good night."

There's no question that I'm going to thoroughly enjoy what happens next.

The club's packed with scantily clad women wearing only the most expensive designer dresses. The men are all in some variation of business suits screaming loud and clear that they're a bunch of stock bro assholes who think they're better than everyone.

I walk deeper into the bar, looking for the man I'm here for. Liam's standing at a high bar table, his date teetering on a chair, her one arm resting on the table for balance. Fuck, she's a mess.

I stay hidden against the wall, waiting for my opportunity. It's dark enough to kill him without being seen, but there are flashes of color, as if the room's being lit by lightning. I'd have to time it perfectly, or everyone would see me snuff this asshole's lights out.

Instead, I wait impatiently as he buys this girl drink after drink until she's slumped over. If I hadn't already been royally pissed at him, this would've done it on its own.

I crack my neck and follow him to the restroom. He stands there, dick in his hand, not noticing I came in. "Liam, is it? I thought I told you I didn't want to see you again."

My voice rings out in the tiled room, the music outside dulled by the closed door. He looks over his shoulder, one brow raised. "What the hell is it to you—-"

He pales, shifting away from me. "I...I'm sorry."

"I haven't even told you why I'm here yet." I step closer and enjoy the way he trembles at my approach. Dick still in hand, clueless of his surroundings, but he's smart enough to know he's not safe here. The urge to channel Damon and cut it the fuck off is more tempting than it should be.

He swallows hard and says in a last-ditch effort, "We're in public. Anyone could come in."

I smirk and click the dead bolt closed, and horror takes over Liam's face. I don't give him time to react, closing the space between us, gripping the hair on the back of his head and slamming his nose into the wall. Blood splatters the white tile when I repeat the motion several more times before hauling him back so he can look at me.

He's in rough shape. His nose is collapsed, mouth bloody, empty spots where he's missing teeth. I slam my fist into his gut, not quite satisfied that he's gotten the message.

Liam's lips tremble, spit forming at the side as he begs, "Please stop."

I let go, and he drops to the sticky floor at my feet. "Why would I stop when I haven't gotten what I came for yet."

He crab walks back on his hands, tears in his eyes. "Why...what do you want?"

I can't help myself from screwing with him a little, letting him think there's hope for him to make it out of

this room. "Leave Scarlet Laurent alone. Make a public announcement stating that you are a cheating bastard who doesn't deserve her and that she called off the engagement because of it."

He nods, but there's a gleam of something else, something sinister in his eyes that has the hair at the back of my neck standing up. He thinks if he survives this, he'll still be able to blackmail her.

He wipes his sleeve over his chin. "She wants to marry me."

"Does she though? Because a little birdie came to visit me earlier and said that you're trying to coerce her. That couldn't be true, right? You wouldn't stoop so low."

"Of course not. I don't have to manipulate some bitch to marry me."

My boot slams into his chest, and his air wheezes out in a loud whoosh.

"Wrong fucking answer. Try again."

He's crumpled over, mouth opening and closing, but no words come out.

I place my hands in my pockets, relaxing like I have all the time in the world. "I found your files, Liam. I'll admit you did an okay job encrypting them, but in the end, they were easy enough to hack into."

Startled eyes meet mine, and he begins to shake at the realization I know all about the sick shit he's been pulling.

I tilt my head to the side, taking in his pathetic state. "The only thing left is a physical copy, and

I'll be honest, I think you're just cocky enough to keep it on your person. So I'll make you a deal. You can either hand it over, or I can waterboard you in the urinal until you give it up. Your choice, really."

His entire body jerks, and there's a green tint to his skin before he pulls a chain from around his neck and hands it to me.

I spin the object around and open the lid, revealing the USB.

"Now...now that you have it, please just go. I promise I won't go near her."

I tuck the object into my pocket. "Apologize."

"I'm sorry. I'm sorry..."

"Not to me. To her."

"What?"

"Take out your phone and tell Scarlet just how much of a sorry bastard you are."

He pulls out his phone from his pockets, his hand so unsteady he's barely able to take it out. It rings several times before her voicemail picks up.

Liam looks at me, but I stare back blankly.

"I'm sorry, Scarlet. I've gotten rid of the video. Of course you don't have to marry me." His missing teeth give his voice a lisp as he struggles to get the words out. He glances up, then back at the phone. "I'm worthless compared to you. I won't bother you again."

I grab his phone, ending the call, and smile at him. "See, it wasn't too hard, was it?"

"I did what you said." He goes to get up, and I push him back down.

"There's something else I want to know. Where did you get the video, Liam? That's not something you should have been able to get a hold of." I'm not lying. The fact that this lowlife somehow managed to get access has been bothering me.

Tears stream down his face. "It just showed up in my email. I swear. I don't know who sent it."

"I believe you." It's significantly more likely than him coming across the video on his own. It also means someone bigger is in play here, someone who wants something from Scarlet.

"Can I go?"

The hope in his eyes is pathetic.

"Don't be stupid." I chuckle before landing a punch into his temple, hard enough to make him see stars. "You're not going anywhere."

I drag him into the stall and bury his face in the putrid water, not letting go as he thrashes in my grip.

I lift his head, allowing him a few breaths.

"You said you'd let me live."

"Hmmm. Did I? I guess I lied." I press his head down, submerging him up to his ears.

The water ripples, splashing from the bowl, and I make a note to toss this suit out. I don't release him until his body's limp, no longer struggling to breathe. Death by toilet is one hell of a way to go.

I kick his feet until he's fully hidden by the stall and

lock the door behind me. He'll just have to stay there until I can find someone to clean this shit up.

My jacket sleeves are wet, and I have to fight back nausea when I pull it off. Fucking disgusting. I calmly wash my hands, taking my time to make sure they're meticulously clean before drying them off.

I make my way through the crowd to the bouncer I saw earlier. He's in the corner, watching to keep things running smoothly. If he does this for me, I'll put in a call to have him moved over to Elysium.

He notices my approach. "Everything go as planned, sir?"

I nod, then point toward Liam's date. She's now fully supported by the table. "Get her home. Bill me whatever the cost."

"Of course," he replies easily.

"I left you a mess to clean up in the men's room. Do you think you can handle it, or should I call someone else in?" I'm well aware that not everyone's fit for this type of work, and I'm giving him an out.

"I've got it, sir."

"Good. I'm trusting you."

A slight flush covers his cheeks, and he lowers his head. "May I ask what he did?"

"He fucked with what's *mine*."

Chapter 9

Scarlet

I RELISTEN to the message Liam left. I'll admit Matthias works fast. I knew he'd get it done, but even I'm impressed by just how quickly he had Liam backpedaling.

My hands are still shaking a day later from walking into the Everette private room at Elysium and demanding he help me. There was an 80-20 chance he'd tell me to go screw myself. After all, I am just another *Laurent* to him.

Ten years, *ten years* since we spent that one horrendous week together, trapped in the hellscape of my family's making. Since then, I've built a life around me, brick by brick, one where I'm more than capable of taking care of myself.

Which made it all the more humiliating to have to ask Matthias for help. Swallowing my pride had tasted sour, but there's not much I could've done about it.

Getting the video wiped from existence isn't something I could trust just anyone with, and despite the fact that Matthias has actively avoided me for a freaking decade, I knew I could trust him to get it done.

Of course, I completely overlooked the fact that he'd ask for something in return, and now I'm living my teenage nightmare, indebted to my childhood crush.

I pull my hand away from my mouth, realizing I've been chewing on my nails, and the once pristine blush polish is now chipped. Dammit.

Putting my phone down, I get back to my computer. We have a large potential client coming in who we've been working with for the last several months. He wants us to provide permanent legal counsel for multiple of his companies. It's a deal that's felt too good to be true, especially since he's been anonymous this entire time, but he's finally agreed to meet in person today.

I've been working on this presentation for weeks. As a junior lawyer on this team, I'm backing up the partners. The only reason I was able to land this job in the first place is because I did a yearlong internship while I was in my final year at Stanford, and I dipped into my family funds to sweeten the deal. I may hate my family, but that doesn't mean I can't make use of the privileges my inheritance provides me. Even with that, I know how precarious my job is and how important it is that this presentation goes well. The last thing I want is to make my boss look bad.

Morning light streams through my office window. It

takes up the majority of the east-facing wall, never failing to make the room feel welcoming.

I've already sent the file over to my boss, but just in case I've missed something, I double-check my work for the fifth time.

There's a light knock, and I get up, opening the door, expecting to see my boss. For a second, I forget where I am as my eyes skim over Matthias. He's tall, dark, devious, a man who could eat me alive.

His large shoulders take up the entire doorframe, blocking the bustling office behind him. I groan internally, tamping down the heat swirling low in my stomach. The man's grown into some kind of sexy, godlike giant.

I clear my throat. "What are you doing here?"

"Is that any way to welcome someone who just did you a favor?" He enters my office, the door closing behind him, and I involuntarily step back. A wolflike smile curls the corner of his lips, and he stalks closer, driving me back until the back of my thighs hits the edge of my desk, halting my retreat.

My breath catches as his presence surrounds me, causing my body to hum even without his touch.

I stare down at the buttons of his perfectly tailored crisp black shirt.

"Look at me, Little Sparrow."

I clench my fingers at my sides to hide the way they tremble and shake my head. "Don't call me that."

He raises his hand, cupping my face, and guides it

up with his thumb. "Don't look away from me when I've come to see you."

I rip my face away and stare right at him. Not looking away from his dark gaze. I push all my frustration into my voice, praying that it covers the slight shake in it. "What do you want?"

His teeth run along his bottom lip as he takes in my words before reaching into his pocket and handing me a USB.

"All handled. Your asshole ex won't bother you again."

My stomach twists as the small device presses into my palm. How could I forget this is why he's here?

He doesn't move away like I expect him to. Instead, his mouth moves closer to mine until his breath tickles my lips, and I can almost taste whatever sweet mint he's been chewing on.

"I've come to call in my payment."

I jerk a little, but he keeps me still with a firm grasp of my jaw. I knew it was coming, but I didn't know it would be so soon.

"What...what do you want?" This time, I can't hide the tremble in my voice. The thoughts swirling around of what he can want when he's so close.

"Kiss me, Scarlet."

His words are an echo of mine from all those years ago. One that has a million memories flooding my head filled with promises he'd made. I push them away, trying to find some semblance of clarity.

"What?" I say breathily.

"There's no running away now, Little Sparrow." His lips brush mine. "Kiss me."

Before I can even comprehend what I'm doing, my desires from my past take over, and all rational thoughts leave me as I close the distance between us.

His mouth isn't soft; it's hard and demanding. Like he wants to own a part of me and show me just how much I need him.

I kiss him back, pulling him closer, losing all sanity as he pushes his knee between my thighs and devours me until my lungs burn.

"*Fuck*, my memories didn't do this justice." His open mouth kisses along my jaw and down my neck, where he sucks on my sensitive skin, and I tilt my head to the side, giving him more room as I grip his hair and hold him closer.

There's a knock on the door, snapping me into reality, but he doesn't let me go even when I pull away, instead sucking my bottom lip into his mouth and biting it.

"This isn't over."

There's a twinge in my heart, and I remind myself that this man told me I was nothing to him while pushing me away and disappeared from my life and has done nothing to make me trust him since. Bracing myself, I shake my head.

"Yes, it is."

He lets me push him back, and I go to the door,

swinging it open to see my antsy boss. She's a few years older than me, with tight, curly black hair braided into micro braids that she's pulled back into an intricate bun that I could only wish I could achieve. Her cream jacket is the perfect complement to her deep brown skin.

"He's not here yet."

Still in a daze, I can't piece together what she means. "Who?"

"The client. He didn't show."

Shit. I'd forgotten all about the meeting.

I can feel Matthias step behind me into the doorway even before he says anything.

"You must be looking for me."

Chapter 10

Matthias

"Do you two know each other?" Mrs. Robertson asks, looking between Scarlet and me, but my attention is caught on the pink crawling up my girl's cheeks and the way her heartbeat is visible in the curve of her neck. She's doing everything she can to push that kiss behind her, but she can't.

"We're childhood friends," I reply when Scarlet stays silent. I love that I left her speechless.

My fingers flex at my sides as I prevent myself from closing the door in the lawyer's face and taking my future wife on her desk like my cock's demanding I do.

We're not there yet—she still has a few more days of freedom, and I'm not going to fuck it up, no matter how rock hard I am.

My reaction just reaffirms why I needed to stay away from her all this time. I can't be in a room with her for

five minutes without wanting to own every single one of her moans.

"Mr. Everette?" Mrs. Robertson says, drawing my attention back to her, and this time, it's Scarlet's turn to smirk at my complete loss of attention.

"I'm sorry. I was distracted." I pull myself away from what I've wanted most and get back to business. "You have a presentation for me?"

Scarlet's boss looks between us, her brows pulling together, but she doesn't say anything. I'll have to be more careful in the future.

"Of course, right this way." Mrs. Robertson leads the way toward the conference room, where there's a large TV with a presentation already set up. My girl's forced to sit next to me in order to avoid the situation, looking more suspicious than it already is. She passes me a folder that's filled with documentation.

I glance at them briefly, already familiar with the document. Hacking into Scarlet's computer and watching her work has been one of my favorite hobbies.

"Those are your copies. I'll also send you the digital copy." Her tone is crisp and businesslike, and I want nothing more than to break it apart.

Mrs. Robertson dims the lights slightly to remove the glare on the TV and begins an elegant presentation.

Unfortunately for her, I have no intention of listening to a word of it, too captivated by my proximity to my future wife.

I should keep my hands to myself, but I've never

been able to do what I'm supposed to, so I slide my hand onto the bare skin of her knee.

She jolts, legs hitting the table, and glares at me, hand attempting to slap mine away.

Her boss clears her throat. "Is there a problem?"

"Sorry. Just killing a bug," Scarlet replies, and her boss turns back to the PowerPoint.

A chuckle rumbles the back of my throat, and I lean in so only Scarlet can hear me. "I'm a bug now?"

She stiffens, and I run my thumb back and forth until her body relaxes beneath my touch. That's my girl.

I inch higher but don't breach her skirt. If she wants this, she's going to have to show me. If she doesn't, I'm satisfied with just being able to touch her.

My thumb skims her sensitive skin, and her breath hitches in her throat, goose bumps forming on the back of her neck and down her arms.

Come on, Scarlet. Take what you want.

She clamps her thighs closed and glares at me.

"You're going to get me fired."

"Unlikely."

My dick hardens almost painfully. I can't help but notice her reasoning had nothing to do with not wanting me. I shift so my fingers graze higher beneath her skirt.

A shiver rolls through her, and a needy sound escapes her lips, drawing Mrs. Robertson's attention back to us.

Scarlet looks at the desk, as guilty as a schoolgirl, and

tries to push my hand away, but I just grip her thigh harder, holding her in place.

I straighten my posture and smile. "I appreciate your time. As I recently purchased your company, I'm happy to welcome your law firm on as my council."

Scarlet jerks, her gaze narrowed. "You've got to be kidding me."

"I would never kid about you."

She stands, apologizing to her boss, and rants under her breath. I think I catch something about *assholes, conceited dickheads*, but I can't be sure.

I let her go, knowing she won't be free for long.

Five days, Little Sparrow.

Then you're mine.

Damon: Did one of you assholes buy a law firm?

Me: I bought Scarlet's law firm.

Bash: Damn Matthias, you're just like Damon.

Xander: I hope it's not fucking contagious.

Chapter 11

Scarlet

"STUPID, STUBBORN MEN," I grumble under my breath as I cover the deep red mark Matthias left on my neck. I can only thank God it didn't darken until I got home from work.

No matter how many times I've rolled it over in my mind, I can't for the life of me understand what's changed.

He went from evading me since I was fifteen to kissing me breathless.

A thrill runs through my traitorous body at the memory. It responded to him so easily, completely taking over my mind, like he owned it. It's like he consumed any semblance of sense I had.

One does not kiss boys who've ignored you for ten years. Not a hard concept to understand, and yet I'd succumb to his mouth willingly.

I remove the giant rollers from my hair one by one,

careful to guide each curl into the perfect position. No one ever accused me of being low-maintenance. Even for events that I don't want to go to, like tonight, I spend hours getting ready. I started with a head-to-toe body mask that makes my skin silky smooth while telling myself the entire time it's not in case I run into a certain billionaire.

My dress is a deep burgundy, so dark it could be mistaken for black, that dips low on my back, the fabric brushing my tailbone.

I look in the mirror and smile, my lips painted a scarlet red.

Matthias showed up to my work today and played with me, and tonight, I'm going to spend my time completely ignoring him as I should have done all along.

Oliver is waiting in a black suit and tie by the door like usual, giving me a small smile. Although our relationship has always been completely professional, he's still been a steady force in my life. One that I'm going to need tonight.

He holds out a light jacket for me. "Are you ready to go?"

I slide it on before pausing and rushing back to my room.

"I can't believe I almost forgot this." I tie the black mask around the back of my head, being extra careful to keep my hair perfectly styled.

I walk back out to where Oliver's standing.

"How do I look?"

"I'd prefer not to be murdered for answering that."

My brows scrunch together. "Why would I murder you? I'm the one who asked."

He ignores me completely. "Let's go. You don't want to be late."

Chapter 12

Scarlet

THE EXCLUSIVITY of this event is what draws so much attention, and I'm not surprised to see the lined-up photographers as we pull up to the Everette hotel. For four brothers who like to stay out of the spotlight, they sure put on a good party.

I lower my mask, blocking my face from view before Oliver opens my door. The black town car is one of many lined up to drop off partygoers. The immaculate designs and attire are all a cover for the darkness that lies beneath. The Order Of Saints isn't exactly bad, but power always stirs resentment, and over the years, I've learned that living this life comes at a cost.

There's a tentlike structure that reaches all the way to the car, made of a bloodred velvet-like fabric that makes it near impossible for the paparazzi to get a clear shot. The entire thing is designed to keep others out, to

maintain the secrecy of the Order while simultaneously rubbing it in people's faces.

I've spent my entire life coming to these events, and the starry-eyed response I had as a kid wore off a long time ago. It was at one of these events that I met the man my father sold me off to. It was a sham of an arranged marriage. One where my father was more than happy to sell his teenage daughter to get the funds he wanted.

This time, it's different though. My heart kicks up as I make my way through the fabric tunnel lit by wide globes on either side.

The hall itself is decorated beautifully, as always. The theme is a midnight tryst. Whoever designed it used the opportunity to create divisions in the space, with low-hanging drapery giving it an enclosed, private feeling. Mixed with the masks, it's as if, even in a crowd of people, no one will be looking. Which is a thousand percent untrue.

Nothing happens here without everyone knowing.

I make my way through the throng of people, careful not to be pulled into a conversation. I'm barely tolerated at events like this. I'm not naive enough to think these men believe I deserve to remain here. Not after what my family did.

I let my gaze skim the crowd, not even bothering to lie to myself about who I'm looking for.

I still haven't decided if that's to seek Matthias out or hide from him. He left me completely confused and more than a little overwhelmed after our last meeting.

The fact that he bought the company I work for both impresses me and pisses me off.

He wants more access to me, but I can't for the life of me sort out why. Why now?

Taking a sip of champagne a server generously brought me, I slowly circle the room. I've been doing this for ages, slowly watching everyone, learning their secrets while keeping my own.

Secrets are power, after all, and I've used them to maintain my position more than once. Not that I truly care about being a member of the Order. Women don't participate anyway, but there's always been something I can't quite place tying me to this world.

"Fancy seeing you here." A voice comes from directly beside me, startling me out of my thoughts.

"Bash!" I stumble back, and he catches me easily with one arm, then lets me go.

He lifts my hand to his mouth and kisses my gloved knuckles. "You look ravishing, Miss Laurent."

"You look all grown up." I smirk, because he does. Gone is the little boy stuck in the room with his brother. He's dashing in his black-on-black tux, standing at least half a foot taller than me. He's not wearing his mask, leaving the devious gleam in his eyes on full display.

"Does that mean you'll hide away with me tonight?"

He's got this whole roguish charm going for him, and I'm starting to feel bad for all the hearts he's broken.

Damon approaches and shakes his head. "You know I can't stop him."

At first, I think it's directed at me, but Bash yanks his hand away and gives a cheeky grin.

"Right. I don't want to die tonight."

"Why do people keep saying that?" It's not like I'd kill him for touching my hand.

He grins. "Because it's likely, and I want to live. I'm too pretty to die this young."

I huff out a laugh. "You're being ridiculous."

"Am I though? I better go before I get into any more trouble." He bows low and looks at Damon. "Save me?"

The eldest Everette raises a brow but turns to me. "I have to get back to my wife. If you find time, come say hi. I'm sure she'd love to see you."

There's so much love in his eyes it makes me go all gooey. "Of course. I'd love to."

He grips Bash around the back of his neck and drags him through the crowd while whispering to his now very pale younger brother.

Alone again, I slowly weave my way around the dance floor, where couples move in choreographed dances that could be found in the nineteenth century. Out of the corner of my eye, I catch the tail of a brilliant pink dress. Misty's grinning up at Damon as they move together as one, standing out in the crowded room.

"May I have this dance?" the younger Volkov asks, bowing low in front of me. His silver mask reflects his red hair. He wears it longer and ties it low in the back. I don't really want to dance, preferring to stay on the periphery. Unable to fight the polite etiquette that was

ingrained into me from a young age, I let him take my hand.

"Congratulations on your ascension." I step in with the other dancers. This one requires intricate steps and changing of partners.

He's cut off from answering until we're brought together again. "Thank you. My father is quite happy."

I tilt my head at his answer. Not quite what one would expect from someone who just took one of the most prestigious roles in the world. I examine him a little harder, but there's nothing in how he holds himself that seems anything but excited to be here.

The steps continue, and I'm once again switched to another partner, but instead of the older, portly gentleman I expect, a gold mask is looking down at me.

Only years of practice prevent me from missing a step when his hand meets mine. The moment of contact sends an electric current shooting up my arm, and I pull away, only to have him catch my fingers. Matthias's deep brown eyes take in mine as we move together through the steps. His scent fills my nose, a nostalgia coming with it as I breathe him in.

Matthias slides his hand up my waist, a move that's not a part of the dance, and heat floods to my core. The room feels small around us as his touch burns me through my dress. I swallow hard as unwanted memories of our kiss come thrashing in, causing my breath to hitch in my throat.

He hasn't said a word, and yet he still has all of my attention.

A slow smile curves his lips when he lets me go, switching to his next partner. Mr. Volkov saves me from embarrassment, an easy hand guiding me back into formation.

He lowers his head so only I can hear. "You okay?"

My pulse wooshes in my ears as I try to gain control of my body, pissed that just the slightest touch from Matthias has my body out of control.

The song comes to an end, and I give a meek smile. "I'm fine. Just thirsty."

"Let me get you a drink."

"I'm alright on my own. Besides, I think the girls will throw a mutiny if I keep you much longer."

He looks around and smiles as if just noticing the countless eyes on him. I can't tell if he's oblivious or skilled at this entire thing. Whatever he is, by the way the girls around us blush, it's working.

"Are you sure?" he asks out of obligation.

"Yes." I laugh at the way he visibly relaxes. He's nineteen max and clearly enjoying his new notoriety. "Go have fun."

After ten minutes of people-watching, familiar white hair catches my attention. I'm not positive it's Liam's friend until I spot the tattoo on his wrist when he lifts his hand to take a sip of his drink.

I haven't seen Liam in the last few days, not that I'm surprised after Matthias spoke with him. No matter

what was said, I'm sure it wasn't pleasant for my ex-fiancé.

Trip and the other man are whispering to each other, and suspicion seeps into the back of my mind. There are any number of things they can be talking about, but there's something that feels off about the entire thing. I inch my way closer, trying to make out what they're saying.

My ears prickle when I catch a few words before they fade.

"You know the Laurent..."

"Are you sure..."

"It's the only way."

Their back-and-forth conversation has the hair on my neck standing up. Every instinct in my body goes into full alarm. These men aren't here for just the party.

As if sensing my eyes on them, they both glance around the room before one nods to the other, and they both head toward one of the halls.

My fingers tap on my hip, mildly comforted by the hard steel under the fabric.

If they are talking about me, nothing good will come from following them. I gnaw my lip, running the outcomes through my mind. If they catch me, I can just pretend I'm lost, heading to the restroom, but depending on the severity of their secret, they may not just let me go.

Counterpoint: if they are talking about me, it's in my best interest to know exactly what they're planning.

Making sure my mask is firmly in place, I trail several feet behind them.

Their strides are twice as long as mine, confined in my tight dress and four-inch heels, and I try not to run to keep up with them in the ballroom.

I can only make out a word or two per sentence. Each one makes me all the more wary.

Call me paranoid, but I know firsthand what happens when men are left to plot for their personal gain.

The hall is dim, lit only by ambient lighting, and the walls are draped in the same velvet to keep the feel of the event, providing me with the perfect cover. I slip off my shoes, knowing that the clicking sound would instantly give me away and try to recover the ground between us.

If I can just get a little closer, I can figure out what they're planning.

This time, I might even be able to stop whatever they're planning.

My heart rate spikes when one of the men stops, turning toward me. I stumble backward, knowing I'm totally screwed if he spots me.

Milliseconds before that can happen, a hand clamps over my mouth, and a solid body pushes me into an alcove covered by velvet fabric.

My breath catches in my throat as I push against my assailant, only to be pulled closer, a familiar scent wrapping around me.

"What do you think you're doing, Little Sparrow?"

A shiver runs through me as his lips brush against the shell of my ear.

Too close. He's too close.

He lifts his hand from my mouth, lowering it until the base of my neck is cradled between his thumb and fingers.

"None of your business." I push against him, hands on hard muscles, his heat soaking through the fabric into my body.

He chuckles low in his throat as he runs his nose along the curve of my neck. "Everything about you is my business."

I huff out a laugh, doing my best to stay quiet in case the two men are still close by. "Since when? Seriously, I thought you couldn't stand me."

Matthias pulls back, a hint of light catching his eyes, watching me. I feel myself grow wet when he presses closer, and the hard ridge of his cock indents my stomach. "Does that feel like I can't stand you?"

"I don't understand you." Mortification seeps in at the slight tremor in my voice.

"You will." He opens his mouth, his tongue hot on my skin as he makes his way up my jaw.

My head tilts involuntarily to the side. The heat of him has stolen my ability to think, and the man knows it.

He grasps my chin, angling my face the way he wants it before capturing my mouth. The feelings he stoked within me the other day come to life as if they

never went out. He burns beneath my skin as his hands travel down my sides and slowly lift the hem of my skirt until he can grasp my bare ass.

He hooks the lace fabric of my thong and tugs on it, a low growl reverberating in his chest.

"We can't do this," I breathe, leaving it up to him to stop.

His fingers press against my entrance. "Tell me to stop."

I try to push the words out but can't.

Matthias chuckles as he sinks two fingers into me, and I curl against him, burying my moan into his chest.

"You can lie to yourself all you want, but your body is so honest."

He grinds his cock into my clit while stroking his fingers deep, stealing my last coherent thought.

Matthias drops his face to my shoulder, his hot breath panting against my neck as he takes me higher.

I whimper as my orgasm grows closer, and he nips my earlobe. "I love the sounds you make."

He presses harder against me, his movements faster, less contained, and my release starts to break around me.

"Yes. Yes," I cry out as pleasure ricochets through me. "Matthias."

He groans low in his throat and bites the side of my neck, his body shuddering in my arms.

My knees are weak; the only thing holding me up is his body pressing me into the wall.

He drops his forehead to mine, our breaths mixing together, and smirks. "I haven't come in my pants since high school."

Shock rocks through me. "You what?"

His smirk turns into a smile. "You haven't said my name in over a decade. I couldn't help it." He nuzzles his nose against mine. "Say it again."

Suddenly, it's as if I'm standing at a precipice and he's asking for so much more than his words. I pull back and search his gaze, looking for the joke.

"Why are you doing this?" My heart aches. I feel like I've left myself wide open.

He leans in and places a kiss to my forehead before creating space between us. "Just say it one more time."

Frustrated, I push him even further, and his eyes widen at the force. Must be surprised that a scrawny girl like me has that much strength. If he keeps picking on me, he's going to see so much more of what I can do.

"Let. Me. Go."

A muscle in his jaw ticks, and his eyes darken on mine, holding my gaze for several seconds before he steps to the side. "Of course."

I blink back tears as I rush through the gala, not caring if anyone sees me. I have to get out of here before the full force of what I just did hits me. I'm such an idiot.

Oliver's already standing with the car door open when I come out of the building, and I climb in, closing the door behind me.

I curl into a ball, holding myself together. It's only then that I realize I've lost a shoe.

A laugh floats from me at the ridiculousness of it all.

This isn't a fairy tale, and I'm not a helpless girl who needs saving.

Maybe it's time I show him that.

Chapter 13

Matthias

I WAD up my black silk boxers and toss them in the trash as I walk out of the restroom. I should be embarrassed for coming in my fucking pants, but all it takes is the thought of how wet she was wrapped around my fingers to have my cock rock hard again. The way she moaned into my neck, her breath hitching with each thrust, her pussy clenching around me, had me coming undone.

I haven't touched a girl since I made her that promise when we were teenagers. I haven't even jacked off without her image in my brain.

My attention was so focused on her that she guided me with her little sounds, the desperate way she pushed into me when I hit the perfect spot or rubbed her the way she needed, drawing a map for me to get her off.

The second she said my name, she owned me, my cum soaking my pants. It won't be long until I'm buried deep inside her. It's unlikely I'll last long that first time,

113

but I'll just fuck her until the feel of my cock stretching her is her only thought. I'm so close to making her mine that my brain short-circuits every time I get near her.

The hall's still full of Saints, their silver wolf masks catching the dim light around them. This is one of the few events the members of the Order are allowed to wear their masks outside of the Vaults. They show off their wives and mistresses as they move around the room, mingling with other members of the society.

I make my way to the only gold-masked members, the Lords themselves. Bash and Xander turn to me as I approach, both wearing matching grins.

Bash is the first to speak. "Where did you disappear to?"

I straighten with the overwhelming feeling of wanting to keep what happened between Scarlet and me private but also knowing he's stubborn enough to keep being a pain in my ass.

Xander examines me, his sharp gaze taking everything in. "You're not the only one who vanished. Somehow, I doubt it was a coincidence that you and Scarlet Laurent left at the same time."

"Mind your business." A muscle ticks in my cheek.

My brothers' easygoing image is more of a facade than anything. They're both entirely too observant, picking up on the most minute things.

A laugh busts out of Bash, a cocky smile on his face. "Since when have we ever done that?"

Xander tilts his head to the side and raises a brow.

"You went from ignoring her to following her around like a puppy."

"Please don't tell me you're stalking her." Bash smirks like he already knows the answer.

"I guess it depends on what qualifies as a stalking."

Bash huffs out a breath. "Yeah, I don't think it's that complicated. Probably one of those things where if you have to ask, you're definitely doing it."

"So tell us, big brother. How have you been keeping track of your girl, because there's no way you haven't been?" Xander asks.

I shrug. "Her guard, Oliver, works for me."

"Damn...you hired him to spy on her!" Xander laughs. "That's fucked-up."

Bash snorts into his drink. "I can't believe you're actually worse than Damon."

"I've had longer to practice," I say, not feeling an ounce of shame.

"The real question is why pay attention to her now?" Bash cuts in.

"Figured I should warm her up a bit before I make it so she can't escape."

"*Jesus*," Xander exclaims. "You and Damon are fucking creepy. You know that?"

Bash smiles at Xander. "I don't know. Seeing this softer side of Matthias is kind of cute."

"Fine." Xander turns serious, a coldness wafting off him that would scare the hell out of anyone else. "Don't forget we owe her. Hurt her and we'll hurt you."

"You're not going to have to worry about that. I'm going to spend the rest of my life giving Scarlet exactly what she needs. Even if she doesn't know what that is yet."

"And that's you?" he asks.

"It sure the fuck is."

Damon walks up to us, handing me a drink. "What are you talking about?"

"That Matthias has you beat in the stalker department."

"Ah, so you finally told them."

Bash's eyes go wide. "What? You knew and didn't tell us?" He places his hand over his chest like he's been wounded. "I thought we were close."

"Trust me, I was as shocked as you are." Damon glares at me. "Not to mention the hard time you gave me when it came to Misty."

"Speaking of which. Where is your beautiful wife?" I ask, knowing the compliment would piss him off. All Everette men are territorial, but the two of them have something extra going on.

"I sent her home with Nicholas. We have this meeting tonight. It better not go long—I've got plans." His lips tip up at the end.

Bash scrunches his nose. "Ew. Don't think about our sister like that."

"I should kill you for your mind even going there," Damon says, his tone flat, and our two youngest brothers smartly take a step back.

Xander holds his hands up in surrender. "Let's just get this fucking meeting over with."

Chapter 14

Matthias

WE GRAB the cloaks we stashed at the Vaults' entrance and pull them over our masked heads. Not that anyone could mistake who we are. The gold wolf mask clearly indicates we're the Lords of the Order of Saints. The Order is split up into an unquestionable hierarchy: the Lords at the top, followed by the Saints in silver masks, and finally, the Unsainted, men who anticipate joining but haven't yet been initiated.

I'm glad that's not what's happening tonight. The blood ceremony is boring as fuck.

Instead, we're holding an open forum where Saints can bring matters to us for assistance. We're stronger as a collective. It never fails to turn into a giant bitch fest, and not for the first time have I wished we didn't have to do this. But the Order is built on tradition that even the Lords can't change. It's what makes us strong.

Bash is first through the door, heading into the

Vaults. Saints line the way to the front, making a path for us. Arched stone walls behind them, and four thrones stand tall on the stage that stands above everyone else. Ours are slightly further back than Damon's. Of the four Lords, he is the highest, and I'm more than proud to support him.

There's no jealousy between the four of us. It's our united front that makes us strong. We'd bonded when they tried to shatter us apart. It backfired—our capture was another way to seal us together. I know it messed Xander and Bash up just as much as it did me, but it's that trauma bond that makes us unbreakable.

Saint Volkov is the first to approach the dais. He's a new member, only initiated a few weeks back. "Lords, may I request assistance with a business matter?"

"You may," Damon replies, the formality of it all itching at my skin. I'd been raised for this. My father was the Lord before us, but I've never wanted it.

"We had a competitor to our security business move into our area. They're undercutting our prices and driving us out of the market."

Damon drums his fingers on the arm of his chair, his tone bored. "Why should I care?"

"It'll cost us our company. The Volkov family will lose our fortune." The Saint has let too much emotion enter his voice. Even here, where we are all supposed to work together, the members are constantly looking for weakness to pounce on.

"And you want us to stop them?" Damon sucks on his teeth. "I grant you—-"

"Wait." A Saint steps into the aisle, risking his life cutting Damon off. The room goes eerily quiet.

Damon stiffens, his eyes narrow beneath his mask at the man who stepped out of turn. The look would freeze most men but doesn't stop this one.

"I own the company moving in. It wouldn't be fair to cut our profits just because they can't compete."

"Fair?" Damon tilts his head to the side and leans back, letting himself appear relaxed. "What have any of us done for the sake of fairness?

In a different place, this would be an opportunity to vote, but the Order of Saints isn't a democracy, and there's only one opinion that counts.

"Work it out amongst yourselves. Don't bring it up to me again."

The man in the aisle smiles like he got exactly what he wanted, and a chill rolls down my spine. I don't fucking like him.

Volkov's chin drops to his chest as he makes his way back to his place. His turn is over.

Saint after Saint brings up concerns, and it's hours before we get out of there. Cool air meets my face as we leave the Vaults into the street. I check my watch. It's 3:00 a.m., and looking at Damon, I can tell he's pissed.

My back aches from the hard chair, and I roll my neck, content with the way it cracks.

"I'm really starting to question why we do this," Bash groans.

Xander nods. "Agreed. You don't need us. Why do we have to be tortured too?"

My teeth shut with a snap, and all three of my brothers look at me. "What do you think will happen if we stop showing a united front? Was Anthony not proof enough that people are still scheming to take us down?"

Bash looks at his feet. "Sorry. I was just screwing around. You know I stand with you."

"I know, and *they* know it too."

I get into my car, already pulled up for me. It's late, and I'm exhausted. I should go home, but I don't turn off at my exit, instead taking the all-too-familiar route to the other side of town.

Scarlet's house is pitch-black, and not for the first time, I wish I'd set cameras up in her place. After feeling her skin in my hands, I need to see her. Oliver sent me a text hours ago that she was tucked in at home, but I couldn't suppress the need to see Scarlet myself.

I pull the car into the alleyway and climb onto the hood before jumping up to reach the fire escape. Her bedroom window is a few feet to the right, just out of reach. Moonlight illuminates her face, relaxed with sleep. She looks so peaceful, and a small part of me hates that I'm about to change that.

Not that I have a choice. She's been on borrowed time, and it's almost up.

Chapter 15

Scarlet

> Matthias: Good morning, Little Sparrow. Did you sleep well last night?

FREAKING A-HOLE. I flip my phone over, leaving him on read as a small act of defiance. I polish off my third cup of chai tea and stare at my laptop screen. The words blur together until the lines are an unrecognizable sea of snakes. I've been at my office since 5:00 a.m. I figured if I'm going to be awake this early on a Saturday, I might as well distract myself with work.

There was absolutely no shot of getting any sleep last night. Not after... A shiver rolls down my spine as the memory of rough fingers sliding across my neck, a hot mouth pressing against mine, infiltrates my thoughts.

I've been at the office for hours in my futile attempt to think about literally anything other than what I did

125

last night. I'm not even sure how it happened. One second, I was following those two creepy guys, and the next, I was pinned against a wall with Matthias's hand covering my mouth.

My thighs press together as heat pools between my thighs at the memory of his fingers buried deep inside me.

Dammit. I drop my head to my desk, groaning. I haven't lasted more than five minutes without thinking about him.

He's supposed to be indifferent to me. At least all previous signs pointed to the fact that he was, but there was nothing in the way he touched me last night that said he didn't want me. Instead, his touch was almost desperate in the way his hold tightened on me. His breath fanned over my neck as he forced my orgasm out of me, making me cry his name. Nothing could've prepared me for him finishing in his pants. The thrill that went through me at having some kind of power over him. Like I made him lose control just as much as he does me. A twisted part of myself knows I could get addicted to that. To that feeling of Matthias needing me.

My phone buzzes on the table beside me, pulling me out of my spiral.

> Unknown: Hi! It's Misty.

> Unknown: Damon gave me your number. I hope that's okay.

> Me: Hi, of course no worries.

I try hard not to be awkward. I know how to deal with cold society women, but I'm not so sure how to process someone who's genuinely nice, and I'd bet my last dollar that this girl is the real deal. I'm damn good at reading people, but even if I wasn't, I'd know just by the way Damon Everette is simping after her. The guy is like a freaking puppy after his wife.

I quickly add Misty to my contact list, and a smirk curls my lips at the thought of the big bad Damon completely whipped.

> Misty: I thought you might want to come by tonight. Damon's out with his brothers and it could be a fun girls night.

> Misty: Of course I understand if you're busy...no pressure or anything.

I let out a breath and pull myself together. If there was ever a day I could use a drink, it's today, and there's the added perk that Misty just might have some information on what the hell has gotten into Matthias.

> Me: I'm not sure Damon wants me there.

> Misty: LOL. You should know I make up my own rules. Pissing my husband off is half the fun.

I knew I liked her for a reason.

Me: What do you want to drink?

I'm surprised when Oliver pulls off the highway into an older part of the city. I'd expect Damon's place to be right downtown, but this is just a regular neighborhood. We stop in front of an older-looking brick building, and my curiosity is officially on full blast.

If it wasn't for the security guard out front with the Everette Industries logo on his vest, I'd think Oliver followed some kind of weird Google map error. The kind that accidentally drives you off a cliff instead of your destination.

I get out before Oliver opens my door and ignore his raised brow. The gesture reminds me of the Everette brother who shall not be named.

One that I'm going to drink into silence tonight.

Misty comes bursting from the entry, lavender hair bouncing around her and a wide smile on her face.

"You're not supposed to be out here, Mrs. Everette," the guard says, eyes darting everywhere as if looking for some unlikely attacker.

There are rumors that something went down with the Everettes. Nothing was confirmed. There's no way a family like that would let any sign of weakness come out.

"It's fine. I'm not going anywhere," Misty huffs

seconds before wrapping me in a hug. She's warm and soft, and suddenly, I understand exactly how she caught Damon. She's a light in a world of darkness.

"Hi," I breathe out, pushing the word out against her tight embrace.

"Oh, sorry!" She releases me, taking a step back, cheeks pink. "I know I can be a bit much. I'm working on it."

"Please don't do that," I say, giving her my brightest smile. One I've hidden for years. "There's no such thing as too much." I hold the paper bag with two bottles of wine clinging together up toward her. "I think we're going to be great friends."

Misty leads me upstairs to her place, smiling as I step inside. Color fills my vision, and a smile grows across my face as I take in the cheerful decor that perfectly matches her.

"Cool, huh? Grab a seat, and I'll grab the glasses." Misty gestures toward the sofa, and I take a seat. I sink into the cushion, practically melting into the corner, where two large pillows support my back.

It takes a second, but in the sea of color, I notice small hints of the eldest Everette brother living here. Crystal liquor set, black jacket slung over the dining chair. Somehow, none of it feels out of place, like Damon's stuff somehow makes the rest shine brighter.

"Your place is really nice."

Misty hands me my wineglass, then sits on the other side of the sofa, pulling her feet up to tuck underneath

herself. We look like a pair of college students getting ready to gossip.

I've heard a million different things about Misty and Damon, ranging from the mundane to the outright crazy. It would be rude to ask, right? I, of all people, know how fast false information spreads around here.

Misty's keen eyes land on mine, a small smirk curling her lips.

I swallow hard, feeling like I was just caught sneaking notes in class. "What?"

"You can ask. I know you're dying to." She takes a sip of her wine. "I invited you here; it's only fair that you get to ask first. Come on, I know you must be curious."

I'm not going to bother pretending I don't know exactly what she's talking about. "I don't believe rumors."

She gives me a reassuring smile. "I believe you."

"It's just that..." I pull my legs onto the couch, happy I wore trousers to work, and face her. "Did he really throw you over his shoulder at the bar and drag you up to their private room?"

"Sure did." She laughs, then leans in, her voice a mock whisper. "But that's not the good stuff."

"Good stuff?" There's a giddiness filling my chest that I haven't felt in years.

"There's the whole marriage of convenience thing."

"Convenience?" Shock ripples through me. There wasn't a single thing in their interactions that ever gave me a hint that it wasn't real.

"Oh no, don't get me wrong. The marriage is real. It was like a weird trick he pulled to make me stay near him."

"Why doesn't that surprise me." I take a long drink of my wine, the smooth taste coating my tongue and warming my body.

"He did stalk me for a bit. But don't worry, I had him take the cameras out of here."

"The what?" I choke on the wine, leaning over in an attempt to breathe. A small hand pounds on my back.

"Don't look at me like that. I'm not the only one with an Everette brother obsessed with her. God only knows what Matthias is doing."

Shock mixes with confusion. "I don't have cameras in my place. I've checked."

She smirks.

That's a skill I didn't realize I needed.

She looks toward the balcony. "It led to some fun times though."

I flip through the last few times I've seen the Everettes out, and I can't remember seeing any of them with a particular girl around. "Who's the other person who has an Everette brother obsessed with her?"

"No need to deny it. I'm literally dying to know what's happening between you and Matthias."

"N...nothing."

"Girl... Matthias could barely form words. He was so focused on you last night. Then there's the whole you both disappearing at the same time thing."

Heat crawls up my cheeks, and I finish my glass of red before asking, "Was it that obvious?"

"Only because we were already watching you. Do you think those boys would give up a chance to see Matthias act like that?"

"Like what exactly?"

"Like some kind of obsessed teenager whose crush just walked into prom." She tilts her head, studying me. "You have to have noticed by now?

"I think I need something stronger to have this conversation."

Misty laughs and gets up, walking to the kitchen. She comes back with two shot glasses and a chilled bottle of vodka.

I scrunch up my nose. "I don't think I can drink that straight."

"Don't worry, this is some kind of smooth, rich Damon special that doesn't burn."

I've been rich my entire life, and I'm pretty sure all alcohol burns, but I throw the shot she hands me back, letting the cool liquid hit the back of my throat. It does burn, but in a different way, and I can see what she means.

She raises the bottle. "Another?"

I smirk. The vodka is already going to my head. "One more."

I down the shot, chasing it with a sip of wine. "I'm not exactly sure what's going on. He's kinda driving me crazy." A low, frustrated sound that I don't dare call a

growl leaves my chest. "Like why did he suddenly start acting this way?"

"That is cryptic." Misty tops up a shot for each of us.

I lift it to my lips and grumble, "Annoying," before tipping it back. "Was I just supposed to wait for him? Does he think I've been waiting this entire time?"

She tilts her head. "Have you been waiting?"

"No," I rush out too fast to be believable.

"Not even a little?"

I drop my head into my hands, the room swirling a little too much around us, and groan. "I have horrendous taste in men."

Misty's clear laugh fills the space. "You never know. He may surprise you?"

"He choked me once. Did you know that?" Of course, that happened when he thought I betrayed his brothers, and he couldn't even go through with it. But it definitely doesn't scream we're meant to be together.

"Like in the good way?"

I cough, nearly spitting out my drink. "The what?"

"Never mind... Do you want me to tell Damon? Pretty sure I can convince him to kill him."

Shaking my head no, I reply, "I deserved it."

"I doubt that. I may not know you well, but Damon told me what you did for them."

"There was a misunderstanding, and I may have let Matthias believe I betrayed him." A flush of anger rolls over me. "Not that he'd let me explain."

"Maybe...you know, have a conversation?"

"It's not that. I'm positive he knows why I had to do what I did back then, but that just makes the last ten years piss me off even more." I roll my neck and hug my wineglass to my chest. "Did you know, prior to this week, he hadn't said a single word to me since we escaped my family's place? Not a single one."

She raises one brow, tilting her head to the side as she examines me. "I've seen him in a room with you."

"What?" I'm starting to feel like Misty knows way more than I thought she did.

"Once I figured out his pattern, I knew that if I followed his gaze, I'd find you. I'll admit it made you like a mystery."

"It's not much of a mystery. We kissed when we were teenagers, then he refused to see me. Actually, it sounds pretty run-of-the-mill teenage romance."

She raises one brow. "Romance?"

"Whatever. You know what I mean."

A smirk pulls at the corner of her lip. "So is there a chance you might be able to rekindle whatever's going on between you two?"

I think through the kiss in my office, then the way he held me last night, and have to tamp down my body's reaction. There's still the underlying sting from when he rejected me. I haven't spent the last decade making myself stronger just because a guy I used to like showed back up in my life.

"Am I just supposed to be grateful that he finally

deigned to speak to me? Welcome him back with open arms?"

"Hell no. Making him squirm is half the fun. Plus, I'm looking forward to all the stuff he does trying to win you over."

I take my shot before wiping my mouth on my sleeve. Not very ladylike. "He bought the company I work for."

"Yeah, that sounds like something an Everette brother would do. Wait. Aren't you loaded?"

Normally, that question would throw me off. More than a few people aren't happy that I got to keep my family money, but I can't help but be honest with her. "Yeah."

A slow smile takes over her face. "I have an idea."

Chapter 16

Matthias

MY FINGERS DRUM on my thigh as I sit in my car in Elysium's parking lot. I left my brothers with full intentions of going home, but my last update from Oliver has me sitting in place. Scarlet's gone to hang out with Misty, and I can only imagine what the two of them will get up to. I've kept myself closed off from pretty much everyone, but Misty's observant in a way that most people aren't. Which means she has more than enough information to ruin everything. I'm trying to ease Scarlet into the idea of being with me, and by the way her body responded to me last night, it's working. *Fuck*, her moans had my dick hard all day. I've never wanted Scarlet to make things easy on me.

Not that I'd mind working hard for her, but I have no doubt the two of them will be nothing but trouble together. A thrill ripples up my spine, knowing that, soon, the two of them will be family.

> Damon: You should come get your girl.

> Me: Oliver's got her.

Even typing the words pisses me off.

> Damon: You are not going to want her alone with him in this state.

> Me: What's that supposed to mean?

> Damon: They polished off a bottle of vodka.

Fuck.

> Me: I'll be there in a minute.

> Me: Take care of her Damon. I'm trusting you.

> Damon: You know I will.

Damon opens their apartment door before I can knock. "You got here fast."

He says it with a knowing smirk that I promptly ignore.

"Where is she?"

"Don't worry. She's fine, just passed out."

I scan the room, and sure enough, Scarlet's wrapped in a large crochet blanket where she's tucked into the corner of the couch.

"How did she get like this?"

"I'm not sure, but my wife and I are going to have a long chat about it."

I choke on my laugh. "Please, that girl has you so whipped it's not even funny."

He doesn't bother denying it, just stands back so I can lift Scarlet, legs dangling over one arm and supporting her back with the other. She snuggles into my chest, nose pressing into me before mumbling, "Ou— smell—ood."

I brush back the hair that's fallen into her face, but she's out cold again.

"Thanks for calling me, Dam."

Damon laughs. "Just be prepared for whatever plan they came up with. They had notes that I could barely make out, but whatever it was, it had to do with you."

I kiss the top of Scarlet's head. "I don't doubt it."

Damon's gaze softens on me. "I'm happy for you. Don't mess it up."

"Don't worry. There's no getting away from her now," I say and hold her tighter as her fingers twist into the fabric of my shirt.

Four days left, Little Sparrow.

Scarlet clings to me when I try to put her in the passenger seat, and a part of me feels like an absolute asshole for being so happy about it. There's no fucking way she'd want me to see this, but I'm not disappointed that I have. Fight it all she wants, I'm going to prove to her that we've always been meant to be together. Not that she doesn't have the right to be pissed. I've always

known she would be, but I just don't care. At least not enough to stop me. I left her alone because it's what she needed. She needed to break out of the holds her family had on her. The space and time to spread her wings and stand on her own feet.

I know if I'd stayed, then I wouldn't have been able to keep away from her, and even if she's pissed now, back then, she'd have given in to me. What kind of man would I be if I didn't listen to her only wish?

I disentangle Scarlet's fingers from my shirt and adjust her on the seat. She's already snoring softly by the time I get her seat belt on her. She's so fucking adorable like this.

Forcing myself to back away, I take several breaths before rounding the car and climbing behind the wheel.

For the first time ever, my girl is coming to my place, and I'm not sure how I'll ever let her leave.

It's quiet this late at night, only a few hours before dawn, but I take my time, making sure to drive as carefully as possible. My girl is in no state to be shifted around. She moans, shifting so her shoulders press into the seat, and rests her head on it.

"Where did you go?" Her voice is soft and breathy, and it pulls at my heart. It's been a long time since I heard her speak to me like that.

I wrap my fingers around her thigh, steadying her. "I didn't go anywhere."

"Liar."

I swallow hard at the thought of her waiting. I'd

140

watched her over the years any chance I got. She'd gone out on her share of dates. Not that I'd let her have an actual relationship. Oliver clued me in when anyone got too close. One of my main hobbies was chasing any guy that got near her, more than willing to provide the necessary incentive to stop them from coming back. They're lucky none of them died because I definitely didn't have a grip on myself when I saw them get close.

Not that I ever gave her space. She couldn't know that though, and even now, I'm the one waiting for her.

My place is off the main road, only a few blocks from hers, situated in the most exclusive part of the city. There'd been two other offers that I'd easily doubled.

One of my men approaches me when we pull up, ready to take my keys.

"You all good, boss?" He looks into the car where Scarlet's still passed out, her shirt buttons popped open, revealing the top of her breast.

"I suggest you look away before it's the last thing you see."

"Yes, boss." He's smart enough to turn his gaze, facing the marble stone wall of the building.

I watch him until I'm sure he's not going to turn around before reaching in and lifting Scarlet in my arms. She barely weighs anything, even with the defined muscles I can feel through her clothes. I'm not surprised she spent the last several years working on her self-defense, not after how she was raised. My girl's a fighter. Always has been.

Her fingers grip my shirt, tugging herself closer to me, and I hum in the back of my throat as her nails dig into my flesh. The need to meld her body to mine has been fucking painful for years. Even if it's only in her sleep she needs to be close to me, I'll take it. I know this is going to take more than a simple *I'm sorry*, but one day, she'll understand. Because I can't accept any other future where she's not my wife.

The doors swing open the second I start climbing the stairs, and a guard stands watch, gaze averted as I make my way in, precious cargo in hand. They're all connected via earpieces, giving each other the heads-up.

My place is at least double the size of hers. I'd originally got it because I thought she'd like a second place downtown and did my best to match her style. It's our other place that I'm dying for her to see. The one only my brothers know about. Not that they've ever understood why I had it built.

I take the curved stairwell to my room. She burrows deeper into my chest with each step, and I can't help but slow down. Tomorrow, she'll go back to not trusting me, but tonight, she knows she's mine.

My room's dark, only lit by the moon shining through the floor-to-ceiling windows overlooking the city, the soft light casting across her face.

I set her gently in a seated position on the bed. "Little Sparrow, I need you to wake up."

She makes a sound of disapproval, not even bothering to open her eyes.

"So fucking cute." Keeping one hand on her, I reach into my nightstand dresser and pull out one of my T-shirts. It's black, and I've owned it for years, making the fabric soft and so worn the fibers separate until it's nearly see-through.

I kiss the top of her head, then drop my mouth to her ear. "I'm going to undress you."

Goose bumps rise down the column of her neck, and I can't stop myself from running my nose up her sensitive skin. Her scent rocks into me, driving the blood straight to my cock. Any other time, I'd have her laid out bare in front of me, but not like this.

Not when she's only holding on to me because she's wasted. Not when it's unlikely she'll remember in the morning.

When I fuck my girl, I want every single second imprinted in her mind until the only thing she can think about is how my cock fills her up.

The buttons of her shirt easily release from their slots as I make my way down her chest. My knuckles graze the path down her sternum, her soft belly. She moans, arching into my touch, and I bite down hard on my lip to prevent myself from devouring her. A few more days until I've met the requirement of her wish, and then I'll have her laid out on this bed, begging for more.

I push the fabric off her shoulders, careful not to let her go, and swallow at the sight of her black-lace-covered breasts.

I reach back and snap the clasp with one hand, letting the sheer fabric fall down her arms. Rose-colored peaks over pale cream skin have me coming undone. This girl has no idea what she does to me.

I slide my shirt over her head before I can go any further, the fabric barely a barrier between us.

She makes a whining sound in her sleep, and I kiss her temple. "Soon, Scarlet. Just a little longer."

"Now," she pleads, and I groan low in my throat, barely holding my shit together.

I nip her ear and stroke my thumb over her taut nipple. "I'm not having sex with you when you'll regret it."

I guide her to lie down and release her pants, sliding them down her legs and dropping them on the floor. There's moisture on both sides of her thighs. I rip myself away, taking several steps back so I don't cave and bury my nose into her cunt.

The tip of my cock's leaking, so fucking ready for her, but I push it beneath my pants' waistband. I'm not giving up this opportunity to hold her, which means I have to keep my shit together.

Circling the bed, I get in beside her and tuck her into my side. She curls around me, heat sinking into my bones.

"Don't leave me."

Her plea is like a knife to my chest.

"Never again."

Chapter 17

Scarlet

METAL WARMS under my palm as I look down the black barrel of my gun. The force of my shot reverberates up my arms and into my body as the loud crack echoes through the room, dulled by my earmuffs.

After waking up at Matthias's place, I knew I needed to blow off steam, or I'd hunt him down and massacre him. I'd been alone, hungover, wearing only his freaking shirt. The thing engulfed me like a dress, and I only had fuzzy memories of him changing me into it.

The graze of his rough knuckles, the prickle of his stubble against my neck. A shiver rolls through me, and I fire off three more perfect shots, hitting the target dead in the center.

He left a freaking note explaining he had to leave early for work and I shouldn't worry. *He* contacted my office to let them know I wouldn't be in. The anger sizzling in my veins right now is only a shadow of what I

felt reading that note. The audacity to call my job. He may own the company, but I didn't need my boss thinking I'm sleeping with him. I ignore the reasons I was drinking in the first place, shoving our kiss into the recesses of my mind and lining up my next shot.

I woke up to their doctor standing over me, IV in hand. The man had fear in his eyes, like if I didn't let him proceed, he was the one who would suffer the consequences.

The note on the nightstand had me grinding my teeth.

Don't be stubborn, Little Sparrow.

The IV drip did wonders for my aching head, and I hated to admit I was a little bit grateful Matthias had thought ahead. It didn't last long when I had to do the walk of shame and Oliver was already standing outside waiting for me. He was smart enough to look away after a death glare from me.

The shooting range is hot, the concrete building meant to keep bullets in, but that means there's barely any air circulation. I'd discarded my top hours ago, leaving me in just my sports bra and leggings. There's no one here; I always rent out the entire place for the duration of my stay. I don't think anyone's currently plotting to kill me, but the odds aren't zero. Not when my spot in the Order of Saints is still up for grabs. Of course, the most guaranteed way to take over for my family is to marry me, but if I'm dead, then there's at least a spot to compete for. At this point, I may have to beg Damon to

open up a few more spots just to take the pressure off me.

I reload my gun, the magazine clicking in place before lifting it again. My shoulders ache from the repeated motion, but I'm happy for the pain. It reminds me that even though it hurts, my body's strong. Breathing in deeply, I let it out slowly and squeeze the trigger.

My shot goes a little too far to the right, and I have to recenter myself. Back straight, body loose but engaged, I focus down the barrel to where I want to hit.

"You look hot like that."

I swing to the side, gun forward pointed directly at a smiling Matthias's face.

"Are you kidding me! I could have killed you."

He grips my hand still holding the gun at his chest and lowers it to my side. "Nah, you wouldn't do that."

Matthias steps into me, his heat radiating off him, and my already pounding heart feels like it's about to crack through my rib cage. He slides his finger over my jaw and runs his thumb across my lip. "Or maybe you would?"

"Don't try me." One wrist caught in his, I push the other one against his chest, but he doesn't budge.

Smirking down at me, he says, "What? Is that how you treat the guy who came to rescue you last night?"

His heartbeat drums into my palm, the tempo rapidly increasing the longer we stand here. I search

between his eyes, but there are no other signs of what he may be feeling.

My voice is too soft when I ask, "Why didn't Oliver just take me home?"

The muscle in his jaw visibly ticks, and his fingers tighten before releasing. "I wasn't about to let that happen."

A thrill rolls down my spine, causing me to shiver. There's something in the way he says it that has my brain short-circuiting.

I pause, unable to respond. His chest is twice as wide as mine, taking up my line of sight. Another crisp black shirt, black belt, and matching black leather shoes. I follow the line of his shoulder down to where his thick fingers wrap around my wrist, overlapping, making it look fragile in his touch, but it's not worry that's curling low and warming between my thighs.

"Why are you here?" Cutting off my thoughts, I beat down the growing heat rapidly filling my stomach and narrow my eyes at him.

Matthias steps closer until there's barely an inch between us. He's so close I can make out the specks of gold in his deep brown eyes.

He leans in, and his breath fans over my lips as he says, "Checking on you."

"Why?" I scrunch up my nose.

He tilts his head slightly. "Do you remember what you asked for last night?"

"No." I swallow, my throat thick. The air is charged

around us, blocking out all other noise. The heartbeat under my palm sets the pace for mine. Suddenly, I don't care about anything other than feeling his lips on mine.

"Let me remind you." He leans in, closing the distance between our mouths, and I don't fight the pull of his kiss. Embers he stoked the other night flame to life, like they've been waiting for this. For him.

His fingers trail up to my side, curling around the dip in my waist and holding me firmly in place. His thumb stroked the bottom edge of my sports bra until I'm close to begging for his touch.

He breaks the kiss, moving to my neck. My toes curl, and a moan escapes my throat as he runs his tongue up my sensitive skin. He groans low in his throat and does it again, shooting shivers down my spine.

"I'm sweaty."

I try to pull away with the last of my sanity, but his grip tightens, and he licks me again, this time delving his tongue into the nook of my collarbone.

He runs his teeth along the same path. "You're delicious."

"We're in public," I breathe out frantically.

He hums low, grabbing the gun from my hand and placing it out of reach. "I love that that's your only resistance."

Umm, no? I have a million reasons this isn't a good idea. He's playing some game with me I have to figure out before I get hurt—

"Stop thinking so much." He captures my lips, grip-

ping my ass, and lifts me onto the counter, spreading my legs so he can stand between them. He's supporting me with one hand banded around my back as he pushes one of my knees to the side until he can press the hard ridge of his cock against my core.

"We shouldn't be doing this."

"You're right." He kisses my neck as if he said nothing.

My grip tightens on his shirt as disappointment curls in my stomach, an ache blooming in my chest. Of course he agrees. It's always been him to push me away.

"Look at me."

My eyes meet his, and he searches my gaze.

"Whatever you're thinking, you're wrong." He runs his nose along mine. "I want to be here."

He grinds his hips against me, pressing his cock harder. "Feel that? If we keep going, I'm going to embarrass myself by coming in my pants again."

I tilt my hips, creating the friction I need. His eyes close, and a shudder rolls through him. "You have no idea what you do to me."

He makes me want to find out. Excitement mixed with nervousness tingles throughout my limbs. Whatever comes next, I'll have never done it before. I should feel scared, but somehow, I feel safe in his hands.

"I'm going to make you come now, Scarlet."

"What? Here?" My thighs try to pull together to release some of the tension, but he's still holding them

apart. Just his words make me want to beg. I shouldn't be doing this.

"Okay—"

The words are not even out before he's lowering my back to the cool counter. He leans down, kissing my stomach, circling my navel with his tongue as he slides my pants and underwear off at the same time. A shiver rolls through me, and I swallow hard, every sensation new to me.

He moves back, eyes hot on my core, and cold embarrassment snaps me back to reality.

"I...I can't."

"Yes, you can, baby. Just breathe." He lowers his face, breath fanning over my core.

I dig my fingers into his scalp and tug at him until he looks at me.

"I've never done this before."

A satisfied smile curves his lips, and his already hungry look turns ravenous. "I know."

He licks up my seam without looking away, taking his time.

It feels like sin, lust, and temptation all wrapped into one, and I want him to do it again.

He doesn't need me to ask, descending his hot mouth on me. He tips my hips back, delving his tongue deep into my core, and I scream out a moan.

He chuckles and bites my thigh. "I've pictured this countless times, but nothing I thought of had anything on the reality."

I'm still trying to process that when he slips a finger inside of me. The stretch, combined with his mouth, has every thought melting from my mind.

The only thing left is the craving for more. Like there's a deep yearning for something only he can give.

My fingers dig into his hair, and he groans, sliding a second finger into me.

The world swims as every muscle tightens in my body, as if he's pulling invisible strings only he can see. My hips rock uncontrollably against his face, tilting with each thrust of his fingers. I'm so close it hurts, and he doesn't disappoint, curving his fingers deeper and sucking hard on my clit until my release ricochets through me.

He doesn't stop until he's wrung every ounce of my orgasm out of me.

He pulls up, wiping his mouth lasciviously.

"Run along now, Little Sparrow. Or I won't be responsible for what happens to you."

Chapter 18

Matthias

I WIPE my thumb over my bottom lip as the door closes behind her and slip it between my teeth. Her sweet taste fills my mouth, drawing a low groan from the back of my throat.

"Enjoy your three days of freedom, Little Sparrow."

Chapter 19

Scarlet

I'M careful not to snag my clothes on the exposed nails lining the narrow hallway. It's barely wide enough for me to walk without having to turn sideways. The only light is coming from the cracks around the door seam up ahead. I've spent a lot of time making my way through these narrow passageways, learning each turn in order to move about the house freely. But tonight is different. The walls seem to be squeezing around me, and the air is heavy, making each breath harder than the last. There's noise up ahead, and I should turn away, hide somewhere deep within the castle where no one can find me, but I can't stop myself from moving forward. The closer I get, the clearer the sounds. There's a muffled thud that repeats itself over and over like a bat hitting a rug. I move closer, careful to stay hidden behind the door, and press my ear against the wood. It's then that I can hear the low groans that accompany each hit. It's a pained, whimper sound

that has every nerve in my body coming alive. I carefully shift so I can see through the minuscule crack and gasp. It's me lying on the ground, hair splayed out around me and blood trickling from my mouth. My brother Christopher's standing above me, screaming about how I'm a traitor and a dirty whore. That I sold myself to the Everette brothers. My copy stares up at him, defiance in her eyes, even as his foot comes slamming toward her. The image flickers, and instead of me getting ready to take the blow, Matthias is in my place. He's sprawled out on the ground, collar chaining him to the wall and his handcuffs pinning his wrists together. That doesn't stop him from spitting in my brother's face, daring him to do his worst.

Matthias is so young and so much smaller than the last time I saw him. There's fear in his eyes that I was too naive to recognize before, but that doesn't stop him from antagonizing Christopher again, each time drawing all the attention to him and away from my door. A bat materializes out of nowhere into Christopher's hand, and he swings it down toward him. It's too fast, too hard. I push against the door, crying out for them to stop, when my father appears in front of me, a sneer on his face. Thick fingers wrap around my neck, and he hauls me off my feet, pinning me to the wall. I quake against his hold, scratching at his arms, but my father's grip doesn't loosen. He laughs at what a waste I am and how he should've disposed of me long ago, that pretending to love me disgusted him.

The air chokes from my lungs as I watch the hate burn in his blue eyes that match mine.

Those blue eyes turn black, and instead of disdain, they're full of betrayal as Matthias screams at me for hurting his brothers. I struggle to speak, needing to explain that everything will work out in a minute, that he just has to wait. That I would never betray him.

Matthias won't let go, his grip turning harder and harder, but it's the tears in his eyes that have me going still. There's pain written all over his face, and it's directed at me.

He's repeating the same words over and over again, but they don't make sense. Wake up, Scarlet. Wake up!

I snap awake, shooting up into a seated position as I gasp for breath. I haven't had that dream for several years. Tears burn my eyes as I force myself to count to ten over and over again until some semblance of sanity returns to my body, allowing it to take over itself again. I pull my knees to my chest, my cream sheets surrounding me as I try to work through the feeling of helplessness, reminding myself that it was a long time ago. I'm not that girl anymore, and my brother and father are dead.

Cool air raises goose bumps along my arms. The window on the far wall is cracked open, the latch undone. I search the room, but I'm alone. There's not even a shadow out of place. Dropping my chin against my knees, I sigh, then force myself out of bed. I must have opened it at some point last night.

A chill rolls through me as I pull myself out of bed and close it tight, locking it firmly in place.

I check the clock at the blaring green numbers announcing it's 4:00 a.m. Too early to go to work, too late to go back to sleep. The feeling of helplessness is still weighing heavily on my mind as I crack my neck back and forth, grabbing a pair of leggings and a hoodie from my dresser. I'm not that girl anymore. If that same thing happened today, I'd have my father squirming on the floor and my brother between the sights of my gun.

I shove my feet into the stretchy black legging fabric. There's only one thing that's going to stop this haunting feeling.

I send Oliver a quick text, knowing when he wakes up, he'll lose his mind when he finds out I've left the house without him.

Pulling my hoodie over my head, I let it drop over me, making me look bigger than I am before I step out into the cool night. My sneakers are silent as they tap with every stride across the paved sidewalks. The entire area is washed with the orange glow from the overhead streetlights that disappears into pure blackness between the houses.

I breathe in through my nose and out through my mouth, tempering the rhythm of my heart. I'd discovered running as a form of therapy shortly after everything went down. It's like I quite literally got my wish to escape, and there was nothing holding me in place. The freedom I feel while my feet thrust me forward at a pace

most people can't keep up with provides me with an unexplainable thrill. I'm sure it's similar to the adrenaline skydivers get, but for me, it's the freedom each step provides me. Unfortunately, it's become my own form of addiction. More than once, Oliver has caught me pushing my one-hour run to two, chasing the high that the long distances push through my veins. Sometimes it feels like I'm running toward someone, like if I can just push myself a little faster, I'll be able to grasp onto them.

Other times, I want whatever's chasing me to catch up, to wrap me in their arms and force me to finally be still. To finally feel safe enough to not have to flee anymore.

It's those times I know I've lost it because no matter what, I know no one can make me feel safe like that. It's completely left to me.

And I've done a great job honing my small body into something dangerous. Something that can kill without a thought. If it wasn't for my small stature, I'd have nothing left to fear, but no matter how strong I become, how fast I am, there's always someone bigger and faster out there.

My heart rate's a steady beat as I make my way out of the residential area and onto the main road. It's lined with stores, the lights still off in the early hours. I'm concentrating on the darkened glass so much I almost miss the large silhouette that steps out in front of me.

My feet slide to a stop as I halt my forward momen-

tum, my hand immediately pulling out my pepper spray from my pouch and holding it at the ready.

My pulse is pounding in my ears, and any control of my breathing is shot with the sheer adrenaline coursing through my veins. The person blocking my path is big, at least a few inches taller than me. I'm still debating whether I can take him or if I should take my chances running when he steps into the light, showing his familiar face.

I take a step back, still hesitant. "What are you doing here?"

"I didn't mean to scare you. I'm just waiting for the cafe to open."

Jeremy's the guy I went on a single date with prior to Liam. I honestly thought we'd hit it off, but he'd ghosted me from that point on. It should've been a blow to my self-esteem, but if the guy's willing to ghost me, I have no time for them anyway.

The sign on the cafe door says it opens in five minutes. It's not completely out of the question that us meeting here is just a coincidence and he's not a complete stalker. After all, he's the one that stopped calling me.

It's the hairs still standing tall at the back of my neck and the pit in my stomach that has me still on edge.

"Do you live around here?" I ask, feeling out the situation. If he does, then I'm probably just overreacting.

"Not far." He takes a step closer, and alarms go off in my head.

Something's not right.

I plaster on my most disarming smile. I just need to get out of this situation, and then I'm good. "It was good seeing you, but I'm going to be off now. Got to keep up my run."

I take a step to the left, fully intending to cross the road, when he says, "I had fun with you that night. It still doesn't sit right that someone could stop us from getting to know each other before we really gave it a shot."

My brows pull together as I try to make sense of his words. "What do you mean someone stopped us?"

"Don't pretend you don't know what I'm talking about. I was so bruised I could barely walk for a week." His tone has dropped low; any of the friendliness from before has vanished, replaced with aggression.

I study him as he stands there waiting for my reply. The lights cast a halo around him, face half in shadow, half exposed. There's a hardness to his jaw, a muscle ticking in his cheek that gives his intentions away. He has no intention of letting me go.

My grip tightens around my pepper spray, ready to spray this fucker in the face. "I don't know what you're talking about, but you need to go."

"Don't be like that. I thought we'd be a good fit together."

"Thanks, but I'll pass."

Any pretense of friendliness drops from his face, and his eyes grow cold. "Listen, I never wanted to date you in the first place. He said I just needed to get you alone."

A chill crawls up my neck. "Who said?"

"This job is way more trouble than it's worth." Jeremy's voice is drowned out by the sound of squealing tires coming around the corner.

A familiar blacked-out sedan hops the curb and stops feet away from us, causing my potential assailant to jump back. I don't have time to question Jeremy further before Oliver stands between us, his entire demeanor on edge. He'd actually look scary if his hair wasn't rumpled like he'd been dragged out of bed.

"I didn't do anything." Jeremy sounds frantic as he stares at my significantly larger bodyguard. There haven't been many situations where he's had to step in, but he definitely comes in handy when he does. Jeremy looks at me, pleading. "Tell him, Scarlet. We were just talking."

I ignore him completely because even though we were just talking, he'd made it clear his intentions weren't innocent. "Oliver, I had it handled."

I need to find out who he was talking about, and I need to do it fast. I'm not surprised there's someone looking for me—after all, I'd be a great catch—but hiring someone to collect me is going a bit far.

My guard's mouth drops open. "You shouldn't have been out here."

"Relax, I brought pepper spray. He was so close to getting a face full of it." I shrug. Honestly, I expected Oliver earlier. I guess it makes sense—it was still stupid early when I texted him.

"You bitch!" Jeremy yells, and I shake my head.

"Really not the time, Jeremy." Well, now I'm officially happy this guy ghosted me. He's a complete psycho with an obvious death wish.

I'm pretty sure if I don't do something soon, Oliver is going to off him in the street, and how the hell am I supposed to explain that?

"Take me home, please. My run's ruined anyway," I say with a smile, Oliver's glare not affecting me at all.

He's all bark and no bite.

It's only after I get into the back seat of the car that I put the pepper spray away and watch through the window as Oliver warns him off. Whatever he says has Jeremy nodding and slumped forward, almost like a disciplined dog.

Oliver gets in and doesn't say a word, clearly going for the mature silent treatment.

"I'm fine," I say, not ready to talk about what Jeremy had revealed. I need a few more pieces before I'll be ready to deal with this situation. Oliver's worked for me for years, but I learned long ago that there are some things I need to take care of myself.

His eyes glance back through the rearview mirror before looking forward.

Okay, so I probably shouldn't have done that, but it's not like I wasn't prepared.

It's the pounding of my heart threatening to break my ribs and the way I have to clench my trembling fists that gives away the fact that I wasn't as safe as I'm

pretending I was. That a simple misstep could've let that guy get too close. I clench my teeth and push that thought away. I'm not that girl anymore. Let them get close—it's better for fighting technique that way. What I lack in size and reach, I more than make up for in speed and technical skills.

I drum my fingers on the windowsill, already feeling better when suspicion seeps in. "How did you know where I was?"

Oliver stiffens, his hands tightening on the wheel. "Just a guess."

I close my eyes as the sun turns the sky pink. Damn good guess.

Chapter 20

Matthias

I WATCH as Oliver's taillights disappear around the corner. It drives me crazy that I'm not the one taking her home, but I have something very important to take care of. I step out of the shadows and smile sharply at Jeremy.

"Shit." He stumbles backward instantly. "Hi, I didn't mean to run into her, I swear."

"I thought we had an agreement. You wouldn't go near her, and I wouldn't have to kill you?" I slide a blade from my pocket and take my time picking at my nails. Part of the torture is always the anticipation. I won't have long to get this done, but that doesn't mean I can't enjoy it. "Tell me, Jeremy. Do you think you held up your end of the bargain?"

"Seriously, I was just get...getting...coffee. I didn't...m...mean to see her. You have to believe me." He stutters over his words as he attempts to weasel himself out of this situation.

Unlucky for him, that's never going to happen. "Do I?"

"What?" He's terrified, and he really should be.

"Do I have to believe you? Because at no point did we discuss the importance of you intentionally meeting up with her. Accident or not, you should have run the second you saw her."

He's visibly trembling now, and I half expect him to beg the next time he speaks.

"Does she even know that you attack anyone who dates her?" He takes a step back, body turning toward the road.

I flip the knife in my hand, a flashy move I learned as a teenager. "What she knows is the least of *your* problems."

That's all it takes for him to take off, but I catch his arm before he can take another step.

He's strong but not strong enough to stop me from wrapping my forearm around his neck and dragging him backward into the alleyway where we can have some privacy.

"I've been watching you, and the only reason I let you live is you've been good. I guess you fucked that up now."

"Wait!" is the last word Jeremy gets to say before I slice through his throat, careful not to get any blood on me. There's a gurgling sound emanating from his throat, but it's quiet enough that I'm not too concerned anyone will hear him. It'd be a shame to have to buy out whoever

witnessed this, but then again, it would be worth it to see the light in his eyes go out.

When he's finally done and his body's gone limp, I cut through the fabric of his jacket and his shirtsleeve, revealing his upper arm, where the faint white scar sits on his bicep. The tip of my knife pierces his muscle easily, revealing the black pill-size tracker.

"Can't have people tracing you back to me, now can we."

I clean my knife with his shirt, careful not to touch him more than necessary. No need to stain my clothes over this asshole.

Pulling out my phone, I fire off a text.

> Me: I need a clean up at this location.

I drop a pin and send it to him.

> Beck: Consider it done.

It's only when I get into my car that my hands start shaking. He was entirely too close to getting to my girl.

Maybe I need to rethink the idea of putting a tracker on her.

I go through my calendar, clearing the entire thing. It's time I pay my girl a visit and ask her what the hell she was thinking.

I pull my phone out and send a message to our brothers' group chat.

Me: Family meeting at my place.

Me: Now

Xander: Do you have any idea what time it is?

Me: Do I sound like I care what time it is?

Damon: You woke Misty up. This better be good.

Bash: I'm pretty sure I'm still drunk from last night. I'm going to sit this one out.

Me: Like fuck you are. Get your ass to my place.

Damon: Just tell us why.

Me: Someone tried to attack Scarlet.

Xander: Oh shit.

Bash: Xander come pick me up. I can't drive in this state.

Damon: I'll grab the coffee.

Bash is the first to walk into my place, dropping his coat on the table near the door. Xander and Damon come in immediately after him.

"So did you kill him?" Bash asks as he takes the coffee Damon hands him, gratitude written all over his face.

I raise one brow and cross my arms where I've propped myself up on the wall. I'm way too worked up since getting home to sit. "What do you think?"

Bash runs his hand through his hair, his eyes glassy. He wasn't lying when he said he was still drunk from last night.

"Did you at least get rid of the body?" Damon asks and hands me my own coffee. I set it on the table, not needing another stimulant in my system while I'm already hopped up on adrenaline. My only regret from this morning was not killing him slower.

"It's taken care of. I called in help from the Gentlemen." They're a nearby mafia who we've become close with over the years.

Xander whistles low. "Must've been messy to call in the big guns. We're going to owe them a few favors after what they've done for Damon and now you."

Bash smiles. "They can ask anytime. I'm more than happy to help."

"So what the hell happened?" Damon collapses in the chair across from me. He's wearing the expression every older brother seems to have mastered that clearly states *spit it out, or I'll kick your ass.*

"One of her exes showed up and started pressuring her. When I'd looked into him before, he'd been after her spot in the Order. I should've killed him then."

"What the actual fuck." Bash smacks both hands on the back of the sofa, swaying a little with the motion. "Can't you close that loop, Damon?"

Our eldest brother shakes his head. "The Laurent position will stay open so long as Scarlet's not married."

I rake both hands in my hair and pull at the ends until my scalp aches. "Which makes her the perfect target for assholes looking to join the Order."

Bash looks between us. "Let's say they manage to get someone to marry her. We'd just make her a widow, right?"

I stand from my seat, rage building a fire in my gut. "You really think that would go down nicely? That they wouldn't hurt her to get what they want."

Xander steps between us. "Honest question. Why don't you just marry her? It'll null and void everything. When you have a kid, they'll take that position."

"I plan on it." I roll my neck, taking a deep breath. It's brutal sticking to my plan. With every day, I'm closer and closer to saying screw it.

"I just need to keep her safe for two more fucking days."

Chapter 21

Scarlet

Iτ's 8:00 p.m. by the time I shut down my work computer. I can tell myself I was just trying to get some extra work done, but I know that's a bold-faced lie.

My run-in with my ex shook me up. Between him and Liam, that's two men in the last week who decided to take their shot at my family's spot in the Order of Saints.

I can't be positive that was Jeremy's intention, but considering I'd previously gone on one date with him, I feel comfortable making that assumption. What was his plan anyway? It's not like I would go with him freely. There's always the chance he planned on killing me. Definitely the messier route in all ways. First because of the actual pain of hiding my murder, and second, because it's not a sure way to get my spot. It just opens it for everyone.

Which makes me think he was going to try to force me to marry him.

A tiny part of me wishes Oliver had gotten there a few seconds later, just so I could've seen Jeremy's snot-covered face as I soaked him with pepper spray. From that distance, he'd be crying for a week.

The other part of me knows that underneath my pride, I'm barely holding it together. I put on the brave mask I've worn my whole life and pushed through it, but it's not real. If there was anyone close to me, they'd see I'm fraying at the seams. It's like every day, another string gets pulled, unraveling my life, and I've been left scrambling to grasp the pieces.

Being alone is something I'm used to. It's as much of a survival instinct as it is a habit, but there are times like tonight that I wish I had someone. Someone who knows that I'm really not as fine as I'm pretending to be.

Deep brown eyes with gold-rimmed pupils flash in my mind, and I push down the thought.

Oliver: Rides here.

I grab my coat from the back of my office chair and lock the door behind me. All I want is to get home, take a bath, and pass out. That's not too much for a girl to ask for, right?

Maybe I'll have Oliver take me to a drive-through. I think the chaos of today calls for something extra greasy.

I approach the exit door, swiping my pass to open it,

and I'm met with the rushing sound of rain, so thick I can barely make out the outline of a car parked a few feet away. I step out under the small overhang, and a wet chill seeps into my bones, causing my entire body to shiver.

I knew it was raining, but at some point between leaving my office and arriving down here, it's gone from a drizzle to a monsoon. I close my eyes, tipping my head back, and tighten my grip on my jacket. No part of me wants to wait it out, which means I'm going to have to make a run for it.

I trail my fingers through the curtain of water in front of me, its weight pushing my hand down. This is going to suck. I secure my purse over my shoulder, give myself a pep talk, and push off my heels, but instead of being drenched, I slam head-first into what feels like an immovable wall.

"I've been waiting for you, Little Sparrow." Matthias's low, gravelly voice tickles my ear, his mouth so close it brushes the skin. A shiver rolls through me that has nothing to do with the cold, damp air. He's so warm I can't stop myself from curling into him, all rational thought disappearing as he wraps one arm around my back, pulling me closer.

We're standing under a giant black umbrella, rain droplets tumbling down the sides, blocking out the noise around us and encircling us in our own private space.

The wall I'd painstakingly built around myself today crumbles brick by brick as his warm breath puffs out

against my neck. I don't want to speak; I don't want to break whatever small truce we have right now, where I can pretend he's just a normal guy I like and we don't have a decade's worth of history.

I stiffen. Maybe for him, we don't. Maybe the time we spent in my family's castle meant nothing to him, when those small moments of peace meant absolutely everything to me.

"Hey. Where did your mind go?" he says softly, his chest rumbling against mine. "Come back."

The ache forming in my chest is the exact reason I need to break apart from him.

"Where's Oliver?" I take a deep breath and straighten my shoulders, pulling away from him. My teeth chatter as his heat leaves me.

"He couldn't make it."

I look Matthias over and have to stop myself from curling back into him. He's wearing a dark hoodie that looks like it would engulf me whole and freaking gray sweatpants. Why is it that a man who spends his days in suits and looks like he can kill you at any second can also show up looking like the warmest, safest place on the planet?

"W...why would he c...call you?" My words come out choppy. I'm shivering so bad.

"Come here." Ignoring my attempts to keep distance between us, he pulls me to his side, clamping me in place with his arm wrapped around my hip. The heat of his

front pressed to my side warms me immediately. He dips his mouth close to my ear.

"Let me take you home," he murmurs.

I force myself to pull back again, not liking how much control he has over me. "I just want to go home." Before he can say anything, I add, "To my house."

His brows pull together as if he's trying to figure out how I knew to clarify, but his intentions were written all over his face.

Long, thick fingers curl around my arm as he tugs me with him toward his SUV. He opens the door for me, careful to keep the umbrella covering us. "Get in."

"You don't have to be pushy," I say, getting into the passenger seat. The second the door closes, I'm wrapped in warmth. Hot air is pouring out of my vents at full blast, and the seat underneath me has been pre-warmed, like Matthias knew I'd be a popsicle by the time I got in here. Even with the umbrella, it was inevitable to get wet, but at least I'm not soaked through. I rub my hands together, trying to get some feeling back into them when he climbs into the driver's side, tossing the umbrella into the back.

His entire body bristles as a shudder rolls through him, and it's so adorable I can't look away. He's such a big guy it's easy to believe he's impervious.

"How long were you waiting out there?" I ask.

"Few minutes." He glances at his rearview mirror, giving me the distinct impression he's avoiding eye contact.

My fingers wrap around his without a thought, and they're like ice. "Exactly how many minutes?"

"You worrying about me, Scarlet?"

His head's tipped forward, so his hair falls into his eyes. It's not fair how hot he is when I must look exhausted.

I yank my hand back and frantically wipe under my eyes, trying to remove the inevitable dark smudges. He covers my hands, lowering them so he can do it instead. It's so shockingly sweet that I lean into his touch without a thought.

His thumb sweeps up to my temple, catching a wet strand and tucking it behind my ear. "You're so fucking cute right now."

Rain covers the windows, making it impossible to look out while the drumming sound blocks out the world. I swallow hard, my fingers gripping the center console, my mind whirling so fast I can't make out my thoughts. He shifts closer, taking up the space between us, his mouth descending toward mine, and I don't think I can stop him from kissing me. I don't think I want to.

I suck in a breath, closing my eyes, but the touch of his mouth never comes. Instead, he reaches around me, pulling my seat belt across my chest and buckling me in place. "Safety first."

I groan low in my throat, my fingers curling in a mix of embarrassment and frustration.

"Just go." I lean forward and turn on the music, surprised to hear my favorite song. I let it drown out any

184

possible conversation and turn my face toward the window.

Matthias doesn't push me any further, as if sensing I'm at the end of my rope, and flips on the windshield wipers before pulling out into the dark street. The reflection from the streetlights makes the road practically glow as we make our way through the city. I curl to the side, putting as much distance as possible between us, trying to escape whatever insanity just took over me.

Matthias' hand slides down my thigh, ending just above my knee, where his fingers wrap from one side to the other. His thumb sweeps back and forth in slow strokes that have all my thoughts evaporating and every molecule of my being focused on the way his touch sends electricity between my thighs. I'd be naive to believe he doesn't know exactly what he's doing to me, but the slight pink flush in his cheeks is what stops me from doing anything.

It's like time morphs sucking up the time it takes to pull up to my place. Matthias puts the car in park and grabs my arm when I go to step out. The rain's slowed to a trickle, and I'm sure I can make it inside without too much damage.

His fingers squeeze. "Just wait. I'll go in first."

"Fine." It's not like I don't do this with Oliver each time we come home. It just somehow feels more...intimate? with Matthias.

He gets out, rounding the car before opening the

door. Raindrops collect together on his cheeks as he waits for me to snap out of it.

Shit. I need to get away from him fast.

I get out, rushing to my door, but freeze when putting in my code. My heart kicks up, sending my pulse rushing in my ears. The glass is cracked in a spiderweb pattern, focused on an impact spot and traveling up the pane.

"What the hell is that?" Matthias pushes me behind his back, creating a barrier between me and the door.

"It's...it's probably nothing. Not the first time someone tried to break into a house on this row." There was definitely the appeal of a large payoff since everyone knew these homes were for the rich. Maybe I should move into Misty's apartment building instead?

"Wait here. I'll sweep your place."

"They didn't get in." I fist the back of his shirt and try to stop him.

His entire body stiffens, and a low rumble forms in his chest. It's so primal my body can't help but respond to him, heat flooding to my core. I'm unsteady on my feet when I let go.

"Okay, just make it quick. It's been a long day."

He huffs out a breath and tips his head back in exasperation before shaking it and entering my place. I follow after him, cautious to stay near the door.

"Just like I said. Nothing is wrong." I hide my trembling hands behind me as I prop myself against the wall

and wait for him to do his thing. The exhaustion from the day is settling in. I don't think I can handle another minute of pretending like everything is okay when not a single thing has gone right today.

Matthias comes down the stairs, looking a little less like he's about to kill someone, but I wouldn't call him calm. "It's clear."

"Happy now?"

"No." He approaches me, eating the distance in a few strides. "Let's go."

"What?" I step out of his reach.

"You're coming with me. You can't stay here," he commands like I have no other option.

"Matthias, it's fine." I take another step away. Yes, I'm freaked-out, but this isn't anything I can't handle.

"Staying is not an option." He goes to lunge for me, but I'm faster, pulling out my gun and pointing it directly at his chest. He stills, a slow smile curling his lips.

He doesn't stop coming toward me as he says, "You're really doing this right now?"

I click off the safety, the click filling the space between us. "I said I'm fine. I'm more than capable of taking care of myself, so just go."

The muscle in his cheek flexes as he grinds his teeth together, his fists opening and closing with each passing second.

"Why do you have to be so stubborn, Scarlet?"

My aim doesn't waver. My stubbornness is the only

thing holding me together, and I'll be damned before I fall apart in front of him. "I'm all grown up, Matthias. I don't need to be coddled."

He tips his head back, taking a deep breath in before meeting my gaze. "You're being an idiot right now."

I smirk. "That's my choice to make. As you can see" —I move the gun an inch higher—"I'm more than capable of handling myself."

He runs his hands through his wet hair, water spraying with the force. "You win, Little Sparrow."

"Please...please just go."

His gaze softens, a sadness taking over, but he just turns and walks out.

"So fucking stubborn." He drops his hands. "Lock the door."

I lock it behind him and kick off my heels. My feet ache from a long day, and a sigh of relief escapes me as I flatten them on the floor. I just want to wash today away and pretend like it never happened.

I pour a glass of wine and head up to my room, going directly into the bathroom, where I fill the tub with steaming hot water. I make sure my gun's placed within reach before stripping out of my wet clothes, the fabric clinging to my skin, and climbing in.

Heat envelops me, and I can finally relax. I needed this.

I push back the thought that I really should've gone with Matthias.

If I'd gone with him, I wouldn't have been able to control my heart.

I deserve better than some guy who only cares about me when he wants to.

I want to be someone's everything.

Chapter 22

Matthias

MY BACK'S aching as I hit the automatic control on the side of the driver's seat. I'm too old for this shit. I spent last night camped out across from Scarlet's house. I can't stop the feeling that if I let her out of my sight, I'll lose her forever. I crack open an energy drink and check my phone. Our group chat is going wild, asking where I've been, but I have no desire to hear the shit they'd give me if they knew what I was doing.

Hell, I only told Damon because I know he'd be the same way if it was his girl inside.

Her stubbornness is pissing me off. The only thing stopping me from going into her house and kidnapping her is her wish has run out of time.

There's a knock on the window, and I unlock the doors so Damon can get in.

"You look like shit." He hands me a change of clothes since I haven't left her long enough to go home.

"Screw off."

"Why don't you hire someone so you can take a break?"

"Would you trust anyone if it were Misty? Someone's trying to get to her."

His brows pull together. "I'd trust you."

An uneasiness settles over me. "You have your own wife to look after."

Damon can't help the smile he wears every time he thinks about his wife.

"You're pathetic."

He looks around the car. "And you're not?"

"Whatever. I need something from you."

"Anything."

"Tell Misty to set up a hotel so they can get ready for the Symposium event. At least then I can go home and shower."

"You should know I don't *tell* Misty to do anything, but you should also know she's more than willing to help you in any way she can." He steps out of the car and leans in. "Take care of yourself, brother. Or I'm telling Xander and Bash and sitting back while they make fun of you."

The door clicks closed before I can respond. Bastard would do it too.

I'm just pulling my shirt over my head when Scarlet walks out of her house right on time.

"Get in the car, Scarlet." I get out, walking around to the passenger side, and open the door.

"Aren't you getting tired of this?"

"I wouldn't have to be tired if you'd just come to my house."

"Where's Oliver?"

"I sent him on a different job."

Her eyes narrow on me. "You can't do that. He works for me!"

That slipped out a little too easily. If I'm not careful, she'll figure out just how closely I've been watching her. I repeat the lie that we've been feeding her for years. "Technically, he works for the Order."

She huffs and walks up to the car. She looks stunning this morning, hair pulled back in a twist at the nape of her neck, her light gray dress curving over her form perfectly, leading down long slender legs and tall black heels.

When my gaze finally trails up, it's to see her warm eyes on me.

She smirks at the state of my hair. "I don't think I've ever seen you this way."

"The things I do for you." I smile back.

Pink flushes her cheeks, and I soak in the way she reacts to me. I wonder if she flushes all over like that.

Before I can pull her closer and capture her pretty pink lips, she sneaks beside me and ducks into the car, making a point to click her seat belt so I don't have the honor.

If she only knew how much the fire inside her made me want to fuck some sense into her.

The drive to her work is peacefully silent. She doesn't push me to speak like other people do. Instead, she flips through her phone, acting like I'm not even there.

My grip tightens on my steering wheel. If she keeps this up, I'm going to have her pressed up against the window with her skirt around her hips.

Before I can make that a reality, we arrive at the front entrance to her work.

"I'll see you at lunch." It's not a question.

"I have plans." She shrugs, a smirk on her lips, knowing it'll piss me off.

That digs under my skin. "With whom?"

"Work friends."

Her intentional vagueness just has my curiosity growing more desperate.

"What kind of work friends?"

"Normal work kind."

"Scarlet..." I've had about enough of this.

"You know, you've become awfully nosy for someone who didn't care about what I did up until a few days ago. Maybe you should talk to someone about that."

I want to correct her. To tell her just how wrong she is. That there hasn't been a single second that I didn't care what she was doing. All you'd have to do is see the trail of her exes who magically disappeared to know that I haven't learned to control my impulses. I may have given her freedom, but even I couldn't handle that.

"I'll see you later." I stop myself from reaching out to

her and dragging her back into the car. It's not like she needs to work anyway. Not when I own the law firm. If she wouldn't kill me, I'd have her locked in the car and on the way back to my place. At this point, my willpower is on a single thread.

"Matthias, what's that look on your face? I'm not kidding. I have lunch plans."

"Don't worry, I heard you loud and clear." As it is, she'll already be pissed.

Her eyes bounce around my face, appraising me as if she doesn't trust a single word I say. Smart girl.

"Fine. And don't come pick me up. You're too conspicuous—it looks bad. Just send Oliver like normal."

If she wants Oliver so badly, he might just have to disappear. He's worked for me for a long time, but maybe I've let him get too close. My teeth grind together as I say, "I'll let him know."

The door slams shut with a loud clack, and she walks off without saying goodbye. I watch as she makes her way up the stairs, her tall heels carrying her easily, and don't look away until the door closes behind her.

I crack my neck and pull out, heading to my place. It's good I'll have a few hours until I need to be back.

The work items I tick off during the short drive home make the time disappear. I've been neglecting everything for the sake of being close to her, but my brothers will just have to deal with it. It's only going to get worse.

I'd dismissed my staff early, so I'm not expecting my front door to be unlocked, and I pull my gun from its holster hidden beneath my clothes. Whoever is stupid enough to come into my house is going to regret it.

"Woah, easy there, killer. You nearly shot me." Bash pushes my aim from his face and smiles like I didn't almost take his head off.

I holster my weapon, heart still pounding in my ears, and debate the merit of still killing him. "What are you doing here?"

Xander appears from the living room. "We came to check in on you. You look like absolute shit."

"Of course you're both here," I groan and rake my hand through my hair, knowing there's nothing I can do about this.

"We heard you're sleeping in the car." Bash snickers as he takes a step back out of my reach.

Fucking Damon. Can't mind his own business and had to bring these two into it.

"Screw off."

"Hey, now. Don't be like that. We're just concerned for our big brother." Xander puts on an innocent face, rocking back on the heels of his shoes.

"What do you actually want?"

Bash grins. "How could we miss a chance to see you like this?"

"Get out of my house." I ignore them as I make my way up my curved staircase and to my room. All I want

is to get the grime off me from sleeping in my car. I'm not old enough to feel so shitty.

The shower is hot against my skin as the heat settles into my muscles and eases the ache there. But there's a gnawing feeling that just keeps growing in the pit of my stomach. Like I'm missing something that I can't see. It feels so close, like if I just try harder, I'll be able to track it down and kill it. It feels like something's coming after what's mine, and no matter how many times I try to push that feeling down, it doesn't stop resurfacing.

Scarlet's ex showed up out of nowhere, and then there was an attempted break-in at her place. Her pure stubbornness has me on edge. I'm not an idiot—I know she's strong and capable, but the idea of someone coming after her has my vision going red.

My phone beeps on the counter, and I groan, washing the remainder of the soap out of my hair. I still have another hour before I need to get back, which is just enough time to stop by Damon's and chew him the fuck out.

Scarlet's building is busy, the low hum of conversation filling the lobby. I stop by the entrance, the guard looking up at me, then quickly back at the screen.

"What can I do for you?" He doesn't look up while he asks.

"I'm here to see Ms. Laurent."

He clicks through the keys before shaking his head. "She didn't put you on her list."

I lean over the counter, forcing him to look me in the eyes. "It would be a mistake not to let me in."

"I...I'm sorry...you're not on the l...list," he stutters out, clearly wondering if he gets paid enough for this.

"I'm sorry for the inconvenience, Mr. Everette. You must excuse him. He's new," an impeccably dressed woman says from behind the desk. "Go right in."

Her voice trickles to me as I make my way deeper into the space, heading toward the sound of plates clinging together. "Do you know who he is? Do you want to get us both fired?"

I should feel bad for my reputation, but why feel bad for things that are deserved?

Unsurprisingly, in a building like this, the cafeteria is a full restaurant. Deep green leather booths line the walls, while wood tables fill the center. It's open, the high ceilings letting the light in from the lobby. It's her laugh that catches my attention first, and the first hint of something curling in my stomach starts to form. Scarlet hasn't laughed like that for me in a very long time. I locate her in one of the back booths, tucked in the corner. She's sitting with a woman at her side and two men across from her. In any other setting, it would look like they're on a date.

She doesn't notice me as I approach, instead smiling at the guy in front of her. He's moving food from his

plate to hers, as if sharing like this is normal for them. It's almost intimate.

It's only when I'm within inches of them that Scarlet looks up, her face blanching before turning a brilliant red that's befitting of her name.

"What are you doing here?" she hisses, and everyone at her table turns to look at me.

Unlike her, they notice the rage rolling off me and shrink back.

If my girl notices, she doesn't care, instead standing and walking right up to me, finger poking into my chest. "You're not supposed to be here."

I tilt my head, cupping her hand with mine and pushing her finger into me. "I'm exactly where I want to be."

"You said you wouldn't come."

"No. I said I heard you when you told me not to. They are two different things." Her ears are pink now, anger practically steaming off of her. I lean in closer and whisper, "You're cute when you're mad."

A low growl-like sound forms in her throat. "You're dead."

She grabs my hand and drags me after her, heading straight for an elevator that opens just as we arrive like fate.

I raise my brows. "Are we going to a more private place so you can kill me?"

She doesn't answer, instead staring at the number

ascending to her floor. As soon as the doors open, she walks directly to her office, knowing I'll follow her.

The second we're alone, she whirls on me. "You will never come back here. If you do, I'll have security throw you out."

I laugh under my breath, a low, foreign sound. "Did you forget I own this company?"

"No, Mercer Equities bought it." She leans back onto her desk, a slow smile crossing her lips, my first clue that I'm in trouble.

I take a step toward her, canting my head to the side. What is she up to? "And I own Mercer Equities."

"Correction: you used to own it. I bought the controlling shares a few days ago. Technically, I think that means you work for me." Her smile is brilliant now, curved at the corner, satisfaction written all over her face.

I've never been so hard in my life. "Oh, you're sneaky."

"Now, get out." Her tone isn't as firm as it was, like she's not quite done having fun with me.

I step closer, forcing her to tip her head back to look at me. "Come home with me tonight."

"That's never going to happen."

I reach up and grip her chin, tilting her so her mouth lines up with mine. "Don't say things you don't mean."

Her eyes go wide, and she jumps back. "You're crazy."

"Never denied it." I want to reach for her, pull her to

me, and force her not to let go. There will be time for that later.

She's so fucking stubborn.

I groan, making my way downstairs. Another night sleeping in my car.

A slow smile takes over my face. It's the last time because tomorrow, my Little Sparrow turns twenty-five.

Chapter 23

Scarlet

ON THE WAY home from work, I rest my head against the car window, watching as side streets pass by. I'd stayed late again, trying desperately to come up with a believable reason why I can't go to the ceremony tonight. It's the season's most extravagant event; everyone will be expected to be there. At least I know I can bail on pretty much everything after this.

Of course, it's on my freaking birthday. All I want is to stay at home in my pj's, watching trashy TV. Is that too much for a girl to ask? Instead, I'm going to be paraded about like some kind of display piece for everyone to examine.

Oliver pulls in front of my town house, coming around the hood to open my door. He gives me a warm smile before passing me a small box. "Happy birthday, Ms. Laurent."

"Thanks, Ollie." Tears prickle at the back of my

eyes, and I fake a laugh to cover the slight wobble in my voice. After years of keeping today a secret, I didn't think there was anyone who even knew about it.

"It's Oliver, miss," he corrects like he always does.

"Oh, come on. You even got me a present. Can't you be normal just one time?"

He arches a brow. "Do you want me to take it back?"

"Don't you dare." I tug the pink box to my chest, protecting it with my other arm.

He bows his head slightly, his steady professionalism back in place. "After you, miss."

The cracked glass pane has already been replaced. Everything looks back to normal, no signs of any damage. The only difference is the thin steel threads woven through the glass, making it shatterproof.

Oliver does his standard checks while I wait in the hallway, back pressed up against the wall, and open the small cardboard box. My chest tightens. He got me a single cupcake, with swirled pink frosting and sprinkles on top. When was the last time I had any sort of cake?

"Do you like it?" Oliver asks, startling me. I didn't notice him approaching.

I smile at him. "It's great. Thank you."

"Of course, miss. I'll be back to pick you up at seven sharp." He says it like the gift is no big deal, disappearing into his car.

Meanwhile, I'm stuck staring at the little piece of confectionery. It's almost too pretty to eat. Almost.

I lean against the counter, getting ready to dig in,

when I see the candle tucked in the side, along with a pack of matches and a small note.

Happy birthday, Ms. Laurent. May all your wishes come true.

I read it over again. It doesn't feel like something Oliver would say. A little too wistful for a guy like him. I laugh, inserting the candle into the top of the cake. He probably googled the top five things to write on a birthday card.

Happy birthday to me. The acrid smell of sulfur burns my nose as I light the wick, wax rapidly melting down the side. I think over the note right before I blow out the candle.

I'm twenty-five, own my own place, am college educated, a lawyer, and respected at my job. Nearly all of my dreams from all those years ago came true. So why is there a hollowness in my gut?

I did all of the things I set out to accomplish, but now I'm standing on the precipice of *now what?* Warmth fills my chest as I remember the other things I told Matthias while we were being held captive. I want the family I never had. Parents who love their children for being who they are and not what they can be used for. I want to hear the pitter-patter of feet running up stairs or the bubbling sound of laughter.

I toss the candle into the sink along with the wrapper before biting into the moist sponge-like cake. The sweet taste of strawberries fills my mouth. I moan and take another bite, wiping the icing off my lips with

my thumb. I'm not sure I want to know where Oliver picked this up because I can totally see myself buying out the store.

My phone beeps, the alarm telling me I'm out of time and need to get ready. I finish the last morsel of cupcake before tossing the wrapper into the garbage and heading to my room.

It takes me two hours before I'm ready to put on my dress. The emerald drapes diagonally across my legs, with a gold band around the middle cinching the waist. I picked it out to go with the Grecian theme of this evening. I may not want to go, but like hell I'm not going to look good while I'm there.

I stand, adjusting my dress so it slithers to the floor, the tall slit traveling up my thigh. It perfectly fits every curve. Unfortunately, that includes the soft pouch of my stomach. I refuse to be embarrassed, even though I'd prefer to have at least two layers of Spanx on.

Oliver calls out from downstairs, and I take one last glance in the mirror. I've curled my hair and pulled it up, letting pieces fall around my face. The entire look has a soft, romantic vibe to it.

I take a deep breath and exhale slowly. All I have to do is get through tonight, and then I won't have to worry about any of this until next season.

Chapter 24

Scarlet

"Ms. SCARLET. Please allow me to be your escort tonight." A man in a silver mask bows low in front of me. I recognize him as Eric Momont, heir to the Momont fortune and my predetermined date for this evening. This event is designed to force all of the unmarried participants to socialize together, and what better way to guarantee success than to have mandatory partners for the evening?

"Do I have a choice?" I laugh. It's not this guy's fault he's stuck with me.

A sly smirk curves the corner of his lip, and he holds out his hand for me. "No, but we can pretend."

"Mr. Momont." I bow and take his hand, allowing him to cradle it in the crook of his arm.

"Please call me Eric." He's cute, sandy-brown hair brushed back from his face, and there's a glimpse of dimples every time he grins. There's a boyish charm to

him that is the complete opposite of Matthias. The image of his larger frame fills my mind, and I clear my throat, giving my head a shake.

Not the freaking time.

"Only if you call me Scarlet."

He gives me a dazzling smile. "Ready?"

"As I'll ever be," I grumble.

"I'll do my best to make this the least painful as possible." He laughs.

I find myself relaxing with him. His self-deprecating humor makes quick work of disarming me.

"Good luck with that," I reply and allow him to lead me through the entrance, where we stand at the top of the stairs.

My breath catches in my throat as my eyes take in the grand entrance before me. The replica of an ancient Greek feast is stunning, with a low ceiling adorned with intricate displays of vibrant flowers. Their sweet scent envelops me, beckoning me further inside. On one wall, olive trees stand tall and proud, their branches reaching toward the ceiling as if trying to escape this underground venue. And above all this beauty, thousands of twinkling candles cast a warm glow that mimics a summer night sky.

I'm so caught up in it I almost miss the way the crowd hushes with our entrance. The women look up at me with disdain, the men with appraisal. If this event is designed to encourage matrimony, I'm quite the catch.

After all, if one could marry off their son, they could have two seats in the Order strengthening their family.

Not for the first time, I'm seriously debating my sanity for coming back here.

As if pulled by a magnet, I turn toward Matthias. He's standing a few feet from the bottom of the steps, dark eyes on me. A flush crawls up my neck, and my breath catches as his gaze burrows into me, branding me everywhere it touches. Even from here, I can see the way the muscle in his jaw ticks when his gaze lands on where my arm is draped around Eric's.

Dark eyes bore into mine, and he takes a step forward before Bash stops him with a hand on his shoulder, a wide grin on the younger brother's face.

"You okay?" Eric's voice is close to my ear, drawing my attention back to him. Guilt rises in the back of my throat. I may not want to spend my birthday here, but that's no excuse for ignoring him. After all, he didn't get to choose his partner either.

With the aim of enjoying tonight as much as possible, I follow him down the stairs. The treads are narrow, and my heels are high, causing me to rely on him more with each step.

His grip tightens, and he tilts his head closer for only me to hear. "I've got you."

I expect to feel warmth in my chest, but there's nothing. Not even a bubble of excitement. Why can't I be into guys like him? Sweet, sensible, *safe* guys.

I ignore the voice in the back of my head telling me it's because I already have a very specific type.

The dance floor is full by the time we get there, and I lift a brow in question to Eric. "Starting off dancing?"

"I didn't think you'd want to mingle and converse."

Sweet and attentive. "You'd be right. Come on."

This time, I'm the one guiding as I make my way through the moving couples and take the stance my body's memorized years before. I can do this in my sleep, but I let him lead me anyway, twisting and twirling me around the floor until my breath comes out in shallow pants. I laugh when he dips me low, my head only feet above the ground, and pulls me back up. A little too close for etiquette.

"You're a good dancer," I say.

His eyes are warm on mine, voice barely above a whisper. "So are you."

There's a pause between us, but no matter how much I search for it, there's no familiar tension pulling us closer. This guy could be my brother at this point.

"I'm cutting in." A low command comes from behind me.

"We're not done with our dance," Eric protests, looking between Matthias and me as if trying to decode what's happening here.

"I'm not asking," Matthias growls deep in his throat, and a shiver tingles my spine, sending heat pooling between my thighs.

Eric's brows are pinched together, but he knows

going against a Lord would be social suicide. He gives me an apologetic bow. "Save me a dance?"

"I will—"

"Not going to happen," Matthias cuts me off, hand on my hip, pulling my back into his chest. We're too close, the position completely inappropriate for the setting.

Eric glances between us, then to where Matthias's hand cinches my waist possessively, then back to me. "You sure you're going to be okay?"

Matthias's chest vibrates against my back as he hisses, "Are you questioning my intentions?"

Eric bows his head. "Of course not."

Then he flees.

Dammit.

I spin on Matthias, poking him in the chest. "What do you think you're doing?"

"*Me?* The fuck are *you* doing, Scarlet?" His brows are pulled low over his eyes, and his voice is rough.

"You do realize that this is a part of the event, right?"

He glances away. "That doesn't mean you should be dancing with him."

"Why?" I ask, searching his face. Why won't he look at me?

He runs his tongue over his teeth and entwines our fingers. "It doesn't matter."

I try to disengage, but he just pulls me harder, dragging me off the dance floor, completely ignoring the whispers and prying eyes that surround us.

"Matthias," I hiss. "Matthias, everyone is watching."

"Let them." He practically drags me toward the back of the room where there's an exit sign. I have to scurry to keep up so I don't make an even bigger scene by falling on my face.

It's a narrow stairwell, clearly meant for staff. The second the door closes behind us, he spins me, pinning my chest to the wall and crowding me from behind.

His breaths are hot on my neck. "Are you purposely making me jealous?"

"Are you actually crazy?" I struggle to get out of his hold, but he just pushes me harder into the cool wall so that there isn't a single inch that he's not touching.

He runs his nose up my neck, inhaling directly behind my ear. "You smell delicious."

Strong fingers curl around my throat, squeezing gently as he flattens his tongue and runs it along my skin. I instinctively tilt my head to give him more access. My fingers curl into the stone as his hand traces every inch of me until it makes its way down my abdomen. My breath hitches when his foot taps mine, spreading my feet wider, making room for him to cup my core. The silk does nothing to dampen the intense feeling of his touch.

"Matthias," I gasp.

"That's it. Say my name." His fingers curl, pushing against me, and my knees grow weak.

He catches me, arms banding around my waist, before spinning me to face him.

It's too dark to make out all the details, but his eyes

catch the light as they peer down at me. Hunger is written in them as he grips my ass and pulls me into him until his hard cock presses into my stomach.

"Feel how much you turn me on." He slides his hand further between my thighs. "Are you wet for me?"

He takes his time dragging my dress higher until it's above my waist.

Squeezing my bare ass, he drops his forehead to mine, a low rumble in his throat. "You're not wearing panties."

He pinches my ass before dipping between my folds from behind, his thick fingers filling my entrance.

"I knew you'd be soaked for me," he groans.

I shake against him as he fills me, stroking me back and forth. I rock into him, mind lost, but I want more. I *need* more of him.

He chuckles against my neck and presses his thigh between mine, applying pressure to my clit. "That's it. Take what you want."

The woven fabric of his pants creates the perfect friction. Tension tightens in my stomach, growing deep in my gut as he fucks me with his fingers.

I'm shivering in his arms, every muscle twitching with my ascending release. He grips my chin, twisting my face, and his mouth captures mine just as my orgasm crests, capturing my cries.

I collapse against him, unable to hold my own weight, my heart pounding in my ear. I need to get away

from this man before I do something I won't be able to take back.

I push him back, taking in gasping breaths, and take a step toward the door back into the hall.

"Where do you think you're going?" He grips my wrist, tugging me back.

I need to rely on the last strands of sense I have left. "Back to the party."

"We're not done," he commands.

I can feel wetness coat my thighs in response, but I yank my arm again. "We shouldn't have started to begin with."

"Oh, it's way too late for that, Little Sparrow," he says, then lifts me off my feet, the hard edge of his shoulder digging into my navel as he tosses me over and quickly ascends the stairs.

I wiggle in his arms. "Let me go, Matthias!"

He slaps my ass, the sharp crack echoing in the narrow stairwell. "For once in your life, stop being so stubborn."

"I am not stubborn. You are out of your mind. Now, let go of me."

Matthias shifts me down to my feet, and I relax.

"Was that so hard?"

Chapter 25

Scarlet

MATTHIAS SMILES before opening the door to where a car's waiting directly outside. "Get in the car, Scarlet."

"Not going to happen, Matthias." I sneer out his name like I did when we were kids.

"You can get in on your own, or I can make you."

"Oh yeah?" I shift so I'm in my fighting stance, arms at my sides, ready to move. "I'd like to see you try."

There's a glint in his eyes as a low laugh rumbles from his chest. "You're gorgeous."

His words throw me off-balance, the last thing I expected him to say.

He takes advantage of my lapse and grabs me by the waist, practically tossing me into the back seat of the car before climbing in. In what can only be described as crawling, I struggle to the other side, hindered by my dress, and pull opposite the door handle only to have Matthias's large chest press against my back, pinning me

face down into the seat, his hand landing firmly on the lock.

A quick sideways glance to the front shows the divider in place, no help from the driver.

"You're not going anywhere." He bites my ear and digs his cock into my ass.

I suck in a breath as he rocks into me again, the downward pressure causing my clit to rub against the seat. I try to push him off me, but he easily grabs my wrists, transferring them to one hand, and pins them out in front of me.

A low rumble forms in his throat. "I want to bury my cock into you right here."

A shiver rolls through me, goose bumps erupting along my neck. "I can't—"

He nips my ear. "I'm controlling myself, but if you keep wiggling underneath me like that, I'm bound to snap."

His words have the opposite effect, and I can't stop myself from pushing against him. His breath is hot on my neck as he runs his tongue along the curve.

Lust fills every molecule in my being as he dominates me, cock rocking against my ass, hand tightening nearly painfully around my wrist.

I gasp for breath, panting into the leather fabric as his hand travels beneath me, pinching my already hard nipple between his finger and thumb.

I moan, face buried in the seat.

He lifts my hips just enough to push the hem of my

dress above my waist, allowing my legs to spread further apart.

He uses the space to thrust his hardness against my core.

I hate the barrier between us, and I whine deep in my throat as I move against him, searching for more.

"Matthias," I hiss through my teeth.

"*Fuck it.*" The sound of his zipper lowering fills the narrow space, and my body trembles beneath him. Never in a million years did I think I would lose my virginity in the back of a car to Matthias Everette, but nothing in me wants to stop him.

Our bodies shift when the car comes to a halt.

"I'm going to kill him." Matthias nips my neck before pulling back and flipping me over.

The door opens behind him, and heat fills my cheeks.

"Look at me, Scarlet."

I meet Matthias's dark eyes. He's panting just as hard as I am, face flushed red. "Wrap your arms around my neck."

I don't stop to think, wrapping my arms around him without protest.

He grabs me by my ass and envelops my legs around his waist, kissing me hard as he hauls me out of the car. I cling to him as he devours my mouth, taking any rational thought with him.

I vaguely process the fact that we're moving into his house, the doors opening without us stopping. He takes

the stairs two at a time, one hand banded under my ass and the other holding me tight so with each step, his hard cock pushes directly into my clit.

"Don't...." I moan. "I'm going to come."

He doesn't stop, rocking against me, shattering my mind with my second orgasm of the night. I collapse, body heavy, and rest my head against his neck.

"That's it, Scarlet," he says as he lowers me, discards my shoes, and slips my dress above my head, leaving me naked in front of him, then guides me back to sit on the bed.

Matthias wraps his lips around the peak of my breast, sucking my nipple between his teeth. My core pulses with need, and I don't bother to fight my moans. Not with how his tongue expertly laps over my sensitive skin. Any thought or worry I have vanishes.

His calloused palm grazes up the smooth skin of my waist before taking the full weight of the breast he's not tasting in his hand and pushes down hard on my nipple, stealing a gasp from my lips. The way he nips and sucks has my hips rolling to get closer to him, chasing friction to get to my release. I wiggle, trying to move forward, momentarily distracted by the effort.

Matthias pinches my nipple hard, and I let out a mix of a squeal and a moan. When he has my full attention, his dark eyes stay on mine as he licks the sore tip to ease the pain.

Shit, that was hot.

"If you want something, ask." He drags me forward

until my butt is balanced precariously on the edge of the mattress. He steadies me with one hand and grips my knee with the other. "Open for me, Little Sparrow."

I should fight against him, but I don't want to. Even as he ignored me, there has always been a part of me that wanted him. Wanted him to choose me in the end.

I spread my legs and suck in a breath when he drops to his knees in front of me. In all the years I've known him, I've never seen him bow to anyone. His big, powerful body is between my thighs, looking up at me with lust-filled eyes. The power that always surrounds him is flowing through me. His words replay in my head. *If you want something, ask.*

"Touch me."

His hands slide up my bare thighs, pushing my legs wider until his shoulders rest between them. He waits until I vibrate with need before running his thumb along my slit. I can feel myself grow wetter as his gaze follows the strokes of his thumb, but nothing prepared me for Matthias dropping his face between my knees and dragging his tongue over my clit.

He sits back, a sly grin barely pulling at the corner of his lips, and his inky black gaze pierces mine. "You taste delicious."

Right now, he's the wolf, and I'm the lamb.

I moan out his name, digging my fingers into his hair, forcing him back to me.

He groans, and his grip on my thighs tightens before he licks me again. His movements turn feral as he

devours me, pulling needy sounds from my throat. I've never come this many times, but I can already feel my next orgasm building. His tongue thrusts inside me as he buries his face between my legs and works me like I know his cock will.

He replaces his tongue with two fingers, slowly drawing them in and out of me before adding a third. It's tight, and he can barely fit them, but the pressure is intoxicating.

My orgasm burst through me, sucking the breath from my lungs when his teeth graze my clit. I scream his name, chanting it until it makes little sense.

This man owns me at this moment, even if I never tell him.

He stands, lifting us both onto the bed, placing himself beneath me. My fingers fumble as they undo his shirt buttons, needing to feel his skin against mine. He helps me remove it, tossing it to the ground. Tanned muscles fill my vision, and I trace one of his brown nipples, causing a shudder to roll through him.

I could get drunk on this. I swallow hard, needing more than just his touch.

He freezes when my fingers work at his belt and trouser button, opening it, and helps me work them down his ass. Of course, he's not wearing underwear, and I'm met by the angry, swollen head of his cock.

His entire body jerks when I run my thumb over the tip, smearing his precum. His dark gaze narrows on mine

when I lift my thumb to my mouth and suck off his taste.

Matthias growls, then raises so his forehead is pressed to mine, and takes several breaths before saying, "I always knew you'd be the ruin of me."

I huff out a breath. "If one of us is going to be ruined, it's me."

He pulls back, gripping my jaw hard between his thumb and forefinger. "Listen to me, Little Sparrow. You could never be ruined." He strokes my cheek until I nod.

I kiss his chest, running my tongue along the valleys between his abs as I make my way down. I wrap my fingers around his cock as I lick the wetness from the tip. His eyes roll back, so I do it again.

I bite my lip before admitting, "This is the first time I'm doing this, so I might not be any good."

"I'll help you." His hand wraps into my hair, causing several bobby pins to fall out, and guides my lips to his cock. "Stick out your tongue."

I shiver as heat rolls through me, and I do as he says.

"Now, take my cock into your mouth." I lower, wrapping my lips around him and earning his moan of approval. "That's it."

He applies gentle pressure to the back of my head, and I take more of him. He flinches beneath my touch, hips ramming upward, forcing me to take even more.

"There you go. Good girl," he grits out between his teeth.

I swallow around him when he hits the back of my throat, taking as much as I can.

He grips my hair hard enough to sting and thrusts his cock into my mouth, taking over the rhythm. I hum at the loss of his control and take him even deeper.

"Scarlet." He grunts out my name as hot liquid fills my throat.

I lift my head, smiling. "Did I do good?"

"Jesus Christ." He hauls me underneath him and kisses up my neck, so soft it could be mistaken for affection. The thought warms my chest before I can push it down. We lie there collapsed, catching our breaths for several minutes before he gets up.

"Do you want some water?"

I swallow hard, my throat dry. "Yes, please."

He goes to the desk, where there's already a pitcher filled, and pours me a glass, bringing it to me. "You first."

I drink the cool liquid, letting it soothe my bruised throat.

Matthias sits on the bed beside me and grabs something from the bedside table before stroking my cheek with his thumb. He trails his hand down to mine before entwining our fingers and bringing them above my head. "So fucking perfect."

Cool metal wraps around my wrist with a soft click, replacing his warmth. My eyes shoot wide when I try to pull my arm down, but it won't move, handcuffs holding it in place.

"Matthias?" I say, shock rolling through me.

He trails his thumb over my lips, then pushes it into my mouth. "You're mine."

"This isn't funny, Matthias." I jerk on my wrist until the steel cuts into my skin. "Let me go."

"Never." He shakes his head.

"What?"

The room starts to swirl around me. My eyes grow heavy. I'm too stunned to stop him from kissing my temple and whispering in my ear.

"Happy birthday, Little Sparrow."

Chapter 26

Matthias

"ARE you sure you know what you're doing?" Damon asks as he slides a crystal glass filled with aged whiskey across the table that seats eight. It looks empty, with only the two of us.

I swallow the amber liquid, welcoming the burn at the back of my throat, and drag my hand over my eyes. The look of betrayal she'd given me right before she passed out will stay with me forever. "She's the one for me, Damon."

My older brother huffs out a breath and pinches the bridge of his nose. "I'm not sure drugging her was the right way to show her that."

"She might not immediately appreciate it, but I know what she needs." I glance toward the closed bedroom door where I laid a sleeping Scarlet down. Even in her drugged state, she'd clung to me. She might not understand what she's feeling, but I can help her

with that. I have no problem showing her she's meant for me. I will keep her here for as long as it takes her to see we are already bound together. That there's never been anywhere else for her than with me.

Damon's phone vibrates on the table, and he flips it over, a slow grin pulling at his lips. His obsession with Misty is the only thing that rivals how I feel about Scarlet.

"Get home to your wife. Just don't forget to be here tomorrow."

He's already standing before I get the words out. Impatience practically radiates off him as he makes his way through the house. He turns in the doorway, and his brows pull together. "I haven't seen you this content in years. I can't say I really understand your strategy..." He chuckles under his breath. "But God knows I wasn't able to stay away from Misty. You've waited a long time for the girl you love. You should have told us."

"I couldn't talk about it. It was all I could do to not think about her. How the fuck do you think I survived all these years? Now, get out of here before your wife gets pissed off at you, and in return, you get pissed at me."

He steps out onto the veranda that wraps around the house. "I'll be back tomorrow."

"Come alone. I don't need anyone feeling bad for her and breaking her out. That includes your soft-hearted wife. I know what I'm doing."

"I'm not lying to my wife, Matthias." A muscle ticks

in Damon's jaw, and his fists clench at his sides, reminding me just who I'm dealing with.

My left brow raises. "Then just don't tell her where we live."

He gets into his black SUV, slowly pulling out of the long gravel driveway.

Our bedroom's dark when I walk in. Only a small light on the nightstand illuminates the space and casts Scarlet's face in a gentle, warm glow. I'm soaking it up, knowing full well she's going to wake up full of rage, and this is likely the last opportunity I have to see her like this for a while. Pulling myself away, I enter the en suite, stripping down my clothes, and step under the water, not caring that it's still cold. My hands clench, remembering her smooth skin under my touch, the small wanton sounds she made, and the way she moved against me.

She can lie to herself all she wants, but her body's too honest.

My dick's already hard just thinking about her. I grab the black cloth from the shelf and cover it in her body wash, the scent taking me under. She smelled so good with my face buried between her thighs as they tremble while pressed against my ears. She'd given herself to me, taking my cock like the good girl she is. I hate myself for betraying that trust, but it's my turn to do what's right for her.

I dry off, throwing on a pair of black boxer briefs before crawling into the bed behind her, propping

myself onto my elbows. Her brows are pulled together, making them crease in the middle, and I run my thumb along the seam until it flattens. I suck in a breath when she turns into my touch, humming. I can't help myself from pulling her into my arms until her head rests on my chest, and I tug her leg so it wraps around my thigh and rests between my legs. She shifts against me, breathing deeply.

"Matthias." She murmurs my name, fingers curling into my chest, and it's nearly my undoing.

I'm about to say fuck it and take her here, but it's her next words that stop me. "I hate you."

My fingers stroke the length of her back until her body goes limp.

"I'm going to make you change your mind. Even if it takes another ten years." I kiss her forehead and promise, "I'll always wait for you."

Chapter 27

Scarlet

I CAN FEEL my heartbeat in my temples, like a drummer attempting to crack my skull from the inside. I roll over, burying my face into my pillow, blocking out the light. Matthias's fresh scent has memories flashing back.

The way my body responded to Matthias, craving more from him, has mortification rippling through me. Tears burn at the back of my eyes. I'd let him closer than anyone else. He freaking drugged me! How could I have been so naive after all this time? He's shown me repeatedly that he's more than happy to leave me wanting.

I rub the sore circle where the handcuffs had been. At some point during the night, he must have come in and taken them off. The thought infuriates me, and I groan and toss the pillow across the room, a Tiffany lamp wobbling on its base. I'm off the bed just in time to save it. The colored glass panes in flower motifs are gorgeous, and it would've been such a shame for it to drop. Now

that I'm up, what I can only guess is one of Matthias's shirts hangs around my thighs, engulfing me. It feels like he's claiming me, and I want to rip it off to show him just how wrong he is.

Except my search reveals there's no other change of clothes, and there is no freaking way I'm leaving this room naked.

Carefully, I crack the door open, unsure of what's outside. I suck in a breath as I walk into a paneled hall with warm woods and detailed wallpaper. Large windows fill the space with light; it feels like something from a magazine. I trail my fingers along the windowsill, looking for the crank to open it. There are multiple ways to escape a building, but windows are by far the easiest way out.

"I wouldn't do that if I were you." I nearly jump out of my skin, like a spooked cat, when Matthias approaches from the other end of the hall. A shiver runs along my skin at the sight of him. His hair is messy like he just woke up. He's wearing a soft black shirt and gray sweatpants that hang low on his hips. I swallow hard, taking him in. He's broad and looks so adorably rumpled that it doesn't fit with reality. It's like instead of kidnapping me, I'm waking up in an alternate timeline where he's waiting for me. The way I want to wrap my arms around him and press my nose into his chest, breathing him in, scares the crap out of me. This isn't how I should be thinking about my captor.

I'm normally smarter than this. Hell, I'd killed the

men who'd tried to get away with it last night. So why do I feel so warm and fuzzy with his gaze on me now?

"And why not?" I cross my arms and lift my head high. There's no reason he needs to know I've truly gone insane.

"I have men stationed around the house."

"To lock me in?" Why does my chest hurt?

"To keep you safe." He rakes his hand through his dark hair, managing to make himself even sexier. "You'll find each exit point is locked."

"What—"

"Just until you accept that you live here now."

"That's never going to happen," I scream at him, a simmering heat curling in my stomach. The audacity.

He shrugs like he's not keeping me hostage. "And that's exactly why they're locked."

Matthias steps closer and reaches for my hand, but I rip it away from him. I hadn't realized I'd let it drop to my side.

"Don't you dare touch me."

His eyes cast down and look to the side as his throat bobs. "You're safe. Just come with me. There's hot coffee for you."

"I'll pass." I turn back, hoping there's a lock on the bedroom, but I'm stopped by his wide hands gripping my waist.

I'm lifted and thrown over Matthias's wide shoulder.

"Let me go!" I slam my fist into his back and squirm in his hold.

He grunts, arm binding me harder. "Be good, or I may drop you."

"That's exactly the point, asshole."

"Relax. I'm just taking you to the kitchen."

As he says it, we enter a light-filled space. There are windows lining the entire end of the wall, nothing but grass for what looks like miles except for a giant oak tree with a tire swing hanging off it. It's surreal how pretty it is.

He lowers me to my feet. I turn toward the room, and my mouth falls open. It's styled in a modernized French country. The kitchen takes up the other side of the space, with long marble counters. The oven is an eggshell blue with silver and gold accents. I've never lacked for money, but this is an entirely new level. I can't even imagine who designed this. It's so freaking pretty.

"Close your mouth. You're drooling." Matthias knocks his curled finger under my chin, and I snap my lips shut.

He's so close, his shirt brushing against my hand. My instincts are failing me because rationally, I know I should pull away, but all I want is to move closer. I turn my head into him as he leans down, our lips nearly touching. Deep brown eyes swallow mine as we breathe in each other's air. I lift onto my toes, my lips grazing his, before he's the one that steps back.

Mortification has my fists clenching and my arms wrapping around myself in protection. It should've been me that put space between us.

He's already turned and walking into the kitchen by the time I get my thoughts together.

I approach the counter cautiously, the smell of bacon making my stomach growl.

"Sit."

"No, thank you."

"Why do you have to fight everything I say?" He slides a coffee toward me, and I look at it dubiously.

He chuckles, a small grin pulling at his lips. "If anyone here should be worried about being poisoned, it's me."

My head still hurts, and my brain is still foggy. Actually, that's probably why I'm acting like a fool. I lift the coffee to my mouth, surprised that it's exactly how I make it. I refuse to let on that I've noticed. No reason for him to see that he's impacted me in any way. He's playing a game that I don't know the rules of.

I lower the cup too hard, hot liquid sloshing over the side as the ceramic connects with the counter with a loud clack.

"Woah, careful." Matthias reaches out, pulling my hand toward him across the counter and under cold water from the tap.

I jerk it back, narrowing my eyes. I need answers, and I need them now. "What the hell were you thinking?"

He leans forward, hands planted in front of him. "I had to do something. You've been so stubborn these past few days that you left yourself wide open to be kidnapped. I'm done playing it your way. You may be fine getting yourself killed, but I'm not."

"You were so afraid I'd get taken that you kidnapped me yourself? That doesn't make any sense, Matthias."

A low growl escapes his throat. "I can't kidnap what's already mine."

"You are nuts."

"I've never said I wasn't. Now, eat." He hands me a plate. There's a cheese omelet, bacon, and hash browns.

My mouth is already watering, and I haven't even taken a bite.

"You'll feel better once you get some food into you. You've been asleep for nearly two days." He slides over a fork and knife.

I suck in a quiet breath as my hand wraps around the knife. Never in a million years did I think he'd hand me one. I slide my thumb over it and frown when it's completely dull.

"You daydreaming about killing me, Little Sparrow?" Matthias's smirk fills me with heat, which I do my best to ignore.

I stab my eggs with my fork and chew, ignoring his question. I haven't figured out how I feel about any of this.

The central air clicks on, and I rub my arms against the chill, my fingers catching on a Band-Aid.

My brows scrunch together as I gently peel it back. There is a half-inch vertical incision held together with surgical tape.

I glare at him. "What the hell did you do to me?"

"It's a tracker."

"You cannot be serious."

"I'm so fucking serious. You attract trouble like a magnet."

Fire licks under my skin as I process it all, and I stand from the table, not stopping myself from lifting my plate and throwing it at his head.

He's barely able to dodge it, and it crashes against the wood cabinet. It would be a shame if it left a dent.

Matthias wipes a bit of egg from where it landed on his cheek and smiles. "You missed."

I clench my teeth together and form a fist, my entire body trembling. "You are such an asshole!"

"I'm happy to be your asshole for now."

For now? What does that even mean?

I turn on the spot, tension still pulling my shoulders together, and march to the bedroom I woke up in. I need to get as far away from this man as I can.

There's a lock on the bathroom door, and I sigh in relief. This is probably the most privacy I'm going to get. The room's large. A white soaker tub rests in front of a window overlooking a field. The windows are tinted for privacy, but it doesn't hinder the view. The shower's just as luxurious. I slide my hand behind the floor-to-ceiling

glass door and twist the water on. Slowly, the steam fills the space, trapped inside its cage. It feels like every single one of my muscles ache, so I slip off my borrowed shirt and step under the water, letting it seep into my skin until my body finally relaxes.

He can't keep me here forever. Eventually, someone will notice I'm missing. Right?

I don't have a lot of close friends, but I do have a boss. Not to mention, Misty would notice. A knot forms in my stomach because she may already know and let this happen to begin with.

If I don't stop thinking about this, my thoughts are going to drive me insane, and the only thing I should be concentrating on is getting out of here.

The shelf is lined with bottles, and I swallow hard when I realize they are all the same as mine. Same shampoo, same conditioner. I look through the glass at the vanity and spot the same toothpaste and the style of toothbrush I like.

There must be something wrong with me because that screams red flag, but instead, my heart is pounding in my chest that this man took the time to care.

I get out of the shower, disappointed in myself, as I wipe myself down and enter the bedroom.

Matthias is there, leaning against the doorway. He's cleaned up, wearing a black suit that wraps around his wide shoulders and narrows at his waist. His jacket's undone, revealing where his white dress shirt skims his

abs. Why does he have to look so good? I internally groan, forcing myself to look away from his chest. There's a soft white dress in his hand.

"I'm not wearing anything you give me."

He tosses it on the bed.

"Then you'll be getting married naked."

Chapter 28

Matthias

"LIKE HELL I'LL MARRY YOU," Scarlet screams, all worked up, her hair wild around her. She closes the distance between us and jabs her finger into my sternum. "You've lost your mind."

She's so fucking cute, all I want to do is lean down and kiss her, but that's not going to get her to calm down any faster. "You can either do this sober or drugged. It's up to you."

Her mouth drops open, eyes wide. I can almost see the wheels turning in her brain.

I'm just fast enough to dodge her fist, which grazes the corner of my ear.

"Almost," I say, chuckling, and leave the room, leaving her seething behind me.

Damon leans against the kitchen island, wearing a black dress shirt and crisp pants. He's wearing an

amused smile as I come closer. "You didn't tell our brothers?"

I go to rake my hand through my hair but stop myself before I can mess it up. I'd taken extra care with my appearance this morning, not that Scarlet noticed, but you only get married once.

"Are you kidding me? Do you have any idea how much shit I'd take? Not to mention, I don't trust them not to take her side and steal her away. I really don't want to have to kill one of them."

The door opens, and the officiant steps in. His eyes dart around the room as he sets papers down on the table. He's not a part of the Order, but he's in enough debt to our family that he has no choice but to do what we say.

"Gerald, we all set?"

He jerks his head toward me and gives me a minuscule nod. If he's already this nervous, he might faint by the time my Little Sparrow comes out.

I go to her and bang on the bedroom door. "You've got ten seconds until I physically force you out."

"Screw you." Her voice is muffled through the solid wood, but her tone's easy to make out. A sick part of me wants her to push it a little bit further. I might enjoy having her fight in my arms as I tie her to me permanently.

A hand lands on my shoulder, and I turn to face Damon.

"You sure about this?"

I knock on the door again. "Dead. I've never been more sure about anything in my life."

Damon laughs. "She'll try to kill you."

The idea of her, fire in her eyes as she takes a swing at me, has my cock twitching. I'm one hundred percent a sick fuck. "I'm looking forward to it."

"Scarlet, get your cute ass out here."

"Ten. Nine."

"I never agreed to this," she yells back from the other side of the door.

"Don't you remember? You agreed ten years ago," I reply and keep counting during the long pause. "Eight. Seven."

"We were kids." Her voice has lost some of its edge and is tipping closer to curiosity.

"We're not kids now. Six."

There's a thud that sounds distinctly like her head landing against the door. "I'm not coming out."

"Five. I dare you to test me."

There's no movement from the other side.

"Four." It comes out like a warning.

The door swings open, slamming into my forearm, and I grunt against the pain as it spreads up my arm. She's radiant in the white dress, and I have to choke in a breath. I've been planning this for months, but I'm in no way prepared for the real thing. Her hair's wild, pulled on top of her head into a messy bun, as if in protest.

"Good girl. I knew you'd make the right choice." I bite the corner of my lip as my dick twitches in my

pants. She looks freshly fucked, and if today wasn't so important, I'd tell everyone to leave and drag her back to bed.

"How does it feel to be the same as every other guy who wants to use me?" Her chest rises and falls rapidly, her eyes narrowed into slits.

I grab her chin, squeezing around her delicate bones. "I'm nothing like them. All they wanted was to use you. I don't need your spot in the Order."

"Then what do you want?" she mumbles through clenched teeth, unable to open her mouth against the pressure of my hand.

I lean down, resting my forehead against hers, basking in the way she gasps in a breath.

"Everything."

She fists my shoulders, but she doesn't push me away, and I use the opportunity to run my nose along hers.

"I'll make you happy."

She huffs out a laugh and seethes. "I hate you."

"Liar."

She shoves my shoulders, and I let her push me back several feet. If we get any closer, I'll be fucking her here, not giving a damn about our audience.

The officiant clears his throat. "Um...if y...you're both ready, we can begin." He's standing with his back toward the window, an open space in front of him. I'd spent more time than I want to admit figuring out where to do this without going outside.

Wrapping my fingers around Scarlet's wrist, I drag her with me.

She winces, and I immediately release her, turning her arm. The faint bruise circling her wrist from the cuffs I'd locked her in has pain piercing my chest.

I press my lips against the mark left by the handcuffs. "I'm sorry."

Instead of pulling away like I expect, she searches my features. "Are you really worried?"

"I know it's hard to believe me now, but I've never wanted to hurt you."

Red rims her eyes, and she sniffs. "Well, you have."

There's so much more pain in her voice than a simple bruise. Knowing that I'm responsible for that hurt is nearly my undoing.

I entwine our fingers. "It's over now."

"What's over?"

"The wait."

"May the witnesses please step forward." The officiant's entire body visibly trembles.

We need to hurry this up before he faints.

Damon steps to my right. "I'm the witness."

The officiant goes white as a ghost. "I...I'm sorry, but two witnesses are required."

"Fine." I open the front door and call out, "Oliver, get your ass in here."

He's quick to come but stumbles back when he sees what's happening. His brows pull down, and his eyes narrow as he takes in the scene in front of him.

"You're going to be our second witness," I state.

He looks at Scarlet, and there's a softness in his gaze that I want to tear out.

"What are you doing here?" Scarlet's mouth drops open, her eyes wide on her longtime guard. The gears turning in her mind are practically visible on her face. "Why are you here, Oliver?"

He glances away, then back to her. "I can't say."

"Tell me!" she screams, her voice cracking.

"He works for me," I answer flatly. It's too late to take back all the things I've done, not that I would if I could.

Her head snaps to me, shaking from side to side in denial.

"He always has." I should have known better than to let her find out this way.

She rears back. "He can't. He couldn't have–"

I sigh, getting ready for what comes next. "He does. Now, let's get started."

"I can't do this. You'll have to find someone else."

Oliver meets my eyes head-on, knowing there's a good chance I'll kill him. The only thing saving his ass is the knowledge that Scarlet wouldn't forgive me if I do.

"You." I point past Oliver at one of the guards stationed at the front of the house. "Get in here."

He looks to his left and right, clearly hoping I'm speaking to anyone else before giving up and entering the house.

Unlike Oliver, he doesn't resist. Our men have

been trained to do what they're told, and ever since what happened with Misty, they've been on extra alert.

"Anything else?" I ask the officiant, my voice low, challenging him to request anything else.

"No...no...we're ready."

"Good."

The officiant starts running through the normal words, and Scarlet takes a step back. Her chest heaves, and her cheeks are pink as she processes everything. She's going to run.

She twists, but she doesn't make it a foot before Damon's holding her in place.

"I'm really sorry about this," he apologizes.

"Hurt her and you're dead," I say.

My older brother nods. "Understood."

"How do you think Misty will react about you participating in my coerced marriage?"

There's a sly smirk on his lips. "I think you'd be surprised how much she'll understand. So long as you don't fuck this up."

"Do you, Scarlet Laurent, take Matthias Everette to be your lawfully wedded husband?"

"No." She spits the word, and the officiant freezes.

"Continue," I command, and he does.

"Do you, Matthias Everette, take Scarlet Laurent to be your lawfully wedded wife?"

"I do."

"By the power vested in me by the state of Mass-

achusetts, I now pronounce you husband and wife. You may kiss the bride."

I grasp the back of her neck and force the kiss on her. She refuses to open for me, teeth clamped shut. I grip her ass, pressing her against my hard cock, and she gasps. I use the opportunity to shove my tongue in her mouth, devouring her.

The hands that push against my chest change to pulling me closer as she melts under my touch.

Goddammit, I want her, but I know she'll hate herself if this continues. I break the kiss. "You taste so fucking good."

She rears back, hazy eyes going clear. "I'm not signing anything."

"You are mistaken if you think that'll stop this."

"I don't want you to touch me." Her neck flushes a pretty pink that crawls up to her ears.

"You shouldn't lie to yourself, Wife."

I can practically see the smoke pouring out of her ears, and I shift back, dodging her punch. She's fast, having spent years honing her skills, but not quite fast enough.

She lets out a frustrated grunt and stomps toward her room.

I take a step after her, but Damon stops me.

"Give her some space."

Everything in me wants to follow her into our room and make her see just how much she wants me. No matter what she says, I know she'll be wet, her body

reacting to my every touch, but I'm looking for more than just sex from her.

"Fine. Let's go," I say.

Oliver slides his phone into his pocket the second I step outside, as if he's expecting what's coming next. I grab him by the collar and slam him against the exterior wall.

"Who the fuck do you think you are to question my orders?"

He doesn't say anything, simply taking whatever his punishment will be.

"You're lucky she trusts you. Stay here and keep her out of trouble."

"Yes, boss," he deadpans, and I have half a mind to punch him for his insolence.

I get into the car, and Damon smirks. "That was very mature of you."

"Fuck off."

His laughter fills the car. "I can't fucking wait to tell Xander and Bash they have a new sister."

Warmth spreads in my chest, and my shoulders relax. Whether she admits it or not, I know family is what she needs.

Chapter 29

Scarlet

WHAT THE HELL was I thinking? I can't wrap my head around the fact that I'm married to cold-as-ice freaking Matthias Helios Everette. The man is frustratingly confusing, switching from cold to hot like it's the most natural thing in the world. The last day felt like jumbled dreams. I can't believe I almost had sex with him, only for him to drug me and handcuff me to his bed.

Nothing about this makes sense. What he says now and what he's shown me for the last decade don't add up. He basically told me he thought I was nothing but Laurent pond scum. Unfit to be his friend. Proceeded to avoid me completely for years, but then he forced me to marry him?

The worst part is I'm not even sure how I feel about it. The sad little fifteen-year-old, heartbroken girl in me is ecstatic. She's practically jumping for joy that this man is finally paying attention to us. It's the same

twenty-five-year-old that knows it's not enough to just mess around a few times. That it doesn't guarantee my heart won't end up shattered. That being said, marrying me is going pretty far if this is all just some big game.

I just wish I had a clear sight of what's happening.

Frustrated, I force myself to stand and make use of my time alone. I'd watched Matthias leave with his brother, giving me the perfect opportunity to search the place and try to figure out a way out of here. There's a large oak dresser along the far wall, the finish gleaming in the bright sun. It doesn't look new though—someone must have taken great pains to fix it up. The drawers slide open easily, the tracks switched out to modern bearings, but it's what's in them that surprises me.

Neatly folded clothes fill the rectangle space. I pull out a shirt, surprised to see it's from one of my favorite brands. I'm a little pissed that I didn't check earlier since I was forced to wear the dress he gave me. A little voice had whispered to go out naked like he'd threatened, but I'm not sure I could have handled the punishment for that.

Not to mention the guilt from the bloodshed it would have caused.

I dress in a white eyelet shirt and a pair of jean shorts that fit me perfectly. Everything about this place seems to match my style, from the decor to the perfectly curated wardrobe.

I'm not sure if that's creepy or sweet.

Dammit, creepy. Definitely creepy...Right?

I slide my fingers over every windowsill—no harm in double-checking, just in case. There are alarm systems set up for each one, so there's no chance I can break it without everyone knowing. I glance out the window over the long field, where guys with semiautomatic weapons patrol. Not that I'm worried that they'll shoot me; what would be the point in that? I hate to admit it but... if I'm being completely honest, it's kinda nice knowing the area is protected.

I'd spent years learning how to protect myself, and it's gotten me out of trouble. Still, having help is a feeling I'm not quite used to.

Not to mention, I went from the frying pan into the fire. Somehow, I managed to avoid one marriage only to end up married to one of the most powerful men in the Order of Saints.

Not that I've ever cared about his title; to me, he's still that boy, bruised and bleeding, staring at me like I was going to be the last happy thing in his life. I'd protected him then; I shouldn't be surprised he wants to protect me now.

There's nothing in the hallway that can help me get out of here, so I search the kitchen.

No surprise there's nothing sharp stocked in here. He's underestimating me with the dull knives though. It'll take some time without a whetstone, but I'm sure I can sharpen at least one. I open a cupboard, and I'm not sure if I should laugh or roll my eyes that all the glasses

and plates are plastic. This man is not leaving anything up to chance when it comes to arming me.

I'll give him credit for that. I've spent my entire life taking advantage of being underestimated.

There's buzzing from the counter, a black phone I hadn't noticed lit up. I grab it just in case there's anything useful, and I'm surprised to see a text from Matthias.

> Matthias: You're wasting your time searching the house.

I spin to search the place but don't spot any cameras. Sneaky asshole.

> Me: Stop watching me. Perv.

> Matthias: Stop being stubborn, and put the knife back.

I laugh. Of course it wouldn't be that easy. I slam the knife into the drawer.

> Me: Happy?

> Matthias: With you? Always

A knock on the front door has me spinning on my heels. Matthias wouldn't knock, and I can't for the life of me think who it'd be.

I don't have time to open the door before Oliver's

standing in the doorway. His undereyes are dark, like he hasn't slept for days.

I'm still pissed at him, but he may be my only shot out of here. He'd definitely be the only one willing to go against my husband.

"Thank you for what you did earlier. You aren't in too much trouble, are you?" I ask, nervous that he'll pay a price for being on my side.

"I'm fine. Your *husband* seems to have a soft spot for you. Please don't complain about me, or I won't survive."

"I'm sure he wouldn't actually kill you."

"He absolutely would." He huffs out a laugh, then steps to the side, letting a man through beside him. I recognize him as Dr. Clark, the same one who set me up with an IV a few days ago. Apparently, he's on retainer for whatever the Everette family wants.

Oliver pushes the doctor forward until he's standing fully in the entry. "You have a visitor. Try to go easy on him."

He's dressed in business-casual clothes, like he'd rather be on his yacht. "How are you feeling today?"

"Like I was drugged and kidnapped. How about you?"

He looks at the ground but doesn't try to do anything to help me. "I'm Dr. Clark. Matthias asked me to do a workup on you."

"You aren't coming anywhere near me." I stumble back, catching myself on the chair.

"It's just a simple checkup. Please let me do my job."

The doctor's voice shakes, and I sigh, taking pity on him. "Fine."

"Please sit." He gestures to the chair, and I take a seat.

He approaches warily, keeping his movements slow. He holds up a black cuff. "I'm just going to check your pulse."

I hold out my arm and watch out the window. The entire thing feels intrusive. It's one thing to go to a doctor when something is actually wrong; it's a total other thing to have my *husband* randomly send one. I'm not sure I'll ever get used to calling him that. After all, it's not too late for an annulment.

The doctor runs through a few standard tests, his fingers trembling when he places the stethoscope to my chest. I'm not sure what he thinks will happen to him, but I'm not going to jump up and attack him. It's not his fault he was dragged into this mess.

"You are in perfect health." He starts loading up his bag faster than should be possible.

"What's all of this about anyway?" I ask.

He tilts his head. "Standard check when you're trying to conceive."

"I'm going to kill him."

Chapter 30

Matthias

THE CLUB'S quiet during the day, only a few workers stocking the bar for later. One of the men nods at Damon. They don't dare look at me; I've spent most of my life making sure no one will attempt to get close. I've fanned more than one rumor that I'm nothing but a psychotic killer. That works for me. Unfortunately, with the added mystery around me comes eyes whenever I turn my back.

I take the stairs to the family's private level two at a time and swipe my room's key pass. The door opens with a beep, and I'm immediately met with my younger brothers. They're both grinning like assholes.

"Did you really force Scarlet to marry you?" Xander says and kicks his feet up on the coffee table. He's lounging back in a comfortable pose on the long leather couch.

I glare at Damon.

"Do you really think I'd miss the opportunity for these two to make fun of you after all the shit you said to me when I was trying to get Misty?"

"It's not the same."

"It's fucking worse." Xander stands and stalks toward me. Unlike my other brothers, there's no humor in his gaze. "She saved us. You ignoring her was already fucked-up, and now you pull this bullshit?"

"Do you think I'd do anything to hurt her?" I ask.

"It doesn't have to be intentional to hurt someone, asshole."

"Xander's right. She's our sister now, which means we're not letting you mess with her anymore," Bash adds, his eyes slits.

I deserve the looks they're giving me. After all, I did take it further than I should have. I was never supposed to bring her home like that. The look of betrayal in her eyes damn near killed me. It was like I'd finally broken through her walls and earned her trust, then stomped all the fuck over it.

"I love her," I say honestly. "I've always loved her."

"We know." Xander and Bash speak at the same time.

"I'm keeping her locked in that house until she realizes she loves me back." I don't care how it makes me look. I can't stand the idea of letting her get away again.

Xander's brows pull together. "What if that never happens?"

"I'm surprised you'd even ask me that, Xander. It's

simple—if she doesn't love me now, I'll wait for her. I'll do whatever I need to do to show her I'm worth loving back. I'm not above begging."

"You aren't winning us over on the whole you-aren't-going-to-hurt-her thing." Bash takes a large drink from a bottle with a label I don't recognize.

"What do you want me to say? That I'd get down on my knees and beg her? That I'll bend to her every whim if it makes her happy? That I'll uproot my life if she asks me? Because there is nothing I won't do for my wife. She could ask me to walk off a bridge, and I'd ask her which one. Don't fool yourselves—she's not the one being strung along. I gave up any hope that I could live without her a long time ago. All I can do is do my best to show her I'm worth taking a risk on. That even though I've hurt her, I did what I did because it's what she needed at the time. Not because I decided for her, but because it's what she asked for."

I scoff, knowing damn well my life's in danger. "Don't worry. She can give as good as she takes."

"My money's on her killing him." Bash smiles.

"I'm not taking that bet," Xander joins in.

Damon breaks up the boys. "Does she know where she is yet? That could change things."

"No." I shake my head, picturing her reaction. "I'll let her figure that out on her own."

Damon pulls up in front of my place. There are guards stationed around the perimeter. I'm not leaving anything up to chance.

The house is dark; all the lights are off. Hopefully, my Little Sparrow is asleep.

"Good luck in there." He chuckles.

I'm more nervous than I expected. It's not clear if the time I gave her helped her come to terms with her situation or if I'm about to take a lamp to my head.

I get out of the car, leaning in, and say, "What do you do when you piss Misty off?"

"I don't piss her off."

"Never?"

He lifts one brow at me. "I do everything in my power to make my wife happy. You should consider doing the same."

"I'm fucking trying." I slam the door shut. With each step I take closer to her, my heart pounds faster in my chest. I suck air in through my nose and push it out through my mouth. I have to have my shit together.

I swipe my thumb over the keypad. It's only keyed in for a select few guards, my brothers and Oliver. Anyone else has to get permission directly from one of us. I flick on the light as I enter, ready to dodge whatever she throws at me, but all I'm met with is silence. Too quiet. I search the open space, not seeing any signs of my wife, and head toward our shared bedroom. My breath comes out quicker with each step.

She's going to be tucked in our bed.

She's going to be tucked in our bed.

She's going to be tucked in our bed.

But that doesn't stop the way my gut twists. If anyone's capable of getting out of here, it's her. I push the door open quietly, not wanting to wake her, and my heart slams into my chest. The force of it feels like it'll break bones. The bed's perfectly made, not a pillow out of place. No one's gotten into it since I made it this morning. My pulse rushes faster with each second as I search the room, as if she'll magically appear.

"*Fuck.*" My muscles strain, and I rake my hand through my hair, fighting my grip until it stings my scalp. I push the feeling down, forcing myself to breathe. There's ten men outside, and I've got a tracker on her. There's no way she's escaping me. I scan the room again, and this time, my eyes lock on the closed bathroom door. It's locked, the handle stiff, and I pull the keys from my pocket. There's nowhere she can hide from me. Slowly, I slide the door open inch by inch, mindful not to hit her with it in case she's close.

My chest caves with my exhale, spotting her tucked into the tub, covered in one of the spare blankets. Her eyes are closed, lashes flickering in her sleep. I drop my head to hers, breathing her in. "You're going to be the death of me."

With an arm under her legs and another supporting her back, I lift her out of the tub and pull her against my chest. She stirs, and I freeze, not wanting anything to wreck this moment, knowing the second she's awake, she

won't let me go near her. Warmth hums in my veins when she turns her face into me. She may not realize it yet, but subconsciously, she already knows she's mine.

I lower her to the bed, tucking her under the blanket, and take a second to just look at her. I've been waiting for her for so long that my heart aches at the sight. I run my thumb over her cheek, pushing back a stray strand of hair. Fuck, if I keep this up, I'm going to cry.

Stripping, I walk around the other side of the bed and climb in after her, wrapping her in my arms from behind. Her scent fills my nose as I press it into the nape of her neck, each breath a drug I can't get enough of. I place a kiss in her hair and tighten my grip.

"I'm never letting you go."

Chapter 31

Scarlet

Hot, steady breaths fan the back of my neck, stirring me from my sleep. I dreamed of my father's eyes as he explained I was betrothed and the way my future husband leered at me. It was deep brown eyes with golden, glowing centers that cut through the nightmare and morphed into Matthias and me standing behind a hedge, hiding from the rest of our world. I'd hidden my feelings then, too afraid to be just another one of his conquests, but in my dream, he'd pressed me against the wall and taken my mouth until I gave in to him.

A soft kiss is pressed below my ear, and I startle. Arms hold me in place, stopping me from jumping off the bed.

"Good morning, Little Sparrow." He shifts me and flips me underneath him, those same brown eyes staring down at me. The dream's messing with my head because my heart kicks up like I want him to kiss me.

Shock registers when my mind clears. "The door was locked."

He gives me a sleepy smile, filling my chest with warmth. "I have the key."

"Of course you do." I need to get away from the way he's looking at me before I do something stupid. I push against his chest with all my strength, but he doesn't move. "Get off me before I bite you."

A low rumble vibrates from him directly into my chest. "That's not the threat you think it is."

"I hate you." I sneer, putting every ounce of betrayal into my voice.

His brows pull together, the light going out before he lifts off me.

I despise the way I miss his heat and scramble until my back's to the headboard and my feet are between us. There's a swirling, sticky sensation in my stomach as I try to process what the hell is going on with me. It's like two sides of my soul are crashing into each other: the one screaming at me not to trust him and the other one begging me to give in.

"Let me help you blow off some steam," Matthias says without coming closer.

"Are you going to let me punch you?"

He smirks. "Something like that."

Matthias gets up, grabbing a few things from my drawer and tossing them at me. "Get up and put these on."

"Don't boss me around." I refuse to get up out of spite.

"Just put them on, and don't be stubborn for once in your life. You're going to enjoy this." Matthias sighs, pinching his nose, and looks up at the ceiling. Getting under his skin like this could become addicting.

I raise the gym shorts that look strikingly familiar to the ones I owned previously. I'd think he brought my clothes over if it wasn't for the tags. "Fine. Get out."

Dressed in shorts, a sports bra, and a tight-fitting tank top, I come out of the room to a waiting Matthias. He's changed into a pair of deep blue gym shorts and a crisp white T-shirt that pulls over his wide chest.

He smirks at me, catching me checking him out, and I look away.

"Don't get cocky. You know you're hot."

He comes closer until his shoes brush against my sneakers. "You think I'm hot?"

"Only on the outside."

He places a hand to his heart. "Rough."

I chuckle under my breath and force myself not to stare at his chest. "Are we leaving?"

He hums. "Yes. I think a little outing will be good for you."

A thrill goes down my spine. This is likely the best shot I have of escaping him. There's no way he'll bring all these guards with us. I shudder at the idea of digging the tracker out of my arm, but there's nothing to be done about that.

"Don't even think about it." There's a clanging sound, and cool metal snaps around my wrist.

I hold up my arm and let the two-foot chain dangle between us. "You've got to be kidding me."

He wraps a blindfold around my eyes, blocking out the light.

A low laugh rumbles in his throat. "When are you going to learn? I'll never underestimate you."

"I'm sorry about this." The car stops, and his arms wrap around my waist, pulling me over the console.

"You could have uncuffed me." I roll my eyes, not that he can see them under the fabric.

"Not a chance." He grips my hand, entwining our fingers, and leads me forward.

There's the creak of a door opening, and then his heavy palm presses against my back. "There's a step here."

I lift my foot and move forward, and I'm immediately hit with the citrusy scent of cleaner. It's completely silent, so wherever we are, we're alone. Damn, he's not going to kill me, right?

"You know, everything you think is written on your face." His front is to my back when he lifts the blindfold from my eyes.

I suck in a breath. Every type of gym equipment fills the space. Squat rack, pull-up, a range of weights. The

three walls are painted a dark gray, and the other is lined with mirrors. It's the prettiest gym I've ever been in. Nicer than the one I've been training at, and that's saying a lot.

"You like it? It's our private gym. I'll take you here whenever you want." Matthias steps up beside me, a gleam in his eyes.

His offer doesn't make any sense. Why would he be the one to take me? "What if I want to go during the day? Can't Oliver just take me?"

"Like I said, I will take you whenever you want," he deadpans.

"Are you going to just leave a meeting because I ask?"

"Yes." There's no humor there—he's completely serious.

My neck heats, and I swear I can feel my ears turn pink. "You're being ridiculous."

He gives me a knowing smile. "You're cute when you're flustered."

Tingles travel down my spine, and my tongue glues to the top of my mouth. How does he just say things like that?

He points at the ring located in the center of the gym, saving me from my embarrassment. "Ready to kick my ass?"

"Wait. You're going to fight me?" A bubbly sensation fills my chest, and I hop from foot to foot. My smile grows, knowing he's going to regret this.

He's watching me. "Just keep smiling at me like that."

The bubbly anticipation turns to heat, and I have to squeeze my thighs together. *Shut it down, Scarlet.* I can't let him see me like this. He handcuffed and blindfolded me, for Christ's sake.

He doesn't push me. Instead, he sits me down on a bench near the ring. "Stay here."

I'm itching to get up just because he told me not to. Hasn't he realized I don't like to be told what to do?

"Why are you always thinking about running?" He's back with a small white box in his hand.

"Why do you always make it so tempting?"

His tongue wets his bottom lip, and I fail not to watch it.

His eyes are on mine when he sinks down to his knees, sending my heart thundering.

"What are you doing?" I squeak out.

"Give me your hand." I've already given it to him before I can think about pulling away. His large body below me, brown eyes looking up, has twisted my brain.

He patiently wraps my knuckles with white tape, taking care to align each row perfectly. His head is bowed, hair tumbling over his forehead. His touch is warm, familiar, everything it shouldn't be. Without thinking, I brush a strand back and run my finger along the jagged scar.

He stills, eyes shooting to mine. "You did a horrible job."

I scoff. "Are you kidding me? You wouldn't stop moving."

He gives me a cocky smile that makes me breathless. "Yeah, because you kept jabbing me with that needle."

"Well, if you didn't open your stitches every night, I wouldn't have to sew you back up in the morning," I taunt back, easily settling into this game we used to play.

I'm not sure who starts it first, but we're both laughing. My head's thrown back, and my heart feels light. There are tears in my eyes by the time I can finally regain my composure.

His gaze is warm. "I like you like this."

"Like what?" I ask, still breathless.

"Happy."

My heart aches, and I have to force myself not to reach for him. How does he do it? How can he ghost me for a decade, show up and kiss me senseless, then freaking kidnap me and still have me wanting to go to him? "Don't be ridiculous."

"Come fight me, Little Sparrow. I can take it." He runs his thumb along my bottom lip and frees it from my teeth.

I stand, needing distance between us. "Don't cry to me when you get hurt."

"That's if you can land a blow."

I come in close, needing to neutralize his reach, and throw a jab into his gut.

He grunts and tries to grip my arm, but I dance away before he can touch me.

"First hit goes to me." I grin.

"I let you have it."

"Sure you did." Adrenaline tingles under my skin as I hop from foot to foot, keeping myself loose.

He dashes forward, trying to grab my waist, but it leaves him wide open for a hit to the jaw.

I pull it back at the last second so it's nothing more than a tap. "Don't worry, I'll go easy on you. I remember you were quite the whiner."

"Low blow. You promised not to bring it up again."

I dance backward on my feet, shifting into my fighting stance, and wait until the moment he comes in to attack again. This time, I easily dodge and swing around his back to wrap the crook of my elbow around his neck.

There's laughter in my voice when I say, "I'm pretty sure I didn't. Plus, our promises don't count anymore."

His hand closes around my wrist. "Why? I kept mine."

"What?"

I jerk back, but Matthias tightens his grip, keeping me in place. He kicks my feet from under me and flips me onto my back, putting his weight on top of me. "I told you I'd marry you when you turned twenty-five."

Stunned, my world spins around me, tipping on its axis. Cracks slice open what I believed to be true, and I

desperately try to hold them in place. I search his eyes, warm on mine. "You remembered?"

He drops his head to mine. "I waited for you."

It feels like he's splitting me open, and I grit through my teeth, "Don't lie to me."

I push at his shoulders, trying to buck him off, but he grabs my wrist and pins them to the mat with one hand, gripping my jaw with the other.

His mouth is hard on mine, biting my bottom lip when I refuse to open. I gasp, and his tongue fills my mouth, a guttural groan vibrating from his chest, reverberating through me. I want to grab him and pull him closer. I want to bury my fingers into his hair and never let him stop.

While he pushed me away, I was able to pretend like he didn't take up my thoughts.

Now he's kissing me, broad shoulders pushing me into the mat, like he's exactly where he belongs. Like he hasn't been the reason my heart ached and I've cried myself to sleep.

The question that's been swirling in my mind over and over tumbles to the forefront as his stubble scrapes my face.

Has he felt this way the entire time? Did his heart latch onto mine like mine did his? Has it been torture?

I search his gaze, looking for that same feeling that's been rooted inside me. At fifteen, he was able to capture all that I am. I can only imagine the damage I'll let him do now.

I rip my mouth away. "What do you want from me?"

"Haven't you figured it out already?" He places a featherlight kiss to my forehead. "Everything. I want everything."

Matthias gets up and pulls me with him. "We're meant to be together, Scarlet, and I'm going to make you believe it."

There's a deep ache in my chest as emotions slam through me, years of actions coming head-to-head with his words. "I'd like to see you try."

It's the realization that I mean it that has me silent the entire way back to the house.

Chapter 32

Scarlet

THE SOFT FABRIC of my robe warms my skin. I'd forced myself into a cold shower the second I got home. What the hell was I thinking, rolling around with Matthias like that? I can still feel the weight of his body against mine. His kiss took over my senses until I didn't care that I was supposed to resist.

It's the impossibility of his words that throw me off-balance. The way my heart ached in my chest like he'd just cracked it open and looked inside.

"I told you I'd marry you when you turned twenty-five."

Never in a million years did I think Matthias would ever say something like that to me. I bite my lip and pull on a skirt that swings out from my hips, large folds rippling the fabric. He handcuffed me, drugged me, kidnapped me, then forcibly married me. Now I'm

supposed to believe it was all because of some promise we made when we were kids?

I cover my face with my hands, sighing out a breath as my eyes sting. I want it to be true so bad. That's the exact reason I need to get out of here. I can't think properly when all I can see is him.

I pull on a thin shirt without a bra, needing all the help I can get, then open the bottom drawer, using the charade of digging for something, but I don't take anything out. Leaving it open, I step out of my room. The chilly air causes my nipples to harden, and a little part of me hates this strategy, but with every eye on me, I need to use every advantage I have.

As expected, there's a guard standing right outside the door. He's wearing black tactical gear and a gun strapped to his chest. The way his belt is stocked with a variety of weapons is more than a little overkill. My heart rate speeds up with every second I wait. I'm not sure what Matthias will do to me If I'm caught.

That's not true. I know he won't hurt me.

One knock is all it takes for the guard to turn toward me, his eyes lowering to my tits before snapping up. "What is it?"

My hand cups my ear, and I mouth some words in my best attempt to fake the inability to hear him. Putting on a show, I huff dramatically and point at the front door. His eyes dart from the door to me, and he shakes his head no, turning away.

I pound the glass with my fist using all of my strength, making it rattle. The hard surface groans, and the guard's eyes go wide. If I break it, I will definitely get hurt, and he knows it.

"Fuck," he cusses and punches in the key code. The door cracks open, but I push against it, throwing all of my weight until it's wide enough for me to fit through.

The clear night tempts me to make a run for it now, but that's not the plan. No, the plan is to take advantage of this poor guy. I almost feel bad for him. *Almost.*

I lift onto my toes before he can stop me, and he visibly shivers when I bring my lips to his ear.

"I need some tampons." I don't. My period isn't coming for weeks, but he doesn't know that.

Pink flushes his cheeks. I'm playing dirty with this one, but hey, it's not my fault this guy is embarrassed by girly things. "I'll let Matthias know."

Images of big bad Matthias standing in the store, flustered by the million options before picking out tampons, makes me smirk. I pull back from the guard, having acquired what I need just as his phone starts to ring.

"You better get that." I step back into the house, smirking at the now pale guard.

He brings the phone to his ear and flinches as the door shuts, lock sliding into place. My heart's thundering, sending my pulse rushing through my ears, elation building inside me, but I'm not done yet. I flip the sharp

blade of his knife that I lifted from him so it's pointed up, the flat side pressed against my wrist. The folds of my skirt engulf my hand. I can practically feel the cameras on me as I make my way back into my room.

Grateful that I had the foresight to leave the drawer open, I crouch, angling my back to the camera, taking care to keep the blade tucked so it's invisible. This is the riskiest part of my plan. I knew I could get it away from that guard easily enough, but all it would take is a camera I didn't locate coming from a different direction, and I'd be screwed. My throat tightens, making it hard to swallow as I transfer the knife to the back of the drawer, then take out an oversized sweater.

I pull it over my head, the hoodie dropping to mid-thigh and warming me. Matthias's fresh scent envelops me and has a calming effect. I countdown the seconds with each inhale, waiting for a guard to come busting in and confiscate the blade. After what feels like forever but is only a few minutes, my shoulders drop. I did it.

There's a bubbling feeling rising in my chest, one that sends shivers down my spine. I lean into it, wanting it to fill me completely. Brown eyes with gold centers have my chest aching. There will be no going back from this.

I scan the room. Everything is still in place, except for my laptop placed on my nightstand. How did he even get this? Stepping closer, I see the white note placed on top.

Behave

- Your husband

I crumple the note, head into the kitchen, and let out a long breath at the hundreds of emails waiting for me. It's going to be a long night.

Chapter 33

Matthias

I GROAN, leaning my head against the sofa cushion as I search through Liam's computer drive. I hacked in before killing him but haven't been able to trace down who sent him the video. I've taken a deep dive through his email network, and it's the first time I've had hope I'll find anything.

Scarlet's safety is my priority. Someone who had access to the security film of her killing her father took the time to set her up. I can't brush it off, but that doesn't mean I'm not miserable being away from her.

I want nothing more than to go home to my wife, pin her to the wall, and fuck her senseless until she understands exactly how serious I am. The sheer amount of willpower it took to come to my place in the city instead of following her into ours is something I should win an award for.

Not to mention how hot she was blindfolded and

handcuffed to me. Did she notice the way she leaned her weight against me? Somewhere deep inside her, she instinctively trusts me to take care of her. Now, I just need her to feel that way all of the time.

"You look pathetic," Bash says from the large leather chair beside me. I decided to escape to my house, not knowing this annoying ass would show up.

I glance up from my screen, glaring at my youngest brother. I miss when he looked up to me. Then I didn't have to take his constant shit talking. I'm so looking forward to the day some girl puts him in his place. He won't know what hit him.

Bash tilts his head. "What are you smiling about?"

Unable to hide my smirk, I say, "How much I'm looking forward to your downfall."

He huffs through his nose. "What's that supposed to mean—"

The encrypted files finally open, revealing exactly what I've been looking for. My fingers fly over the keyboard, so close to finding whoever tried to fuck with her. It doesn't take long for me to hack into the person's phone, locating them after finding their name.

I jolt up, standing from the couch, already making my way to the door. I shove my phone into my pocket as Bash grips my arm.

"Tell me what the hell is happening. You look like you're going to kill someone."

"That's exactly what I'm going to do. I found the guy

that sent the video of Scarlet killing her dad. I've got his location."

"You thought you'd leave without me? I'm coming too."

A muscle tenses in my jaw, and I give him one last out. "This is going to get messy."

"Dude, she saved our lives. Plus—" He smiles, and it's fucking devious. "—she's my sister."

He might be my little brother, but he's all grown up now.

"Where are we going?" he asks, already pulling out a gun from a locked cabinet.

"We're going hunting."

"Where did you get the video?" I ask, the tip of my knife grazing down the asshole's arm. Blood trails the blade, but I'm careful not to cut too deep. He needs to last long enough to get the answer. It didn't take long to realize he's just a middleman, which means I need to dig his source out of him. We've been at this for the last ten minutes, and the man's already covered in marks.

"Go fuck yourself," the man hisses from where he's leaning against his mangled car. The entire left side is dented in from where I crashed into it, pushing him off the road.

Bash slams his fist into the guy's gut. "Wrong fucking answer. Try again."

He smiles up at us, looking entirely too confident for the situation he's in. "You can't protect her. He's got eyes and ears everywhere."

A shudder rolls down my spine, and my grip tightens on my knife. Knowing for sure someone's out there wanting to hurt her has all my hair standing on end. I need to find them and shut them down before they can come near her. "Who? I'll pay you triple whatever he offered."

He tips his head back, exposing his neck. "You can't buy this type of loyalty."

I grab him by the collar, slamming him into the crumpled steel of his car door. "You're going to tell me, or I'll fucking kill you."

"Too late." Blood pools over his lips, coating his chin and throat as he slumps to the ground motionless.

What the hell? He shouldn't have died from what I've done so far. I'd been saving that for later.

Bash flips him onto his stomach, revealing a long gouge that runs the length of his back. It must have hurt like hell. He'd just been playing with us, waiting out his time until he died.

"Fuck. He's the only lead I have, and now he's useless." I slam my foot into his back, frustration crawling through my veins.

Bash grips my shoulder and pulls my attention to him. "We'll figure this out. No one's coming near my sister."

I turn back to my men, who are cleaning the space.

"Bring him to the Vaults. I want everyone to see what happens if they come after my wife."

Damon and Xander are already waiting when Bash and I show up to the Vaults.

"Why the fuck didn't you call us." Damon shoves my robe into my chest hard enough to knock the air from my lungs.

"We had it handled."

"You had it handled?" Xander yells. It's so unlike him I take a step back. "You rammed your car into theirs. Do you have any idea how fucking dangerous that was?"

"It worked, didn't it?" Bash gives Xander a cocky grin, and I have to catch Xander before he can punch his little brother.

"If you're mad, be mad at me. It was me who brought him, after all," I cut in.

Damon shoves me again. "Oh, don't worry. I'm fucking mad at you."

"They aren't kids anymore, Damon," I say.

He glares at me, brows pulled low. "I know that, but ramming a car?"

"There's more to this than me taking Bash on a joyride. Shady things keep happening. At first, I thought they were one-offs, but now I think they're all connected. Scarlet's asshole ex showed up out of nowhere, trying to get her to go with him. I should have

found out how he knew where she'd be. I'm still pissed at myself for killing him too fast. Then there's the attempt to break into her apartment."

"You're just telling us this *now?*" Xander cuts in.

"Tonight's the first time I've had any semblance of a lead. Liam showed up with a video of Scarlet killing her dad. There's no way a guy like him should have had access to it, so I've been hacking his computer since then. I decrypted his files and figured out who sent it to him. That's who we were after tonight."

"Fuck," Damon whispers under his breath.

I continue. "Before the asshole died, he told us that whoever he was working for had eyes and ears everywhere. Whatever this is, it's not just about Scarlet's position."

"So what now?" Xander asks.

"I won't let her leave my side until we figure this out."

"We'll help—" Bash starts, but we're cut off by two men carrying the bloodstained body down the stairs.

Damon whistles under his breath. "You really beat the shit out of him."

"You'd have done the same."

"I fucking did." Dark eyes that match mine gleam, and for a moment, I regret not cutting off this fucker's cock.

We put on our gold wolf masks but don't bother with the hood. There isn't a single person in there who doesn't know who we are.

Xander and Bash each take one of the unconscious man's arms. Our guards aren't able to follow us into the Vaults. Instead, my brothers drag him through the aisle, leaving a trail of blood. All eyes are on us as they take in the scene. It's a show of power, one that can't be mistaken for anything else.

I take the no longer breathing body from my brothers and turn it so it faces the crowd. His back propped against the dais beneath where our throne-like chairs sit.

Blood pools from his mouth, ears, nose. The red slashes from the cuts down his chest are easily seen through his open shirt.

No one steps forward to claim the man, knowing full well they'll be pinned right beside him.

My brothers take their seats, overlooking the crowd, but all eyes are on me as I walk to the edge of the dais and press my foot into the back of the soon-to-be dead man's head. "This is a reminder of what happens to anyone who fucks with us. You're going to wish you had it as good as this guy if you so much as think about coming after what's mine."

Chapter 34

Scarlet

THE FRONT DOOR OPENS, and the smell of roasted chicken hits my nose before I spot Matthias. His hair is wet, pushed back from his face, and his brows are pulled low, giving him a sleepy look that doesn't belong. His attention lands on me, and all signs of wariness vanish without a trace, leaving behind his piercing stare.

"Waiting for me, Little Sparrow?" He steps closer, and I take a step back in a dance we're both familiar with.

"Hardly." My breath hitches when the tips of his shoes brush the tips of my toes. There are dark circles under his eyes, and I don't know why I care, but I can't help myself from asking, "Tough night?"

"Nothing to worry about." He tilts his head to the side, scanning me before stepping back and placing the food on the kitchen counter. My mouth waters when he places mashed potatoes and a box of chocolates next to

the chicken. He fills two plates with food without asking me what I want.

"I'm not hungry," I say.

He laughs. "You're a terrible liar. The guards said you haven't been eating properly."

My eyes dash to the window, and I glare at the guard. I take it back—I don't feel bad for him at all. *Tattletale.* Thank God he didn't catch me earlier; he'd have definitely told Matthias.

"What are you looking at?" Matthias's voice is rough, a darkness filling it he doesn't normally use on me.

"Huh?" I look at him, then back at the guard. "Don't tell me you're jealous."

A thrill starts to climb up my spine at the thought of this man being upset about me just *looking* through his window. A glimmer of an idea filters through on just how fun it would be to press Matthias's buttons. What the hell is wrong with me? Matthias is a sea of red flags, and I don't have a boat.

He glares at the unknowing guard. "My patience is completely worn-out tonight, Little Sparrow. I dare you to test me."

"You should have thought of that before you went and locked me up here." I stand firm.

He sets the plates down on the kitchen table, then turns, lifting one brow.

"Eat."

I fold my arms in front of my chest, not budging. "I said I'm. Not. Hungry."

"I'm not joking." His gaze turns pitch-black as he stalks toward me, forcing me backward.

"I don't want to eat with *you*." I grip the glass of water from the counter and toss it at his face milliseconds before he can get a hold of me.

He stands there, water trailing down his chin and falling to the floor, blinking at me, mouth half-open before he laughs. He wipes his hand over his face, shoulders loosening as his entire body shakes, and his laughter fills the space between us. He looks so young and happy, something I haven't seen in such a long time. Not since before my family captured him and his brothers.

He and Damon used to laugh like this when they were up to no good, constantly causing trouble at whatever events they attended. Warmth fills my chest seeing him like this now.

I twist my lips against my own smile. "Like I said. I don't want to eat with you."

It takes a second, and then he gives me a cocky grin. "There's the fire I love."

I'm still stuck on the word *love* as he lifts his shirt over his head, wiping his neck and face, leaving him in nothing but his black pants, clinging low on his hip bones. Dammit, he's so broad I can't look away from his tanned chest, the way his muscles form peaks and valleys. Matthias flexes under my gaze, and I snap back into reality.

"It's funny you think you have a choice." He lunges forward, catching me by my waist, and hauls me up.

"Put me down!" I try to shift my weight and gain purchase to throw him off-balance. My fists clench, and I grunt when he easily evades all my attempts to make him put me down.

"Anything you want." He seats himself at the table with me on his lap. His hot, bare skin presses against my side, warming me through my sweater.

"Are you out of your mind?!" I yell, trying to squirm my way off his lap.

He grunts. I can feel him getting hard beneath me, and his lips skim my ear. "I wouldn't do that if I were you."

I freeze, core throbbing as he presses harder against me. I'm panting, trying to regain my breath, when he lifts a piece of chocolate to my mouth.

"Come on, take a bite."

My stomach growls in response, and he chuckles, the vibration traveling through my back.

I've lost it because I lean in, taking the morsel from his fingers with my teeth. I close my eyes, humming as the sweet taste melts on my tongue.

Matthias runs his thumb over my lip. "See what happens when you stop being so stubborn?"

I'd kill him right now if I wasn't so hungry.

Instead, I sit with him, back stiff as he feeds me my dinner piece by piece.

My eyes feel heavy as exhaustion takes over me, and I find myself slowly relaxing into his chest until his arms cradle me.

"Let's go to bed." He kisses me behind my ear, sending a shiver down my spine.

My chest squeezes, almost regretting what's about to happen next, but I can't turn back now.

Matthias lifts us both from the chair, carrying me to our room. I can't stop myself from breathing him in and filling my lungs with his scent. This will be the last time he holds me like this, and I want it to last longer. Bile rises into the back of my throat when he gently lowers me to the bed, leaning in closer, eyes searching mine.

"What are you up to, Scarlet?"

My heart comes to a dead stop before slamming into my ribs, knocking the wind out of me. "Just get out."

Matthias cants his head to the side, observing me. "Okay...I'm going to wash up."

"Not in here!" I call after him, standing as if to grab his arm. He's been using the bathroom down the hall, and I hadn't calculated for this.

He smirks down at where my fingers brush his bicep and grins. "Did you want to come with me?"

I choke out a breath, biting the corner of my lip. There's something about his smile that makes me want to lift onto my toes and press my mouth to his. I need to play this perfectly, and kissing him is not a part of the plan. At least not yet.

"Just clean up after yourself," I scoff.

"I always do." He has an unnatural ability to make everything sound dirty.

The second the door to the bathroom clicks shut

behind him, I head straight to the dresser. I purposely chose this drawer because it houses my pajamas, but that doesn't stop the rhythm of my heart from racing. It's like I just walked off a building, and my body hasn't figured out I have a parachute yet.

I bring my clothes to the bed, and under the cover of my sleep shirt, I slide the blade between the mattress and the frame, pushing it backward until it's hidden by the dresser.

I'm so amazed that I pulled it off that I nearly jump out of my skin when Matthias walks out, toothbrush in hand. His eyes are sharp as they scan me. The hairs on the back of my neck stand up at his appraisal as I try to keep my anxiety from my face, using the best tool I have.

I hold my shirt up, covering my not-bare chest. "Get out. I'm changing."

The suspicious eyes turn dark, toothbrush pausing mid-stroke.

"I said get out!" I yell.

"You have thirty seconds to get your ass into bed." He turns and heads into the bathroom, and I catch a peek at his broad back as the door closes.

Why does he have to be so freaking hot? It's unholy.

I rip my shirt off, replacing it rapidly, and do the same with my skirt. My sleep shorts are tighter than I'd normally wear. I internally groan, knowing getting the wrong size is likely intentional on his part.

I tuck the blanket up to my ears, pinching my eyes

closed and counting in my head. I can do this. I just need to distract him long enough to get the upper hand.

The bed indents with his weight, and I have to use a hand to stop myself from rolling into him.

"You're not sleeping here, asshole." I say it, but I'm counting on this happening. Matthias is easy to read, and the chances of him sleeping anywhere else are slim to none.

He hums, mouth close to my nape. "Why not? This is my bed?"

"Listen—"

Matthias covers my mouth with one hand, turns me to face him, and presses his forehead against mine. "I've already given up too many nights without you."

His words are sweet enough to kill. They make me want things I can't have. I need to do this now, or I'll never find the nerve again. I wrap my fingers around the knife and twist so my mouth presses against his. He doesn't open immediately; instead, his eyes stay hot on mine. *Come on. Close your eyes.*

I run my tongue along the seam of his lips, and it's like a band snaps in him. His mouth opens to take over the kiss. He tastes like mint toothpaste, and I let the sensation fill me for one more second before raising my hand.

Matthias freezes the moment the cool tip of the blade touches his throat. I've positioned myself so I'm lifted on my left elbow and my knife in my right hand, the edge grazing his skin.

"You are going to let me go, Matthias, or I'm going to slit your throat." I pray that he doesn't hear the tremble in my voice. The way that my mind screams at me to drop the knife. I'm not going to kill him, but a hard hit to the temple with the handle will at least knock him out. Then, I can threaten the guards with killing his unconscious body. The chances of me getting away are next to nothing. I have to get past the guards, dig out my tracker, and I'm not sure there's anywhere I can go that he can't find me, but I can't just sit here and let this happen. I'm never going to allow myself to be someone's captive again.

The asshole smirks at me, his grin growing until it's a full smile. He grips my hand, but instead of pulling away, he digs the blade in deeper.

Shit. I jerk, but he holds me in place.

"Go ahead, Little Sparrow. I'll die a happy man."

Blood drips down from the cut as he pushes it deeper. Tears sting the back of my eyes. This isn't what I wanted. "Please, let me go."

"I don't think so." He grips my wrist hard enough to hurt and reaches over to his nightstand. His arms are so long he doesn't have to move his torso as he grabs his phone, turning on the camera so he can see what he's doing.

"What...what are you doing?" I can't breathe as he slides his hold upward to cup my fingers in his, then slowly manipulates the blade to cut an S inches below his neck.

I gasp. "What the hell are you doing?"

"You seem to be confused about what's happening here. I'm just showing you how permanent you are."

"By what? Carving my name?" I ask, eyes wide.

"Exactly. Now, don't move around too much. Wouldn't want to fuck this up." He's watching through his phone as he carves the *C* into his skin.

"You are out of your freaking mind!" There's something wrong with me because my core aches to be touched. I rub my wet thighs together, fighting the urge to climb on top of him.

"Help me out before I mess up the *A*." The knife slides, and I stop it before he can permanently write it backward.

"I can't believe I'm doing this." I take a deep breath when he lets go of my hand, tilting his head up, giving me full access to his neck. He's so vulnerable to me, in the exact position I needed him in earlier, but this time, I can feel his gaze branding me. I should slice his thick neck—I should do so many other things, but my hand moves on its own, meticulously carving each letter. The tail of my name follows the path beneath his collarbone.

He watches me, hot breaths brushing my skin, but doesn't so much as flinch as I finish my name. There's a twisted sense of satisfaction when I look at the raw letters, blood trickling from them.

He holds his phone up, examining my work. "So much better than your stitches."

His laugh is contagious, and I press the knife to his throat. "I can still kill you."

Strong hands cup my ass and shift me until his thigh is pushing between mine.

"You can kill me tomorrow," he says, then takes my mouth.

I drop the blade, pushing it off the bed before burying my fingers into his hair and forcing him closer. He moans in the back of his throat, flipping me beneath him. I gasp as his hand travels up my side and cups my bare breast. He sucks my nipple into his mouth, rolling his tongue over the tip before biting. I scream, fingers tugging at his hair as the pain mixes with pleasure. I'm way over my head with this man, and he knows it.

He pushes my shirt higher, then attacks my other breast, teeth scraping the delicate skin as his fingers pinch and pull my other nipple. It feels like a punish- ment, one that I don't want to stop. I'm gasping for breath, back arched, mouth wide as he makes his way down my stomach and presses his mouth to my core, blowing hot air. I'm shaking by the time he pulls my shorts off, discarding my underwear with them.

"Beg for it," he says, mouth grazing my clit.

I shake my head no, and he licks me from back to front.

I moan, scrambling for more when he removes his mouth. "Beg for it."

"No," I grit through my teeth. I can't. Not even when my entire body fights against me, wanting nothing

more than his touch. But I can't. Not after everything. Tears pool in my lashes. I thought there was something truly special between us back when we were kids. Forged in our shared trauma, but he brushed it away like it was nothing. Broke my heart like I meant nothing to him. He'd said I was just a Laurent, putting me in the same bucket as my father and brother. Nothing has ever hurt as much as those words he'd spit out at me all those years ago.

"I still hate you," I say, fingers digging into the blanket. I wish I was telling the truth. The truth is I've never hated him, not for a second we were together or the ten years we've been apart.

He kisses my thigh, and it's softer than I expect. "I know. I just don't care."

I look down at him, his dark eyes already on me.

"I won't make you ask for it." He nuzzles his nose against my clit. "Tell me no and I'll stop."

"That's not fair. You're playing dirty."

He lifts my leg and kisses the side of my knee, eyes meeting mine, but I can't make the words come out to tell him to stop. His mouth moves lower, driving me crazy.

I want this. Need this. And he's making it possible for me to pretend that I don't. Letting me claim I didn't ask for it. That it's all him initiating when we both know that's a lie. I bite back a moan as he runs his tongue along my thigh. Each of his kisses moves closer to my core. By the time he gets to my apex, I'm shaking and can't stop

myself from gripping his hair, pulling him closer. He chuckles under his breath and pushes my legs wider, licking the crease between my core and thigh.

So close, so close.

Tears of need fall down my cheeks as he licks me again. "Hmm? Did you say something?"

My back arches painfully, and I'm barely able to support myself. Matthias wraps his arm around my back, catching my weight and holding me in place so I'm able to rest against him.

He places a featherlight kiss over my clit. His breath is warm when he says, "Last chance to say no."

I couldn't say no if I wanted to. I can't even breathe.

He waits a second before groaning and burying his face into my pussy. He runs his tongue from back to front until I'm grinding against his face, needing more. I feel hollow, needy in a way I don't understand.

Matthias nips my thigh, then pushes a finger into me. I cry as he rocks it back and forth.

His head drops to my stomach. "You're so tight."

"W...what?" I'm trying to comprehend when he cuts off all my ability to think by sinking another finger into me. He rocks them back and forth, pressing upward with each stroke, hitting a spot I've never discovered on my own. I'm crying, one hand gripping the sheets above me, the other shoving his face into my clit until he sucks harder. It's like time splits into a million pieces, no longer a part of reality when my orgasm crashes over me in wave after wave. It feels like it's never going to end.

I flinch, my clit too sensitive when he tries to lick it again.

He raises unto his elbows, face directly above mine. "Good?"

I don't bother opening my eyes. "You know the answer to that, asshole."

He kisses my neck, hot air brushing my ear. "I want to hear you say it."

His tongue licks the curve of my collar bone, and my eyes roll back in my head. "It was good. So good."

"Good girl." He kisses my temple, pulls off his boxers, then rests back so he's kneeling, weight resting on his calves.

The way he's looking at me has heat pooling between my thighs. There's a tinge of fear there. I've never done this before. I swallow hard, preparing myself for what happens next. It's only natural for this to lead to sex, and it's not like I'm especially attached to my virginity. That doesn't stop the nerves from crawling under my skin.

He fists his hard cock, and the tip weeps with precum, dripping down the sides. He's so thick I don't think my fingers could touch if I wrapped them around.

I swallow. Has he always been that big?

"Are we going to have sex?" I say, barely above a whisper. If he wasn't so close, I doubt he would have heard me.

He moves forward, lifting my ass up to meet his

cock. He runs it along my seam, coating it with my wetness.

I can't breathe with anticipation as he slides his cock through the narrow gap between my thighs.

"Not while you still hate me." He pushes forward, the friction causing me to moan.

"Tighten your legs," he says, voice trembling. He's as undone as I am.

"I can't. They're like Jell-O," I answer honestly.

He wears a satisfied smile as he bands his arm around my thighs, squeezing them together. "That okay?"

"Yes." I moan as the head of his cock glides over my clit.

"Fuck." He thrusts forward, his cock pushing between my tight thighs like he's fucking me. Each of his movements is more uncontrolled than the last. His tip hits my clit with each press of his hips until I can feel my orgasm growing.

"I'm...I'm going to come." My voice cracks as pleasure builds within me.

"Me too." He moves faster, head falling back as he chases his own orgasm. His body is shaking as he pounds harder. My release hits me seconds before his hot cum covers my stomach, filling my navel.

Matthias falls forward, kissing me, soft, warm lips on mine. "You feel unbelievable."

Emotions swirl inside me, overwhelming my senses.

I want to yell at him while begging him to hold me closer. It's too much. It's all too much.

As if sensing my distress, he gets up out of bed and grabs a wet cloth from the bathroom, wiping my stomach clean.

There's blood dripping down his chest, but he doesn't move to clean it.

"You need to do something about that, or it'll get infected."

He lifts a brow. "Worried about me now?"

Matthias kisses my forehead and gets off the bed, leaving me cold at the loss of his heat. "I'll go. I'm sure you need space."

I do. Of course I do. But why do I feel like crying as I watch him leave?

Chapter 35

Scarlet

GROANING, I bury my face into my pillow and punch the soft mattress. *Are you freaking serious right now?* I carved my name directly below his neck and collarbone. His neck! Then I proceeded to have one of the hottest experiences of my life that didn't even include sex! I press my face deeper into the pillow. Maybe if I just suffocate myself now, I can forget all of this happened.

There's a knock on the bedroom door. I can't handle seeing Matthias right now. Actually, there's no way he'd knock.

I flip around, lifting on my elbows.

"Scarlet, it's me." Oliver's familiar tone comes through the door.

It's been a while since I've seen him, and I'm still livid with him for lying to me all these years. The worst part is he made it hard for me to trust myself. There must have been signs along the way that he was feeding

my every move to Matthias, and I was just too clueless to see it.

I collapse back on the bed. "Leave me alone."

"It's not the time, Scarlet. Get out here."

It's the raised pitch of his voice that has me getting up. In the seven years that I've known him, he's been nothing but calm. A steady presence in my life.

I grab my robe from the hook and open the door a few inches. Oliver's standing there, eyes darting in every direction.

"We need to go now for this to work." A muscle ticks in his jaw, and his breaths come out too hard. Something's not right here.

"Go where?"

His gaze snaps back to mine. "Anywhere you want so long it's away from here. It's my turn for surveillance of the front. If you want to leave, this is your only chance."

There's a weight crushing my chest, pushing the air from my lungs. After all the wanting to leave, I should be elated, but there's this gnawing ache in my chest. I'd have to be crazy to stay. After all, Matthias has done all of this on his own terms, not giving me a single choice. I take a deep breath and push the voice at the back of my head that's telling me I want to stay into the recesses of my mind.

Matthias will always be my first love, but the boy he was has grown into a man I could never have predicted. One that simultaneously makes my hair stand up on the

back of my neck while sending shivers of anticipation down my spine.

I swallow hard as my emotions swirl around me. The way I felt last night, the power that went through me as I marked Matthias with my name, makes me want to stay by his side. It sparked something in me that I buried deep inside.

I can feel myself falling back in love with him with each second we spend together, but I'd been in love with him once, and he'd torn my heart out. I close my eyes, trying to hang on to that hurt and replay his words that cracked me open before.

"Don't tell me you got the wrong idea?"

"Just because you helped me out for the last week doesn't make us close."

"Let me make it easy for you. I don't want to see you or hear your voice. I don't want to be in the same room as you."

"You may have helped us, but you're still a Laurent."

I swallow hard as the pain crashes through me just as strong today. I believed that he loved me then. That we were fated to be together. I'd trusted him then. I can't make the same mistake now.

"Let's go." Bracing myself, I step through the doorway. This is the right decision.

"Uh...are you not going to get dressed?" Oliver takes two giant steps back.

"Shit." The blood drains from my face as I grab the front of my robe. Twisting on the spot, I rush to my

dresser. That could have been bad. It's like I've turned my brain completely off. I throw on a pair of black jeans and a T-shirt before glancing around the room to see if there's anything else I need. The glint of the blade, tip still painted in red, sits on the nightstand. My hand hovers over the knife for several seconds. He didn't take it. Why didn't he take it?

My chest tightens, and I have to fight against it. Screw this. It's just a knife, not a declaration of love.

I grab the handle and walk out of the room, where Oliver's waiting for me with my favorite pair of boots.

He glances at his watch. "We have less than a minute to get to my car. Hurry."

I slip my boots on, not bothering to tie the laces, and race after Oliver. Time ticks away as I push through the door, onto the veranda, and down the wood steps. Oliver has the door open, and he's already rounding the corner to get into the front seat. I just need one last look. I turn my head, knowing I'm wasting precious seconds, and stumble backward, my butt hitting the ground.

The house is exactly what I wished for when Matthias and I were stuck in that room. When I told the only boy I trusted my dreams that I never believed would come true.

It's a farmhouse, painted eggshell blue with white trim, with a wood shake roof. My eyes burn, and my breath catches. There's a wraparound porch and the tire swing hanging from one of the tree's sturdy branches.

Tears pool over my lashes and run down my cheeks.

He built it for me. Everything he's said comes crashing to the forefront.

"I told you I'd marry you when you turned twenty-five."

"I waited for you."

"We're meant to be together, Scarlet, and I'm going to make you believe it."

"There's the fire I love."

"Anything you want, Little Sparrow."

"I've already given up too many nights without you."

I thought this was just some kind of sick, twisted game. One where my heart was the only one on the line. All of this time, he's been waiting for me...

My heart aches, and I press my palm against it. I need to hear him say it. I need to understand exactly what's happening. Why did he let me go when I would have stayed with him? I never would have gone to Stanford if he'd asked me to stay.

"Get up. We have to go." Oliver's in front of me, holding out his hand.

I shake my head furiously, unable to form words.

"Scarlet. He's seen me on the cameras by now. He's going to kill me if we stay any longer."

I lift my gaze to the man who's protected me all these years, but I can't bring myself to follow him. "I can't leave. Just go without me. I'll deal with Matthias."

"Get in the car, Scarlet." He grabs my arm, but I pull it back. "This chance won't happen again."

I meet his eyes and shake my head. He's done so much for me. "I'm sorry. Just go."

He looks me over, as if debating the merits of lifting me and tossing me into the car. I square my shoulders, ready to fight him off.

"Fine, have it your way." He looks across the field.

Matthias's men are running from different directions, one calling out not to shoot.

I nod. "Go."

Oliver's tires squeal, gravel kicking up behind him as he books it out of here.

I lift myself off the ground and slap away the hands that try to grab me.

"Don't touch me. I'm going back."

One of the guards holds his gun at me, and I laugh.

"I suggest you lower that."

Another guard, slightly older, calls into his radio to have everyone stand down. "As long as you go back into the house, we won't touch you."

I almost want to fight just because he's telling me what to do. This is probably why Matthias calls me stubborn.

"Move." I shove my way past the men, back up the stairs, over the porch I've always wanted, and into the house of my dreams.

The door clicks shut, audibly locking.

Now, I wait.

Chapter 36

Matthias

I DROP my head into my palms, digging my fingers into my hair. I nearly fucking lost her today. She was so close to disappearing from my life. The only thing saving my sanity is the video of her looking back at the house and the clear expression on her face. It may have taken ten years off my life, but knowing she's the one who chose to stay, that I'm not forcing her to be here, soothes something deep in my soul I didn't know was hurting. I've never wanted to be her cage.

I'm going to face whatever comes next head-on. No more secrets, no more half-truths. She needs to understand exactly what she means to me. I get out of the car and make my way into the house.

"You're back," Scarlet states from where she's curled up on the couch. The sight knocks the wind out of me. She's wearing one of my shirts, the collar exposing her shoulder while she tosses popcorn into her mouth. The

sight is so domestic, like a glance into the possible future, that I lose my breath. I'd gladly get down on my knees if it meant coming home to this every day.

"You're still here."

She shifts on the sofa, tucking her feet beneath her, and her back straightens. "Explain what's happening."

I don't bother to insult her by asking what she means. She's right. I owe her answers. Her pulse is visible at her throat, the rhythm pounding at the same speed as mine. I've been waiting years to have this conversation, but that doesn't mean I'm not terrified to lay my soul out.

I force myself to relax, leaning against the couch, and grab a handful of popcorn. Her brows pull low over her blue eyes, casting them in shadow as she takes in my relaxed posture.

There you go, Little Sparrow. Be mad at me. Be anything but indifferent.

I move the popcorn to the coffee table and move closer to her, hating the way she shifts back, maintaining the space between us.

"There hasn't been a single day in the last ten years I haven't wanted to be with you." I search her face, reading every little change in her expression.

Her eyes go wide, light catching the corners, before she slams a mask down between us. "Don't lie to me."

I curse internally, needing her to believe me. "I'm not lying. I got blackout drunk just to stop demanding to know why you made that fucking wish. I hated the fact

322

the only thing you asked for was within my power to give because I knew I could never deny you."

She's shaking her head no, a pretty pink flush crawling up her neck. "What you are saying doesn't make sense. You never said a word to me from age fifteen until I went to college. You literally ran away from your house the two weeks I stayed there. You had plenty of opportunities to reach out, even after I went to college."

"Because it fucking hurts to be near you and not be able to touch you." I reach for her face, and this time, she lets me, round blue eyes on mine. I run my thumb along her cheekbone, and she leans into me. I take a deep breath and cut myself open. I drop my forehead to hers, breathing in each of her exhales. "You're mad at me, but you could have come to me. I would have knelt for you even back then. I wouldn't have been able to hold myself back if you did, but you didn't because *you* knew you weren't ready. Getting away from all of this bullshit isn't something you could have done if you were with me. The best thing you ever did was move to California. You know you needed that. You know it was good for you."

"I would've stayed with you." Her voice cracks, and my heart aches with it.

"And you would've regretted it." I swallow hard and run my nose along hers. "You are worth the wait. I'd have given you forever if you'd asked me to."

Tears pool on her bottom lashes, and I pull her into my chest, basking in the way her fingers curl into my shirt, pulling me closer.

"I want to believe you," she whispers, and I tighten my grip.

My fingers stroke her hair in slow, calming motions. "Don't worry. I'll keep showing you until you do."

"You better," she murmurs into my neck, and I cradle her face, angling her until she can see me.

"I love you, Scarlet. I've always loved you. I loved you enough to let you go."

I push a stray strand of her hair behind her ear, gently grazing my fingers along her cheek. Scarlet's head tips back, and she gazes at me through her lashes. It's the way her cheeks flush to that perfect shade of pink, and her mouth opens slightly, like she's welcoming my kiss. I let myself get lost counting her freckles, the way her dark lashes skim over her cheeks, the small lines that crease the corner of her eyes. The way her cupid's bow arches perfectly into a plump pout. I run my thumb along her bottom lip and slide it down, opening her mouth further. I've been craving seeing the small changes in her face as we got older. The way one only can when they're close like this. She barely moves, and her nose runs along mine, the sensation sending a shiver down my spine.

I cup her cheeks between my hands and kiss her forehead. "I'm going to fuck you now."

She trembles in my arms, hot breaths washing over me. "I've...I've never done this before."

"I know." I lean in, opening my mouth above hers until we're inhaling each other's exhales. There's a weight to the air around us, one that pushes me closer

and has her rising into me. Our lips merge, and a groan forms in the back of my throat. We've kissed countless times, but there's something completely different now that she knows how I feel. She's warming in my arms, more accepting of my touch.

She's lost all of her resistance she held onto for so long. I place kisses across her jaw and nip at her neck, marveling at the way she leans into me. The only noise in the room is the soft sounds of her panting. I suck on her delicate skin, marking her along the curve from her jaw to her collarbone, leaving my marks along the way. I want every person who goes near her to know that she belongs to someone. That she belongs to me.

Laying her flat against the sofa, I lift her shirt, bringing it to her mouth. "Bite."

Her eyes widen, but she secures the fabric with her teeth. I growl and run my tongue between her breasts, kissing the hollow of her neck. "I could do this forever, tasting you like this."

A shudder runs through her as a small hum forms at the back of her throat. I flatten my tongue along her nipple, swirling around it. The way her body responds, guiding my every move. She likes it when I run my thumb under her breast, then palm it gently. She moans whenever I suck her peak into my mouth.

I'm greedy and want to hear more.

I twist so my body's between her thighs and trail my knuckle down her stomach, following closely with open-mouth kisses. She's wearing a thin pair of black leggings,

and I have to grip the cushion to stop myself from tearing them off her. I'll wait—I can fuck her until she passes out, but tonight, all I want is to make her feel good, to make her want me the way I desperately want her.

Blue eyes meet mine, and she lifts her hips when I pull her pants off her, chucking them on the ground. She's left in only my shirt, still held by her teeth, leaving her on display for me. I've never seen anything so beautiful in my fucking life. She deserves to be worshiped. I have no problem getting down on my knees at her altar.

I flatten my tongue over her clit in an echo of what I did to her nipples. Swirling my tongue, listening as her moans get louder. I want so much more. I sink a finger into her core, groaning at the way she sucks me in, then add another, making room for myself. She's shaking, fingers curling in my hair, begging me without words.

I scissor my fingers back and forth, slowly stretching her. My cock's huge compared to her tight pussy, and I'm not skipping this step. I want her to come apart when I slide my cock into her for the first time, and she can't do that if it hurts. I grip her ass, angling her better, and push a third finger into her. This time, she gasps.

I still, letting her adjust. "Breathe for me, Little Sparrow."

Her eyes are slits when she lets go of the shirt and takes a deep breath.

"That's it, baby. I've got you." I love the way she listens to me, trusting me to lead her through this. I'm going to take such good care of her. When she relaxes, I

start again, slowly increasing my speed until she's rocking into my fingers, greedy noises coming from her.

My cock's leaking, soaking my pants, but like hell I'm going to take her before she's ready. I suck her clit between my teeth and curve my fingers, smiling when she screams out my name, body trembling as she comes on my tongue.

She collapses back, tears in her eyes as she looks at me with awe. It's a sensation she needs to get used to because I've been waiting a decade to be able to pleasure her like this.

Her lids close, exhaustion taking over, and I lick up her neck, teeth grazing her chin. "Wake up, Scarlet. We're nowhere near done yet."

"Good." She wraps her arms around my neck, circling my waist with her legs as I lift us, walking to our room.

This next part needs something better than a quick fuck on the couch. I'll leave that for later.

I stand between her thighs, shivering as her fingers undo each button of my shirt. She kisses each new inch exposed as she slowly reveals my chest. A shiver trails down my spine when she kisses a line below her name etched into my skin.

She shifts down until her tongue flips over my nipple, drawing a low moan from my throat. "Do you like this?" she asks, blue eyes meeting mine hesitantly.

I could come just by the way she's looking at me. "Fuck, I love anything you do to me."

She bites her lips before sinking her teeth into my chest, forming perfect teeth marks around my nipple.

"I'm trying to be good," I groan.

She licks the pain away and meets me with hooded eyes. "Be good later."

My head falls back, every muscle in my body tensing. I nearly came just at her words. "You're really going to be the death of me. You know that?"

She removes her shirt and grins. "I've had plenty of opportunities to kill you, but you're still here."

I drop my forehead to hers. "I think this time you will succeed."

She nips my bottom lip, then moves back until she's fully laid out on the bed. I groan, pushing my pants down and fisting my cock. She's delicious laid out for me like a dessert I get to eat. She's fucking mine now, and I'm going to savor every bite. I slide her legs up so they're bent at the knee on either side of me. Placing a gentle kiss to the inner corner before I move over her, elbows resting on either side of her head, I nuzzle her neck and graze the shell of her ear.

"Are you okay?"

"I'd be more okay if you hurried up," she huffs, using her feet to tug me closer. There's fire in her eyes, which her family tried to douse, but it's just a part of who she is. That doesn't take away the way her body's shaking, this time not in pleasure, and her teeth gnaw on her bottom lip.

I pull it from between her teeth and stare into her eyes, promising, "I'll be gentle."

She nods, fingers curling onto my shoulders as I reach down and slide my cock up and down her slit, getting her used to it.

"I'm going to push in now." She's so wet I'm completely coated as I notch my cock to her entrance.

She nods again, eyes squeezed shut as I slip the head in, stretching her around my cock.

I grunt—she's holding me so tight it's almost painful. I brush my fingers over her temple and lower myself so our noses meet. "You have to relax. Breathe with me."

She follows each of my inhales and exhales until I can feel her relax around me. I lower so my lips brush hers. "Good girl."

I take her lips as my cock slides into her. She winces when she's taken half of me in, nails scratching my back.

Tears form in her eyes, and she clenches her teeth as I push in a little further.

"Does it hurt?"

She shakes her head no, but it's written all over her face.

"You're lying to me." I slide my hand between us and draw circles over her clit with my thumb.

Her head falls back, jaw dropping open with my touch.

I kiss her jaw, loving how she responds to me. "Better?"

"Yes," she rasps.

I grip her leg and thrust until she's taken all of me, pausing for her reaction.

She's panting, wide blue eyes on mine, and for the first time, I can see her love there.

I rock into her in controlled motions, giving her time to tell me to stop. Each time she takes me in, her pussy clenches around my cock.

I groan and kiss her until my lungs burn. "I'm not going to last long."

She nips my bottom lip, digging her heels into my ass. "Harder."

As if she released something wild inside me, I can't stop my hips from bucking into her. Each of her moans drives me faster until I've lost my fucking mind. Her legs clamp around me, and I press harder against her clit.

"I'm close," she cries.

"Me too."

She runs her nose along mine. "Come with me, Matthias."

That's all it takes for me to spill into her, emptying myself and filling her pussy. It takes everything in me not to collapse. Instead, I roll onto my back, bringing her with me.

I stroke her hair, just taking in the elated aftermath of being inside my girl.

She's touching the marks her teeth left around my nipple. "Sorry about this."

"Don't be. I liked it." I guide her face to mine. "How about you? Are you okay?"

She smirks. "I'm fantastic."

"It doesn't hurt even though it was your first time?"

She laughs, a glint in her eye when she says, "Pretty sure my first time was with a pink toy."

I cough, then catch my breath. "Do you have more toys?"

"I'm twenty-five and a virgin. What do you think?"

I grip her ass and slide my fingers between her thighs until they rest against her core. No matter what she says, I know she's sore.

"You *were* a virgin. This pussy belongs to me now."

Chapter 37

Scarlet

MATTHIAS CARRIES me to the bathroom and sits me on the vanity. I grip the counter to keep my balance as he runs his fingers between my thighs and pushes the liquid pooling there back inside.

His lips drop to my ear. "I don't want to waste this."

He kisses my temple, then stands, turning toward the tub and running the water. I watch as he fiddles with it until he deems the temperature's right before turning back toward me.

I go to get off the vanity, but his sharp words stop me. "Don't move."

He stalks toward me with dark intent, and I'm captivated. My mouth waters with every inch of his deep tan skin. His forearms are lined with thick veins that highlight his defined muscles. His shoulders take up my line of sight. But it's his massive dick that has me dazed. Was that really inside of me?

He chuckles, pulling me out of my gawking. In any other circumstance, I would be embarrassed at being caught, but Matthias's heated gaze travels from my eyes to my lips and back with so much lust I can hardly breathe.

He leans forward, lips barely brushing mine, but pulls away when I move to close the distance. Instead, he lifts me from the counter like I weigh nothing and carries me to the bath. He slowly lowers me into the tub, the hot water warming me inch by inch until I'm fully submerged.

I'd been so distracted by the man holding me that I'd forgotten how cold I was. I lean back against the porcelain and watch Matthias as he moves around the room, holding my breath to stop myself from doing something embarrassing, like calling out to him. It doesn't matter that I'm sure he wants me.

He dims the light, casting the room with an intimate glow, an almost secret feeling, one that allows the possibility of things we would never do in the light. My gaze follows him until he sits behind me on a small stool I hadn't seen. I stiffen when his large hands land on my shoulders.

"Relax, Little Sparrow. I've got you." He applies delicious pressure with his thumbs, working out the knots in my neck from holding myself so tightly. He guides me deeper into the tub until my head dips into the water, wetting my hair before helping me back up.

He washes my hair, massaging my scalp with

talented fingers, and I have to bite back my moan. "Feels good."

His fingers tighten in my hair, pulling my head back to meet my eyes before shaking his head. "From now on, I will always make you feel good."

Matthias's fingers slide south from my shoulders over my collarbones, then skim along the top of my breast. The lightness of the touch has me arching into him.

Frustration floods me, and I let out a whimpered sound when his touch leaves my skin.

His hands are back on me before I can say anything, the soft fabric of a cloth moving over every inch of me. The space fills with the girly, citrus scent of my body wash, one that Matthias has no business owning. I tilt my head back, and my eyes flick up, and he leans over, kissing my forehead, his lips too gentle for such a dangerous man. My eyes close as I surrender myself to him. I don't want anything to break this moment.

His touch is magnified as he runs the cloth up my arms, then over my chest. Heat pools low in my stomach when he takes extra care with my breasts, then grazes all the way down my stomach, stopping just above where I desperately need him. I wiggle and shift, trying to get him to move, but he just chuckles into the crown of my head before cleaning my hips and thighs.

By the time he lifts the cloth out of the water, my breath comes out in short pants. Not daring to open my eyes, I can still feel his presence behind me. I'm

desperate for air but unable to take a deep breath in anticipation of his touch.

I struggle to speak, but he stops me, his voice a low command. "You're going to do exactly what I say, Scarlet. Keep your eyes closed and your mouth shut."

His command flares through me. Something about him taking control settles me, and instead of fighting him, I relax further into the warm liquid.

He lets out a low hum of approval, and his strong fingers grip my legs, separating them, before he inches his way upward.

I suck in a gasp when he stops his ascent at the juncture. My lungs burn with each moment he waits.

The anticipation is killing me, and he knows exactly what he was doing.

His one hand holds me firm in his grip while his fingers run over my wet folds, giving me no warning before he buries them deep inside me. A strangled cry breaks from my mouth as he moves them, pressure building within my core. It feels like every nerve ending responds to him. Like he owns my body and knows how to control it. And for right now, he does. I'm so close to my release I can't stop my hips from rocking and fucking myself on his fingers.

"That's it. Come for me."

Tension grows until tingles form in my lower back and radiate through my body. I'm so close but can't push myself over the edge. Frustration builds under my skin, making my movements jerky.

Matthias drops his mouth to my ear, his breath heating the sensitive skin. "Kiss me."

I twist my head toward him and gasp when his palm presses against my clit at the same time his mouth captures mine, sending my orgasm crashing over me in waves. He doesn't remove his fingers until he's wrung out every ounce of my pleasure.

His mouth leaves mine, and I gasp in my breaths, having no idea when the last time I'd taken in a lungful of air. Breathing was the last thing I cared about.

Matthias moves from behind me, and I immediately miss his closeness. I need him back more than I care to admit.

His arms are around me, lifting me from the tub and helping me stand on the mat in front of him. He takes his time drying me off with a large fluffy towel, and all I can do is stare as this man, who'd always been a dark presence in my life, takes gentle care of me.

I follow a rivulet down his pecks, then follow it as it trails between the corded muscles of his abs. I swallow hard, needing more than just his touch.

His entire body jerks when I run my thumb over the tip, smearing his precum. His dark gaze narrow on mine when I lift my hand to my mouth and suck his taste off before fisting his cock and stroking it in the same rhythm he fucked my pussy. His eyes are hot on mine as his hips buck into my fist. He's so large I have to add a second hand. It doesn't take long for him to come all over my hands.

Matthias growls, dropping his forehead to mine, and takes several breaths before saying, "I always knew you'd be the ruin of me."

I huff out a breath and clean myself with my towel. "If one of us is going to be ruined, it's me."

He pulls back, gripping my jaw hard between his thumb and forefinger. "Listen to me, Little Sparrow. You could never be ruined." He strokes my cheek until I nod, then sweeps me off my feet, carrying me to the bed.

Chapter 38

Scarlet

I BLINK AWAY the sleep as I wake. Matthias's deep brown eyes are already on mine, his face lying on the bed so we're facing each other. All the feelings that rose inside me yesterday, the acceptance, love, understanding, are mirrored back at me. The late-morning light is soft, like a halo around him, and the way he's looking at me, like I'm his reason for breathing, has my heart twisting in my chest.

He gives me a sleepy smile, dark hair ruffled from my fingers. He reaches over, callused thumb grazing my temple as he pushes my hair behind my ear. "Good morning, wife."

"Morning." I turn into the pillow as my cheeks flush, and a slow smile curls my lips.

He leans in, stealing a kiss from the corner of my mouth. "Don't hide from me. I want to see all of you. I've dreamed about this day countless times over the years.

341

Each time, waking up felt like a punishment." He kisses my jaw, pressing his forehead to my temple. "I was worried if I went to sleep, I'd wake up and none of this would be real."

"Was handcuffing me a part of your dreams?" I lean into his chest, tucking my head against his shoulder.

"Sometimes."

Everything about him at this moment screams that he loves me. That he really has been waiting all this time. From the way his fingers stroke my hair, to the way his voice is soft and low, even while teasing. It's like he doesn't want anything to break this moment, and it's sending warmth flooding through my heart. So many things about us shouldn't make sense, but I'm starting to realize there's nothing I'd let tear us apart. Somehow, this man who everyone else fears is everything I need.

He runs his knuckle along my knee. "Are you sore?"

I wince when I shift around, pain in my lower back and between my thighs. "A little."

"I'm sorry. I tried to be gentle. You just felt so fucking good." There's real concern in his eyes, and I stop him with a touch.

I face him, a smile taking over. "I never expected you to be such a sweet talker."

He buries his face in my shoulder and kisses his way to my ear, sending shivers rolling through me. "It's not sweet-talking if it's true."

I trail my fingers up his bare back, loving the way his muscles flex under my touch. This big, powerful man is

all mine. I trace the lines of his pecs and down his abs until his stomach concaves at my touch, making room for me to go lower.

He captures my hand, stopping me. "I have something for you."

"What?" All I need is right in front of me, but he pulls away before I can say anything, reaching over to his dresser.

He's hiding something in his palm when he turns back, and a light flush creeps up his neck before coloring his cheeks. His eyes search mine, holding my gaze until it's hard to take my next breath.

"I wanted to give this to you when we got married, but I was afraid you'd toss it immediately." Matthias opens up a small black velvet box, revealing the perfect teardrop diamond on a simple gold band. I lift it up and hold it to the light. It's got to be at least eight carats, if not more.

I bite my lip and fail to hide my smirk. "You're right. I definitely would have trashed it. What a shame that would have been." I hand it back to him and hold out my fingers so he can put it on me.

He kisses each of my knuckles before sliding the ring over my finger, where it sits perfectly. My smile grows. "It's gorgeous."

"Not as gorgeous as you."

A laugh bursts from me, and he rolls me beneath him.

"You think I'm lying, Little Sparrow?" He nips my

neck and whispers in my ear. "I don't think you have any idea how devastatingly in love with you I am. I've tortured myself to always be your wind and never your cage. I may have kidnapped you, but if you'd truly asked to be let out, I would've let you. But you never asked, Scarlet, because the truth is you never wanted to leave."

Realization fills my chest. In all this time, I never asked for him to let me go. I wanted to be here. My eyes sting as emotions I can finally acknowledge tumble to the forefront.

"I...I love—"

Matthias kisses me, cutting me off. "Tell me you love me when you're pregnant with my child and full with my cock."

He kisses a line down my throat, and I arch into him, pressing my chest into his. Just as I'm about to beg for more, the doorbell rings.

Matthias groans like he's being tortured, then says, "Ignore it."

It rings again, and he grunts, getting up from the bed, and pulls on his boxers, all the while murmuring adorable death threats to whoever's unlucky enough to bother us.

I watch his ass disappear from the room and collapse. How the hell is he so sexy?

It doesn't sound like anyone's being murdered out there, so I get up, throwing on his button-up shirt from last night.

"Fuck." Matthias is in the doorway, holding two

containers and scanning me from head to toe. "I'm going to replace all of your clothes so you can only wear my shirts."

"Do that and I'm dyeing all of your clothes pink." I do up another button but leave the top two open, enjoying the heat in his gaze.

"Get back into bed." His growly command has my nipples hardening and my ass hitting the mattress.

He sets the containers down on the nightstand and crawls on top of me. "You're lucky I'm worried about hurting that pretty little pussy of yours, or I'd fuck you senseless for your sass."

My arms wrap around his neck, ready to tell him I don't care if it hurts, when the sweet scent of syrup fills my nose, and my stomach rumbles loudly.

Matthias lifts off me, manipulating my body easily so I'm upright against the headboard.

"Sooo, we're really not going to have sex?" I ask.

"Not while you're still sore." He opens the container and lifts a piece of french toast to my mouth, his other hand cupping underneath to catch any drips.

"Seriously? We're eating this in bed?" My mouth drops open, and he uses the opportunity to slip the piece between my teeth. The warm, sweet liquid coats my tongue, drawing a moan from the back of my throat.

Matthias glares at me, brows pulled together.

I slip the fork from my lips. "Don't tell me you're jealous of my breakfast."

J Wilder

"Of course not," he huffs, but the tips of his ears turn pink as he feeds me another piece.

This time, I moan louder, and he collapses so his face rests on my stomach, placing light kisses there. "You're doing that on purpose."

"Maybe."

He grabs a piece of fruit and brings it to my lips. "Keep eating. If you're pregnant from last night, we want to keep you healthy."

He says it so matter-of-factly it almost doesn't register. My mind swirls around his words, my lungs unable to take in air. There's an undeniable warmth building in my chest that shouldn't be there. One that says I don't hate that idea nearly as much as I should.

"I'm...on birth control," I stammer.

"I hate to break it to you, but you've never taken birth control a day in your life. It was easy enough to switch them to sugar pills and recently to prenatal."

"How?" I'm still not firing on all cylinders, asking the wrong questions. "What if I'd had sex with someone?"

He tilts his head, biting his lips against a smile. "Do you really think I'd let that happen? That I'd ever let anyone close to you?"

Rage burns in my stomach, and my heart beats in my ears. He's the reason I've been ghosted countless times? That I was still a virgin at twenty-five!

"Ugh!" I push at his chest, but he just leans in,

kissing my stomach again. "We're not done talking about this."

"You want a half dozen kids, we need to start now," he murmurs into my stomach.

I can picture those little faces vividly. They have his eyes, the gold-rimmed centers catching the light as they blink up at me with thick lashes and dimpled smiles.

"Hmmm." He kisses my stomach again. "You like that idea."

"You still shouldn't have done it without asking."

"I'm not sure if you've noticed this yet, but I'm done fucking asking. I did what you wanted for a decade, and now I'm taking what's mine."

"And that's a half dozen kids? Do you even want that?"

"I want it with you."

There he goes again, melting my insides with his sweet words. "Not fair."

He tilts his head and raises a brow. "Who said anything about fair?"

"While we're on the topic of fair, I have a favor to ask you." There's a pit forming in my stomach as I wait for his answer. He is so not going to like this.

He runs his thumb over the line forming between my brows until it smooths out. "Anything."

"Let Oliver come back." He's worked with me for years, and I know he did what he did because he truly believed he was helping, and in any other situation, he'd

be right. I can't stand the idea of it turning around on him when he was just trying to protect me.

Matthias jerks, eyes wide in astonishment. "You mean in a body bag?"

"No...I mean as my personal guard, like he's always been."

"I'm sorry, I can't trust him anymore after this. He tried to take you away from me."

"Well, I trust him more. When I found out he'd been reporting everything I did directly to you, it really pissed me off. He was supposed to be my guard. He earned that trust back when he put what I wanted first, knowing you'd try to kill him."

Matthias drops his head to my stomach. "Anything but that."

"I'll forgive one year of you ignoring me."

His eyes slide up, and he looks at me through his lashes. "Two."

"Deal."

"Tell him if he fucks around again, he's a dead man."

I ruffle his hair. "You don't have to worry about that now because the only thing I want is you."

He lifts so our foreheads touch. "Now who's the sweet talker."

Chapter 39

Scarlet

MY BACK RESTS against the arm of the sofa as Matthias and I relax, watching a show. It's been two weeks since Matthias and I first had sex. Two weeks of blissful honeymoon gooeyness that would have made past me vomit. He's absentmindedly massaging my calves, kneading the muscles with deep strokes that have heat trailing between my legs. From the glint in his eyes, I have no doubt he knows exactly what he's doing to me.

A slow, lascivious smile curls his lips, and he leans over me, kissing down my neck and over my collarbone. At some point last night, he changed me into one of his giant shirts, and he's making quick work of lifting it above my waist.

He licks up my throat and gently bites my chin. "Let me lick it better."

My head drops back, wetness already slicking between my legs. I'm pretty sure I'd let him do anything

to me. I moan in the back of my throat when he sucks on my nipple through my shirt. It's still tender from his touches last night, and I wiggle away from him. He catches my hips and places gentle kisses over my tip.

"I really lost control last night. Are you sure you're okay?" His hands rest on my bare thighs, thumbs stroking back and forth less than an inch away from where my body's begging for them.

"Keep going."

He descends, kissing a path down my stomach until his head is buried between my thighs. He licks me once, sending shivers down my spine, when our phones ring simultaneously.

"Ignore it," he says and licks me again, his hands squeezing my ass and raising me higher.

My phone rings again, and I push his head away. "I need to get that. It'll be work."

He growls, pressing his face against my core. "Quit."

I raise one brow. "No."

He responds, looking at me through his lashes, breath still hot on my clit. "Then answer it."

"Are you crazy?"

Before I can do anything, he's already answered the call and pressed the phone to my ear.

"Hello," I rasp out.

"Just because you own the company doesn't mean you can abandon your clients. We're going to get sued."

"I...I—" My breath hitches as Matthias runs his tongue from my back to my front.

"You don't have an excuse?" she asks, and I can practically feel her disappointment.

"I'm so, so sorry." I swallow hard, stumbling on my words when Matthias thrusts his tongue into my core.

Clearing my throat, I try to continue. "I have a family emergency. I should have done more to get a hold of you."

"You're lucky I know you sent out emails to all the clients recently and caught up on your work. Next time, you'll find yourself without a mentor, owner of the company or not. I need someone I can depend on with me."

I'm sure I'd feel bad if sparks weren't traveling down my stomach and forming a knot against my clit.

"I understand. I'm all set. It won't happen again." I have to fight to get the words out and pray that she can't hear how hard I'm breathing.

"When will I see you at the office?"

Matthias raises one brow and shakes his head no.

We will see about that, but for now, I just need to get off this call.

"Soon, I promise. Until then, I have my computer, and I'm all set to work from home."

"Are you okay?" Her concern almost makes me feel bad, but Matthias's teeth scrape my clit as he sucks it hard.

"Yes," I gasp, barely breathing as my orgasm crashes over me again and again.

I'm shaking all over when Matthias holds the phone to me on speaker and mouths, "Say goodbye."

"I have to go. See you soon," I hurriedly tell my boss before my husband can do something I'll regret.

He clicks the phone off before I can say anything else and places a light kiss against my mouth. He tastes like me.

He hums against my lips. "All better?"

"Asshole," I say, but there's no disdain in my tone. I'm loving this as much as he is.

A mischievous smirk takes over his face like a warning. "You're right. I should have licked there too."

I grip his hair, holding him in place before he can travel down any further. "I need to go into the office tomorrow."

He's already shaking his head no before I can finish what I'm saying.

"Scarlet, my brothers and I are trying to figure out just who's coming after you. We don't think your ex was motivated on his own. Then there's the fact that someone tried to break into your house."

I go to argue, but he holds up his hand.

"Please, don't be stubborn about this."

I cross my arms. "I have to go to work. It's non-negotiable."

He pulls out his phone, and his thumb flies across the screen. "Fine, I'll clear my schedule."

"What?" I shake my head no. "That's totally unnecessary."

"Either let me come with you, or don't go at all."

I roll my eyes. "Just don't get in the way."

"I'd never dream of it."

"And don't scare my clients," I warn.

He laughs. "No promises."

"I'm not kidding. If you're coming to my office, you have to be good."

"Don't worry. I can be good. Plus, I have more important things on my mind than terrorizing your workplace." He lowers onto his forearms and grazes his mouth against my stomach, placing delicate kisses over his shirt. "I'm hoping you have twins that look just like you."

Heat flushes my cheeks. "Please be serious."

"Look at me, Scarlet," he commands, and I obey. "I'm dead fucking serious about this. We've wasted entirely too much time, and I've been waiting too long." He runs his hand over my still-flat stomach, his gaze out of focus. "Soon."

It's his phone that breaks the moment this time, and he groans into my navel when he sees who it is.

"I forgot I'm supposed to meet up with my brothers. Will you be okay here by yourself?"

"I've been taking care of myself for a long time. You don't need to watch me every second."

He tilts his head to the side, then glances away. "Who says I wasn't watching you then?"

I laugh and push against his shoulders. "Get out of here."

He leans in and takes my lips in a sweet kiss that has my body melting beneath him. "I'll be back early. Be good."

"You really shouldn't give me orders. You know it just makes me want to do the opposite."

He huffs out a breath and sits on the side of the sofa. "If you can't be good, at least promise me you'll be safe."

I nod. "Don't worry. You heard my boss, I have to catch up on work."

"You really can quit, you know. It's not like you need the money."

I could, but that's always been an option for me. To sit back and live off my family's dirty money. I've used it for the necessities of life, because even I'm not stubborn enough to let it go to waste, but when it comes to things like this, it has to be all me.

"It's never been about the money. It's always been about me standing on my own, by my own strength."

Matthias surprises me when he smiles.

"I'm proud of you." It takes him several seconds to finally stand, and even then, he doesn't turn from me. "I'll see you soon. No sneaking off."

It's only now that I can see the way his brows pull together and his fists clench at his sides. He can laugh it off, but there's some part of him that's worried I'll disappear again.

I wrap my arms around his middle and rest my chin against his muscled stomach, looking up at him. "I'm craving Italian for dinner. Bring some home for me."

He relaxes in my arms and runs his thumb along my cheekbone. "Anything for you."

The afternoon air is crisp with the oncoming fall. I pull Matthias's sweater closer around me. His smell combines with the scent of approaching rain. I'd found the oversized sweater in his closet and couldn't stop myself from putting it on. Tea in one hand and a computer bag over my shoulder, I make my way to the porch swing that overlooks the front lawn.

Three guards stand rigorously, all eyeing me like I may bolt at any given second. I guess I can't blame them. I nearly made it out of here, and I'm sure that didn't go down well with my husband.

Husband.

The title fills me with a tingly warmth. He may have gone about it in the most asshole, overhanded, giant brute of a way, but that doesn't change the fact that he's mine. I should probably stop planning his murder for it. I sit on the swing, pulling the blanket already resting there over my lap, and sip my warm drink, giving the guards a little wave. Hopefully, they'll be able to relax a bit once they realize I'm not about to disappear on them.

The swing is deep, big enough to fit a twin mattress. It's filled with squishy down-filled pillows that form around my back when I relax into them. If I have to work, I can't think of a better place to do it.

My hand grazes my stomach when I reach for my bag, and I freeze. There really could be a little Matthias in there. Deep brown hair and dark eyes, but I'll never let them hold the same hurt he carries around. Instead, they'll glow with warmth as I wrap them in my arms and promise to always protect them. Matthias deserves that. Another chance at happiness, and...so do I.

Chapter 40

Matthias

I ENTER into our private room at Elysium, and the loud music from the club mutes behind me as the door clicks shut. All three of my brothers are here, waiting for me after Damon sent out his immediate meeting text.

He screwed up my plans of keeping Scarlet beneath me and full of my cock all day, so he better have a good reason for this shit.

"I heard you finally convinced your wife to like you." Bash slow claps. "All you had to do was drug her, kidnap her, and lock her in your house. Honestly, isn't that a little pathetic?"

He's sitting on the leather sofa, feet kicked up on the table, giving off I-don't-give-a-fuck vibes that aren't fooling any of us. He might be the youngest Everette brother, but he's as curious about why we were called here as I am.

"Fuck off." Ignoring him, I stand next to Damon. He

hasn't looked up since I walked in, too consumed by whatever's happening on his phone.

"This better be good. I was busy." I say to my older brother, waiting for him to snap out of it.

He gives me a sharp look, then back to his phone, finally putting it in his pocket. "You aren't the only one who wants to get back to their wife."

Fair. Damon's been so inseparable from Misty I'm surprised she's not here. Luckily, my older brother's wife loves his paranoid ass enough to let him keep up with the countless cameras at her place, so he can check in whenever he wants.

Xander comes up from beside us and hands me a whiskey on ice in a crystal tumbler. "Drink this. You're going to need it."

The cool alcohol burns my throat as I down it in one gulp. "Enough with the lead-up. Tell me what you found out."

Damon hands me an iPad with a file already pulled up. It's a picture of a black car with what appears to be two men inside.

My brows pull together as I try to make out the blurred license plate. They're using some kind of image blocker technology, making it impossible to read. "What is this?"

Damon glances at me, then away. "According to the information you sent us, this car has been following Scarlet."

"You're only telling me this now?!" I yell. I'd trusted

them with handling this because I've been too busy with my wife. Leaving her for any length of time pisses me off. Rage burns through my gut, pinching my throat. "Who the fuck are they? I thought we took care of this?"

"It's a new car every time. We haven't been able to track any of them. Whoever's after her knows what they're doing." Xander hands me another drink, and a rock forms in my stomach.

Fear lances up my spine. Every second they're out there, my wife's at risk.

Damon cups the back of my neck, pulling me closer. "We will figure this out before anything happens. Until then, don't let her out of your sight."

The only thing stopping me from hitting his hand away is the memory of what happened to Misty. He'd never willingly let me go through any of that.

There's a hardness to my older brother when he tightens his grip. "We will kill them, Matthias. No one's ever touching our family again."

Bash's usual playful tone turns cold. "No one's getting anywhere near our sister. We owe her a lot." He gives me a playful wink. "And as soon as you stop hoarding her away like a damn dragon, we can all get together."

I rake a hand through my hair. "I'm not hoarding her away."

All three of my brothers give me knowing looks.

It's not so much that I'm hoarding her away as I'm fucking terrified she'll be taken from me. At first, I

thought it was some lowlifes who thought she was the best way to get into the Order of Saints, but the longer this goes on, the clearer it's becoming that whoever's after her is more organized than we expected.

"Do we know for sure it's not another family trying to overthrow us?" I ask, already knowing all the measures we have in place. We have tails on all the main members, tapped phones, hacked computers. No one can do anything without us knowing about it. Which means whoever the hell this is, they aren't a member of the Order.

"It's definitely not one of the Saints, but we can't rule out the fact that they want Scarlet's place in the Order." Damon cracks his knuckles. "You should make your marriage public."

It makes sense—if they're after the Laurent seat, that avenue has been closed since I forced her to marry me. That doesn't ease the nausea crawling up my neck.

"If that is their plan, they'll have to kill me," A coldness takes over me, filling my veins until there's no warmth left. "And I'd like to see them try."

"Whoever is behind this won't take the news of her marriage well." Xander says, eyes sharp on mine. "It might be better to keep the marriage portion a secret, so at least they'll be less drastic until we can find those assholes."

"There's no way they don't already know. Whoever this is has been trailing her for a while. We were able to pull up street camera feeds and track them down.

They've been following her since she came back to Boston."

"What the fuck are they waiting for?" Bash asks.

"My guess is, it's personal," Xander answers his brother and confirms what I was already thinking.

Bash looks between us, brows pinched together. "We made sure everyone who was involved back then died, and I know she didn't tell anyone else about the Order."

"It makes sense though. This all started with the video from that night resurfacing," Xander says.

I run my hands down my face, the overwhelming need to get back to my wife nearly taking over my mind. Each second I'm away from her is going to drive me insane.

"How many guards do you have at your place?" Damon asks, typing on his phone again.

"Four."

"Double it." He looks at me and smirks. "Oh, and Misty's coming over for a visit."

The gleam in my older brother's eyes tells me nothing good will come from this.

I'm not expecting to see Scarlet curled up on the couch. Her laptop's open on the coffee table in front of her, papers she must have asked someone to go get for her scattered around. I may have to go pay her boss a visit if she's going to overwork my wife. The only thing

holding me back is Scarlet will likely try to kill me if I do.

Warmth fills my chest, knowing she's more than capable of accomplishing it. If my girl wants me dead, I'm not going to stop her.

I drop to my knees in front of her, brushing the hair from her face and tucking it behind her ear. She looks so young like this, all of the worries she usually carries around are absent from her expression. I swipe my thumb along her cheek, chest clenching around my heart. One day, she'll always look like this. No worries holding her in place. None of her past coming back to haunt her. I can promise her that. Now that she's within my care, nothing will ever happen to her.

"What's that serious face about?" Scarlet's sleepy voice drifts up to me, pulling my attention.

Her clear blue eyes are hooded, lashes fanning over her cheeks in slow blinks. My girl's barely awake. I kiss her forehead.

"You're not supposed to be working this hard." I wrap one hand around her back and the other beneath her legs, lifting her with me.

She buries her face into my chest, taking in deep breaths before sighing. "It's your fault."

"You can't blame me for everything. It's not my fault you were too stubborn to move in with me of your own free will. "

She slides one eye open, glaring at me before closing it again. "Matthias, I'm tired."

Her words gut me, knowing she means them in more ways than one. She's been fighting for her place in this world, desperate to separate herself from her family's wrongdoings. Even the thought pisses me off. She was more of a victim than we were, stuck in that fucking castle with her demented family.

"I know, Little Sparrow." I pull her closer, making my way to our room. "I have you."

Chapter 41

Scarlet

THREE SHARP RAPS on the door let me know Misty's here. I open it to a whirlwind of colors as she enters the space. Her natural warmth makes it feel like she's been here countless times before.

"Girl, this place is amazing." Misty looks around my home, eyes wide as she takes in all the details. The tones and shades are muted compared to her, but it's obvious she likes it anyway. "Did Matthias really do all this himself?"

I shrug. "I'm pretty sure he hired a designer, but yeah, the planning was all him."

"He really nailed your style."

I'm not quite sure what she means by that. This place doesn't look anything like my town house. I'd styled that one myself to perfectly fit my needs.

Misty raises a brow. "You don't believe me? It's welcoming while being sophisticated. The clean lines

are softened by the textured textiles. Modern windows mixed with old wood details. You've got to admit, it's perfectly you."

Is it really? Am I really a mix of contradictions that Matthias somehow sorted out? Whether Misty's right or not, there's no question that I feel at home here.

Deciding to change the subject, I grab her coat and hang it on the small metal hook. "I'm not going to lie, I didn't think Matthias was allowing visitors."

"Hmmm." She sits on the sofa, tucking her feet underneath her and covering them with the wide hem of her dress. "I didn't give Damon a choice, so I'm pretty sure he didn't give Matthias a choice. Not to mention, I doubt that man can deny you anything."

"You do realize he drugged me, handcuffed me, then brought me here against my will and forced me to marry him, right?"

She looks me up and down with a smile growing on her face. "You've got to admit, it's sorta romantic."

I collapse on the sofa beside her, positioning my legs to mirror hers. "Sure, in a weird Stockholm syndrome kind of way."

"What I want to know is how he managed to convince you to marry him. Damon had sneaky ways of his own, but I don't think Matthias had the same leverage on you."

"Wait?" I lean back against the armrest. "So you don't know?"

"Know what?"

I almost feel bad for Damon because I have a sinking feeling this is not going to go over well. It's one thing for your brother-in-law to get into trouble; it's a whole other thing when it's your husband.

I wince but throw him to the wolves anyway. After all, he deserves it. "Your husband was there to keep me in place during the entire ceremony, so I couldn't leave."

A twisted smile forms on her lips that doesn't meet her eyes. "I'll kill him for you."

I laugh; it's full and loud, coming from somewhere deep in my stomach. She just looked so freaking serious, like if Damon walked in at that second, she'd have no trouble attacking him. Knowing him and how much he loves his wife, he'd probably be happy about it. I haven't decided if that's sweet or messed up yet.

Mind you, we're all a little messed up.

"That feels extreme. Can't you hold out on a night of sex or something?" I'm kidding, but she blushes anyway.

"I really don't think I can do that."

It's my turn to blush, and I cough to cover my nerves. "Pretend I didn't mention it."

"Deal." She wraps her arms around her knees, now tucked to her chest. "If you had an issue with the whole drugging and kidnapping thing, why didn't you run?"

"I did. Twice."

She jerks back, eyes flaring. "Well, Damon left that out in our evening gossip."

I lift my shoulders, then let them fall. "I'm not sure he knows about it."

"Tell me! It'll feel good to have one up on my husband for a change."

"The first time, I threatened Matthias with a knife, and it ended with him carving my name into his neck." I draw a line hollow of my neck and trace below my collarbone.

"Okay, that's kinda hot. I wonder if Damon will do that." She's smiling wide, and not for the first time, I understand what Damon sees in her. It's not her preciousness but the life she breathes into the room.

"He definitely will if you ask."

She scrunches her nose. "It's kinda messy. Maybe a tattoo?"

"Matching?"

"Maybe." She hums in the back of her throat. "Your second attempt must have ended well, too, since you're still here, after all."

"The next day, my guard helped me escape, but I couldn't leave him. I gave up."

"Did you give in, or did you finally get out of your own way and recognize this is what you wanted?"

She drums her fingers on her knee. "Do you love him?"

"I...I d—" Pause. If I'm going to say that, I'm going to tell him first.

She laughs, butting through my nerviness. "You don't have to say anything. It's written all over your face."

I cover my cheeks, knowing the heat in them is giving me away.

"He looks at you like you're his world," she says quietly.

"Well, he's kind of obsessed with me now."

"Not just now. If I saw him staring off into a room, I knew I'd find you on the other end. That man has been absolutely smitten, probably his entire life."

"Well, we didn't really get close until we were fifteen."

"You cannot convince me it didn't start sooner than that." She drums her fingers on her knee. "You should set up a family dinner. I know the guys want to come visit."

"Really? They haven't shown any interest."

"Are you for real? Matthias has shut down any attempt to come here. He's not going to let them until you ask."

I roll the idea of having the Everette family over in my mind, and I'm surprised to realize I like the idea. "I can ask, but there's no guarantee he'll be okay with it."

Misty tilts her head, a mischievous smirk curling her lip. "You really don't know how much power you have, do you?"

The keypad on the door beeps before Matthias steps in. My mouth waters just looking at him in his white collared shirt, sleeves rolled up to his elbows and the first few buttons undone. His hair's messy like he's been dragging his hand through it, and it's giving off just-had-sex vibes. My

thighs rub together on their own as I take him in and process the fact that I'm married to this man. That I'm going to keep seeing him come through that door for the rest of my life.

His dark gaze is hooded on mine, a lazy smile curling his lip as he walks closer. "Miss me, wife?"

There's a thud in my chest, and my breath catches at the way his voice curls around my nickname. If it wasn't for Damon following after him, I'm pretty sure my clothes would spontaneously combust.

The eldest Everette brother steps around us like we aren't even there and goes directly to his smiling wife. She leans back on the sofa, head resting on the cushion as she takes him in. I can practically feel the love sparking between them, and for the first time, it feels familiar.

"I'm taking you home, Nymph." Damon's command is low, and Misty visibly shivers.

She tilts her head, her eyes gleaming. "What if I'm not ready to go?"

I swear the tension is wafting off them, and if they don't leave soon, they'll be making out in my living room.

Hot lips caress my neck, and Matthias's raspy voice fills my ear. "They're like this all the time."

"I wasn't asking, wife." Damon lifts a giggling Misty up and over his shoulder, landing a sharp smack to her ass that has her sucking in a breath.

He stalks out of the room, and Misty winks at me before she disappears out the door.

"Do you think we look like that?" I ask.

"I hope so." Matthias places a gentle kiss on my head. He sits beside me, pulling me over his lap so I'm resting against his chest, and nuzzles his nose into the crook of my neck.

Goosebumps erupt everywhere he touches.

"Did you have a good night?" I ask, snuggling in and letting his scent fill my nose. I'm still not used to being able to touch him like this, but I'm not complaining.

He'd gone to some Order of Saints meetings, ones that sounded too dull to care about, but at least he got to spend some time with his brothers. I've been monopolizing every second I'm not working with him.

"The only thing good about it was coming back home to you." He kisses my forehead, and his hand runs up my arm.

I hum in the back of my throat as his words wash over me. "You really do know how to sweet-talk a girl."

He grips my hips, lifting me easily so I straddle him, and says, "It's not sweet-talking if it's true."

My lips brush his as I say, "Kiss me."

He doesn't hesitate to devour my mouth, his tongue rolling against mine as he grips my nape and manipulates me to deepen the kiss even more. His cock hardens beneath me, and he growls low in his throat when I rock against him.

I pull back, sucking in deep breaths, trying to get myself under control. "Hold on. I want to ask you something."

Matthias runs his nose along mine. "Anything."

"I want to hang out with your family. Misty said you've been keeping them away." He stiffens, and I slide my fingers through his hair until he relaxes. If it wasn't so ridiculous, I'd think he was jealous of me wanting to hang out with his own brothers. Doubt crawls down my spine. "They're important to you. I already know them, but I want to be a part of your family. Is that okay?"

He stares down at the space between us, not lifting his head to mine. Maybe he doesn't want me to see them because he doesn't want me to get too close. They've always been nice to me, but I couldn't blame them if there's some leftover resentment for my family's actions.

"Matthias?" My voice is dry, and I swallow hard.

My heart calms, then squeezes when he finally looks at me, a cocky smile on his face. "I've been waiting a long time for this, Little Sparrow. I've got to warn you though. It might be intense. Especially Bash and Xander. They've been practically begging to come here."

"Really?"

"Of course. You're their sister."

Chapter 42

Scarlet

THE OVEN BEEPS, and I reach in to grab the casserole pot, only to have Matthias's large hands circle my wrists holding me back.

"You're going to burn yourself."

"Oh my God." My brain clicks into place, processing the fact that I'd been so frantic I'd nearly burned my hands by reaching in without oven mitts.

I'm pulled back into a strong embrace, Matthias's chin resting on my shoulder. "Why are you so nervous?"

"I just...it's the first time we're all meeting like this since you and I got married." I rest my head back on his shoulder and lean into him, letting him take my weight. I ask the thing that's been bugging me since he agreed to have them over. "Do they know I tried to run from you?"

His chuckles rumble through my back.

"Don't laugh at me." I struggle to pull away, but he bands an arm around my waist and holds me in place.

"I'm sorry. I promise I'm not laughing at you."

"Sure sounds like you are," I huff.

"It's not that. It's that they've always been on your side. Had I let them anywhere near here, they'd have helped you escape. Traitorist bastards."

I twist in his arms, fingers balling in his shirt. "Seriously?"

Strong fingers massage into my tight shoulders. "Yeah, they definitely like you more than me."

All the strain leaves my muscles, and my head drops to his chest. "Alright then. Let's get everything ready."

———

As if they perfectly timed it, the second I put the last plate on the table, there's a loud knock on the door.

"Open up, big brother!" Bash yells and bangs again. "You can't keep her from us forever."

Matthias mouths, "I told you so," then swings the door open.

Bash tries to sneak in, but my husband steps in his way. "Whatever you're planning, knock it off."

"Hey, that's not fair. I wasn't planning anything."

Xander walks in, squeezing behind Bash. "He's lying. He has a whole-ass plan to sneak Scarlet out of here."

"The fuck you do." My husband lifts his youngest brother up by his throat until his feet barely meet the floor.

Bash frantically taps out on his shoulder until Matthias releases him.

"It was a joke! I was just playing around." He winks at me. "Plus, if she wanted to leave, she's more than capable of doing that herself."

Heat flushes my cheeks, knowing I'd tried just that.

"Move out of the way." Misty's familiar voice comes from somewhere behind them. She's too small to make out from behind the Everette men.

The three brothers fall back as if she's their leader and make room for her to pass.

Matthias bows his head in an awkward show of respect. "Thank you for joining us."

She smiles wide. "Aww, you're sweet, but I definitely came here for your wife."

Damon slides his hand around Misty's waist, securing her to his side. "Smells great in here."

"Did you make all this?" Xander asks while examining the array of bowls and serving dishes on the island.

"Matthias did most of it." I shrug, not wanting to take too much credit. I'm not a bad cook, but he definitely stepped up.

"Matthias?" Bash lifts a brow. "Our brother cooked this?"

"What? It's not that hard," Matthias grumbles under his breath, cheeks turning pinker by the second.

Bash leans toward me, placing his hand on my shoulder, and fake whispers, "This isn't some elaborate plan to try to kill us, is it?"

Matthias lifts his brother's hand off me. "You keep pushing it and you'll wish I poisoned you."

Damon comes in and pushes Matthias back. "Easy there. No need to threaten your family."

Xander snorts, then coughs. "You're one to talk."

My husband rests his chin on the top of my head. "I'm already regretting this."

I slip from under him, peering up. "Don't say that. I want them to like me."

"They already do like you." He rakes his hand through his hair, messing it up. "Too much."

I lean in close so only he can hear me. "Are you really jealous of your brothers?"

"I'm jealous of anyone who gets your attention." He runs his thumb over my mouth and pulls down my lip.

Heat floods my stomach and swirls in my core. The possessiveness in the way he looks at me makes me want to cancel everything and just let him follow through on the promise his eyes are making.

"Ugh...I'm going to lose my appetite." Bash makes a gagging sound that has me pulling back from my husband.

I squeeze through everyone and put a stop to the nonsense. "Let's eat."

Plates in hand, they pile food on top and take a seat at our ginormous table. Even with its size, the four grown men make it look tiny.

I smile at the sight. "It kinda looks like you're sitting

at a kiddy table. I can almost picture your mom coming around the corner."

The atmosphere in the room shifts. It hasn't been hard to see how strained their relationship has grown with their mother. There was a fair bit of gossip surrounding her being a cruel bitch to Misty.

I look at my new friend and press my lips together, wringing my hands. "I'm sorry, I shouldn't have brought her up."

She smirks. "Don't worry about it. Damon took care of it."

All four brothers look a little too pleased, and I almost feel bad for their mother. Not quite though.

Matthias passes me a heaping plate with turkey and mashed potatoes smothered in gravy with sides of corn and cheese broccoli. I take a deep breath, letting the smell fill my senses. My stomach growls, and Matthias raises one brow at me.

"I thought we talked about you eating lunch?"

We did...I may have skipped it anyway. Oops. "I tried."

He puts my fork in my hand. "Eat."

Even an unimpressed Matthias is hot.

I take my first bite, buttery goodness washing over my taste buds, and hum.

"I take it back. This is delicious." Bash says from my left side.

We're sitting three on each side, Misty, Damon, and

Xander on the opposite and Bash on my left while Matthias's on my right.

I can already tell my husband is regretting our positions.

Bash leans over the table, going closer to Misty. "Did you know she saved our lives?"

He smirks, as if remembering a good moment instead of a traumatic one. "You should've seen her. I thought she was some kind of fifteen-year-old avenging angel. Blood dripping down her arms as she broke us out. She pulled two knives from her pocket and told us to stick the pointed end into anyone who comes near us. Her fucking dad walked by when she was leaving, and she unloaded a clip in him."

Bash wraps his arm around my shoulder, still addressing Misty. "I fell in love with her right then."

Matthias growls, the room turning cold. "Get the fuck away from my wife."

Bash's mischievous grin is still visible, even while he's looking down at his plate. He's trying to give off the appearance of innocence, but I have no doubt this boy is devious. If left up to his own devices, he'll get into nothing but trouble.

"So, Bash. How about you? Are you looking to settle down?" I ask.

He snorts and has to take several gulps of his wine before being able to speak. "Not a chance. Why bother settling down when you can have fun forever." He points at Damon and Matthias. "These guys are old."

"Fuck off," Matthias replies with no heat behind it. It's clear this gentle teasing is a part of their day-to-day life.

Xander opens a new wine bottle, and it goes around the table. I go to fill my own cup, but Matthias covers it with his hand.

"What are you doing?" I whisper, not wanting to advertise his craziness to everyone.

He kisses my temple. "Just in case. We don't know for sure you aren't carrying my baby."

That sounds entirely too pleasant.

There's an itching feeling at the back of my brain, trying to tell me that something's not quite right. That I'm forgetting some very important details. My fingers trail over my stomach, but I brush it off. I'll remember if it's important.

"I want to hear all about my brother kidnapping you," Xander says.

Bash adds, "Right! He wouldn't let us in on any of the fun."

Whatever's bothering me is lost in the banter between my family. Warmth fills me, and my chest aches as they pull me into the conversation with them. My experience with family is cold, brutal, and sick. Everything was a transaction, and we only seemed happy when we put on our public facade.

Everything about them feels genuine, like this is an everyday occurrence. It's so comfortable I want to sink into it and save it forever.

Matthias leans in and presses his lips to my ear. "You belong here, Scarlet. They'll love you just as much as I do if you'll let them."

His words replay over and over. *If I'll let them.*

I let out a breath and join the conversation.

It's time to let go of the fear of rejection and let myself be happy.

Misty gives me an all-knowing look from across the table and rests her head on Damon's shoulder, who immediately adjusts to let her closer.

I smile when Matthias does the same with me.

I belong here.

Chapter 43

Matthias

SCARLET'S eyes are closed as she drops her head back, long golden-brown hair catching the wind behind her, and kicks herself higher on the tire swing. She looks like a goddess, painted in warm pink light from the setting sun, on the background of long green grass going for as far as the eye can see. I undo my tie as my legs eat the space between us. She'd stiffened when the crunch of gravel under tires announced my approach but relaxed after confirming it was me.

She looks lost to a world of her own making, and my chest squeezes, wanting her to share it with me. What is my Little Sparrow dreaming about while that soft smile settles on her face?

"You're staring." She says it without opening her eyes.

"I can't help it." I step closer, not wanting to break her blissful moment but not wanting to stay away.

Her smile widens, and she tilts her head back, peering up at me. "Give me a push?"

She lets out a shocked squeak when I grasp her blanket-covered hips and pull her backward.

"What are you doing?" Her eyes are wide, and her fingers tighten on the rope drilled through the top of the tire.

"I'll have you know I'm an expert swing pusher."

"You're awfully confident."

It's the gleam in her eyes that has a giddy playfulness pushing me forward. "Xander told me so."

I release her, letting the momentum pull her forward, and watch as she tips her head back and the blanket trails like a cape behind her. She laughs without restraint, a clear bell-like sound causing me to chuckle with her. She's never looked freer than she does now. Like there's nothing tying her, except for me pushing her higher until her breath catches.

"Okay! Stop," she cries out, voice light with laughter.

The swing slows to a stop, and she looks up at me with wind-pinkened cheeks. "I never really pictured you as a kid playing with your brothers."

Curling my fingers around her arms, I help guide her to a stop. "You say that like you think Bash ever gave Damon and I a choice. He could be painfully annoying when he didn't get what he wanted."

She laughs again. "They were definitely trouble when they were younger."

I laugh and wrap my arms around her, lifting her from within the tire and into my arms. "They still are."

Scarlet's fingers curl into my shirt, and she takes slow breaths as I sit on the cool grass, positioning her between my legs so her back rests against my chest.

"You've been gone for a while." She doesn't meet my eyes when she says it, instead looking at where the sun is disappearing behind trees in the distance. Her lack of attention doesn't hide the way she picks at her nails and her teeth gnaw on her bottom lip.

I entwine our fingers. "You miss me?"

Her weight collapses into me, and she huffs. "I'm bored."

Nuzzling the curve of her neck, I kiss along her delicate skin. "We can't have that."

A shiver rolls through her, and goose bumps rise when I suck her earlobe between my teeth. Blue eyes meet mine through dark lashes as she twists to face me, her chests rising and falling, matching the quick tempo of mine. It's been hours since I've had her in my arms, but it's felt like torture.

There's something left unsaid that has me pushing her further instead of lying her down like I want to. "What's wrong?"

"Am I a hostage?"

It's like a punch to the stomach. "I've never wanted to be your cage."

"That's ironic." She holds her wrists together, miming handcuffs.

"I can see your point. Kidnapping you was a little extreme. I won't apologize for it though. You were being so fucking stubborn, and I waited a long-ass time. Your father tried to sell your life from beneath you. That pervert tried to marry you off to a man who would have locked you away and only brought you out to show off. Used you as a tool to build connections and display his power. I've never wanted to take anything away from you."

She's silent for several seconds. "You did take something away. You took *you* away."

"I heard you tell Damon that if someone wanted you, they'd be willing to wait. Why do you think I wouldn't be? I've loved you since we were teens. It was hard to step back and give you what you needed, but I've always known you'd come back to me. Do you think if I'd admitted I loved you back, then you'd have left? Or would I have become just another cage?"

I lift her so she's fully facing me, her knees on either side of my hips, and cup her cheeks. "Even as a kid, I knew you were my soul. Letting you fly was the least I could do. But you're mine now, Little Sparrow, and even though I will spend the rest of my life lifting you up so you can soar, I'm never letting you go again. I'm done waiting."

She turns into my palm. "I'm not going anywhere."

"You couldn't even if you wanted to. Whatever semblance of masochistic patience I clung to evaporated the second I touched you."

I drop my forehead to hers. "Felt your breath on my skin."

Our mouths brush. "Felt your lips pressed to mine."

She opens for me, and I deepen the kiss. "Tasted the sweetness of your tongue."

My arm bands around her waist as I flip her beneath me and lay her down on the blanket, settling myself between her legs without breaking the kiss. She shivers, and her breath catches in her throat when I push my thumb below her panties and into her wet folds.

She moans, and I brush my lips against her ear.

"Heard the way you whimper when I touch you." I adjust so I'm sinking two fingers into her, stretching her wider to get ready for my cock.

"Your guards are here." The way her hips buck into my hand undermines any worry in her voice. She doesn't want to stop this any more than I do.

"They value their eyes too much to look."

I move to undo my pants and notch my cock to her entrance before filling her completely.

"How you gasp when my cock fills you."

"Matthias." Her nails dig into my shoulders. She's so tight it's hard to move, so I move slowly, giving her time to adjust. She goes pliable beneath me, and I slam my cock forward, growling against her lips, eyes never leaving hers.

"Fuck, I'm addicted to the way you say my name."

Scarlet presses her head against the blanket, arching

her chest upward, and I suck her nipple through her thin dress.

"So good. More." Her quiet pleas have me coming undone, and I rock into her harder.

There's a tingly, tightening sensation that grows in my spine, then down through my balls, and I groan, fighting against it.

"Come with me, Scarlet." I slide my hand down her stomach and over her bare skin.

Her eyes snap open, tongue wetting her bottom lip as I circle her clit with my thumb, working her higher.

"I'm close," she gasps, and I keep my motions steady, knowing that's what she needs.

"M...Matthias," she cries, and her pussy clenches around me, pulling my release with hers.

I brace my weight on my forearms, not wanting to crush her, and pant as I try to catch my breath. "I love you, Little Sparrow."

"I love—"

I cut her off with a kiss. I wouldn't be able to stop myself from fucking her again if she said those three words, and I need to get her inside. The night air's cooling rapidly, and she's covered in goosebumps.

Wetness pools out of her when I remove my cock, coating her inner thighs. Fuck, she's stunning, spread wide for me and covered in my cum. I scoop it up with my fingers and push it back into her core. "It would be a shame to let any of this go to waste."

She squirms, and pink takes over her cheeks. "Have you always been such a pervert?"

I lean down and kiss her stomach, rubbing soft circles beneath my palm. "Get used to it, Wife. I'm going to keep this pussy filled with my cum until I'm a dad."

A smirk curls my lips. "Then I'm going to do it again and again until you have the half dozen jelly-covered faces you want chasing you around."

"You're okay that I want so many kids?"

"Are you kidding me? I can't fucking wait."

Wind blows through the yard, and she shivers, teeth clicking together. I pull the ends of the blanket and wrap them around her, lifting her in my arms. "Come on, let's get you inside."

Chapter 44

Scarlet

WARM WATER COATS my back as Matthias pulls me closer to his chest. He's tucked my legs on each side of him so I'm sitting on his lap, facing him. The tub is big enough for two people, even taking into the fact that he's practically a giant. I rest my cheek against his peck, tracing my fingers over the letters of his freshly healed scar, and let the soothing way he strokes between my shoulder blades relax me further.

He's good at this, always knowing exactly what will put me at ease. From the way he washed my hair to how he knew exactly how to hold me. Whereas I feel like a fumbling disaster when it comes to him. It's not like I have years of experience with this kind of thing. If anything, it's the exact opposite.

I scratch my nail along Matthias's shoulder. He's the reason I'm so inexperienced, and I still haven't decided if it's annoying or endearing.

Does being so good at all of this mean he's had plenty of practice? Have other women laid against him, felt the heat of his skin as he's coaxed them to do whatever he wants? He'd been an absolute player when we were teens. All the girls wanted to get their chance with him. Their demure smirks and false laughter grated on my skin every time one of them caught his attention. He'd give them a cocky smile, and they'd fall all over him like he was theirs.

I can only imagine that continued throughout his life. More so once Damon became the head of the Order of Saints. Countless women willing to do anything to have a taste of an Everette brother.

A coil forms in the pit of my stomach, and the back of my throat tastes like acid as I picture another woman lying on him just like this, his arms wrapped around her. It's not that I'm worried he's going to leave me. Not after everything he's done to get me here.

I can't believe the fact that he kidnapped me is actually giving me relief right now. The confidence to know that I'm the only one he wants.

It doesn't stop the way bile coats my tongue that I'm not the only one. I guess he's not the only possessive one in this relationship.

"I can practically see the gears turning in your head. Just ask me." Matthias's low voice rumbles against my ear as he tilts my head up to look at him.

"It's nothing." A flush crawls up my neck and cheeks, and I'm grateful for the heat of the tub to hide

my reaction. The idea of him knowing I care about something so trivial as a grown man being with other women... I am though. I'm not even annoyed that he prevented me from being with anyone. I'm frustrated that he was.

I suck on my teeth before asking, "Were you with anyone while you waited?"

His eyes go round, and I raise my hand, cutting off his answer. Actually, I don't want to hear him say it.

"Forget it. Of course you were."

His calloused fingers wrap around mine, and he brings them to his lips. "I've never touched anyone since the first time I kissed you."

Memories of that night, him locked in that room and me asking him to be my first kiss, flood my mind. His young eyes had looked at me with such warmth as he cupped my jaw and brought his lips to mine.

Ten years. It's been ten years since that happened, and he's telling me he hasn't touched anyone since? There's a dangerous, bubbly sensation building beneath my ribs.

"No one?" I ask, my voice too breathy to be firm.

He brings his mouth to mine and kisses me deeply. "Only you."

I let him pull me into him, losing myself to his touch, when a thought creeps in. "Wait, were you a virgin?"

He bursts out laughing, causing the water to splash over the rim of the tub. "No. Do you not remember how I was back then?"

I can't look at him. My heart swells until my chest feels tight.

Strong fingers brush the hair from my face. "If I'd known back then, I wouldn't have ever touched anyone else."

His gaze stays hot on mine, imploring me to believe him. He'd been a bad-boy player, up to nothing good, who grew into one of the most dangerous, influential men in the world. And he's always been all mine.

A thrill sends goosebumps down my spine as the power of that thought hits me.

I huff out a laugh. "It's probably for the best you messed around back then. One of us needed to know what we were doing."

"You like what I do to you." A low rumble reverberates from him into my chest as he nuzzles my shoulder. The weight of his cock hardening beneath me has me going still. We've already had sex more times than I can count today, and my body's sore just thinking about it.

I push him away with all my strength, but he doesn't budge. "Don't you dare."

His hot tongue flattens on my neck, licking a path to my ear. "Just one more time."

Heat floods between my thighs, and I can't help but rock my hips against him. "That's what you said last time."

Matthias rests his forehead against mine, his breath fanning over my lips as his cock notches against my

entrance. We both gasp as he sinks inside of me, filling me completely.

"Every time you tell me no, your pussy sucks me in deeper."

He nibbles on my jaw, and I let my head fall back.

"One more time."

I'd been surprised when Matthias handed me yellow flannel pajamas with teddy bear heads printed on them and told me to get into bed before disappearing back into the bathroom. They're soft and warm, and the second I put them on, I could feel myself growing sleepy.

I'm adjusting myself under the blanket to get comfortable when the bathroom door opens. I can't stop the laugh from busting out. Matthias Everette, Lord of the Order of Saints, is standing in the threshold, wearing a matching set of yellow flannel teddy bear pajamas.

He grins widely at me and gives a mock bow. "I thought you'd like this."

"You're ridiculous." I say it, but he's right. I do like it. There's something about him being silly with me, unashamed to do something as out of character as wearing matching pj's, that has my heart skipping.

I'm nearly overwhelmed with the reality that this man is mine.

He crawls into the king-sized bed and immediately pulls me into the middle.

He rests his head on my stomach, drawing circles with his thumb. "I'm switching the bed for a double."

I choke on a laugh. "What?"

"You're too far away." His tone is playful, but he still sounds half-serious. I can't even imagine him trying to fit into a double bed.

This man is ridiculously endearing.

"How am I supposed to take you seriously?"

He moves so he's between my thighs under the covers, arms on either side of my waist, and places delicate kisses below my navel. "I'm so fucking serious, Little Sparrow. If I can't feel the pulse of your heart, you're not close enough."

"You're insane."

He nods, nuzzling my stomach with a small hum of agreement in the back of his throat. He's been obsessed with touching me there since he brought me to this house, taking every opportunity he gets to touch me.

Warm anticipation fills me at the idea I could be pregnant right now. Matthias' constant optimism has been slowly seeping in. I hadn't been thinking about kids, and now I'm hoping some miracle happened and I'm already pregnant?

I try to count back the days in my cycle, but the past weeks are fuzzy. My periods have always been irregular, and I've given up tracking them in my app. I can't be sure when it was, and even though the likelihood is extremely low, I can't help but think I should get a test.

I brush back a strand of Matthias's deep brown hair,

loving the way he leans into my hand. If I even hint at the possibility, I'm sure he'd run to the store right now, but I don't want him to leave. Not when his weight is covering me and I'm so close to sleep.

Soon. I'll get tested soon.

"What are you thinking about?"

I jerk back, breath catching in my throat as his searching eyes meet mine. He's entirely too observant, and I flounder to come up with something else. "I need to go back to the office."

I blurt it out, but at least it's something I actually want to talk to him about. I need to recover some form of normality in my life before he tries to lock me away again. I roll my eyes at the thought. I'm going to have to do something about his protectiveness because he's only going to get worse.

"No," he replies flatly.

"I'm not asking you, Matthias. This is my job. You promised to lift me up and not lock me away."

"Did I?" he huffs. "That doesn't sound like me."

"Matthias, I need this."

He lets out a long sigh. "Fine, but you're bringing a guard."

"Who?"

"Me."

Chapter 45

Matthias

SCARLET LEANS TOWARD HER MONITOR, pen perched in her fingers as she rolls the cap along her lips in thought. She's been at it for days, never distracted from whatever she's working on. I tried talking to her the first day she came back to the office, but she only lifted a brow and said firmly, *"I said you could come. Not that you could distract me."*

God, she's hot when she's in full lawyer mode. My eyes follow the thin chain of her necklace to where it forms a V above her top button. I gave it to her her first day back, the blue sapphire reminding me of her eyes.

I've spent the last several days sitting at her small round table, ignoring my own work while I take her in. From my observation, as a new member of the company, she takes on a lot of the smaller, menial tasks her coworkers don't want to do. Every time someone asks her

to complete a task, she jumps at it like it's an opportunity rather than a chore.

There's a soft knock on the door, and a woman in her mid-thirties peeks in, a wide smile on her face. I recognize her from the several other occasions she's appeared. S...Samantha? Stephanie? Synthia? Whatever her name is, I'm getting the distinct impression, by the way her attention is focused on me, that she's been coming up with new reasons to drop work on Scarlet.

Scarlet lets out a small groan, and I smirk as my wife narrows her eyes on her unsuspecting coworker. There's a flush to her cheeks, and her finger taps aggressively on the table as she watches her coworker approach me. She's giving me some warped imitation of a sexy look that has my stomach turning. With each approaching step, Scarlet's brows pull closer together, and I swear she sneers behind closed lips.

"How can I help you, Rebecca?" Scarlet asks, her tone clipped.

Rebecca? I wasn't even close.

The woman startles and looks back at my wife, who's now leaning back in her chair with her arms crossed. In the days we've been here, she's been nothing but happy to take on more work, so the sight of her glaring through her lashes has my head tilting to the side. My girl's getting possessive, and I fucking love it.

"I...I'm here with some work I need you to do." The woman hands some papers over that Scarlet immediately scans before handing them back.

"Scott gave these to me yesterday. Just like Julie gave me the work you brought in this morning." My wife's smile is sharp when she says, "Please check with the others before coming to see me. I'm terribly busy, and the constant interruption for things I've already handled is distracting."

Scarlet types on her computer for a second before glancing up. "I've just sent you the completed files. Hope that's all for today."

Rebecca is a red that rivals my wife's name as she looms over the desk. "I'm a partner at this firm."

Scarlet stands, placing her hands on the desk and leaning in. "And I'm the owner. If you keep looking at my husband like that, you won't be anything here."

Fuck me, that's hot.

Scarlet snaps back into her professional tone like nothing happened and sits down, speaking to the woman, whose mouth is still wide open in shock.

"If that's all, you can go."

It's completely silent as the woman walks through the office until the door clicks behind her.

"You're jealous?" I ask, tone playful as I take in my wife. Somehow in the last five minutes, her hair's come undone around her nape, and wisps around her ears give her a bit of an untamed appearance that goes perfectly with the vibes she's throwing off.

Her head cocks to the side, eyeing me like an eagle. "Should I be jealous?"

"Never. I just think it's adorable."

It's her turn to blush, and she glances back at her screen. "I just didn't like the way she was looking at you."

I fight back my smile.

"Thank you for not smiling back." She mumbles her words.

My smile breaks free. "Of course."

If she keeps this up much longer, I'll be locking the door, pushing her skirt above her hips, and fucking her against the desk.

My phone vibrates on the table, breaking me free from the thoughts.

> Damon: You've been MIA. You need to come to the meeting. I can't cover for you.

> Me: I'm busy.

> Damon: Staring at your wife doesn't count as busy.

> Me: You're one to talk.

> Damon: Get over here, and I'll distract our brothers so you can get home early.

> Me: Fine.

I slide my unused laptop into my bag. "I have to take you home."

Scarlet's head whips up to mine. "What? I'm about to meet my client."

She doesn't flinch while she stares me down. There's a hint of disappointment behind her eyes that has me caving. I never want her to think I don't respect her. That doesn't mean I can leave her unprotected.

"I'm going to kill Damon for this." I rub my palm over my face. I don't like the idea of anyone but me staying with her.

"Bring in Oliver," Scarlet says, like she's unaware of the wrath that creates within me.

"Hell will freeze over first."

She stands, walking around her desk, and places her hands on my chest. I suck in a breath of her vanilla scent and let it out slowly.

She gives me a small smile. "You trusted him to be my guard for years. You know he's capable."

My teeth squeak with the force in which I grind them together. I thought he was fucking capable all the way up until the point he tried to steal my girl.

"He's loyal to me, Matthias. That's what matters." Scarlet lifts onto her toes and places a kiss on my chin.

I grumble under my breath, but she's not wrong. The little asshole betrayed me, but he did it for her. I may hate him, but at least I know he'll put her first. "I'll kill him if he even thinks about taking you away."

She smirks, knowing she's won. "He won't. It's not what I want anymore."

It takes a half hour for Oliver to pull up and another five minutes for him to get out of his car. He's slow to approach me, muscles coiled to the point his veins are visible in his neck.

"I'm surprised I'm still alive."

So am I.

He's lucky I wouldn't risk my wife being upset over him. "The only reason you're not on a missing poster is because you were doing it *for her*. Any other reason and I'd have spent my time cutting you into little pieces."

The guard I'd entrusted with Scarlet years ago visibly shudders, but he doesn't cower when he says, "You may be my boss, but I'll never be completely loyal to you. If she wants to run again, I'll help her."

I smirk, knowing that's never going to be a problem, then slam my fist into his gut, causing him to double over.

He chokes on air, struggling to breathe as I lean in close and say, "My Little Sparrow knows she's mine now. She's not going anywhere. Not without me."

Chapter 46

Scarlet

Rays from the setting sun cast my office in shades of orange and pink. I've stayed later than I planned with the excuse of catching up on work, but the truth is I don't want to go home while Matthias is still busy with the Order of Saints.

"Mrs. Everette, it's getting late," Oliver says from where he's leaning against the far wall. His arms are crossed over his chest, and he's wearing a familiar blank expression on his face. Ever the professional, he walked in here hours ago, gave me a curt nod, thanked me for saving his life and his job, then got into place. Not that I was expecting much else from him after all of these years. The most I've seen him break character is when he'd been pleading with me to get into his car before Matthias' men caught us. Apparently, even my unshakable guard gets desperate when faced with being murdered by my husband.

"Just a few more minutes." I shuffle the papers on my desk and check my email for the millionth time. I don't know where the hesitance to leave is coming from. I'm used to being at home, but there's something about tonight that's holding me in place.

My phone vibrates, and I already know who it is.

> Matthias: You should be home, wife.

> Me: I'm going. I'm going.

> Matthias: If you don't leave right now, I'll take it out on that guard of yours.

I glance up to Oliver, who's none the wiser to the fact that his life's being threatened yet again, and sigh. If it wasn't for this uneasy feeling hounding me tonight, I'd already be in the bath. I stand and grab my coat from the counter, but the second I lean forward, acid climbs up my throat, causing me to gag. Like a rope tied into a knot, my stomach twists over itself as nausea rolls through me.

I barely make it to the trash can next to my desk, thanking God there's a bag before falling to my knees and emptying my gut.

The queasiness doesn't subside until I've ditched what feels like every bite of food I've eaten in the last twenty-four hours. I'm not sure how long it's been, but there are steady pats on my back when I finally recover.

"Are you okay, Mrs. Everette?" Oliver asks while handing me a bottle of water. His brows are knit together, and sweat builds at his temples.

I guess it shouldn't surprise me that a puking girl is out of his comfort zone. "I'm fine now. Sorry about that. I don't know what came over me—"

I cut off my words as the weight of what's happening lands on me. The first time I had sex with Matthias was... And we've been doing it consistently each day. Sometimes multiple times... My cheeks warm just thinking about it.

Pregnant.

I glance up at Oliver while taking a tiny sip of water, not willing to give my stomach anything else to reject.

"Oliver, I have a favor to ask."

***

I peel my eyes open as Oliver pulls the black town car into the roundabout entry to the Empire Hotel. The valet's already opening my door before I can process what's happening.

"Why are we here?" After the nausea disappeared, I was immediately hit with a wave of exhaustion, making the details of us getting here a little fuzzy. I distinctly remember Oliver running into the store for me like I asked and coming out with a small opaque bag.

Then, one slow blink later, we're at a luxury hotel between the farmhouse and my office.

Oliver reaches a hand down to me and guides me out of the car. "I thought it was best to go somewhere close because you aren't feeling well."

"Really?" I tilt my head, examining the intricate hotel logo scrawled in gold along the glass doors. I can already picture the pinched line between my husband's brows.

I send him a quick text explaining what's happening, then let Oliver help me out of the car.

I'm tired and hungry as we make our way through the lobby toward the elevators, where a man's waiting, holding it open. My shoulder aches from the strap of my computer bag digging into it. Just a little longer and I'll curl up into that bed. I cross both my fingers. God, if I am pregnant, please don't let this be how I'm going to feel the entire time.

"Here, let me take that." Oliver lifts my bag, taking my purse with it.

I sigh with instant relief as we head up to the penthouse. I lean against the elevator wall and give the man who held the door open for us a small smile. I may look like crap, but that doesn't mean I shouldn't be polite. I can just imagine the field day the press would have if the new Mrs. Matthias Everette ended up being rude. Not that I think he'd care.

The stranger ignores me, choosing to face forward, and it's honestly for the best. I don't have the energy to pretend like I'm anything but miserable. That, plus the growing anticipation of what I'll find out when I get up to my room, is taking over.

The man gets off one floor below ours, not bothering to look back. His shoulders are wide, and it looks almost

artificially rigid, like there's something underneath, but the doors close before I can take a guess.

"Here you go." Oliver draws my attention back to him, handing me a white plastic bag just as the elevator dings to our floor.

"It's in here?" I fist the handles, the material crinkling in my hands. How could something that can reveal such a life-altering thing be so light?

Oliver swipes the key to the hotel room. "I'm not sure how many you'll need, so I procured six."

Six.

My brain is repeating words as it struggles to catch up with the situation. Less than an hour ago, I was pretending to work so I didn't have to go home. Now, I'm entering a hotel bathroom so I can take one of the biggest tests of my life. Kicking off my heels, I head towards the bathroom.

"Do you need anything?" Oliver is right behind me, and I swivel on my feet. The large man nearly collides with me as he struggles to come to a halt.

"I think I've got it. You can wait out here." I start to close the door and see the way the blood drains from my guard's face upon realizing where he was about to follow me.

Unfortunately, not even Oliver's comically mortified expression can save me from the nerves crawling up my skin. I pull out a box, using my nail to crack open the seal and reveal the small white stick.

There's a loud thudding in my ears, and my vision is

going fuzzy around the corners. It's only once my lungs burn that I remember to breathe. The test itself is easy. It's the wait that's killing me.

I'd left my phone in my purse, so I have nothing but my thoughts to distract me while I watch the second hand click by, counting down until the test results will be ready.

Ten. Nine. Eight. Seven. Six. Five. Four. Three. Two. One.

My trembling fingers hover over the paper instructions. I draped over the test to stop myself from staring at it for two minutes straight.

I gnaw on my bottom lip, wishing Matthias was here for this. Hesitation has my hand pausing midair. I should have waited for him, but there's no turning back now. I lift the cover before I can chicken out, and my breath catches at the sight of a plus sign dead in the center.

The air whooshes out of me, and I stumble until I sit on the tub's edge. My heart's beating erratically, some kind of weird beat unsure if it's excited or terrified. I have no experience with what a healthy family looks like, and I'm suddenly overcome with fear that I won't be able to provide one. My mother died before I can remember, and my father was absolute scum. Even my brother was a sadistic asshole.

My chest squeezes as I lay my hand against my flat stomach. "It's going to be okay."

Unsure if I'm telling myself or our baby, I get up, tossing the test into the garbage, and make my way into

the room to wait for Matthias. All I want is for him to wrap me in his arms and tell me we can do this. That we're going to make the kind of family that we didn't have. That nothing is going to hurt our child the way our family hurt us.

Chapter 47

Scarlet

OLIVER'S WAITING for me the second I open the door. There are clear, defined lines creasing his forehead as he stands ramrod straight. I guess I'm not the only one freaking out.

"I'm pregnant." A calmness settles over me as I say the words. Every worry I'd been tumbling over is eclipsed by how right it feels.

Oliver stiffens, his shoulders pulling back as he looks at me and pulls out his phone.

I'm not sure what I expected, but it definitely wasn't this coldness.

"Wait, I want to tell Matthias myself," I say as I watch him type something.

He hits a few more buttons and nods. "It's better that he doesn't know."

His words don't settle well, like they're a glove that doesn't fit. He's watching me now, but the warmth I'd

expected, even for him, is completely missing. He's cold, calm, calculated in how he approaches me, clearing the few feet between us.

He tsks. "I had a plan to get you out of here, but this makes it messy."

Nothing he's saying makes sense. "I already told you I don't want to go. I'm happy staying with Matthias."

He smiles, but it's flat. "Of course. I knew you wouldn't come with me after what you did at the farmhouse. All I had to do was get you to him, but you kept messing it up."

Alarms go off in my head, and I take a step backward. "What are you talking about? Get me to who?"

"Where do you think you're going?" The glint of steel is my only warning before he points the muzzle of his gun directly at my chest.

"This isn't funny." I freeze, staring at the man who's been with me for years.

"You're right. The boss is going to be pissed." Oliver clicks the safety off. "Mr. O'Connor will just have to understand. I can't let you live, carrying that bastard's heir."

A tremble travels down my spine, but I don't have time to panic. I push the fear and betrayal into the recesses of my gut to process later. All that matters right now is that our baby and I make it out of here alive. I need to act and pray I don't make the wrong choice.

"Who are you talking about? Who is Mr. O'Con-

nor... I thought..." My voice cracks. "I thought we were friends."

Oliver's laugh is cruel. "You are so naive, Scarlet. You never once questioned where I came from. Even Matthias, with all his skills, couldn't dig anything up on me except what I wanted him to see. I have hated you from the moment we met. I've been biding my time for years, waiting for my boss to give me the go-ahead to ruin you. Haven't you wondered why so many things have been happening to you lately?"

"Of course I have, but you were supposed to protect me." My fists clench at my sides, and I force air through my lungs. I can freak out later.

"You really should be careful who you trust." He lifts the gun higher between us. "I'm sorry to cut this short. I don't want to be here when your asshole husband shows up."

I have one chance to get out of here, but if he calls my bluff, I'm screwed.

"Matthias!" I scream out my husband's name as if he's standing directly behind Oliver. My guard falls for my trick, momentarily taking his eyes off me. It's all the time I need to slam my palm into his chest while simultaneously kicking his foot out from under him. He crashes to the floor, air whooshing out, and his gun clatters a few feet away, giving me just enough time to make a break for the door. I only take three steps before fingers wrap around my ankle and yank me hard. I catch myself on the coffee table, struggling for breath as I desperately try

to kick him off me. Those familiar eyes I've trusted for the last seven years stare back at me as he tries to pull me under him.

Shit. I grab onto the only thing I can and lift the heavy ceramic lamp. Oliver's eyes go wide, mouth dropping open, catching his attention for the split second it takes me to slam it down on his face. The ceramic disintegrates upon impact. Gripping a sharp shard, I move so my knee is on his chest and scream as I drive it into his neck.

Tears well in my eyes as blood pools over my hand.

"You didn't have to do this," I cry at him, even after he stops moving.

I scramble off his stiff body, using my hands behind me as I crawl away. I need to calm down so I can figure out what the hell is happening.

What are the facts?

Fact: Oliver tried to kill me.

Fact: I killed him instead.

My heart starts to calm as I remind myself that he didn't succeed. That it's him lying in his pool of blood, not us. I replay the situation, trying to pick it apart. He made it sound like he'd changed his plan from taking me somewhere to killing me when I told him I'm pregnant. Take me where? This goes way beyond just wanting a position in the Order of Saints. They must know when I married Matthias there was no claiming the Laurent seat, no matter what happened.

I think through the last fifteen minutes, step by

step, from the second I left the bathroom. What had he been doing when I told him I was pregnant? I thought he'd been texting Matthias, but... I have to get out of here.

I force myself up, my legs unsteady beneath me, catching my weight on the wall. Adrenaline is the only thing keeping me going. I need to find somewhere to hide. I have to trust that Matthias will come find me. I can't believe I'm actually grateful for this freaking tracker.

I crack the door open, peeking through the narrow gap to check out the hall. So far, I still have time to get out of here. The elevator opens just as the room locks shut behind me and out steps the same man who'd ridden in the elevator with us earlier.

A sneer curls his mouth. "Looks like you've caused a bit of trouble."

I don't bother glancing down, knowing he's referring to the blood now soaking through my clothes.

"Don't come near me." I realize my mistake immediately. How could I have left the gun? I'd been so thrown off by killing Oliver that I forgot something so basic, so fundamental.

The stranger holds the elevator open. "Now, come with me, and you won't have to get hurt."

My muscles charge with electricity, and my brain screams at me that if I want to survive, I need to run.

I throw the bloody shard at him and don't wait to see if it hits its mark. All that matters is I get out of here and

away from him long enough for Matthias to find me. Because he will. I just need to stay alive.

I crash through the exit door and take the stairs three at a time, using the handrail as my last Hail Mary to stop me from plummeting face-first. Footsteps thunder behind me, chasing me down. Acid burns in my quads, begging me to slow my pace, but I push through. I can't give up now. Being caught is a death sentence.

If I can just get downstairs where there are people... I round the bottom set of stairs and slam through the exit door. A cry breaks from my throat when I exit onto the rear street instead of the road. All I can do is keep going. I fight back tears, desperate to get to safety.

A car door opens in front of me, and I skid to a stop. My feet burn from the rough ground.

A man steps out, a sneer across his lips. "Well, isn't this convenient? I thought we'd have to hunt you down, but here you are."

"Leave me alone—"

A large hand clamps down around my mouth before I can say anything else and pins my arms to my sides, preventing me from reaching for my knife. I kick out, slamming my heel against my attacker's shin, wishing I still wore my shoes. Their spike would've taken a chunk out of them.

The man in front of me says, "Now, now. Don't go hurting yourself. Boss won't be happy."

He steps to the side, opening the rear door.

"Bringing you in catches a pretty penny. So just be a good girl and get in the car."

I can't go in there. Every true crime documentary says it'll be worse at the second location. They aren't moving you for the fun of it. The alley is eerily quiet.

Clearly, I'm on my own to figure this out. I struggle against the hold, slamming my head back, wishing I was tall enough to connect my skull with his face.

The man in front of me tsks. "It's unfortunate you're going to be like that. We'll have to do it the hard way."

I'm lifted off my feet, arms crushing the wind out of me, then shoved into the trunk of their car.

The second my back connects with steel, I kick out, trying to stop it from closing, but it's too late. The lid clicks into place.

I feel like I'm choking, acid crawling up my throat as everything that's happening slams into me. I'm not getting out of here.

The car pulls out, and my entire body vibrates and bounces off the hard walls that only have a thin felt separating me from the sharp metal. My bruised skin is the least of my problems right now.

I shift from side to side with each turn they make, desperately trying to track where we're going. It's useless. Within two turns, I'm completely lost. The only thing I know is from the stops and starts, we're staying in the city.

I can't believe I'm in this freaking mess. I'm smarter than this.

Inhaling deeply, I try to pry open the taillight, but they've blocked it off with a steel plate. All there's left to do is wait and hope they don't bring me to some abandoned hangar or something like that.

My only opportunity to get out of here is to surprise them when they open the trunk.

I count my breaths in my head, trying to keep them steady. I need to be in control of my body if I'm going to make it out of here.

The car slows to a stop, and I have to plant my feet to the side of the trunk to stop me from rolling with it.

Silence surrounds me until the clack of their car doors opening and shutting sends nerves through my gut. I get into position, pulling my knees as close to my chest as the tight space will allow.

Here we go.

.

Chapter 48

Matthias

> Wife: I'm not feeling well. Oliver's taking me to the Empire Hotel.

> Me: Are you okay?

> Me: Why aren't you answering me?

> Me: I'm here. What's your room number?

NEITHER SHE NOR Oliver have answered my half a dozen calls.

With each ring, my blood pressure rises. It goes to voicemail, and I call again. And again.

I snarl into the receiver, "Answer your fucking phone, asshole, or you're going to wish you were dead."

The second I arrive at the hotel, I grab the container of soup I purchased on the way here from the passenger

seat and get out of my car. The valet greets me with a smile.

"Will you be needing assistance tonight?" He's wearing a black suit with gold details around the collar signifying the hotel.

I hand him my keys and tuck a bill into his palm. "Keep this somewhere close."

I don't plan on staying here long, unless Scarlet absolutely needs it. The lack of control over the building's security has me itching. A fact that I know Oliver is well aware of. He wouldn't have taken her here unless he felt like he had no other option. Even the thought that my girl is sick enough she couldn't make it to an Everette hotel has my stomach twisting. I've already called the doctor to come meet us, and the second she's stable, I'm taking her with me.

The valet's eyes widen at the amount, and he gives me a quick nod. "Of course. I'll have it at the ready."

The guest service desk is made of marble, lining the entirety of one wall.

The woman standing behind it gestures me over with a smile. "How may I help you?"

"I need to know Scarlet Everette's room." I drum my knuckles over the table, unable to stop moving.

"Of course, sir. I can look that up and call her room for you." Her fingers tap lightly over the keys in what feels like slow motion. A tick forms at the corner of my temple, increasing in speed with each second I'm sepa-

rated from my wife. At this point, I'll take torture over waiting here like this.

Finally, she lifts the phone to her ear. She waits patiently, a practiced smile on her lips, before setting the phone down. "I'm sorry, sir, no one is answering."

"Call again," I order.

"Sir, I can't—"

"I said. Call. Again," I grit through my teeth, fighting for control. "Please."

She complies, but there's no answer. "I'm sorry. There's nothing I can do."

Every muscle in my back tightens as I try to keep my shit together. This woman is officially keeping me apart from my wife, and it's pissing me off. "She's not feeling well. I have to check on her."

"I'm sorry, sir. I can't do that." She glances behind me, and I catch the security guard starting to approach.

Fuck this. I reach over and twist her screen toward me. A quick glance tells her room number is 402.

The security guard approaches me with caution. "Sir, I'm going to have to ask you to leave."

I turn on him. He's an older gentleman, hair graying at his temples. I'm at least five inches taller and weigh a good fifty pounds more. Unless this guy has a Taser on him, he doesn't stand a chance.

My fingers squeeze his shoulder tight enough to hurt. "You have two options. I can either knock you out here and take your key from you. Or you can come with me and check on her too. Choice is yours."

He searches my face and seems to relax. "You're really worried about her, aren't you? Alright, let's go."

My breath whooshes out as we head to the elevator. I'm going to move this guy over to my hotel and double his salary. Fuck, maybe I'll give him enough that he can retire.

The floor numbers illuminate the closer we get to her. The door hits my shoulder as I squeeze through before they're fully open. The guards close behind me, the universal key card already ready when we get to her room.

I knock. "Scarlet. Scarlet! Answer the door."

There's no response. If she can't answer the phone, she won't be able to answer the door... My stomach rolls. Why can't she answer her phone?

The security guard opens the door, and my heart stops when I step inside.

The familiar sharp tang of blood fills my nose. My gut twists as I round the island, spotting Oliver laid out on the ground, his neck split open in a jagged cut. Acid climbs the back of my throat as I turn, searching for Scarlet.

There's a gasp from behind me, but I don't have time to check on the security guard. Not when my girl could be bleeding out or d—I cut off the thought and search the space. It doesn't take long to see she's not here. The idea is almost worse than if she was because it means someone took her.

I pull up the tracker app on my phone and see she's on the move.

"What the hell happened here." The guard's eyes are blown wide, his face pale as he holds himself up against the counter.

I don't have time to feel bad for him. "Someone will be here in a few minutes. I have to go. Just try to breathe."

I'm out of the room and pushing through the exit, not wanting to wait for the elevator. The handrail is wet beneath my fingers, soaked with crimson blood. I'm taking the stairs so fast my lungs burn with the lack of air, but I can't waste time. My girl's somewhere out there, and she needs me.

The stairs lead to a back street. Light catches on something on the ground, and my heart's like a ticking time bomb, ready to explode. I lean over and pick up the necklace Scarlet was wearing earlier.

I hate the fact that this is how they took her, no doubt shoving her into a vehicle. They are going to fucking pay for this.

I round the front of the building and spot my car. Thank God I paid the valet off.

"Keys, now," I snap, and the valet tosses them to me.

I'm in the car and have it started and rushing down the street without taking a second to catch a breath. The little dot denoting Scarlet's location has stopped ten minutes away. *I'm coming, Scarlet. Just hang in there.*

Fear crackles through the shell of rage I've built

around me, threatening to take me under. Those corn-flower-blue eyes meeting mine all those years ago flash in my mind, and acid burns up my throat.

She protected me then; like fuck I'm going to let her down now.

Switching tactics, I call the only people I trust.

"What's up?" Damon answers, his voice light. He must be with Misty. She's the only one who can make him that way. He must still be at the event that kept me away tonight.

"Scarlet's missing." The words are hard to push out, cracking around the syllables. It feels wrong to say it to the universe, admitting it's true.

"What the hell do you mean she's missing?" he says sharply, his voice frigid.

"I mean she's fucking gone." It's more of a plea than a statement, but I don't care. All that matters is I get her back safely.

"Alright, calm down. Are you sure she didn't just go home?" He tries to sound reasonable, but I can hear him make his way through the crowd, Xander and Bash's voices mumbling through the receiver behind him.

"I found her necklace in the alley. She's gone."

"You should've been watching her."

A fissure forms in my chest, cracking open my ribs one at a time. "Don't you think I know that? Don't you think I hate myself for this?"

"I've got to bring Misty up to our room. I'm sending

Xander and Bash your way. Don't worry. We will find her." He hangs up, and the line goes dead.

I fill my lungs and slowly empty them. Being out of my mind isn't going to help Scarlet right now. I'll leave that to when I have my hands on whoever dared to touch what's mine.

My phone rings, and Xander asks, "What's the plan?"

Bash's voice comes through next. "What the fuck happened?" His tone is vicious, none of his usual playfulness present.

"Xander, go to my house and stock up on weapons, gear, anything you can think of. I'm already on my way to her. Bash, I want you to meet me there. I will gladly kill anyone within a ten-mile radius of her. These boys have no idea just how badly they fucked up."

"I've got you, brother," Xander and Bash answer in unison.

"Thank you," I say, trying to hide the way my voice trembles.

"She saved our lives, Matthias. We'd save her even if you asked us to or not."

"Don't worry about me. I'll be ready. Concentrate on tracking her down," Xander says.

"Where am I heading?" Bash asks, panic clear in his tone.

"Her tracker says she's at North Street. I'll pin you the location." The sound of his engine fills the line.

"We're going hunting," I say and end the call.

Chapter 49

Scarlet

THE TRUNK OPENS, streetlights flowing in, and I don't wait a second to kick out. My feet catch a guy in the jaw, sending him backward with a groan. I smile when I spot the glint of steel in his hand and slam my fist into his wrist, loosening his grip enough to take his knife. A quick slice through his wrist has him falling back, gripping his open wound.

While he's indisposed, I fling myself at the other guy and grab his neck while simultaneously slamming the knife into his ribs. It's hard, sending a shock reverberating through my arm as it strikes bone.

He coughs up blood in my face before he lets go of me.

I use him as leverage to pull myself out of the car, then rip the knife from his chest, unwilling to leave myself defenseless.

A man in a ski mask approaches me from inside the building, a gun pointed at my chest. "Give me the knife."

I flip the knife in my hand, securing it in my grip on the handle. "Why don't you come and get it."

He cocks the gun, bullets loaded in the chamber, and I fight against my instincts to run, knowing I won't get far. If their goal was to kill me, they've had plenty of chances by now.

"Oh, you're feisty," he practically purrs, and I shudder in response. "Fortunately for you, I already have a buyer lined up."

A buyer?

His head tilts to the side. "I'm curious though. What's so special about you that fetches such a high price?"

If he only knew he had Matthias Everette's wife within his reach. Would he go back on his deal? If he does, maybe whoever the other guy is will kill him.

"Whatever you're thinking, forget it. We're here for the money."

Why isn't he coming closer? The two men from the car are still laid out on the ground...is he stalling?

"There's something special about this knife." I hold it loosely by the tip between two fingers until his eyes focus on it, drawing his attention away from my face.

He looks back at me like he's trying to get a read. He clearly didn't do his research before coming after me.

That's too bad.

I flick my wrist, sending the knife hurdling end over

end through the air and landing perfectly in the hollow of his neck. His eyes are wide, hand hovering like they don't know what to do.

He collapses, his body hitting the ground with a thud. When you cut through the major artery in the throat, they fall fast.

Clapping comes from the doorway, and a man exits the building. "Well, aren't you a clever girl."

I look from him to the gun now laid out on the ground and don't hesitate to dive for it, throwing myself at the prone body to get to it first.

I'm not fast enough. The second I grip the handle, a boot comes down hard on my wrist, and tears sting my eyes. I instinctively pull my hands to my chest as the pain crashes through me. He chuckles, kicking the gun away, leaving me defenseless beneath him, covered in someone else's blood.

Struggling to breathe, I look up at my attacker. He's wearing a cap pulled low over his eyes that casts his face into shadows.

"Come on. Don't you recognize me?" he asks, pulling his hat off to reveal striking white hair.

"Trip?" I jerk back, shock rippling through me. He's the last person I expected. "Why are you doing this?"

He huffs out a breath. "I guess I shouldn't expect you to understand. I was only ten back then."

"Back when? Listen, whoever you think I am, you're wrong. Just let me go, and we can forget this happened," I plead.

"Let you go?" His smile is wrong, showing too much of his teeth. "When I just got you where I need you? Do you have any idea what I've done to get you here? Who I've lost?"

"I don't know what you're talking about."

"Of course you don't. You didn't even know I existed. It was all set up for me to inherit, but you had to go and get betrothed to him."

"Whoever you're looking for, it's not me." Even as I say it, his words crack open an idea within me. Prior to Matthias, I'd only been betrothed to one man, but he didn't have a son. I snap my mouth shut. If I'm quiet, this asshole will likely tell me what's happening.

"That's where you're wrong. I know exactly who you are. After all, I've spent the last ten years planning exactly how I dispose of you. I'll give you credit, it wasn't easy. You evaded Liam, and that was after all the time I spent manipulating him. Then Jeremy failed to collect you." He slams his foot into my chest, knocking the air out of my lungs. "Then you went and killed the two people closest to me. Was it fun seeing my friend propped up for the Order to gawk at?"

"I don't know who you're talking about," I wheeze.

"Hmmm...I guess your husband doesn't share everything with you. How about Oliver? Did you make him beg for his life after all those years standing by your side?"

Tears sting the back of my eyes and pool over my cheeks. Rationally, I know my guard was never the man I

knew, but that didn't stop the torment from being the one that killed him.

"Fuck you." I spit out the words. "Matthias will come for me. He knows where I am."

"That's the entire point," he sneers. "As always, you're nothing more than an object for the men to use."

A pit twists in my stomach, but I breathe through my nose. I can't let him have the upper hand. Not if it puts Matthias in danger. Slowly, I move my hand to the left through the pool of warm liquid. My heart's pounding so hard I can barely hear Trip as my fingers finally reach the steel handle of the knife protruding from my attacker's chest. I grip it but don't move. The second I do, he'll shoot me, so I have to time it perfectly.

"You see, I'm counting on all of the Everette brothers to show up. They killed my father and ruined anything he's ever created." Trip steps closer, gun still trained on my chest. "No one would work with our company. No deals, no trades, nothing. We lost it all. We didn't have anything to do with the coup, but they still came for him."

He shifts, and he's finally within range.

I lift so I can hide the fact that I'm sliding the knife up. A laugh bubbles in my throat; I can't stop it. "You're a Vasiliev. I thought they were wiped out."

"You missed one." He smirks. "My father never claimed me. He was close, but then those fucking bastard Everettes killed him."

"Oh my. You've really got it wrong." I slice forward,

443

cutting through his Achilles. I feel the shot go off just past my head as he collapses beside me.

I slam my knife into his throat and say as he bleeds out, "*I* killed your father. He underestimated me too. It's unfortunate you weren't able to learn from his mistake."

His eyes go wide as he grabs his throat, desperate to stop the bleeding.

There's no point, and within seconds, he's out. I scramble up, knowing I have to get out of here. There's no way he's alone if he set up this trap to catch Matthias and his brothers. Panic lances through my chest, sending ice through my veins. I have to warn him.

There's a loud boom from the other side of the building. Just as I take a step towards the door, the sound of gunshots fills the air from the other side of the building.

Too late. He's here.

Chapter 50

Matthias

Xander pulls up to the dock seconds behind me. The sound of waves covers the crunch below our tires. The tracker shows she's in the white building a block ahead of us.

Bash and I get out of the car and head to the back of Xander's Range Rover. The chill rolls down my spine as I throw on my tactical vest. It wasn't too long ago that we'd been doing this to save Misty, and that went to hell fast. If we'd been any later, we'd have lost them both that night.

My fingers tremble as I slide extra magazines into their slots. I can't let that happen again.

Xander grips my shoulder. "It's going to be okay. We are going to take every last one of those assholes out."

"Hell yeah, we are! They're going to learn exactly what happens when they fuck with our sister," Bash cheers, but there's an edge to it.

They're both ready to go, with enough weapons to take down a fort. It's clear they're all in, that they want to get to Scarlet as badly as I do, but going in now without any backup is a suicide mission, and I can't let my baby brothers risk their lives like that.

"Wait for Damon and backup." I turn to them.

"The fuck are you talking about?" Bash replies.

"We're not little kids anymore. This is as important to us as it is to you," Xander adds, adding another gun to his arsenal. "Our men will be here soon. They'll cover us."

I search their faces, but they stare back at me with hard expressions.

"Don't fucking die," I command like I can actually control what happens next.

Bash grins. "Double promise."

I blow out a breath. "Let's go."

We hide in the shadows as we approach the building, scoping out what we're up against. There are only three men stationed out front. They're dressed in plain clothes, nothing like you'd expect going against us.

Bash comes up beside me. "Do you think they're trying to lure us into a false sense of security?"

"I don't think so. Look how they're carrying their guns." Xander points out. "These aren't high-class mercenaries. Whoever was stupid enough to take her likely doesn't have enough money to fund something like this."

I cock my gun and step out into the light. "Let's hope you're right."

All three men are down, bleeding across the pavement before they can turn in our direction.

Bash kicks one of the men's guns away from him. "I know we should be happy about it, but honestly, I'm a little disappointed. No fun at all."

"Scarlet's in there somewhere, and you're complaining it's too easy?" My voice travels through the parking lot, echoing off the buildings.

"Jeez...I was just joking around." He heads to the door first, getting into position, and signals to Xander he's ready.

Bash opens the door, and Xander scopes it out, his gun ahead of him and half-covered by the doorframe. He gives me the all-clear sign and waves me forward.

That's all I need to see before I rush through the empty hallway, fisting my phone in my hand. The tracker isn't perfect, but I can still see the approximate area she's in. If I can just get to the other side, I'll be able to see her. My breath grows rapid, and my chest aches. I need her to be okay.

Five men enter the hall in front of me, cutting off my path. I fire round after round, running at them head-on. Their eyes are wide, fear throwing their aim off. Whoever they are, they're definitely not used to live combat.

Xander and Bash are close behind me, each taking out men ahead. It takes seconds to clear the hallway.

The sound of boots comes crashing down the stairs, and my brothers position themselves to face the attackers.

"Go find our sister," Bash yells just as the first man steps out in front of him, taking a shot between his brows.

I hesitate for a second, not wanting to abandon them.

"We've got this. Just go," Xander calls over the sound of gunshots as they mow the men down. The attackers made a tactical mistake coming down the stairwell. It only allows a few to exit at a time, making it entirely too easy to take out. Like shooting fish in a barrel.

No part of me feels bad for them—they fucked up when they came after my wife.

I glance at my phone as I turn down the next hall-way, and I'm nearly on top of her dot. I suck in a breath, trying to prepare myself for what I'll see when I open the door. I can't lose her. No. I won't fucking lose her.

I swing the door open, gun pointed straight ahead, finger resting on the trigger, then come to a halt.

Scarlet's standing around three dead bodies, a wide smile across her lips. She's dripping with blood, but from the way she's smirking, I don't think it's her own.

"I told you I can take care of myself." She points to the carnage she created, and I've never been so happy that she'd spent the last ten years learning how to defend herself. She'd told me once she'd never be in the same position she was in back then ever again, and she meant it.

"Fuck, Little Sparrow, I love when they underestimate you." I've never been so proud of anyone in my entire life.

My feet are moving without me telling them to, closing the distance between us. I drop my gun as she runs and jumps into my arms, burying her face into my chest. For all of her bravado, her body's shaking, and I tug her closer to me, trying to push all of my strength into her.

I kiss the top of her head. "You did good."

"Did you doubt me?" Her voice is light as she murmurs into my vest.

"You are so much more than I deserve," I say shakily.

She pulls back, tears pooling in her eyes. "I was scared. I tried so hard to hide, but they were too fast."

"Me too, Little Sparrow. I was terrified." I grip both sides of her face. "I can't live without you. Do you understand? My life is nothing without you in it."

I bury my face into the curve of her neck, closing my eyes and breathing in her scent. *She's okay. She's okay. She's okay.*

I say the words on repeat as shudders roll through me. Rationally, I can see she's fine, but my body hasn't quite caught up yet.

A scuffle on the floor has me lifting my head just in time to see a man lunge in to stab her. Rage fills my veins, and I move without thinking, switching Scarlet's and my positions.

Pain radiates through me as the knife sinks into my lower back, but all I can feel is grateful that it's me and not her.

Two gunshots ring out before I can turn around, and warm liquids splatters the back of my neck.

Damon's voice booms across the open room. "You couldn't fucking wait for me, could you?"

I raise a brow at him. "Like you can talk."

When Misty had been in danger, he'd lost his mind.

He looks us over. "You okay?"

Scarlet breaks free of my hold and gasps at the sight of my back. She places two trembling hands against the wound. "You're hurt."

"It's just a scratch, Little Sparrow." I try to ease her mind.

She glares up at me. "You are not okay. We're going to the hospital."

"We can just wait for our doctor. He can stitch me up."

"Matthias Helios Everette. Do not argue with me right now."

My mouth twitches, but I bite back my smile. She'd probably kill me if I did.

"Of course. I'll do whatever you say."

Damon glances between us. "My car's around the side. Follow me."

Xander and Bash are waiting by the Range Rover when we exit the building. Neither of them has a scratch on them.

Bash crosses his arms. "Don't tell me you actually got hurt, Matthias? I'm disappointed in you."

"Fuck off." The pain is getting worse, but I refuse to let Scarlet see it. She's already white as a ghost.

She climbs into the back seat of the SUV after me, tucking herself into my side.

Damon gets into the front, and Bash and Xander follow behind us in Damon's car.

"Apply as much pressure as you can," Damon calls out from the front.

Scarlet doesn't need to be told again and pushes hard.

"*Fuck.*" A hiss escapes my lips as the pain burns all the way up my back. "Go easy on me."

She presses harder. "I'll never forgive you if you die."

I wipe away the tears flowing down her cheeks. "I'm fine, Little Sparrow. I promise."

With the way Damon's driving, it takes less than ten minutes for us to pull up to the emergency room. Someone must have called ahead because there's already a team waiting with a gurney when I get out.

I hold my hand up, stopping their approach. "I can walk."

Scarlet's not screwing around when she says, "If you ever want to touch me again, you'll get on the damn gurney, Matthias."

I'm laid out on the gurney immediately—I'm not going to risk the chance she'll follow through with that

threat. I think I'd rather die than have her close and not be able to touch her.

A firm hand pushes me against the hard mattress. The woman's wearing green scrubs and a stethoscope around her neck. "Don't move. We're heading in."

"I said I was fine."

"We'll be the judge of that." She commands her team like a drill sergeant as they move me into the hospital.

I twist, ignoring the pain, and call back to Damon. "Take care of her."

"I'll protect her with my life, brother."

Scarlet runs up to me and grips my hand. "Don't you dare die."

I squeeze her fingers. "Only because you asked."

Chapter 51

Scarlet

IT'S BEEN an hour since Matthias disappeared through those double doors. Misty brought me a change of clothes, and I washed off as much blood as I could, but I refused to go when they suggested I leave and take a shower.

I can see I'm scaring a few of the other people waiting here too, but all that I can think about is getting back to him.

His brothers have tried to talk to me, but I haven't been able to do anything but stare at where he disappeared deeper into the hospital.

"You can see him now." A nurse approaches, wearing a soft smile. "His surgery went really well."

It feels like I can breathe for the first time since I saw his wound, but I won't feel relief until I see him myself. I'm up and walking toward her, following through the

double doors. She leads us through a labyrinth of halls to where there are rows of rooms lining the hallway.

She points at the furthest one. "He's in here."

I hesitate at the threshold, my fist closed so tight my nails dig into my palms.

Bash comes up behind me, giving me a gentle nudge. "You're blocking the way."

I don't understand how he can be so cheerful in this situation, but that doesn't stop it from dissipating some of my anxiety.

Matthias's eyes lock on mine the second I step inside. I rush to him, gripping his hand.

"Don't ever do that to me again."

"Okay." His smile is lopsided, and that's when I notice that his eyes are still glazed over. He hasn't fully recovered from the anesthesia.

His brothers crowd around us, all talking over each other, but Matthias' focus is on me.

He rolls his head toward me. "You're pretty. Do you want to go on a date?"

I choke on a laugh. "We're married."

"No way? Really? I must be pretty lucky."

Nothing prepared me for how adorable he's acting.

His brothers burst out laughing, filling the space.

"Fuck, I wish I got that on camera." Bash chuckles. "He's never living that down."

A nurse comes in. "I'm going to need all but one of you to leave. This is a hospital."

Damon approaches the bed and places his hand on

Matthias's shoulder. "We'll be back in a bit. Stop scaring your wife."

Matthias grins. "My wife."

"You are never living this down," Xander adds before leaving through the open door.

The guys leave, and I sit in a chair as close as I can to his bed, brushing the hair off his face.

His eyes start to droop when he asks, "Do you love me?"

"Yes." I swipe my thumb along his temple.

His blinks grow long until his eyes close. "I love you too."

The sensation of fingers raking through my hair pulls me from sleep. I blink my eyes open. "What time is it?"

"Early," Matthias answers, wincing as he tries to lean over to kiss me.

I close the distance between us and press my mouth to his, pulling back when he tries to deepen it.

"Do you have any idea how scared I was?"

His voice is hoarse when he says, "Yeah, I think I have a pretty good idea. You disappeared."

"I had it under control." I press my forehead to his, eyes closed, basking in the sound of his breathing. My entire body starts to shake, like it chose this exact moment for my adrenaline to wear off.

"Are you okay?" Matthias grips my arm just as the nausea hits me.

Not now, not now, not now.

I jump up from the bed and rush into the attached bathroom just in time to vomit. All the strength leaves me, and I'm about to fall when strong arms wrap around my waist.

"I need a doctor. Get us a doctor now," Matthias's voice booms, likely echoing through the entire hospital.

"I'm fine. It's okay. I'm fine."

"You are not fine." His growl reverberates through my back.

I twist in his arms. This wasn't exactly how I was planning to tell him, but there's no way he's going to get back into that bed unless I do.

"I'm pregnant."

His eyes flare wide, mouth dropping open, then closing like he's trying to say something but can't. He grips my arms, holding me so we can face each other.

"I'm going to be a d...dad?" His voice cracks.

I push him back, careful not to apply too much pressure. "Yes, we're going to have a baby. Now, get back into bed."

Matthias just stares at me. "I'm going to be a dad."

"Bed, now," I command, and he gets on the bed obediently.

He grips my hand and pulls me onto the mattress beside him. "Are you sure you're okay?"

I snuggle into his shoulder, breathing him in. "Positive."

"There's something I need to say, and I need you to just listen," he says, running his thumb over my cheek.

I look up at him, trying to read his expression, but there's no tell there. "Okay."

"You don't need to do everything on your own. You are not alone. You've never been alone because even if you didn't know it, you have always had me. I have belonged to you for so long I can't remember what it feels like to belong to myself. Loving you has been the reason I wake up in the morning. There is nothing about you I would change. Not your past. Not your dreams. Not your family. Nothing. You are and you have always been it for me. I was a stupid fifteen-year-old kid, but even then, I would give you anything you wanted. I would wait for however long you needed me too. I was happy to sit by and watch you because it's what you needed. But now you..."

Matthias rubs my stomach, and tears pool in my eyes.

"Now you both need me. There's no end to how much I care about you. There's no bottom to the well of my love. I want to be here for you. You don't have to do any of this alone. So pull everything you need from me. I won't break."

He cups my face, holding all of my attention and promises.

"You're mine now. I'm never letting you go."

Chapter 52

Scarlet

WE INVITED the entire Everette family over for breakfast, and our farmhouse is filled with the brothers speaking over each other. Well, our home may look like a farmhouse, but it's anything but small. It's as if Matthias knew I'd want to have our home boisterous with family before I did.

Misty and Damon are cuddled up on the love seat, lost in their own world, as Bash and Xander finish up the dishes.

I can't help the smile overtaking my face at the fact that this is my new life. My home growing up had been a cold, unforgiving place, where nothing but perfection was accepted. I bite my lip as the two youngest brothers make their way to the living room, a constant bickering between the two of them.

"I still can't get over that fucking bastard Oliver. To think, I actually liked that guy," Bash says, collapsing on

our wide leather sofa. He's been rambling on about what happened for the last week. They'd all been shocked when I explained everything.

I pass him a steaming cup of coffee. "It's alright. He fooled us all."

"At least you got to kill him," Bash grumbles under his breath.

My chest stings, a burn burrowing between my ribs. I will always protect myself, but Oliver's betrayal and subsequent death will always be a sore spot for me. There's an underlying guilt that gnaws at me in quiet moments, and it doesn't matter if he deserved it or not.

Strong arms wrap around my middle, and I'm pulled easily onto Matthias's lap. His mouth grazes my ear, sending a shiver through me when he says, "He deserved what he got, Little Sparrow. He's lucky it was you and not me."

"I'm not sure he'd agree with being lucky." The tension that had been growing between my shoulders releases with his words.

"Trust me. You did him a favor by making it quick." Matthias kisses the soft spot behind my ear, his fingers gently tracing my stomach, filling me with warmth.

"Knock it off, you two. I just ate," Bash chimes in again, and Xander looks at him sideways, hitting his shoulder.

"If you aren't careful, you'll be next," Xander says, the gleam of mischief clear in his eyes.

Bash leans over, pretending to puke, sound effects

and all. It's moments like this I'm reminded they're barely adults.

"Be quiet. Misty has something to say." Damon's voice booms through the room, and Bash's and Xander's mouths click shut comically fast.

When Damon's satisfied, he gives his wife a warm smile, helping her up. He's holding her almost tenderly, like she's breakable.

Actually, it's not much different than how my own husband is holding me now. Nerves have plagued me all morning, knowing what I'm going to announce. I'm not sure if the delay makes me feel more or less anxious.

Damon helps Misty bring over a large black box. She's practically vibrating with excitement when she pulls out small blue bags. "I got you all something small."

"Presents!" Bash is up and grabbing his, too impatient to wait. He collapses back, ready to tear into it.

"You're going to open it at the same time," Misty cuts in just in time, and the youngest Everette pouts.

"You're no fun."

Misty looks at him with an exasperated fondness as she hands out the rest of the bags. I take mine, giving her a knowing look, and pass the other one to Matthias.

No one else has caught on. Instead, they're all turning their bags around like they have X-ray vision.

"On the count of three," Misty says, and Damon wraps his arms around her from behind. "One. Two. Three."

I watch Matthias as he pulls out a t-shirt and cocks his head to the side examining it.

"World's Best Uncle?" Bash says, his voice full of confusion.

Misty's mouth twitches as she waits for the dumbfounded brothers to clue in.

"Wait." Xander's word stretched so long it could be four syllables.

"I'm going to be an uncle?" Matthias cocks his head to the side and looks at me in confusion, clearly still hung up on the fact that we're announcing today as well.

Misty and I talked about it and decided it would be fun to announce them back-to-back. That way, both Damon and Matthias get to enjoy the surprise.

I'd gone to Misty's place to tell her the news privately earlier this week, knowing that she desperately wanted a family of her own and wanting to be as delicate with the conversation as possible. There's no way I'd ever want to do something that would make her uncomfortable. So imagine my surprise when she burst out laughing.

"But I thought..." Xander cuts off his words, sensing they may be insensitive.

"We're adopting a little boy. He'll be born in roughly six months," Damon replies.

"Six months! You mean I only have six months to babyproof my entire place?"

Damon raises a brow. "Is there a reason you think my baby will be at your place?"

Bash snorts. "Because I'm going to be the best uncle ever."

"I'll get my place ready too," Xander chimes in.

The brothers all speak over each other in their excitement, keeping themselves distracted as Matthias and I get up.

His strong fingers curl over my waist, and his chest rests against my back, his sturdy presence easing my nerves.

"Listen up. Scarlet has something to say."

Damon's face snaps to Matthias's, clueing in seconds before I say the words.

I take a deep breath. "We're happy to announce that your son will have someone to play with...because I'm pregnant."

"No shit?" Bash collapses against the back of the sofa, a dopey look on his face, but it's Damon who has my attention.

He's crossing the room in three strides before pulling Matthias and me into a bone-crushing hug.

"Easy on my wife."

Damon steps back immediately and looks me up and down as if he'll be able to spot signs. "You're really pregnant?"

"Yup, Uncle Damon," Matthias replies, and the room erupts with noise.

My heart swells as all the brothers are off their feet,

hugging everyone. I can't stop myself from laughing when Bash hugs Xander, his joy overflowing.

It takes a while for the room to quiet down and for us to finally be able to take our seats. Tears of happiness prick my eyes as I glance over at Misty, who's already looking back at me. Loud, boisterous, full of love. I can't imagine a better place to have my family.

Hours later, the last Everette brother finally leaves, and I get to collapse against Matthias on the couch, exhaustion taking over me. My eyelids grow heavier with each blink, and Matthias shifts me so I'm laid out over him, his arms securing me in place.

I rest my chin on his chest, meeting his eyes, and voice the worry that's been plaguing me. "Do you think after everything that's happened, I can be a good mom?"

My husband's arms tighten, and his eyes bore into mine, as if trying to imprint the truth of what he's about to say. "Despite everything you've been through, you are still the most caring person I know. Plus, there's not a doubt in my mind you will be able to protect our kids."

Kids. Plural. I like the sound of that. "Promise me we will never be like our parents."

"You never have to worry about that. We're going to surround them with so much love they won't be able to comprehend how we grew up. They will never know what it feels like to have parents who don't adore them."

I push a strand of his hair back. "You're going to spoil them, aren't you?"

He kisses my forehead. "You have no idea."

My breath catches. "I love you."

"I love you more." He buries his face into the crook of my neck and shifts so I'm beneath him, his hard cock pressing between my thighs.

My mind's blank, and my heart's full as I bask in our new life. One that he's given me everything I've ever dreamed of.

Chapter 53

Epilogue

Matthias

I BALANCE Eve on my hip. She's a runner, so if I have any chance of drinking my coffee, I have to keep her feet above the ground. Her little fingers dig aggressively into the back of my hair, holding herself in place as she watches her siblings attentively.

"Olivia, stop picking on your brother," I tell my oldest daughter. She's got Tucker in a headlock Uncle Bash would be proud of.

"He started it." I don't miss the way her grip tightens slightly before finally releasing him.

"Nuh-uh. You started it." Tucker glares up at his big sister, and I catch his arm just as he scoops a large handful of dirt from the raised garden bed. My poor coffee is abandoned on the ground.

"I'm not going to save you if you follow through with that." I ruffle Tucker's hair, who's eyeing his older sister up as if debating if he can take her. He must decide he

can't because he releases the dirt and wipes his hand across my pants.

I may be a Lord in the Order of Saints, but I've given up on ruling over these three a long time ago. Now, it's a matter of survival.

"Looks like you can use some help." A bell-like laugh comes from the veranda behind me, and I turn to see Scarlet's wide grin. She approaches, still wearing her work clothes, perfectly pressed, not a wrinkle in sight. It's the swell of her stomach that's just beginning to show with our fourth baby that has my attention. If it was up to me, she'd never work another day, instead relaxing at home with me, but she's assured me dealing with lawyers is easier than being outnumbered by our crew of unruly pirates at home.

She kicks off her shoes before walking up to me, placing a peck on my lips.

"You surviving?" she asks, and I deepen the kiss. It's this very behavior that's got us surrounded in the first place.

"Me too. Me too," Eve screams, reaching both arms out to her mother.

Scarlet lifts her into the air, guiding her small legs around her waist and balancing our daughter on her hip.

Scarlet peppers her with kisses until Eve erupts in giggles, pushing her mother's face away.

"Mommy!" Tucker and Olivia come running toward Scarlet, outreached dirty hands trying to grab onto her.

Scarlet laughs, pretending to run. "Mud monsters. We need to get away."

She weaves through the garden beds as our kids chase after her, wide smiles on their faces. They are fully determined to wipe dirt all over her, but she doesn't seem to care, more focused on playing with them than her clothing.

Scarlet slows, crouching down to accept their grubby hugs. Our three children laugh, Eve still tucked into her side when Scarlet falls back and lands firmly on her butt. She looks up at me, smiling, a brightness in her eyes I wasn't sure would ever be there.

When we'd been locked away by her family, all of this had been nothing but a dream. Something I could imagine to help the hellish hours go by. Now, with my family's right in front of me, it's everything I could ever wish for.

Sometimes I'm not sure if I deserve to be this happy.

"Alright, you three, it's time for your baths," Mrs. Cournoutt says from where she comes out of the house. She's an older lady in her mid-fifties who has grown to be an essential part of our family. She's been our nanny since Olivia was born, and I don't think we could function without her.

The kids run up to her. Even little Eve wiggles out of her mother's arms and chases her older brother and sister up the stairs. She's still unsteady, but she's fast.

They disappear into the house, and I walk up to my

wife, who's still on the ground with a soft curve to her lips.

"Welcome home." I reach down and help her up, tucking her into my side. She leans her weight into me, body going limp.

The sky turns a soft orange pink as the sun descends behind the treeline. I turn Scarlet toward me and kiss her softly. "Are you happy, wife?"

"Yes." She hums in the back of her throat, and her delicate fingers trace my cheekbones. "Thank you."

I lean into her touch and ask, "For what?"

"For waiting."

**A Devious Arrangement
Book 3: Bash's book in the Twisted Vows Series.
Girl pretends to be her brother in order to infiltrate a secret society.**

Chapter 54

10 YEARS AGO

Matthias

Me: Where the fuck are you?

How DID Damon get out of this? As the eldest Everette brother, it should be him standing in this brain-melting tedium, not me.

Damon: Father sent me on an errand.

Me: Why didn't he ask me?

Damon: Big bros privileges *wink*

Damon: Don't worry. I'll come save you from the monotony in a bit.

I grab a glass of champagne from a member of the waitstaff walking by. He doesn't bother questioning my name, already familiar with who I am, and what station I have as one of the Lord's sons.

Me: You better.

Not bothering to hide my boredom, I look over the crowd. We're at one of the Volkovs' massive estates. It has the standard marble everything, low-hanging chandeliers, and winding staircases. When I was little, I used to gawk at the high ceilings and intricate details. Now, it's just more of the same.

Members of the Order of Saints aren't like normal people. They've all been initiated into the most powerful secret society in the world. They influence policy, wars, who wins elections and who loses.

Its exclusivity makes it all the more intriguing to those on the outside. They'll never make it in, though, because there's only room for twenty-six families, and none of them will ever give up their spot.

To prevent chaos, the Order is split up into a hierarchy. The Unsainted, members not yet initiated. The Saints, representatives from each family, and the Lord who rules over them.

My father's the Lord, and there's nothing and no one more powerful than he is. The Order is filled with powerful men, but they wouldn't make a step without his say-so. With power comes envy, and for centuries, there's been a fight for the ruling spot. That is, until the Everette family took over and cast out any doubt on who belonged on the throne.

No matter how much of an asshole my father is,

there's a security in knowing he's feared just as much as he's revered.

Honey-brown hair catches my eye and draws my attention. There are at least twenty girls my age in here, all dying for a chance with the son of the Lord of the Order of Saints, so why can't I pull away from her?

Scarlet stands beside her father, the esteemed Charles Laurent, an active Saint in the Order. He treats her like a jewel on his arm, something to show off, and she plays her role perfectly, smiles at all the right times, bows when she's supposed to. Never too loud, too aggressive, too happy. The perfect little society darling.

It grates on my fucking nerves.

Ever since she pushed me down on the playground and kicked dirt in my face when we were children, catching glimpses of who she is underneath her perfect facade has become an addiction.

She's a sliver buried under my skin, a constant reminder of her presence with no way to dig it out.

"Not interested in my sister, are you?" Christopher Laurent asks from directly beside me, startling the crap out of me.

"Fuck no" is my immediate response.

Interested is the wrong word. Each glimpse beneath her flawless facade has me intrigued, like she's some sort of puzzle I can't help but want to figure out.

"Sir Everette." Despite the fact that it's easy to see it grates on him, he bows his head slightly in the deference

that my name commands. He's an Unsainted, and with that, he must obey the rules we live by.

"Laurent" is my only reply.

Christopher's gaze slides to his sister and back to me. He looks just like her—same light brown hair and soft blue eyes—but instead of being slight, he's got at least five inches on me.

"Good, because her future is locked down." His lips twist in a mockery of a smirk.

I hide the surprise from my face. She's barely turned fifteen, and even in our fucked-up society, that's young to marry off your daughter. Not only is it disgusting, but it removes them from the market for future matches.

"Who?" I ask, dreading the answer.

"No one you'd know." Matter-of-fact, like he didn't just admit they're selling out his sister.

I press my palm against my sternum, an uneasy burn forming there, and take a sip of the bubbly liquid from the flute. I'm sure it's the best quality, but it still tastes like ass to me.

I feel the weight of Christopher's attention on me as he studies my reactions to his declaration of his sister's future marriage.

No matter how revolting it is, there's nothing I can say about it. Arranged marriages have always been a part of our society. I change the subject before he can catch on that I'm a little too interested in Scarlet. "You nervous about tonight?"

Christopher stiffens, his wide eyes darting around

the room. He looks like an animal that's just been caught. Not the reaction I was expecting.

"You know the Saint ritual?" I remind him.

He turned eighteen last month, and as a member of the Laurent family, he has the ability to become a Saint in the Order. Everyone knows there's some kind of ritual, but they keep that shit under lock and key. Wouldn't be surprised if it's just to freak us all out.

I could've asked Damon, my older brother, when he went through his earlier this year, but I'm honestly not that curious. As a son of the Everette family, we'll all be Lords instead of Saints in the Order. It all sounds like bullshit to me.

"Nah, I have it all planned out. Nothing's going wrong," he says, his tone a little too rigid. There's a sharpness to his smile when he looks at me, like it's edged with something.

I'm about to question him on it. If he really is worried about the initiation, I can call Damon and ask him what the fuck happens in that room.

"Lord Everette, it's good to see you." Christopher's eyes go over my shoulder, and every one of my muscles tense as the presence of my father approaches from behind me.

"Son." My dad's crisp tone serves as a warning. Whatever I'm doing, he doesn't like it, and I better figure out what the fuck the problem is before he has to explain it.

I straighten to my full height and lower my chin,

hoping this is enough to appease him. "Father, how are you tonight?"

"Take care of your little brothers," he commands, not acknowledging my question.

Xander and Bash sit on a nearby sofa, watching the crowd around them while they whisper into each other's ears. They're definitely plotting something, and keeping them out of trouble is the last thing I want to do.

"But..." I protest.

My father turns to me, just enough to see his sharp glare, and the temperature plummets around me. "Are you questioning me?"

A chill runs down my spine. Whatever warmth he may have possessed as my father has been annihilated by the need for respect as the Lord of the Order of Saints.

"No, sir." I stare at my feet, not daring to look up, remembering the sharp crack of Damon's arm breaking the last time he dared to question our father.

I brace for impact, but thankfully, he walks off in the direction of the back staircase.

Air rushes from my lungs as relief washes over me. I'm such a fucking idiot. I learned young never to back talk to men like my father.

"I better go," Christopher says, moving to follow him.

"Good luck."

He smiles back at me. Something in the way he looks has the hair raising on my neck.

"I told you. I've got this all planned out."

I down the rest of my champagne, trying to discard a lingering unease that's clinging to me. Something feels off about this entire night, and I just want to get the fuck home.

"Miss Laurent. You look delicious this evening." A booming voice catches my attention, and I'm just fast enough to see Scarlet's smile falter before she smooths it back into place. The man can't be younger than sixty, with bushy white eyebrows and a combover that accentuates his receding hairline.

Who the fuck says that kind of thing? I'm expecting her father to step in since he hasn't left for his son's initiation yet, but if anything, he looks even happier.

It's odd that I don't recognize the man. This isn't an open party; every member is associated with the Order in some way. The fact that there's someone here who's not a member doesn't make sense, even if Mr. Laurent personally invited him.

I watch as Scarlet holds her hand out for him like she's supposed to, but she's paler than she was a second ago, and she visibly tenses when the man brings her fingers to his lips and leaves them there for several moments too long. She just stands there, visibly uncomfortable but not pulling away, not breaking a single society rule that tells her to obey the men around her.

I fucking hate every second of it.

The growing tension in my body doesn't start to ease until she pulls away from him, but just before she can

get her hand free, he tugs her against his chest and reaches around to grab her ass.

The crystal glass shatters in my grip, and the group breaks apart with the loud crack. I shift so my back's to them, and Scarlet doesn't see I've been watching her. I've sliced a line across my palm, and if I'm not fast, I'll be leaving a trail of blood behind me.

A quick glance over my shoulder shows Scarlet has escaped, and only her father and the pervert stand in my line of sight. Mr. Laurent should be raging, bringing down the full might of the Order. God knows I'd back him up, but instead, he's smiling and shaking the geezer's hand. A sickening realization descends on me. This can't be the guy Christopher was talking about. Right?

I need a fucking drink, something stronger than the bullshit being served here.

My two younger brothers are still on the sofa when I find them. I reach over Bash's shoulder and grab the silk pocket square from his jacket. Two eleven-year-olds dressed in suits should look ridiculous, but they've been raised for this. Not that they aren't more than capable of causing chaos if I don't keep an eye on them.

"Hey. I was looking good." Bash reaches for the silk fabric, and I lift it out of his reach, pressing it into the cut on my palm.

"I have to step out. Don't do anything stupid while I'm gone."

Both their heads tilt at the same time, and they give me matching grins.

Fucking Irish twins. I love them, but they can be creepy as hell.

"Just don't move, okay? I'll be back in a minute."

"Of course, big bro." They nod simultaneously with too-innocent grins.

I groan. I can't leave them in here alone for long, or they're likely to set something on fire.

"Be good."

The second I get outside, I fill my lungs with the crisp night air, washing away the weight of the overly packed hall. I tuck myself behind towering evergreens to my right that provide the perfect hiding spot. The Volkovs carved out this small area for guests who want to smoke without ruining their perfect image. I'd found it when a valet disappeared behind the cover one day, but I've never encountered anyone in the year I've been coming here. I take out a black flask from the inside pocket of my jacket and twist the cap.

If there's ever been a night I need a bit of numbness, it's tonight.

The cool liquid burns the back of my throat as I drink it down, and I nearly choke on my cough. Thank God Damon's not here, or I'd never hear the end of it.

I watch the parking lot through the small gap in the bushes. There's a seemingly endless line of black luxury cars, all looking nearly identical, even though they're different models. In a world of power, sameness has an odd hold on these people.

I swallow more whiskey, the taste swiftly morphing

from a burn to a smooth warmth. It had been buried in the back of my father's cabinet, so it probably cost a fortune. He'll kill me if he finds out, but thankfully, I never get caught.

The door opens beside me, and I disappear deeper into the shadows. It's only when I catch the red of Scarlet's dress that I step out, grasping her wrist and tugging her into hiding. I cover her mouth and pin her against the wall before she can scream and keep her there, wide eyes on me, until she calms down.

"You're not going to scream, right?" I tease, and I can't help my smirk. There's just something about her that brings out this side of me. Having her this close is a mistake. Her skin's warm from dancing, and her vanilla citrus scent fills my nose. Her soft panting breath, still rapid from the scare of being dragged in here, tickles my neck, sending shivers along my back. I've never been this close to her, and it's fucking with my head. I rip myself away before I do something stupid, like kiss her.

She rolls her eyes dramatically when I cross my arms, putting a semblance of a barrier between us, and whisper, "We need to stop meeting like this, or I'm going to think you're following me."

"You wish," she replies without missing a beat, her voice as soft as mine, but her poised demeanor doesn't snap back into place. Instead, her eyes travel over me, and pink covers her cheeks.

"You blushing for me, princess?"

"Have you always been this delusional?"

This isn't the first time we've run into each other in a tucked-away spot, both escaping the hell that is one of these parties. I've given up on telling her to get lost; I never could follow through on making her. I'm almost used to it now, her presence close in a quiet space, bickering with me about nonsense.

Almost *anticipate* it.

I take a swig and wipe the back of my hand across my mouth. "You looked like you were having fun in there."

Her blush vanishes, a sickening paleness taking its place, and an urge to walk back in there and beat the shit out of that old man settles into my gut. I hand her my flask. "Drink it. You look like you need it."

She chokes on it, covering her mouth as she stifles her cough. "What the hell is that?"

I shrug and take it back, easily taking another drink. I didn't tell her I had the same reaction minutes earlier.

"You're so prissy."

She ignores my comment, instead grabbing my hand that's wrapped in silk fabric. Blood had soaked through, turning it a deep red.

"What happened to your hand?" She takes it in her delicate fingers, careful not to touch the cut.

You happened.

I yank my arm back, hoping to God she can't see the blush crawling up the back of my neck. "None of your business."

Like fuck I'm going to tell her I cut it just because

some asshole old man touched her and made her uncomfortable.

"Another fight? You are such a delinquent." She narrows her eyes at me, nose scrunched up, and I can't help myself from thinking she's adorable like this. So much better than the serene calmness she'd worn before. I press her further, wanting to see more of the fire she tries to hide.

She can pretend all she wants, but she can't hide it from me.

"Is that what you think I am, a delinquent?"

She rips the flask from me with a huff and takes another sip. Her pink lips capture my thoughts as they wrap around the opening. This time, she doesn't cough, giving me a small smile in triumph.

"You might want to take a closer look at yourself before you go calling me names?"

"I'm not the one who's slept with half the girls here." She snaps her mouth closed, and her cheeks flush a deeper shade of pink.

I don't bother denying, stepping closer as an invisible thread pulls me toward her. I close the distance between us until she's forced to tip her head back to look at me. "Are you jealous?"

"Never." Her voice is breathy as her blue eyes meet mine, pupils blown wide in the shadows. Black lashes fan over her alabaster skin each time she blinks as her chest rises and falls in time with mine.

"Liar." It's as if I can't get enough oxygen, like the

only way I'll survive is breathing her in. A voice in the back of my head screams at me that I shouldn't be doing this, but I can't for the life of me think of a reason why.

Our lips nearly graze each other's when my father strides out of the side door, causing the temperature to dip even lower. He's on the phone, his voice angrier than he normally lets on, and I thank fuck I'm not the one on the receiving end.

I push Scarlet behind me, shielding her more.

"Who's there?" My father spins toward us like he has some kind of sixth sense or X-ray vision, and I swear under my breath.

I press my finger to my lips, telling Scarlet to be quiet, and point her to a path, hidden from sight by trees, that leads to another door. Her eyes are wide on mine, her body stubbornly stiff.

"Go," I mouth and push her until she starts moving.

I wait until she's far enough away before stepping out of our hiding spot and making a show of tucking my flask into my pocket. He'll make me pay for it later, but it's enough of a reason for me to be out here, that he won't question it more and look behind me. Scarlet had taken her own risk being out here. It would be social suicide for her to be caught behind there with me. Unlike normal people, the women of the Order are expected to stay pure until marriage. Even the thought of the word makes my stomach churn. Who the fuck still believes in that?

"You're supposed to be responsible for your broth-

ers." He uses the same tone he'd had on the phone, and dread fills my gut.

I swallow hard, looking at my feet. "I checked on them. They're fine. I'm going back in now."

"We'll speak about this tomorrow."

Chills run down my spine, but showing fear will only make it worse.

My muscles don't loosen until he gets into his car, his driver already ready with the door open, and he closes it behind him.

It's going to hurt like a bitch, but the memory of Scarlet's body near mine makes me think I won't regret it.

The squeal of tires fills the air as a Range Rover crashes through the steel gate.

My attention goes back to my dad, but none of his coldness is there. Instead, panic is written in his wide-eyed expression. He's struggling to open the door, but he can't get out.

A sick, coiling dread buries deep in my stomach as a sharp click comes from the car milliseconds before it detonates into splintered pieces. Heat flares against my skin as I'm thrown back, crashing against the marble steps leading up to the entry with a thud.

Ringing in my ears dulls my senses, and I heave, desperate to suck in a breath as the world turns to chaos around me.

Flames take up the space where my father's car was, their heat causing sweat to drip into my eyes.

Thank fuck, Scarlet's long gone.

My head aches from the explosion as I force myself up. There's screaming from inside the building, and I twist, trying to see what's happening. I have to get to my brothers and get the fuck out of here. Despite the heat, chills roll through me as the reality of the situation solidifies. If they've gone after my father, they'll be looking to take the rest of us out next. Bash and Xander's mischievous grins flash behind my eyes, and my stomach drops. They're still so fucking little, and I've left them in there *alone*.

I have to get to them. I can get them out if I can just get to them.

My throat burns, and pain radiates through my entire body as I roll onto my hands and knees, fighting against the thrumming in my head.

My father's words from minutes before loop in my brain. The boys are my responsibility.

Get up. Come on, you fucker, get up.

I clench my teeth against the piercing pain as I stand, surprised at how steady I am on my feet. It's the seconds of inattention that cost me. Arms hook around my shoulders from behind, and I'm ripped backward.

My elbow slams into my assailant's gut, earning me a pained grunt, but he doesn't let go, even as I throw my weight, thrashing against his hold.

"Got him, boss," my assailant calls out as he drags me backward toward a blacked-out truck.

I dig my feet into the ground, but it doesn't slow him down.

Rage is radiating through me, but it's not until Xander's and Bash's small forms are dragged out of the house, kicking and screaming, that I learn what true terror is.

My heart slams into my ribs, fear piercing through me like I'm being stabbed with thousands of shards of ice.

They have me constrained, but that doesn't stop me from slamming my booted heel into his foot with a sickening crunch. His grip loosens, and I use the opportunity to rip out of his grasp, but I don't make it five feet before a solid weight smashes into my temple, knocking me off my feet.

My head swirls with the force of the impact, and I blink away my blurred vision.

Christopher Laurent stares down at me, a cruel smile smeared across his face and a pipe raised above his head.

The iron taste of blood fills my mouth, coating my teeth, and I spit at him. "I'll hunt you fucking down."

He smirks, the bar raising higher. "No you won't."

His arm slashes downward, and everything goes black.

Chapter 55

Matthias

"You can't even stay still when you're out cold," a soft voice says, breath fanning over my ear, quickly followed by a sharp pain and a tugging sensation by my temple.

I fight against an oily fog that's pulling me back to sleep and slit my eyes open. When they adjust to the bright lamp placed inches away from my face, familiar startling blue eyes, surrounded by thick black lashes, blink back at me.

I jerk away, and there's a quick pinch where her hand touches my hairline. My thoughts are thick, like trudging through tar, as I try to piece everything together.

"Where am I?"

"Look what you did," she tsks, ignoring me, and swipes something wet over my skin.

I hiss through my teeth, pulling away.

She grips my head, keeping it still. "Don't be a baby. I'm almost done."

"Almost done what?" My voice croaks as I put more distance between us, and that's when I feel the tug of cold steel circling my neck and follow the thick chain-link cord to where I'm locked to the wall. Memories of being dragged into this room, handcuffed and collared, overtake me.

I'm going to fucking kill them all.

"Listen to me." Cool fingers clutch both sides of my head. "You need to stop moving. You're practically bleeding out at this point."

My jaw clenches, and I grip her arm until she winces, trying to pry herself from my grasp. Tears prick her eyes as I shake her hard enough for her teeth to click together.

"You did this. You took my brothers."

Scarlet shakes in my arms, body trembling as she begs me to understand. "It wasn't me. I didn't do this. I swear."

Each word is more of a plea than the last, and against my better judgment, I find my fingers loosening. Even at sixteen, I've learned to detect a lie. A glance away, a twitch, calculation, but her fear-filled, glistening eyes never leave mine.

"Explain. *Now*," I grit through my teeth. I should kill her, smear her brother's name across the wall with her blood. Show him exactly what happens when you mess with the Everette family.

As if feeling the shift in me, she stutters.

"I don't...I didn't... They're keeping me here..."

Fat teardrops roll over her cheeks, and I fight the urge to catch one.

"What do you mean they keep you here?"

"My brother—" she cries out when my fingers tighten, but she doesn't stop. "He made me come."

Trembling, sobbing, terrified. That's how I'd describe the girl in front of me. It's easy to see she's as much of a captive as I am.

Just a little sparrow caught in her cage.

"What happened to my little brothers?" I demand.

"They're in a different room," she replies immediately.

Hope is sour in my throat. "You've seen them?"

"Yes...just a little. They're together, confined in a bedroom but not chained."

Relief washes over me. They're okay. Or as okay as this fucked-up situation will allow.

"What about my father?" I ask, even though I know the answer.

She looks away. "He's dead."

I release her after she confirms what I already suspected, and she collapses forward, hands pressed into the hardwood floor, gasping breaths wheezing out of her. The twist in my chest has me looking away, giving her time to piece herself back together.

It's the first chance I have to examine my surroundings. Surprisingly, it's a regular room, not a dungeon like

I'd expect these assholes to have. There's a large oak desk, two club chairs pushed out of my reach, and a bookcase that lines the far wall. The odd angle of one of the shelves catches my attention. It's as if it's been pushed forward to open like a door.

"Is that how you got in here?" I ask a now glaring Scarlet. There's a fire in her gaze that does a decent job of covering the fear that lies below.

Good. She should be afraid. If she'd been smart, she'd have moved out of my reach and gotten the fuck out of here.

She rubs at her arm where finger-sized bruises are already forming. "I grew up coming here in the summer. It was to my advantage to spend a lot of time finding hidden spots in this old castle."

"There are no castles in Boston."

She sighs. "Did you really think they'd keep you close to home?"

Fuck. I race through possible scenarios, but nothing good can come from keeping us alive.

Scarlet lifts a needle and thread, reminding me of what she said earlier. Warm liquid slides down my face, and the sensation of blood pooling in the divot above my collarbone makes me want to gag.

She raises one delicate brow. "Are you going to let me finish, or am I going to watch you bleed out?"

I place my hands behind me in a sign of peace and tilt my head forward to give her a better angle. No

matter what else is happening, she's my best bet right now.

She lifts to kneel, bringing her face inches from mine, and I can just make out the rim of yellow and pale purple that surrounds her right eye.

My teeth scrape across each other. "Who hit you?"

She huffs out a laugh. "Who hasn't."

Before I say anything, she digs the needle into my skull, and I have to flex every muscle to keep myself from pulling away.

"Have you done this before?" I grunt out.

"No, but I've seen it done," she says, an apology edging her words.

"Comforting..."

"If you hadn't torn it when you woke up in the first place, you'd already be done by now." Her voice is clipped, none of the trembling that had been present before.

I can't help but smirk. "So this is *my* fault."

"Everything is your fault."

I don't dare move away in fear of her wielding that needle and respond, "You do realize they knocked me out to get me here."

My last memory is of a silver steel pipe barreling toward my head. Just the thought of her asshole brother has my teeth grinding together.

"You shouldn't have let yourself be caught to begin with. I honestly thought you Everettes were smarter than this."

Cornflower blue fills my vision as she waits for a response.

"Me too."

A slight flush crawls up her neck, stopping just below her ears before she goes back to torturing me. "I'm doing the best I can. Just stop moving."

I stiffen under her touch, obeying her request, and use this opportunity to gain information. There's no more powerful weapon than knowledge and who holds it. "How long have I been here?"

"Three days." She's so close, her breath fans over my temple. It reminds me of the moment behind the hedge right before the world got all fucked-up.

I wince when she tugs on the thread, then pierces my skin again.

She smooths her thumb under the cut. "Sorry...I tried using suture tape, but it wouldn't stop soaking through."

"It's fine. Not my first time getting stitches."

Her knuckles brush back a strand of my hair. "The scar is going to be awful. At least it'll be hidden in your hairline."

I chuckle under my breath. "I doubt I'll live long enough for it to scar."

She tenses before tying off the string with a knot and cutting the ends. "You'll get out."

Her fingers shake as she tucks away her supplies. She looks so small, ankles tucked under her knees, dress smudged with my blood.

I force playfulness into my tone, anything to stop whatever's playing in her mind, and lay my hand over hers. Her gaze shoots to meet mine.

My lips curve. "Promises, promises. I'm going to hold you to that."

She pulls her hand away. "Why do I feel like I just made a deal with the devil?"

I cock my head to the side. "I'm not sure I'm the devil in this situation, Little Sparrow."

Voices come from the hall, and her eyes widen. "Pretend you're still unconscious, and keep your stitches covered by your hair."

I smirk, knowing damn well that's the coward's way out. "Now, where's the fun in that."

"You're an idiot." She scrambles up, shutting the bookcase behind her milliseconds before her brother's face appears in the door.

I crank my chain, covering the sound of her hiding spot clicking shut just as the asshole walks in.

"I've been waiting a long time to see this. Matthias Everette on the ground, helpless at my feet," Christopher says, careful not to come within reach.

A slow smile curls the corner of my mouth, daring him. "Why don't you come closer, and we'll test just who's helpless."

"No need for that. You've lost, and as soon as we get Damon, you are all going to die slow, painful deaths." He picks at his nails. "Your little brothers are pretty close, aren't they? I'll be honest, I've never understood the

appeal of sibling friendship. I thought of killing them together, but don't you think it would be more fun to have the one watch as we dice the other one up? Like a two-for-one torture."

I crash forward, held back by my collar, foaming at the mouth like a rabid dog. "Do not fucking touch them."

"Who's going to stop me? *You*?" He smirks, and I want to rip it off his face. "You're all tied up at the moment." He looks down the hall. "You know what? I bet you're close enough to hear them scream."

Steel digs into my throat, the dull edge cutting into my skin, and blackness crowds my vision as I press forward, desperate to get close to him.

Christopher laughs. "I am so happy I got to see you like this. The great Matthias Everette. Nothing more than a mindless bitch."

"Boss, we've got a problem." A guard enters the room, a crisp gray uniform shirt tucked into black pants. He looks more like a rent-a-cop than a threat. He doesn't make eye contact with me. Even tied up, I can feel his fear, practically smell it wafting off him like the animal they've made me.

"I'm fucking busy." He gestures for the guard to leave, but the man doesn't budge.

"It's your sister, boss. She's trashing her room."

Christopher looks up and to the right, his fists clenching and unclenching at his sides. He turns and looks at me. "That cunt's going to regret distracting me."

My heart thuds in my chest. The only thing

replaying in my mind is I can't let him get to her. Not when he's like this. Not when he's clearly still raging to hurt someone.

The sacrifice is easy. I'll gladly take the pain if it means she doesn't have to feel it.

"Pussy." I let disdain and challenge drip from my voice. "You always were a little bitch."

"What the fuck did you just say to me?" His eyes are wide on me, the whites visible on all sides. He looks rabid.

Good, that's how I need him. I can't let him control his emotions. I want them all directed on me.

"I called you a pathetic little bitch." I spit, and it lands on his cheek.

The thread holding Christopher together visibly snaps, his face twisting in rage. His fist comes flying, crashing into my cheeks. Pain radiates through my skull, making my ears ring.

I smile, letting the blood show on my teeth. "That all you got?"

The next punch lands right above my eye socket, the force rocking me back, followed by a kick to the stomach that has me hunching over, unable to breathe.

I force myself to stay upright on my knees. I need to stretch this out as long as possible if I'm going to succeed in taking the heat off Scarlet.

He lands hit after hit until his blows finally slow, the strength leaching out of him. I'm lucky he's so fucking weak, clearly not trained to do lasting damage.

No...why would he be? His victims are always weaker than him.

My forearms slam onto the ground, catching me before I face-plant headfirst. Blood pools beneath my face, running from my nose and mouth. It takes several breaths to find the strength to look up.

"You are going to regret this." Christopher wipes blood off his knuckles. They're split open from connecting with my bones. I have to hide my smirk at the fact that more than one of them is sunken in, a sure sign that he broke them.

His face is ruddy red, chest rising and falling as he tries to regulate himself. He looks worn-out when he tells the guard, "Deal with my sister. I have somewhere to be."

I nearly snort, knowing he'll be going directly to a doctor to protect his precious hands. Like I said, pussy.

Those blue eyes, so similar to Scarlet's, stare back at me. "I'll be back, asshole. I'm going to drag this out nice and slow."

"Looking forward to it."

I don't even dodge his kick, knowing his pride wouldn't let me get away with that level of snark.

The thing he doesn't understand is I'm already fucking crazy. There's nothing he can do to me here that I wouldn't willingly take on for my family.

"They'll never follow you," I bark after him, enjoying the way he stiffens mid-stride. "You have to be

smart to be a Lord of the Order of Saints, and you're a fucking idiot."

His booted foot lands firmly into my gut, causing me to gag on air. "Big words from someone who's chained to my wall."

I struggle to breathe, and my eyes fill with water, but I don't miss the glint of metal on the guard's hip.

Please tell me he's stupid enough to bring my key into the room.

Christopher steps closer and spits on me but has to jump back to avoid my kick.

"Better be careful, Chrissy." I give him my wildest smile, letting my demon shine through. I may be the one chained, but he has no idea what he's gotten himself into.

He seems to sense the shift in the air because there's a slight stutter to his voice as he hisses, "Fuck you," and lets the door slam behind him.

The sharp clack of the lock snapping in place fills the space.

Sighing, I collapse back, eyes drifting to the bookshelf. I can only hope that was enough to keep her safe.

Chapter 56

Matthias

"LET ME SEE YOUR STITCHES," Scarlet says the second she comes through the hidden door in the bookcase. Her hands are full with the same medical aid case she's brought with her the last three days and a small brown bag.

Each day has been nearly identical. Get the shit kicked out of me the night before and wake up to her complaining about me tearing my stitches the next morning.

I take the bag she holds out for me and search through it to see a sandwich and a crisp green apple.

My stomach growls, and her lips twitch.

I raise the sandwich to my mouth, pausing right before my first bite. "You're not going to poison me, are you?"

"I'm not sure you're aware of this, but I don't need to

507

poison you in this situation." Her gaze roams over my chains, then my cut.

"Fair." I take a bite, ignoring the pain in my gums, and hum in the back of my throat. If this is how she's going to kill me, I'm down.

I finish in a few short bites and tuck the apple near the wall for later. I'm not sure what she risks by coming here, but I'm positive neither of us wants to find out.

She holds up a thin antibacterial cloth. "Ready?"

I flinch back. "No fucking way. That shit hurts."

"And you called *me* the prissy one. It's not that bad." She chuckles, and it's a light, cheerful sound, one that doesn't belong anywhere near here. The fact that she's able to make it tells me there's nothing about this that shocks her. I hate the thought of her being the one on the receiving end of her family's pitifulness. She's strong, maybe even stronger than me.

The entire situation pulls on my pride, and I force myself to stay perfectly still as she pokes at her stitches for several seconds.

Her neck is inches from my nose, and the sweet smell of citrus and vanilla fills my senses, momentarily stealing all of the blood from my brain.

Scarlet pulls back, completely unaware of the state I'm in, and smiles. "See? Not too bad. It's ugly, like I figured, but at least you aren't bleeding everywhere."

She grabs a regular face cloth from her bag and soaks it with a bottle of water before rubbing it harshly against my neck.

"Hey." I inhale sharply. "That hurts."

Little nails dig into my skin as she holds me still. "Relax. You're covered in blood. If we get out of here, you'll have to pay me to keep all your whining a secret."

"You don't need to be so aggressive."

She smiles, a glint in her eyes. "I'll try to be gentle."

Ignoring the warmth spreading through my chest, I take her in as she cleans, not bothering to tell her I can do it myself.

She looks better. The bruise around her eye is a faint yellow. Relief releases the tension in my muscles as I scan her, happy there's no signs of new marks. At least I know my plan to keep Christopher's attention on me is working.

She's pulled her hair into a ponytail-bun thing that sits messily at the top of her head. An oversized sweatshirt falls below her thighs, covering bright purple leggings. It's such a far cry from the perfectly styled pieces I'm used to seeing her in.

"Nice outfit."

"You're one to talk." She tosses her cloth back into her bag and sits with her back against the wall beside me, her head tipped back and her eyes closed. She's left herself completely vulnerable to me, and instead of taking advantage, a sense of power flows through me at her trust.

I shake the feeling off and sit in an identical position beside her. She shouldn't be here, but I selfishly don't want her to go. When she's here, everything else washes

away as all of my attention fixes on her. I want to live in these stolen moments. I want them to stretch out forever until the only reality is me and her.

I close my eyes and pretend like we're anywhere else.

We sit in silence for several moments. She's practically vibrating against the stillness beside me. Clearly, my Little Sparrow does not like the quiet. I count the seconds in my head. Five, four, three, two..."

"Do you like sweet or savory?"

"That's really the question you're going to ask me?"

"Come on. You've got to be bored here."

Bored? Not with the way the heat from her arm transfers into mine. I wait until I can feel her ready to wring my neck before answering. "Sweet."

There's something about riling her up that gets to me. To be fair, I don't give a fuck what we talk about when she glares at me like that. I just want her to stay. She helps me forget this fucked-up situation. I'm not stupid enough to think we're getting out. A part of me doesn't want Damon to show up because if they catch him, this is all over.

Christopher's clever. He knows he can't leave any of us alive if he plans on taking the Everette family's spot in the Order of Saints.

Scarlet doesn't force me to answer, instead filling the silence with random, meaningless things that calm me way more than it should.

"You know, I'm kind of jealous of you." Her voice is

soft, and she's staring at a moth fluttering around the ceiling light.

"Me? Chained and about to die?"

She shrugs. "First, you're not going to die. That big brother of yours is going to get you out of here." She sounds so positive that a trickle of hope slips in.

A blankness takes over her features. "Death is its own form of freedom though. At least that's the last decision anyone can make for you."

An eerie feeling prickles down my neck and sits like a rock in my stomach. What has she been going through to talk like that?

I brush back a strand of her hair, my handcuffs clicking together. "Don't give them that kind of power over you."

Her eyes close, breath leaving her. "What if it's my decision? My power for once."

A shudder runs through me as my blood grows cold. "Don't talk like that."

She smiles up at me, a lightness in her tone that makes me think I've imagined everything she just said. "What will you do when you escape? I know what I'd do."

"What's that?" I humor her, not wanting that sadness to creep back in.

"Run." She sighs out a breath. "They're trying to force me to marry some old guy. All this talk about duties and alliances. Like I don't know I've been *sold*."

My teeth grind together. "What do you mean?

They're marrying you off *now*?" I knew she was betrothed, but even in our fucked-up world, the marriage wouldn't happen until after she turns eighteen.

"Yeah, that's why they're keeping me here." She smiles, eyes trained on that moth. "They're worried I'll run away."

Fuck.

She trails her fingers along her neck. "I guess they don't think I need to be shackled to keep me in line."

I bump her shoulder with mine, drawing her attention. "I'm glad they underestimated you."

That earns me a smirk and a minuscule shake of her head. I want her attention back on me. I want to know everything about her, so I ask, "If you could choose, what would your future look like?"

Tears pool at the corner of her eyes. "If I got out, I wouldn't even think about settling down until I'm twenty-five. No men, no expectations, no commitment. Complete freedom."

My chest clenches because I want to give that to her. Rage boils in my stomach, knowing I won't be able to see it happen. Knowing that even if I find a way to get her and my brothers out of here, there's no escaping for me. If Damon does show up and all of us die, I swear I'll get her out first. I'll grant her wish before those bastards get to kill me. I've come to terms with dying. It's enough to know she'll be free.

"Oh yeah? Then what?" I want her to tell me every-

thing so I can survive on the thoughts of her when she's out of here.

She turns to me with a genuine smile. "Then I'll find a guy, get married, and have a half dozen kids. Live in an eggshell-blue house with white trim and a wood shake roof. With a wraparound porch and a tire swing hanging from a tree. I want to be chased around my backyard by jelly-covered faces. Is that too much to ask?"

I can picture her, hair lifted by the wind, as kids that look just like her follow behind. I suck in a raspy breath and scrunch my nose to hide my thoughts. "That sounds awful."

She throws her head back and laughs. "Maybe, but it sounds perfect to me."

"I'll get you out of here," I promise.

A sad smile curves her lips. "No you won't." She starts to collect all her things, tossing them into her bag. "By the end, you won't even want to."

I hate the way she doesn't meet my eyes. She doesn't realize just how impossible her words are. "They won't break me."

"I know." She tilts her head toward me and brushes her fingertips over her lips. "Kiss me."

I swallow hard, not trusting my own ears. "What?"

"I don't want my first kiss to be some gross old guy who's willing to marry a fifteen-year-old girl."

All I see is blue when she says, "I want it to be you."

I twist so that I'm kneeling in front of her and lean forward until my forehead presses against hers. I inhale

each of her breaths as I build up the nerve to speak. "I'll be the one to marry you when you turn twenty-five."

Her eyes shoot wide, but I kiss her before she can say anything. I know I won't be alive by then. I know I'm going to die chained to this wall, but that doesn't mean I can't want it.

I deepen the kiss, running my tongue along hers. She's inexperienced, and I hate the fact that I won't be here to fix that, at the same time loving that she'll be my last. I break the kiss and move to the side, ignoring the pounding of my heart. There's a cruelty to letting me find her here.

"You should run along now, Little Sparrow. Don't come back."

Chapter 57

Matthias

IT'S BEEN two days since Scarlet's visited me, and I try to convince myself it's for the best. I can't keep living in the delusion that I might have her one day. The most I can hope for is she finds a way to get free of all of this.

I roll the apple she gave me between my palms. Even starving, I can't bring myself to eat it.

A sharp, high-pitched scream rips me out of my thoughts, filling every nook and cranny of my room. I stand, moving as close to the door as my chain will allow.

Another scream, this one a begging plea, sends a shiver down my spine. The voice is too young, too innocent to sound like that. It goes on and on, alternating from one small voice to another.

The bloodcurdling noise has every muscle in my body pulled taut as the weight of who it is slams me down to my knees.

"Let them go!" I yell until my throat's raw, but it

never stops. On and on, the sound of young cries eats away at my sanity.

"Please. I'll do fucking anything. Please," I beg the empty space around me.

Tears stream down my face as my breath grows shallow, the screams digging into my skull as the feeling of hopelessness overwhelms me. It's all my fault. If I hadn't been cocky—like my name alone would save me—Christopher wouldn't have gone after my little brothers. He's hurting them to punish me.

Time warps around me as I curl into a ball, not daring to block out the noise. I owe them this. I owe my brothers to be here with them.

Soft hands touch my back, and I whirl around, barely catching Scarlet as she falls backward.

Red-rimmed blue eyes meet mine as words I can't understand pour out of her. She moves closer, as if she's approaching a rabid animal that's too far gone to be reasoned with.

She kneels in front of me, gripping both sides of my face, and brings her mouth to my ear.

"It's not them." She says the words on repeat. "It's not them. It's not them. It's a recording from a horror movie. It's not real."

She grips my ears, tugging me back so our gazes meet. "It's not them. Please listen to me. It's a recording. It's not real."

"It's...it's not real." I replay her words, letting them form on my own lips. "It's a recording."

I search her eyes for the lie, but I don't see it. "How do you know?"

"I checked on them. They're not even on this level. They're upstairs." Tears run down her cheeks. "I promise. It's not real."

I collapse against her, my body trembling with the adrenaline pounding through my veins as I hold her tight like she's the only thing holding me together. Fingers stroke my hair as I fight against the screams still coming from the hall.

Scarlet's breath fans the shell of my ear as she tells me over and over again that it's not real.

Rage builds like an ember in my gut, slowly igniting until my entire being feels like it's on fire.

When she looks at me this time, her eyes are wide, filled with terror. She startles back, ass hitting the ground as she puts distance between us at whatever she can see inside my soul. Good. She needs to get away from me because I'm going to destroy everything in this godforsaken building. Light it up until all that's left is ashes.

"What the fuck are you doing here." The guard from earlier comes crashing through the room to grab Scarlet, yelling for backup.

His mistake.

I grab the apple I'd been saving and slam it into his mouth. The crisp scent fills the air as it knocks his teeth in. He lets her go, hands instinctively moving to take it out, but his distraction is his downfall.

Even with my wrists chained together, I'm able to grip his neck between my palms and snuff the life out of him, not letting go until he's limp. The only thing holding him up is my grip on his crushed windpipe.

I grab the keys from his hip, desperate to get this collar off me, a dangerous giddiness overtaking my senses at the thought of being free. My fingers fumble with the lock, but it's impossible to reach where it's attached to my neck.

"Take it off." I toss the key to Scarlet, who catches it between trembling fingers.

"I'm sorry." Her brows pinch, teeth chattering together. "I can't...I can't let you go. It'll ruin everything."

"Is this some kind of sick joke? Take it off, Scarlet."

"Just wait. I can explain." She grips the key, holding it behind her back. The small motion feels like a knife sliced through my chest, cracking my ribs and splitting me until the sharp blade is buried in my gut.

She steps away, but her mistake is not moving fast enough. I swing my leg out, taking hers from underneath her, and drag her toward me.

I climb over her, hands going over her throat like they just were on the guard. "Give me the key."

She looks to the side, where I can see the silver metal glinting just out of reach.

I tighten my grip. "They have my fucking brothers."

"I know. Let me explain—" My fingers tighten, cutting off her words, and a growl rips from my throat.

"You fucking cunt."

She struggles against my hold, hips bucking against mine, trying to unseat me, but she's too small, too delicate. Too easy to snap.

The firmer I press, the less she fights, the light I've admired the last few days dimming. I should kill her now, revel in it, but my stomach churns, and bile climbs up my throat at the thought.

Delicate fingers gently wrap around my cuffed wrists, and it's only then that what I'm doing really hits me.

Fuck.

I throw myself off her, disgust coating my tongue. "Get the fuck out of here before I change my mind."

She scrambles to her feet, back hitting the shelves out of reach. "You don't understand."

"You're right I don't fucking understand. Did your brother send you here? Was this all some kind of sick game? Were you supposed to worm your way in? Bat your pretty lashes?"

"I can explain—"

My chest heaves as I cut her off. "I hope they catch you. I hope you spend the rest of your days under your old-ass husband, having to take his wrinkly fucking dick. I hope you spend the rest of your life miserable for what you did to my brothers.

"I'm sorry." A sob escapes her lips, and she ducks through her bookshelf.

I slam my fist into the ground the second it closes

behind her, a scream ripping from my throat. The sharp slice of betrayal wreaks havoc like knives through my ribs, tearing me to shreds.

I collapse until my forearms press into the floor, and my head rests against them, taking heaping lungfuls of air as the reality of my idiocy hits me. How the fuck could I let her in?

I wait for hours for what will come next, the dead guard stiff and wide-eyed at my feet. I keep my thoughts blank, not trusting them not to stray too terrified blue eyes.

It's the sound of gunshots that pulls me out of my daze, but it's Damon's face dripping with blood that has me standing.

My eyes search him, unable to process that he's here. He's in black tactical gear, guns holstered all over his body, covered in deep red speckles as if he's been sprayed over his arms and neck.

Xander and Bash come up behind him. Their eyes are haunted, but they have wicked smiles on their lips. Both of them have knives in their tiny hands, tipped in blood.

I shake my head, praying this isn't a dream.

"How," I say roughly, barely able to get the word out. "How did you find us?"

Damon crosses the distance between us, cupping my cheeks with callused fingers over the same spot delicate ones held hours before.

"Scarlet."

I flinch at her name. "No, she betrayed me."

"No, brother. She called me. Set everything up. She told me to tell you she's sorry, but you would have ruined everything if you got out before I arrived."

It's like a punch to the gut. I fucked up. "I have to get to her."

I move toward the bookshelf, breaking from Damon's grasp. "I need to make sure she's okay."

Damon grabs my arm and hauls me with him. "She's already safe. You should've seen what she did to her father on her way out. Fucking beautiful."

A laugh bubbles up from my throat, escaping my mouth in a wild cackle.

She's free.

Chapter 58

Scarlet

I TUCK my knees further under my chin, the narrow hidden hallway making it impossible to get comfortable. My heart pounds as the minutes tick by, each one feeling slower than the last. I've been waiting quietly for Damon for the past few hours, left alone in this dark, cramped space with my thoughts tumbling over themselves as my memories of Matthias's face twisting in betrayal replay on repeat.

My chest burned with a desperate longing to tell him why he needed to stay, but I couldn't risk being overheard.

The plan is simple. The three Everette brothers stay in place until Damon comes and gets them. That way, no one gets accidentally blown up during the rescue mission. If all of the Everette brothers don't survive, none of them will forgive themselves. I may not be

directly responsible for them being captured, but it's my responsibility to fix what my family started.

Everything was on track until that stupid guard walked in with the key.

Matthias loomed above me, grip cutting off my air, and for a second, I believed I deserved it. His voice cracked as he begged me for a reason I would deceive him. Because from his angle, there was no other way to look at it. I couldn't give him the key, and explaining wasn't an option at that moment, which left him breaking apart. Even with all the reasons to kill me, he still let me go, and my heart cracked at the revulsion in his eyes as he spewed his hate at me while demanding I leave.

It'll all come to light soon, but I will never forget the way his face cracked above me.

The first explosion rocks the castle, sending me hard against the door. I'd been careful to give Damon our exact locations to guarantee we wouldn't be accidental collateral in his invasion. I wait patiently for the four planned explosions to go off before pushing open the concealed door that had kept me out of sight. I needed to get into position; I have my own tasks to complete in order for this to be a success.

"You fucking cunt! I know you did this." Christopher grips my shoulders and slams my back against the wall, knocking the air out of me. I'm wheezing for breath as pain radiates along my shoulder blades as they dig into the wood paneling. Shock rolls through me as I'm

slammed repeatedly, my skull connecting with each one. I dig my nails into his forearm, blood dripping from the wounds, but nothing I do slows him down. My feet connect with his shins, but he's too enraged to register the pain.

I hadn't accounted for him being in this room. He should've gone to fight by now. I'd miscalculated just how much of a coward he is, and now I'm going to pay for it.

"Fuck you!" I grit through clenched teeth as I fight through the fog rapidly taking over and spit at him. It's thick as it rolls down his face.

This time, the connection with the wall is hard enough to make my vision go white. Ice fills my veins as the realization overtakes me.

I'm going to die here.

My body buzzes as I slowly lose the battle and accept that my brother's going to kill me. Not that I can blame him. I fully intended for him to die tonight. I can only pray that Damon's more successful than I am.

A loud bang ricochets through the room, and warm liquid splatters my face, soaking my dress. I blink at Christopher's half-missing face. He stands there like his body doesn't realize it's dead for several seconds before crashing to the ground.

"You alright?" Damon's beside me, checking my wounds, his brows pinched together as he takes me in.

My heart thunders in my chest. He's just bought me the time I desperately need. "I'm fine. Go do your job."

He looks me over one last time before releasing me and handing me a gun. "You're fucking crazy."

"Yell at me after." I sway on my feet but catch myself before I can fall. Nothing's going to stop me from completing what I have to do.

We both exit the room, but when he turns to where his brothers are being held, I continue down the hall and out the back door leading to the helipad. Rain beats down around me, soaking through my clothes, but I don't feel the cold. Not when my prey's standing in front of me.

"I knew you'd be here," I yell above the whooshing sound of the helicopter blades cutting through the air. There was no way my father would let himself be caught here.

He freezes in place as I raise the gun and point it directly at his chest. The pilot looks away as if he knows to stay out of this.

"Honey, you're hurt. Just put the gun down, Scarlet. We can sort everything out. You don't have to marry anyone you don't want to, I promise," my father says, voice placating me, but even with death pointed at him, he still can't hide the condescension. I'll never be anything more than a tool to grow the family's influence for him.

"Oh, this?" I pull at my damp shirt. "Don't worry. The blood's not mine." I hate this man more than anyone in this world, so I smile and say, "Your son made quite the mess when he died."

My father lurches forward but stops himself when my finger loops over the trigger.

"You should be proud of me, *Dad*." I sneer the last word and take a step closer. "I'm the reason this is all falling apart. You, of all people, should appreciate that level of scheming. I learned it from you, after all. I contacted Damon and told him where we are. I timed the guard's schedule and knew exactly when security was at its most vulnerable."

"Ungrateful bitch," his voice booms, but I no longer cower beneath it. This time, I'm the one with the power.

"Ungrateful? Ungrateful for what? For you beating me? Controlling everything I do? Locking me up in this gold-plated excuse of a prison? No?" I raise a brow, moving even closer until there are only a few feet between us. "Oh, should I be thankful that you sold me to some perved-out fifty-year-old man? Tell me, *Daddy*. Did you get a good deal?"

"I'm unarmed. You can't shoot me." His voice trembles, his body visibly shaking.

"Says who?" I shrug and squeeze the trigger, watching as red blooms from his chest. I'm near enough that his blood soaks my dress as I loom over him, firing round after round, not trusting a monster like him to be dead.

In the end, no matter how much pain he'd caused, he's only a man, and men can be killed.

I fire one last shot before turning around to see Damon and his two youngest brothers wide-eyed, gaping

at me. My breaths come out hard as I struggle to regain my composure.

It's over.

As if sensing I need a moment to get myself together, Damon calls out to me, "I'll meet you out front."

I nod, unable to speak, holding myself straight only long enough for the three boys to disappear back into the house. Tears stream down my cheeks as I'm rocked with a million emotions. The earth-shattering relief that we survived is tainted by the fact that it's my family's fault that all of this happened to begin with. I'm the only remaining Laurent, and I won't be able to avoid the Order's hatred.

I hold my head high as I walk around the building to where Damon and Matthias are already waiting. The two younger Everettes are huddled together under a blanket only a few feet away.

"You good?" Damon asks. There's a hardness to his features, any playfulness he'd once had carved out of his face.

"I'm fine," I lie, not wanting his pity.

I don't notice my hand still wrapped around the gun until Matthias is slowly releasing my fingers. His deep brown eyes meet mine for several seconds, some unknown secret written there.

He leans in closer, whispering, "You're safe now."

My shoulders drop, and I sway on my feet when he gives me a hint of a smile, easily catching me. However

he feels about my betraying him is buried under the happiness of escaping.

"We'll debrief in thirty minutes," Damon cuts in.

The adrenaline's already wearing off, taking every ounce of my energy with it. I wipe my face, my hand coming back sticky. I'm not sure how much longer I can do this.

"I'm taking her to the hotel," Matthias says, with no room for argument in his tone. Damon's not the only one who's changed. This past week has taken a toll that will leave permanent scars on all of us, no matter that it ended in our favor.

A muscle ticks in Damon's jaw before he gives us a small nod. "Meet me in the lobby tomorrow morning, Scarlet."

"Yes, Lord." I bow my head to him in the respect his position commands. Matthias's warm fingers tip my chin up.

"You don't bow to anyone." His brown eyes are soft but sure as he runs his thumb along my cheek.

Warmth spreads throughout my chest, chasing away my thoughts as he replaces them with himself. We'd made it. I had faith that Damon could get Matthias out, but my plan didn't guarantee me the same. There was a decent chance my father would kill me first.

I let Matthias tuck me to his side and guide me toward a large black SUV. Acid burns in the back of my throat when I don't recognize the driver. I'm stopped

when Matthias leans in, his breath brushing my temple sending shivers down my neck.

"He's one of ours. Let me keep you safe."

My body relaxes into his, my muscles turning into Jell-O as I climb into the car. My limbs feel like they're being held down by weights, and Matthias catches me, maneuvering me until I'm able to lean against the opposite door.

"The hotel's about twenty minutes from here. Get some rest." His heat sinks into my skin as he reaches over me, causing my heart to skip wildly. His lips are so close to mine, and I can practically taste them. My chest clenches as I wait, desperate for his kiss, but he turns away from me, leaving my heart crashing against my ribs, and pulls my seat belt over my lap, clicking it in place.

I'm too tired to be embarrassed, and I let the door take my weight, drifting off to sleep.

My body jostles, shifting up and down in a steady cadence, drawing me out of my dreamless sleep. Matthias is looking down at me, a line between his brows. I hate to see the worry there and want to tell him I'm okay, but I know he'd sense the lie. Instead, I reach up and brush my finger across it, smoothing it out.

"I didn't mean to wake you." His voice is low, barely above a whisper.

I look around at the unfamiliar hallway. The wallpaper looks gilded in gold, with crystal light illuminating overhead. "Where are we?"

"We're at Hotel Savant. Damon's set up multiple

guards around the building and throughout the halls." He says it without me asking, knowing I need reassurance. I'm not sure when I'll ever feel safe again.

He tugs me closer, his familiar scent filling my nose. "Nearly to our room."

Our.

The word bounces around in my head like it can't find a spot to land. There's no reason for us to share a room, but I can't bring myself to protest it. I'm not sure I could make it through tonight on my own. There's a connection built in trauma that holds me to this boy, one that won't ever fade. After everything, there's no one I'll feel safer with than him.

Matthias stops in front of a room and swipes a card over the keypad. It beeps, lighting up green, letting us in.

The bed is calling my name, but there's no amount of exhaustion that could get me to climb in while caked in blood.

I wiggle until Matthias puts me down, then points to what I assume is the bathroom. "I'm going to shower."

He doesn't let go of my arm, instead taking a step with me.

"Alone." I raise a curious brow at him, and he startles back as if just realizing what he's doing.

The water's hot enough to turn my skin red as I scrub off the evidence of what I did tonight. I've never killed anyone before, and it was a hell of a way to start. No matter how evil he was, he was still my father. I stay

in the shower until the water turns from red to clear at my feet. I'm barely able to keep myself up by the time I climb out.

I wrap a towel around myself and step through an archway that leads to a small room with double vanities. This place is bigger than some studio apartments. There's a pile of clothes neatly folded on an ottoman in the middle of the room. I don't have the brainpower to even make a joke about why someone would need to sit while getting ready.

The black oversized shirt slides easily over my head, engulfing me to my thighs. The next item of clothing is a pair of boxers that I eye dubiously. I don't really have a choice at the moment, so I pull them on, pushing any mortification I might feel until later.

Matthias is waiting for me, sitting at the foot of the bed. His hair is wet, and he's changed into different clothes. He must have gone to one of his brothers' rooms while I was in the shower. With each step, my pulse races faster until I'm nearly out of breath. Tears prick at my eyes as I run my finger over my crude stitches that are just above his temple.

I smile softly. "I'm surprised you didn't tear these again."

"I was careful just for you." His tone is exhausted but playful. "Plus, most of the fun was already over before Damon got me out."

My heart squeezes, and I lift my hands from touching him. I'd taken that revenge away from him, and

no matter how solid the reasoning was, I'm sure he'll always resent me a little.

Matthias wraps his arms around me, tugging me closer, then lifting me into the air as he stands.

"Stop thinking so much." He lowers me onto the bed, pulling the plush blanket over me until it's tucked under my chin.

He steps back, and I reach for him, my hand catching his, holding him in place.

"Stay." My voice is weak, but there's no mistaking the plea.

He squeezes my fingers before letting go. "Nothing could stop me. I'm just climbing in on the other side."

I fall into him as he wraps his arms around me from behind, tucking me under his chin. The warmth of his chest soaks through the thin fabric of my shirt and into my back, relaxing my muscles as the steady rhythm of his heartbeat lulls me under.

Chapter 59

Scarlet

MY ENTIRE BODY hurts as I slowly rise from my sleep, the light from the early morning landing on my face. I don't have a phone, but the clock says it's already past nine. Definitely late to my meeting with Damon. I go to get up, only to be pulled backward, an arm banding around my waist.

"Where are you going?" Matthias murmurs into my nape, his voice raspy with sleep.

I laugh, wiggling against his hold. "I'm going to meet with Damon."

He lifts, but I stop him with a hand on his chest. "Stay here and keep the bed warm. I'll be right back."

He hums under his breath and snuggles into his pillow. He hadn't fully woken up, making falling back to sleep easy. He looks even younger than sixteen, with his face relaxed with sleep and his hair wild around him. I brush a strand, careful not to touch where he's bruised.

I'm not sure I have the right to touch him this way or what's going to happen in the future. What I do know is a piece of me will always seek him out. That everything we've been through has tied me to him forever. There's a bubbling sensation in my chest that I don't dare to acknowledge. Whatever's between us feels too big for us, being so young.

I lean down and place a kiss on his forehead, knowing it may be my only chance, then get up and go to meet Damon, grabbing a robe on the way out.

The conference room's open, and I groan when I see Damon dressed in a perfectly tailored suit.

"Come on." I gesture to him, then my clearly under-dressed state. "That's not fair."

He huffs out a laugh. "You seem better this morning."

Am I?

"I'm okay enough. What did you want to talk to me about?"

"The Everette family owes you a great debt." He's so formal in the way he's speaking, taking on his role of the head of the Order of Saints with ease. He stands and comes before me, his head bowed.

I take a step back. There's no way the Lord is bowing to me.

"It's my family's fault to begin with."

He sighs. "Matthias told me you'd be stubborn. Just listen."

I clamp my mouth shut.

"I will use my position as Lord to protect you and will guarantee the Laurents' place will remain open in the Order."

I shake my head. I never expected any of this. "There's no need to do that."

"Scarlet, it's the only way your family's funds can be transferred to you. Even as it is, it won't move over until you're eighteen."

"So I'll be the new Order member?" I tilt my head to the side, scanning him.

He looks away for a moment before answering, "Sorry...even I can't change tradition. The title will pass to your husband when you marry."

I cross my arms over my chest, hiding the way my hands shake. "You're not going to marry me off, are you?"

He steps backward, revulsion clear in his face. "You saved my family. I'll give you whatever you want."

I swallow hard as a lightness fills me. With his words, the ever-present weight lifts off my shoulders. In my entire life, I've never been given a choice, and to have it now has me almost drunk on giddiness.

Smiling, I look him dead in the eyes, letting him know I'm serious. "Don't marry me off to anyone. I don't care how good the match is. I want to go to college, get a degree and a freaking job. I want a life of my own creation with no one telling me what to do."

There's a bubbly, tingling sensation climbing up my chest, threatening to break through in a laugh. I'm

hopping from foot to foot, unable to completely contain the feeling.

Damon glances over my shoulder, then back to me. "What do you want me to do if someone asks me to set you up with them?"

My answer's quick on my lips, no hesitation. "Don't tell me. If someone's interested, I don't want to hear about it until I'm at least twenty-five. If they are really serious about me and not just the title, they'll be willing to wait."

A muscle ticks in his jaw as he glances behind me again. I nearly turn with the curiosity to see what he's looking at. "Are you sure that's what you want?"

My smile's so wide I'm practically beaming. "Positive."

"You've got yourself a deal." He holds his hand out in front of him, and I stare at it for a second before shaking it. "If you ever need anything, just let me know. The Everette family will always be there for you."

"There you go again, being all stiff," I scoff.

Damon softens for a second. "I can see what he sees in you."

"Who?"

Damon gestures with his head to where Matthias is leaning against the doorway. He's wearing different clothes, and his bandages have all been replaced.

I walk up to him and smirk. "What, you didn't like stitches? Had to go to an *actual* doctor?"

"They were crooked." His tone is missing the teasing

I've come to expect. The gold in his eyes somehow dims when he straightens.

"How long have you been listening?" I smile at him.

His eyes dart away from mine. "Long enough."

What is wrong with him? Whatever it is, I'll help him figure it out. "Want to get breakfast?

He raises a brow, and it's like a cold wall shutters his expression, making it impossible to read. "Don't tell me you got the wrong idea?"

"What?" I breathe, a pit forming in my stomach.

He gives me a bored look, folding his arms across his chest, one I'd never expected to see again. "Just because you helped me out for the last week doesn't make us close."

His words dig into my heart, compressing my ribs until I can't breathe as confusion swirls in my brain. "I don't understand."

Matthias straightens, his cold eyes locked with mine as he says the words that tear me apart. "Let me make it easy for you. I don't want to see you, hear your voice. I don't want to be in the same room as you."

The bond that felt tied between us, one shaped by a world we barely survived, pulls and frays with his words. My stomach twists, and bile rises in my throat as thoughts pummel me, but none of them make sense.

"Why are you doing this?" Voice cracking around the vowels, I struggle to keep myself together. His eyes dart to the side, hiding the glimpse of emotion he'd let slip through his mask.

A muscle ticks in his jaw with each clench of his teeth, and I can almost see him build the wall between us brick by brick, cutting off any semblance of connection I thought we shared.

Matthias's cool, twisted laugh sends a shudder down my spine. His lips pull back in revulsion as he hisses at me. "You may have helped us, but you're still a Laurent."

I gasp, lancing between my ribs, stealing the air from my lungs as his words land their intended blow. How could I be so naive to think even for a second that what my family did wouldn't matter. My sheer level of audacity should be embarrassing, but all I can feel is the soul-crunching reality cave in on me.

My chin wobbles as I strain to hold myself together, but I refuse to cry. I knew there would be consequences for my family's actions, and no one suffered as much as Matthias did.

I should've known that any peace between us couldn't last. I just wish I'd done a better job of preparing my stupid heart.

I lift my head high and don't look at him in fear he'll see the tears in my eyes. I'm going to leave this all behind.

My dad, my brother, the old guy that wanted to fuck me. I sniff, pulling myself together.

And Matthias Everette.

Now it's my turn to be free.

A Devious Arrangement
Book 3: Bash's book in the Twisted Vows Series.
Girl pretends to be her brother in order to infiltrate a secret society.

The Everette Brothers

Bash: I caught Damon and Misty making out in the coat closet and I think I'm blind.

Xander: You think that's bad? You should have seen them in the exit stairwell.

Matthias: If you two don't fuck off, he's going to kill you.

Damon: Too late.

Bash: Oh, come on. You know we're kidding. We all saw how much you love her in A Tempting Arrangement.

Xander: Exactly. Plus, Misty's our sister. We love her.

Damon: You what?

Matthias: Relax...

Bash: Don't worry, we love Scarlet too.

Matthias: Nevermind, Dam. He clearly has a death wish.

Xander: Soooo, any of you check out The Wild Ones - J Wilder's Reader Group?

Damon: Nice change of subject.

Xander: What? Seriously, she posts updates, sneak peaks, giveaways, polls. I heard she's really engaged in there.

Bash: Already a member. You guys are slow.

Damon: Misty said she's named after a reader giveaway in that group.

Xander: That's pretty sick.

Bash: Speaking of. If you enjoyed this book, it would be pretty sick if you left a review. I know J would appreciate it.

Matthias: Help give her some motivation to give us Bash's story next. You should see the way this boy falls in A Devious Arrangement.

Bash: Never. Permanent bachelor.

Damon: Keep telling yourself that.

Xander: See you soon!

Thank you!

I want to give the biggest thank you ever to everyone who made this book possible.

I would never have made it without you.

Aly Beck, who magically kept me on pace. Best writing buddy ever. Emily Rath for always being honest with me.

Nicole, Jen, Brittany and Sam. I could not ask for better beta readers.

Steph for the impressive developmental editing. I'll never write again without you.

Lastly, I want to thank my readers. Without you, none of this would have been possible. Your love for my characters has been truly life changing.

READ MORE

A Tempting Arrangement
   Book 1 in the Twisted Vows Series
   READ NOW
   You might say my obsession has become a compulsion in the way I need to know everything about Scarlet Laurent.

Even though I've taken a step into the background, I could never look away from my Little Sparrow.

She's a sliver, buried under my skin, a constant reminder of her presence, with no way to dig it out.

Staying away from her for the last ten years has been a brutal form of torture.

Her times run out and when the clock ticks midnight on her 25th birthday, I'll tie her to me forever.

After all, I can't kidnap what's already mine.

Cozy Obsession Interconnected Standalone. Can be read on its own.

Rule Number Five
Book 1 in the Rule Breaker Series
<u>READ NOW</u>

I had my whole life planned out... until I met a hockey player obsessed with breaking all of my rules.

My 5 simple rules for hooking up keep me from being distracted. And now I'm so close to landing my dream internship. Nothing is going to make me break them.

Even a protective hockey player with clear grey eyes, a sharp jaw, and a body that makes my breath catch.

Until Jax wins a bet and one kiss has me breaking them all.

TROPES:

- Slowburn
- He Falls First
- Friends with benefits
- Jealousy
- Mutual pining

Rules Of The Game
Book 2 in the Rule Breaker Series
<u>READ NOW</u>

He's the star hockey player, my brother's best friend and the boy I've been in love with since I was 7.

The problem? He wants nothing to do with me.

Then why does he sneak into my room when I have a nightmare?

Gets jealous when I go on a date?

And has a tattoo of my birthday on his ribs.

Lucas Knight's a lot of things. He's possessive, jealous and overprotective. And he just might be in love with me.

Angst filled, heartbreaking and kick your feet in the air giddy inducing.

TROPES:

* Brother's Best Friend

* Secret Pen Pal

* Jealousy

* Mutual pining

* You're going to suffer, but you're going to be happy about it.

The Gentlemen Series
READ NOW

She's a kickass thief and the heads of her rival gang, Beck, Nico, and Rush need her help.

Whychoose, Multi-POV, Badass Heroine, Tons of funny banter, All over 20 years old, Forced Proximity

By Jessa Wilder & Kate King

The Blissful Omegaverse Series
READ NOW

In a world where Omegas are cherished, Alphas are revered, and Betas are forgotten I wouldn't have changed a thing.

Growing up in foster care, my friends and I took care

of each other. Ares, Killian, Rafe, and Nox, were my everything: my first loves, my only family, my pack. Until the same night they told me we'd be together forever, I presented as an Omega, and everything changed. By Jessa Wilder & Kate King